GW00859413

Second Sight

Text Copyright © 2018 by Richard Smith

Second Sight

Richard Smith

Prologue

London was on fire. Row after row of houses burned and blazed. Buildings that had stood for generations disappeared beneath clouds of thick, black smoke and a hellish music shook the city. The mournful song of the siren choir rose and fell over a symphony of screeching bombs, thunderous blasts and the pounding drumbeat of gunfire. Houses, factories, cinemas, shops and churches all turned to rubble as a plague of ravenous planes swarmed overhead.

Josef Berg, only twenty-two years old but already a veteran of fifteen missions over five different cities, struggled to breathe as smoke spewed into the cockpit. They were going to crash, he knew that; one engine was already on fire and another smouldered ominously. He struggled from his pilot's seat, fighting to keep himself upright as the aircraft listed to starboard. Glancing down he saw that Niels, his gunner, his friend, was dead; a ribbon of deep crimson trickled down his smooth jaw.

There was no time to mourn however, Niels was dead and he would join him if he didn't get moving. Josef heaved open the stiff hatch and pulled on his parachute knowing that he would likely be killed before he reached the ground. He crossed himself, kissed the St. Christopher's pendant that dangled around his neck, then prepared to leap into a sky on fire.

Before he did, he took one last look at Niels, the boy he

had shared so much with. They'd been at school together, played football together, fought together, and now maybe they would die together. Grief gripped his throat as he tried to swallow the rising feeling of helplessness and dread. He had to stay focused. He had to get out.

All of a sudden the world fell silent, and for one moment Josef was sure he saw something quite remarkable, and quite, quite impossible. Standing beside Niels, dressed only in a plain white nightie, was a girl, about the same age as his younger sister Heidi. She was staring at him, her mouth and eyes agape, with skin as pale and fine as china. Who or what she was, he did not know, though he would remember her face until his dying day. He must be imagining her, he told himself, though deep inside he hoped against all hope that she was an angel, come to see him to safety, or some other, better place. He kissed his pendant again and jumped from the plane, floating with agonising gentleness towards the ground.

The girl in the nightdress did not speak, for she was not really there, and the events that she was witnessing would not come to pass for three days yet.

Though Josef was unable to release his full arsenal upon the cowering citizens of London, many of the bombs fell anyway, tumbling from the ruptured belly of the disintegrating plane and burying themselves in the charred patchwork of buildings, bridges and roads that stitched together the bloodied city.

One of these bombs, the last of them as it turns out, lands upon the end terrace house of Waverley Lane – a street known to the locals as Cowslip Lane for reasons no one can quite remember. The house is home to a girl named Emily Cartwright, the girl in the nightdress.

That Emily's house is not the intended target does not matter, nor does it matter that the plane that delivers that fateful load ends its days in a thousand tiny pieces, scattered over a playing field somewhere in North London. All that matters is that Emily is standing in the only place that can shield her from the full force of the explosion that kills everyone else in the house. All that matters is that all that matters to Emily will die in the smoky ruins of 23 Cowslip Lane.

Chapter One

Emily had only been asleep for a few hours when she disturbed by the dreadful wailing of the air raid sirens. She sat up, blinking the sleep from her eyes, and tried to gather her thoughts. She'd been having a rather strange dream, but even as she tried to recall what it was about the details were slipping away. She had been flying on board an aeroplane; no, not flying, falling. The plane had been crashing. She shuddered at the thought.

Outside the sirens continued to warn of impending danger. Emily put the plane from her mind and glanced across the room expecting to see her sister, Celia, clambering from beneath the bedcovers and slipping on her dressing gown, but Celia wasn't moving.

'Cece? Are you awake?'

'Go away, I'm sleeping,' mumbled Celia.

'Are we going down to the shelter then?'

There was no response.

'Ce!'

Without opening her eyes Celia grabbed one of her pillows and tossed it in Emily's direction. Emily hadn't shared a room with her sister all these years to be caught out like that. She plucked the pillow out of the air without batting an eye.

'Should we go down do you think?'

'Let's wait here for a bit,' replied Celia sleepily, 'if the siren continues we'll go, but you know what'll happen, we'll get halfway down there, then the all clear will sound and we'll have to walk all the way back again.'

Moments later, just as Celia had predicted, the sound of the sirens changed and their ululating cry became one long unwavering note, signalling that danger had passed.

'Told you,' said Celia smugly, wriggling deeper into her blankets. 'Now, can I have my pillow back?'

Emily chucked the pillow across the room with practiced ease making sure it landed right on her sister's face.

'Thanks.'

It had been like this for months now. She'd lost count of the times they'd been woken in the middle of the night, only for it to turn out to be another false alarm. It was almost routine. A year earlier all the talk had been that Hitler would start bombing the cities the moment that war was declared. Most of her friends had been evacuated to the countryside to live with distant relatives, or even complete strangers, so long as it was somewhere safe from the predicted onslaught. After many arguments it had been agreed that Emily and Celia could stay in London for the time being.

Though it was a nuisance having to traipse down to the shelter each time the sirens sounded, Emily didn't think it was a good idea to stay inside. Of course, Germany wasn't *trying* to bomb people's houses, but there were occasions when they aimed for the airfields and missed. Unlike many people, Emily's family were lucky enough to have their own air raid shelter in the back garden. Her father had built it for them before he went away the previous year, but no one liked sleeping down there because it was so cold and cramped. One person in particular refused to step foot inside it, certain as he was that they would never be bombed. That person was Emily's uncle, Frank, who had moved in with them the day after war was declared, much to Emily's dismay.

'Hitler won't bomb London,' he insisted, 'I've always said it.'

This at least was true. Barely a day went by without her uncle making this same confident prediction.

'There's nothing to be gained from it,' he continued, 'it's all just scare mongering. What's it been now? Almost a year? And nothing. The government want to keep us scared so that we won't notice what it is they're up to. But I've got my eye them, don't you worry.'

Her uncle, it seemed to Emily, always had his eye on someone. In fact, he appeared to have so many eyes on so many different people that she wondered how he kept track of them all. Pulling her blankets tight around her, she rolled over, and waited for sleep to claim her. After ten minutes she was still wide awake, and the more she tried to get to sleep, the more awake she felt. Every little sound began to irritate her: the ticking of the clock on the wall, the distant rumble of her uncle's snores, the rattling of the loose glass in their bedroom window, until it was too much for her to take, and she threw off the bedclothes and climbed out of bed. Careful not to wake Celia, who unlike Emily always seemed to be able to get back to sleep after the sirens sounded, she wrapped her threadbare dressing gown around her and tiptoed across the room.

Emily crept down the stairs, making sure to miss the third step from the bottom which made a sound like a startled crow if you stepped on it, and slipped into the kitchen. Taking her father's favourite mug from the cupboard, as she always did when no one could see her, she placed it underneath the tap. In what was by now a well-rehearsed routine, she twisted the handle a fraction of a degree to the left till the water was running at a steady trickle. If she ran the water any faster it would cause the pipes in the attic to bang and clatter, waking the rest of the house. Her uncle had promised to fix them when he moved in. A year later and they still made a dreadful racket. She waited patiently for the mug to fill then took a large satisfying gulp.

Emily opened the back door that led into the garden and took a seat on the step with her mug of water. The night was warm, even in her dressing gown she wasn't cold at all. It was so peaceful; the moon and stars were the only light to be seen for miles around, and the moon's halo bathed the garden in its milky glow. She sat for some time, just staring out at the night sky until she could see the first glimpses of dawn seeping onto the horizon, the dark of the night giving way to the greyish blue of twilight which in turn was washed away by a watercolour sunrise of reds and oranges. It was hard to believe that anyone could want to destroy something as beautiful as this she thought. She wondered where her father might be at that moment, a desert perhaps, or a dark forest looking up at a different sky; surely longing for home. Wherever he was, she hoped he was safe.

Draining the last drops of water from the mug Emily decided to go back to bed, tiredness had crept in with the dawn and if she was lucky she might just be able to get a little sleep before the rest of the house woke up.

Her head had barely hit the pillow when she was awoken by a loud buzzing sound. She opened her eyes and found, to her surprise, that she was not in her bed, but somewhere else entirely. Her cheek was pressed against something hard and cold. It was metal. She was lying on a metal floor which, alarmingly, seemed to be vibrating. Where am I she wondered? And how did I get here?

The buzzing continued. There was something familiar about that sound, but she couldn't quite work out what it was. A breeze blew about her and the strong smell of oil hung in the air and clung to her nostrils. In an instant she knew where she was, and yet she couldn't be. It was impossible. She was on an aeroplane.

Emily had never seen the inside of an aeroplane in real life before, let alone been up in one. Her stomach did a somersault. How was it possible? It couldn't be, obviously. She realised now that she must be asleep, that she must be dreaming, and slowly the details of her dream from earlier that night began to come back to her. She had been in a plane over London, and she had watched a man jump out. There was more to it, she was sure, but it was hard to pin down. Even so, she was certain she had never had a dream as vivid as this before, or ever been aware that she was dreaming whilst it was happening.

She moved slowly forwards. In the cockpit she could see a man surveying the panels in front of him which were filled with a baffling array of dials and switches. Was it the same man from before? She couldn't tell. The man shouted something and then laughed, but what he was saying, and who he was talking to Emily didn't know, it was impossible to hear anything clearly over the rumble of the engines.

Either side of her were two small windows. Gingerly she looked through the porthole and was immediately struck by the vivid blue of the sky which stole her breath from her. Beneath them lay a blanket of white clouds so thick she felt sure that she could have walked across them. The plane sailed over their whipped peaks and the sun glinted off the wing tips. The fear she'd felt just moments before had already disappeared in the excitement of seeing the world in a whole new way. She knew she was dreaming but at that moment she wished she really was up among the clouds, it was the most amazing thing she had ever known and she didn't want it to end, but end it did, and moments later she found herself back in her bed.

Emily smiled to herself. It had been a wonderful dream but she could hear the sound of breakfast being prepared downstairs, and she knew it was time to get up. From the empty bed next to her she guessed that Celia had already gone down. She threw on some clothes and made her way to the kitchen where she found her uncle reading the morning paper and loudly expanding on one his favourite themes, the idiocy of others, and in particular the Prime Minister.

'The problem with Churchill is that he doesn't understand the German mind,' he said with a rueful shake of his head.

Emily wondered what penetrating insight her uncle might have into the German mind, but she was spared his bone-headed analysis by the sound of the pips which signalled the start of the morning news on the radio. Emily sat down on the chair next to her sister, whilst their mother fussed around them setting the table.

The man from the BBC announced in grave tones that the town of Hardstone had been attacked during the night but that no damage had been done.

'That's only a few miles away,' said Celia.

Their mother pursed her lips but said nothing and went back to serving the breakfast.

'Prime Minister Winston Churchill delivered a speech in the House of Commons yesterday commending the bravery of the RAF and promising once more Mr Hitler's total defeat.'

The familiar growl of Churchill's voice came thundering over the airwaves, but it was drowned out by her uncle's derisive snorts.

'Prime Minister, I ask you. Just turn it off, I'm not listening to him. I don't care what anyone says, it should've been Halifax. Halifax was the right man for the job, but instead we got stuck with that old soak. Germany doesn't even want a war.'

'For a country that doesn't want a war they're doing ever so well at finding them,' whispered Emily to her sister who had to stifle a laugh beneath her uncle's gaze.

'It's not in their interest. Let them have what they want over there,' he said raising his voice slightly, the better to talk over her.

'France, Holland, Poland, Austria...' continued Emily.

'Let them have Poland, what do we want with Poland? Every country needs a strong leader, and like it or not, Hitler is strong. I don't agree with everything he's up to, but he's tough, and he's done well for Germany. And now there's a buffer isn't there? Between us and the Russians. Let them fight it out I say. Your dad and I went over twenty-four years ago to sort all this. It was supposed to be the war to end all wars, and now look at us, angling for another one.'

'I wonder who he's going to blame?' whispered Emily to her sister. 'Could it be Churchill perhaps?'

'It's Churchill's fault of course,' her uncle continued unabated.

'Do I win a prize?'

Celia laughed but swiftly transformed it into a cough when her uncle looked at her.

'I don't trust him. Have people forgotten about Gallipoli? Forty-six thousand of our boys died under his brilliant leadership. Then there's Norway, remember Narvik just this year? Another bloody disaster. What will it take before people realise he's just another upper-class buffoon with no understanding of military strategy? And now he's taunting Hitler, forcing him to come at us. We bombed Berlin just the other day. Well a man can only take so much, it wouldn't surprise me if Hitler was bombing London just to spite Churchill. He'll have blood on his hands, mark my words.'

'A few weeks ago you said Hitler wouldn't bomb London, now he's sending planes over daily.' Emily interjected.

'They're only bombing the aircraft bases so we can't bomb them. Churchill forced their hand, they had to come over.'

Her uncle, Emily had learned, was like a storm, he would rant and rave and then blow himself out. Anything that you said would just provoke him, so it was better to say nothing at all. She began to chew her top lip as she always did when she disagreed with something and was trying not to say so. After a rather heated row the other evening Celia had forced her to agree that keeping quiet would be the best course of action in future, a fact she was frantically trying to remind Emily of by placing one finger over her lips and kicking her under the table. Of course, agreeing on a plan and sticking to it were two totally different things.

'I like Churchill,' said Emily, prompting much eye rolling from Celia.

'And what would you know?' snapped her uncle, hauling himself forward in his chair to stare directly at her.

'I know he wants to stop Hitler,' she said, meeting his stare.

'We don't need to stop Hitler. I've told you it's Stalin and the Russians we've got to be worried about.'

'You're an idiot. Stalin's not the one sending planes over. He's not the one who's destroying all our ships and killing all these people.'

'Emily...' said her mother in a voice that clearly indicated she should consider changing the subject.

'Can't I have an opinion of my own?' Emily protested.

'Not while you're under my roof,' said her uncle with some considerable relish.

'But it isn't your roof. This isn't your house. This is our house and I'll have opinions on whatever I jolly well like thank you very much.'

Feeling rather pleased with herself, Emily managed to snatch defeat from the jaws of victory by continuing to talk.

'Dad is away fighting, what is it you're doing again?'

Her uncle turned a dark shade of red she'd never seen before.

'Emily! Don't speak to your uncle like that,' warned her mother.

'My work is vital to the war effort, it's a protected job, I'm not allowed to go.'

Emily knew she'd pushed it too far, for all his faults her uncle was no coward, but stopping now would mean apologising to him and there was no way she was going to do that, so instead she did what she always did and ploughed on.

'Why shouldn't I speak to him like that? He speaks to me however he likes,' said Emily, and out the corner of her eye she could just make out her sister shaking her head in bemusement.

'No, you do not call your uncle an idiot,' her mother snapped. 'Not in this house.'

'Well where can I call him an idiot then?'

'Apologise immediately.'

'No, he *is* an idiot.'

'Right then, you can go to your room, and I don't want to hear another word from you until you've said sorry to your uncle.'

'Then I won't speak ever again,' said Emily with an ugly smile.

Her uncle rocked back on his chair, smirking. 'Best bit of news I've had since the war started.'

Emily stalked past him and up the stairs to her room making sure to slam every door behind her as she went.

Throwing herself down on her bed, she glanced at the alarm clock on the bedside table. A quarter past nine. A new record. It was normally several hours before she got into a fight with her uncle, but today she had managed it in just fifteen minutes. She lay back and closed her eyes trying to calm herself down. Just then she heard a loud, low buzzing sound. She opened her eyes and looked quickly round the room for the source of the noise. There was nothing. She was still tired and wondered if she'd just nodded off for a moment.

She quickly forgot about the noise as her thoughts returned to the fight with her uncle. She knew she'd overstepped the mark by calling him an idiot (though she'd called him far worse in her head). Her mother would be true to her word and force her to apologise. The thought of doing so made Emily feel sick. It wasn't the apology itself that bothered her, so much as the smug, gloating, expression that her uncle would wear as she was forced to deliver it. He'd pretend to accept her apology with grace and understanding, but all the while his twinkling eyes would goad her into saying something else.

Suddenly the buzzing was back; louder this time. At first she thought it might be an insect of some sort, a fly or a bee trapped up against the window, but it was far too loud for that and it was getting louder. She covered her ears but it was no use, it was as though it was coming from inside her head, but it couldn't be. She wasn't imagining it, this was real, she could even feel the floor throbbing. Emily ran to the window to see where the noise was coming from but as she did so she stumbled and fell onto a hard metal floor. The room was gone, she was back on the aeroplane, the one from her dream. But how could she be dreaming if she wasn't asleep? She pinched her arm hard. It hurt but she didn't wake up. Without stopping to think any further, Emily moved forwards through a narrow passage towards the front of the plane. It was as if something was pulling her on.

A glance out of the window told her it was later than before. The sun was disappearing below the clouds and the plane felt cooler. She also realised that they weren't alone. All around them there were other planes racing through the sky. She wondered how many there were. Twenty? Thirty? Maybe more. She knew what was happening couldn't be real, that somehow she must be dreaming again, but she didn't care, she felt as though she was meant to be there.

Emily drifted around the plane unchallenged and unimpeded but curiously detached from the situation. Something nagged at her, but before she could work out what it was the sound of the engines disappeared to be replaced by the chirruping of birds and Emily found herself back in her bedroom lying at the end of her bed.

It was as if nothing had happened. She stood up and dusted herself off checking herself for bumps or bruises. She must have fallen, hit her head and passed out. It was a very humid day, perhaps that was the cause of it, yet she could find no sign of damage except for a red mark on her right forearm where she had pinched herself. How odd that she'd had the same dream again, that had never happened to her before, and the dream felt so real, no different to how she was feeling at that very moment. She was about to go downstairs and tell her mother all about it when she remembered why she was up in her room in the first place. She could hardly say anything in front of Uncle Frank, he'd just laugh at her, accuse her of making it all up or tell her that she should have her head examined.

Emily retraced her steps, trying to make whatever had just occurred happen again, but she couldn't, so instead she opened the bedroom window in the hope of capturing the faintest trace of a breeze. The day which had started so brightly had become stilted and muggy. Dark clouds, heavy with the threat of rain, rolled ominously overhead.

She watched two boys from down the road kicking around a football. Alf, the younger of the two, sent a shot bouncing off the top of the greengrocer's van that was parked on the corner. They both looked round sheepishly hoping no one had seen. If Mr Patterson the grocer had spotted them, they'd have had an earful. They grinned at each other and chased off down the street after the ball, narrowly avoiding colliding with a tall gentleman in a long grey coat whom Emily did not recognise.

The man was smartly dressed and had a shock of blond hair that was swept neatly beneath a grey trilby hat. He paused beneath a lamppost and removed something from his breast pocket. For reasons she did not understand, this man made Emily nervous. She took a step back from the window just as he looked up. Their eyes met for a moment, then he continued with whatever it was he was doing.

'What are you looking at?'

Emily jumped, she hadn't noticed her sister enter the room.

'Some man... I'm not sure who he is,' she replied beckoning for her sister to join her at the window.

'Very smart... and blonde too,' said Celia, as if that confirmed her suspicions.

'So?'

'Well he's probably a German spy isn't he? You're always hearing about them.'

'On Cowslip Lane?' said Emily incredulously.

'Maybe,' Celia replied with a sly smile creeping across her face.

'What's he spying on? Mrs Sadler's carnations?'

Celia laughed, pulled herself up to her full height and began to address Emily in the guise of a German Spymaster.

'Ve must know about zees flowers Herr Strudlebaum. Zey may be zee key to vinning zis var. To England at vance, and be quick about it. Der Fuhrer vants dose carnations as soon as possible.'

Emily saluted and drew her feet together. They both laughed and turned to look out of the window again. The man had gone.

'Where did he go?' said Emily straining to see to the end of the street.

'I don't know, maybe he went inside. He's probably one of the busybodies from the council come to see Mr Wilkinson about his blackout curtains or something.'

Emily frowned but said nothing.

'Has mum been up yet?' asked Celia.

'Is my head still on my body?' replied Emily.

Celia sat down on her bed.

'Just so you know, I think you're right.'

'Why don't you say anything then?'

'What's the point? Then Uncle Frank would be shouting at me too. No thank you. Besides I enjoy watching you. In fact I really admire your debating style, the first person to disagree with you gets called an idiot.'

'Uncle Frank *is* an idiot.'

'Uncle Frank isn't the one who got sent to his room, so who's the real idiot? Besides, it's not nice to call people names.'

'Idiot isn't a name. Who names their child idiot?'

'I was planning to call my first-born Idiot. Idiot Ethel Virginia Cartwright.'

'And if it's a boy?'

'Idiot Bob Cecil Cartwright III.'

'After all those Idiot Bob Cecil Cartwright's that came

before him?'

'Exactly. Only you won't be having any children because you're about to get grounded for about forty years, and by the time you're allowed out the house again you'll be all old and warty and no one will want you.'

Celia screwed up her face and puckered her lips. Emily laughed.

'Like Nurse McCorkadale from school?'

'Yes, exactly like her. And you'll smoke a pipe like she does too.'

'She never smokes a pipe.'

'She does I've seen her.'

'That's probably what gives her that distinctive smell.'

Celia chuckled.

'What are you two up to?'

Emily's mother was standing in the doorway.

'Just talking about flowers and the state of healthcare in this country,' said Celia, giving Emily's arm a sympathetic squeeze before making a discreet exit.

Her mother let out a long sigh. 'What are we going to do with you?'

Emily didn't say anything. She could feel the anger rising in her again.

'You have to control yourself Emily. You can't go flying off the handle just because you disagree with someone.'

'But he makes me so cross!'

'Don't let him.'

'I've tried that.'

'Could you try harder?'

'It doesn't work. He just... it's just what he says... it makes me so angry. Father's away fighting, and everyday someone round here gets a telegram telling them that their father or their husband or their son has been killed. What if...?'

Emily paused and composed herself.

'What if Uncle Frank is right? What if this war is a huge mistake? Is dad risking his life for no reason?'

Her mother sat down on the bed and gestured for Emily to do the same.

'When I was at school, there was a girl who was always picking on people. She was a nasty piece of work. She bullied anyone she considered to be less than her, which was pretty much everyone. We never said anything, we all let it go, we were too scared of her.'

'Why didn't the teachers stop her?' asked Emily.

'The only reason the teachers would ever have stopped pupils hitting each other at my school was to prevent the blood from staining the floor. Anyway, we tried everything we could think of to make her go away. We gave her what she wanted time and again, but she always came back for more. So one day I just snapped. She started picking on a friend of mine and I stood up to her, I told her not to.'

'What did she say?'

'Nothing. She just hit me.'

'Oh.'

'Right in the face.'

Emily's eyes widened in disbelief. It was hard to picture her mother as a schoolgirl, and harder still to picture her getting into a fight.

'What did you do?'

'What could I do? I hit her back. I had to. I was a lot like you are now, couldn't keep my mouth shut, didn't know when to back down. Besides, I'd had enough. She needed to learn that we weren't going to take it anymore.'

'What happened?'

'Well she hit me again, even harder this time. In the end the Master had to break it up. We each got the cane and a letter home to our parents informing them of our 'foul and disreputable behaviour.' Then I got hit all over again, this time by my father. Four strokes with his belt. I swear I can still feel it.'

'Was it worth it?'

'Well she wasn't a problem after that, not for me anyway or for any of my friends. What I'm saying is this:

21

sometimes you have to do the thing you don't want to do because nothing else has worked. We tried giving Hitler what he wanted but it turns out that what he wanted was simply more, more of everything. More land, more troops, more Empire, more power. In the end we had to say 'No. No more.' Your father is putting his life in danger so that we can live in freedom and at peace. You should be very proud of him.'

Emily smiled.

'So, what you're saying is that I should hit Uncle Frank?'

Her mother rolled her eyes.

'No, that is certainly not what I'm saying. The girl I hit was being a bully, Frank is just... well...' her mother let out another long sigh. 'It's different with your uncle. He's been very good to us these last few months, he does a lot for this family that you never see. He's always has an opinion on everything, so let him bluster and blather. What harm does it do? Let him have this. Your father is a hero, off fighting for his country, but he can't go. He's the eldest and he's always looked out for his little brother, but now he can't; he can't do anything to protect someone he loves so much and it hurts him, it really does. I think that's why he says these things. It's his way of showing that he wants your father to come home.'

Emily nodded. 'I just wish he could find another way of doing it.'

'He's suffered a lot of disappointments in his life has Frank. He wasn't always like this, loud yes, opinionated certainly, but not angry. Believe me. When I first knew your uncle he could be quite charming when he put his mind to it.'

'Charming? Uncle Frank?'

Emily stared at her mother in disbelief. She might as well have told her that he came from Mars. Her mother laughed.

'I'm serious. There was more than one girl who carried a torch for Uncle Frank when he was younger.'

'Why didn't he marry any of them? Do you think that's why he's always so cross?'

'There's very rarely just one reason why anyone is like they are; people are much more complicated than that, but maybe it played a part. And of course he was very close to his sister, but she died young, when she was only a little bit older than you and Celia.'

'What happened?'

'She went out one evening and never returned. Your father doesn't like to talk about it. My point is, before you judge Frank too harshly remember that he's already lost a little sister and he's terrified of losing his little brother too. Show him some respect, try and be polite, let him have his opinions. He's not so bad. And I'll have a word with him, see if I can do anything to help.'

'Thank you' said Emily as her mother folded her into a huge hug.

'And later you're going to apologise okay?'

'Can't I just apologise to you and you can pass it on?'

'No, you have to do it in person and you have to mean it or it's not worth a lick. Also, he'd never believe it unless he heard it with his own ears. Now, come down and finish your breakfast.'

Then seeing the look on Emily's face she added, 'Don't worry, it's safe! Frank's gone to work already.'

After breakfast Emily headed out into the back garden. It was only small and it had become a lot smaller since her father had built the Anderson Shelter in the corner of it. She had helped him dig the hole for it in August the previous year. It had been hard work; that summer had been a glorious one, long and hot, the result of which was to leave the ground as hard as rock. Of course, it wasn't just her garden that was getting smaller, across the country gardens were becoming unrecognisable, first with shelters being put in, then whatever remained of the grass was dug up to be replaced with vegetable patches. *Dig For Victory* was the slogan on the posters around town, but Emily couldn't help feeling a little resentful that the war effort was taking up all the spaces she had to play in, for it wasn't just gardens that were disappearing but public parks as well.

Their air raid shelter had fallen into disuse; like a lot of families they had built it when war seemed inevitable and all the talk was that the Germans would attack London from the air. Despite the recent raid at Hardstone, so far most of the bombing had been against the RAF bases scattered across the country and not, as was feared, the cities. Now it was rumoured that they would instead come by the sea, landing at Dover or Southampton. The talk had reached such a fevered pitch recently that Emily half expected to hear the sound of hobnailed boots clacking on the cobblestone streets at any moment.

First however, they needed to knock out Britain's air defences which is why they sent planes over daily; bombers to destroy the airfields, and fighters to protect the bombers. It was not uncommon to see an aerial dog fight between a British Hurricane and a German Messerschmitt. They would race across the skies leaving white vapour trails in their wake. This, along with the specially fashioned vegetable gardens and the sudden appearance of sand bags around every public building, was one of the many new sights they'd had to get used to since the war started.

Their shelter was made out of several curved panels of tough corrugated steel, and was set about four foot into the ground to better protect it from any bomb blasts. It was also partly covered by soil and plants in a futile effort to make it blend it with its surroundings. There was a small door at the front and several sandbags that could be pulled across too. Inside, up against the walls there were two thin benches, some old cushions and a few tattered blankets. Pressed to the back wall there was a small square table with a round tin on top of it which held candles and matches so that they would have some source of light in the event of a long raid.

Emily thought about the times they had spent in there when the war had begun. Together they'd sat whilst the air raid sirens sounded in the street outside, listening for any noise, any sign at all that might indicate that the German planes were overhead. Sometimes these alarms lasted only a few minutes, other times it was several hours, and even, once, the whole night. At first the fear had been almost unbearable, just the four of them sitting, waiting, the minutes and hours slowly ticking by. It was hard watching her mother trying to pretend that she wasn't terrified, and to see her normally bellicose uncle fall quiet. They had each tried everything they could to keep their minds occupied, singing, playing cards, but they had all heard the horror stories about the destruction an air raid could wreak.

Although Emily did not like staying in the shelter, it did have its uses. As her father wasn't around to play with her anymore, it was handy to have a sloped surface she could use to stop the flight of her cricket ball. When she was bored and had nothing else to do Emily passed her time attempting to win back the Ashes for England.

Garden Cricket required five things: an alleyway or small strip of glass, a short plank of wood, a bat, a ball and someone to play with. Emily had four of those things. Crucially she lacked anyone to play it with, but, as she had so often in the past, she would take on the role of bowler and practice bowling towards the shelter where the 'stumps' (an old wooden plank about as wide as a piece of writing paper) were located.

Whenever Emily bowled there was only one man she would be, Hedley Verity, the pride of Yorkshire. Verity, it was said, was the only man who could make Don Bradman, universally acknowledged as the greatest batsman to ever play the game, look nervous. Adopting the crisp, measured tones of Howard Marshall, the BBC's voice of cricket, she provided a running commentary on Verity's duels with Bradman, Gregory and Badcock.

'Verity comes round the wicket this time, it's a quicker

delivery, Mr Bradman has played and missed. I am quite sure Mr Bradman was not expecting that. That's a very good over from Verity.'

Most of the time Emily as Verity triumphed, but occasionally she allowed Bradman to rack up a big score before being brilliantly bowled in an inspired over that would remove most of the Australian upper order.

'He's bowled him. The turn just got the better of the batsman there and it's taken the bails clean off.'

Emily collected the warm round of applause that greeted this crucial wicket with polite nods to her team mates and the crowd at the Pavilion End. Now all that was left to do was polish off the tail-enders before tea. She marked out her short run up and prepared to humble the Australians once more. Before she could do so however, she noticed something very odd. In the distance she could see large shadows dancing across the roof tops. They looked like the shadows of aeroplanes, but when she looked up there were no planes to be seen. Emily listened intently but all was quiet. There was no sound of engines, no air raid sirens or cries of alarm. The whole of London was curiously still. A shiver ran up her spine as the shadows passed right over her, leaving her in shade. One after another after another sailed by, yet still she could see no planes. The sky above was clear blue, the only thing to fly overhead was a small bird who had just been startled by the neighbour's cat. Moments later her mother appeared at the back door.

'Emily?' she called.

'Did you see that?' said Emily still staring up at the sky.

'See what?'

'The shadows?'

'What shadows? Whatever are you talking about?'

'I saw… there were shadows on the ground, the shadows of planes, lots of them.'

'I can't see any planes. Don't talk nonsense. You had me worried for a moment.'

'But they were there, I saw them. Shadows of planes coming this way, they passed right over me and then... and then they were gone. I'm not making this up,' she insisted, seeing the look on her mother's face.

'Are you feeling okay?'

'I'm fine... Honestly I'm fine,' she said as her mother continued to look at her, 'I could've sworn... it doesn't matter.'

'Well,' said her mother, a note of concern in her voice, 'come back inside then, I need some help chopping the vegetables.'

'All right,' said Emily, 'I'll be there in a minute.'

Her mother returned to the kitchen and Emily packed away the cricket things, one eye on the heavens, convinced that the German planes would come roaring overhead at any moment, but, with the exception of the platoon of watchful barrage balloons that bobbed and swayed above the sandbagged city, the skies of London remained clear.

Chapter Two

Emily was thrown from her feet as the sky erupted around her. Puffs of black smoke appeared then vanished in an instant. The noise was almost unbearable, the mad cackle of gunfire and the growl of the engines meant she could hardly hear herself think. The plane juddered and throbbed then lurched violently to one side, and for a moment Emily was convinced that it would tear itself in two, before somehow it righted itself once more. She looked out of the window at the ground below. The once grey buildings now glowed a menacing orange, as forty or fifty fires billowed and raged pouring thick black smoke into the sky, and the normally murky green water of the Thames blazed an angry red as it snaked its way through the belly of the city. London was dying.

A huge explosion rocked the tail of the plane, and the roar became a whine as if the plane itself was letting out one final scream of horror. Suddenly Emily was aware of a searing heat so intense she thought it might melt the skin from her bones. A young man, barely a man really, emerged from the cockpit looking around him, a boy soldier playing at war now fighting for his every breath. He covered his mouth so as not to breathe in the poisonous fumes that were filling the aircraft. He pushed his way towards a small hatch at the side, pulled on his parachute, and kissed the chain which hung around his neck.

Emily stumbled backwards and found herself standing next to the body of a man. She looked back up and saw the pilot starring at her. She opened her mouth to scream but if any sound emerged she could not hear it over all the noise. The man kissed his chain again and then leapt out into the pockmarked sky. Meanwhile the plane began to totter and sway before finally slipping forwards, nose tipping towards the ground as it started to pick up speed, like an owl swooping down upon its prey.

'Emily?'

She heard a voice calling her name.

'Emily are you all right?'

The dream vanished. She opened her eyes and she was back in her bedroom. Her sister's face loomed over her.

'Are you okay? You were having a nightmare, I didn't know if I should wake you, but then you started to scream and I thought...'

'I'm fine,' she said, rather more harshly than she had intended, 'I'm okay really.'

Celia backed away giving Emily the space she needed to sit up.

'What were you dreaming about? Can you remember?'

Emily hesitated. It was only a dream after all, what was there to say? Celia would probably laugh at her but it was so unsettling she needed to tell someone.

'I keep having this dream, well I think it's a dream anyway...'

'What do you mean you think it's a dream? Of course it's a dream silly.'

'It's just... it's so realistic, it's like I'm actually there.'

'Actually where?'

'On an aeroplane. I keep dreaming I'm on a plane, a German plane, and it's flying across the ocean; only this time it wasn't the ocean it was over London, and all around there was gun fire and bombs dropping on buildings.'

'You've been reading too much,' said Celia pointing at the dog-eared copy of HG Wells's *A World Set Free* that lay on the bedside table. 'We've been at war a year now and they've mainly attacked airfields and ports.'

'I know,' said Emily.

'Even the Nazis won't attack civilians.'

The doubt must have shown on Emily's face because Celia continued.

'It won't be like Spain, that was different. This was only a dream Emily, you need to forget all about it.'

'I can't. You don't understand, I'll be walking along and suddenly I'm on the plane, and it feels real, as real as this moment right now.'

'But it isn't real.'

'I know it isn't real but that doesn't change how it feels,' said Emily frustrated.

She wished she hadn't said anything but it was too late.

'A few days ago it happened during the middle of the day. This isn't day dreaming or nightmares: this is something different.'

'Are you feeling okay?'

'No of course I'm not. I know what dreams are, I've had dreams, and this doesn't feel like dreaming.'

'But what else could it be?'

Emily could barely bring herself to say it. It sounded stupid, even in her head, but she couldn't think of anything else.

'Maybe... I don't know, maybe... I somehow travel to the future.'

'But you were in your bed the whole time, I saw you.'

'Ok, alright then perhaps I don't *physically* travel there, perhaps I just see it. I see what's coming.'

Now she had said it out loud it did seem ridiculous. Apparently Celia agreed.

'I don't know what's more worrying, the fact you think the Nazis are going to destroy London or that you think you can see the future.'

'I know it seems mad, but I'm telling you I'm not crazy.'

'The chorus to the song sung by every crazy person in

the history of the world.'

Emily felt her temper flaring once more.

'I'm not mad. I'm not overtired. I'm not worried. Something is going on. I don't know what but something is happening to me. Ever since these dreams started I've been feeling worse and worse, I've got this rash on my arm that I can't stop scratching. I really think something bad is coming. I think the Germans are going to bomb us.'

'Us? You mean this house?'

'Yes. No. I don't know.'

'Well that's cleared that up.'

'I didn't see everything. I was – they were – flying over London and all around there were fires burning. You've got to believe me.'

'I believe that you believe.'

Emily bit her lip hard to keep herself from shouting. She took a deep breath. 'Promise me one thing.'

'What?'

'Promise me that when you next hear the air raid warning you'll come to the shelter with me.'

'Emily!'

'Promise me Ce.'

Celia sighed but the look on Emily's face told her it was not worth arguing.

'I promise.'

'And you'll help me get mum and Uncle Frank down there too?'

'Uncle Frank won't go.'

'He will if mum does. You promise?'

'You're worrying about nothing. Uncle Frank thinks we'll make peace with Germany soon enough, we'll have to. Then dad will come home and everything will go back to normal.'

Emily said nothing. In truth a small part of her hoped her uncle was right. Like everyone else she had heard the rumours of an invasion. Barely a month went by when there weren't reports of Germans landing somewhere on the coast of Britain and any accident, no matter how innocent, was followed by talk of Nazi spies and sabotage.

'Go back to sleep, you look awful.'

'Thanks.'

'You know what I mean. And in the morning we'll put some calamine lotion on that rash. I think we have some leftover from when I got chicken pox.'

Emily smiled, though there was little more than eighteen months between them, Celia sometimes seemed a lifetime older than Emily. She wished that she was more like her, calmer, more reasonable. She decided to take her sister's advice and try to go back to sleep.

Emily woke the next morning feeling better than she had in days. Perhaps it was because she'd finally confided in someone; she had told Celia and had managed to get her to agree to help if anything happened. She no longer felt alone. She smiled and drew back the curtains much to Celia's displeasure. It was a beautiful day out, sunshine spilled through the clouds like laughter and Emily couldn't wait to play in the garden. Running downstairs two at a time she skidded to a halt in the kitchen where her mother was once again trying to make an exciting breakfast from their grey and meagre rations.

'Morning!' chimed Emily as she entered the room.

'You're up early,' replied her mother, 'is the bed on fire?'

'You're so funny mother,' said Emily giving her an affectionate kiss on the back of her head.

'You don't need to tell me. It's not easy coming up with jokes that good every day you know?'

'Yes, well don't wear yourself out will you?'

'Not when I have such an appreciative audience.'

'What's for breakfast?' said Emily settling herself down at the table.

'Powdered egg on toast.'

'Well if the bread is as fresh as your jokes then we're in for a treat.'

'You know one day that mouth of yours is going to get you into trouble. Elbows off the table,' she said serving up the quivering gelatinous mass that was the scrambled eggs onto Emily's plate. Powdered egg wasn't to everyone's taste, but scrambled it tasted just about palatable, even if it did have a rather rubbery texture.

'Where's Uncle Frank?' she asked through a forkful of eggy toast.

'He wasn't feeling too well this morning so I've told him to stay in bed.'

Emily allowed herself a sly grin which her mother instantly spotted.

'Oi you. It's not nice to take pleasure at someone else's pain. There's a word for that.'

'Nazism?' suggested Emily.

'Schadenfreude.'

'Bless you.'

'And you think my jokes are old.'

Celia traipsed into the kitchen and threw herself down opposite Emily.

'Where's Uncle Frank?'

'Mum says he's not feeling too well and you ought not be happy about that otherwise it means you're a Nazi.'

'Oh... right...' said Celia looking confused.

'Ignore your sister, she's thinks she's Arthur Askey.'

'Arthur who?' asked Celia.

'You know, the comedian' replied Emily putting her fingers around her eyes like a pair of glasses and launching into her best Arthur Askey impression, 'Ay thank yaw'll'.

It drew only a blank look from Celia so Emily went back to devouring her rubbery egg.

'So...' said her mother taking off her apron and hanging it over one of the chairs.

'No!' the girls chimed together.

'What?' Mrs Cartwright replied.

'Whenever you say 'so' in that voice it means you're going to ask us to do something,' said Celia.

'Chores or something like that,' Emily agreed.

'It does not.'

'It does too,' they replied.

'No it does not,' said Mrs Cartwright firmly.

'Okay then, what were you going to say?' asked Celia.

'I was just going to say... I was going to say... so... isn't it nice outside?' she finished unconvincingly.

Emily and Celia exchanged a look.

'So, isn't it nice outside?' repeated Celia.

'Yes. It's lovely.'

'And what else?' asked Emily suspiciously.

'Nothing else.'

'Nothing?'

'No.'

'No chores? No trips to the shops to pick up groceries for you?'

'Well that's very kind of you to offer Emily. Yes, now you mention it I could do with a hand getting the shopping in. I'll give you a list.'

'But you said–'

'I wasn't going to ask, but since you kindly offered–'

'It wasn't an offer, it was a question.'

'It was a trap,' sniggered Celia.

'What cynical children you are, as if I would do such a thing.'

She wore a look of such innocence that Emily had to laugh.

'Give me the list,' she said wearily.

'Thank you Emily.'

Celia raised her arms in triumph and did a little victory dance at seeing her sister's plight.

'I don't know what you're celebrating for Celia, you're going with her. It'll be quicker with two of you.'

Celia stopped dancing and gave a little cough.

'Oh no, I think I'm coming down with what Uncle Frank has...'

'Nice try, but he's got stomach pains, not a hacking cough. I'll give you the ration book. Whatever you do...'

'...Don't lose it,' chorused the girls before their mother could finish.

Mrs Cartwright gave them a list of things to get

including a pint of milk, 4oz of bacon, 4oz tea, 8oz sugar, 3 eggs and a loaf of bread. They were also to be on the lookout for sausages at the butchers because they were Uncle Frank's favourite. Privately Emily thought that the chances of buying any sausages was remote, Mr Playle, the butcher, told her recently he hadn't been able to get any in for weeks.

'Don't forget your gas masks,' said Mrs Cartwright dangling two flimsy cardboard containers in front of them as they tried to leave.

'How are we going to carry all the stuff home if we've also got to carry these masks?' asked Celia. 'Besides, no one goes out with a gas mask anymore.'

'I do and so would your father if he was here.'

It was well known to Emily and Celia that their father would do no such thing. He had hidden his in the Anderson Shelter two days after war had broken out, but as they had promised not to say anything in return for a month's worth of his chocolate ration, they could hardly correct her.

'Come on, there's one each. You can carry them over your shoulders, you know that, then you'll have both hands free for the shopping won't you?'

Emily and Celia reluctantly took the boxes containing their masks and heaved them over their shoulders.

'See you later girls. Come straight home after you've finished, I don't want you dawdling in town.'

'Yes mum,' they replied in unison.

The shops were located on the high street not ten minutes away and the girls were well known in the area. Since the war had started it had been a lot harder to get the food they had grown used to. Every day things like bacon, butter and sugar were all rationed and could only be obtained by using coupons from their ration books. Emily wondered if the day would ever come again when she would be able to walk into a shop and buy as much food as she liked.

Of course, some people were still doing very well for

themselves. Although a lot of food was rationed, restaurants were exempt which meant that if you had the money you could eat out regularly and get around the rationing that way. All the talk at the start of the war had been about how Britain would get through it if everyone pulled together. Emily wondered how much the hardships were really being shared if you could skirt them by virtue of having more money than other people.

Their first stop was at the bakery. Bread was not rationed but there was no doubting that it no longer tasted as good as it had done before the war started; it was greyer and tasted slightly stale even when it was fresh. Not only that but you had to queue for it, sometimes for an hour or more. They were lucky on this occasion, waiting only twenty minutes.

Of course, they understood why the queue was so short once they reached the front; the only loaves left were small and burnt. Mr Thompson the baker must have cut off the worst bits, hence the size. There was nothing else for it however, they would have to take what they could get. Uncle Frank would not be happy, but then when was he ever?

Coming out of the bakery something caught Emily's eye. On the far side of the street was a tall man in a long coat, and a grey trilby hat.

'Do you recognise that man?' said Emily to her sister.

'What man?'

'Him. Over there,' she said nodding towards the far side of the street. 'It's the man from the other day.'

'Who?' asked Celia.

'You know, the man we saw on our street a few days ago.'

'What? The spy who was after Mrs Sadler's flowers?'

'Yes.'

'Are you sure?'

'Of course, I recognise the hat.'

'Anyone could have that hat; it's a very common hat.'

'And his hair.'

'You can't see his hair. It's hidden under his hat,' she pointed out reasonably.

'Look closer, you can see a few strands of blonde hair just sticking out the side,' said Emily tugging on her sister's arm and spinning her to face him. 'It's definitely him.'

'So?'

'What are we going to do?'

'About what?'

'About him.'

'Nothing. First of all, he might not be the man we saw the other day...'

'But he is.'

'...Secondly, even if he *is* the man...'

'Which he is.'

'...He isn't doing anything wrong. He's just standing in the street, wearing a hat. That's not a crime.'

'It is odd though.'

'So are you but that doesn't make you a spy does it?'

'I mean what's he doing?' Emily asked, ignoring her sister's jibe.

'Maybe he's doing his shopping?'

'But he's just standing there.'

'Then maybe he's waiting for someone.'

At that moment the man looked straight towards where Emily was standing. He held her gaze for a moment and then moved off.

'See, he's going. Honestly Emily you aren't half suspicious sometimes.'

'Yes, but he looked right at me.'

'Probably because you were gawping at him.'

'So you don't think he's a spy then?'

'Pretty rubbish spy if he is. What's he going to find out here? That the queues are long and the bread is burnt? That's not exactly a secret. Come on, let's go.'

Their next stop was to Mr Patterson's, the grocer's, to buy potatoes, cabbage and carrots. Mr Patterson didn't like children. He always said that children should be seen and not heard, but Emily had a feeling he would rather children weren't seen either. Both the girls hated going in his shop. It didn't matter how nice they were to him, how meek or quiet they were in his presence, he would never smile or offer them a friendly word. Instead he would watch them intently from the moment they entered, his beady, bloodshot eyes tracking their every movement. Even if he was serving another customer he always knew their exact location, convinced that they would get up to no good if he looked away for just a second.

As a little girl Emily had been terrified of him and, being the loving older sister that she was, Celia would make up stories to frighten her further. This had only stopped when their mother overheard one particularly gruesome tale that ended with Mr Patterson using the blood of young children as fertiliser for his vegetable plot, after which she put an end to Celia's night-time storytelling sessions.

Eager to spend as little time in his presence as possible, Emily and Celia would play a game of 'Rock, Paper, Scissors,' to determine who would have to do the shopping. Unfortunately for Emily, she lost more often than not. Today however, she was determined she was going to win.

'Okay, on three,' she said.

They both held their fists in front of them.

'Wait, on three, or after three?' asked Celia.

'You always ask that.'

'And you always screw it up so we have to play again.'

'I do not.'

'Do too.'

'Do not. Anyway,' she said quickly before her sister could respond, 'I said *on* three.'

'Fine, *on* three,' mimicked Celia. 'Ready?'

Emily looked her sister in the eye, holding her gaze, resolved to beat her this time.

'Ready.'

'One… two… three…'

'PAPER,' Celia shouted as she held out her hand in the shape of a pair of scissors.

Emily, having meant to do 'Rock', found herself confused by the shout, and put her hand straight out like a piece of paper.

'YES!' crowed Celia. 'Off you go!'

'That's cheating,' said Emily sourly.

'No it isn't. I won fair and square.'

'You shouted paper.'

'So?'

'So then you did scissors. I… it confused me.'

'I can't help it if you're easily confused now can I? Go on,' she said with a huge grin on her face.

Emily scowled at her but knew it would be futile to argue. She held out her hand for the shopping list which Celia was only too happy to give her.

A small bell tinkled as Emily entered the store. Mr Patterson was busy serving another customer but without even looking up, she could tell he knew that there was a child in his shop. Breathing heavily out of the corner of his mouth, his eyes scanned the room and fixed quickly on Emily who stood patiently waiting to be served. She might have imagined it but she was sure she saw his nostrils twitching. The shop wasn't as busy as the bakers had been, and she only had to wait a few minutes before she was at the front of the queue.

'What do you want?' he croaked.

'A cabbage please,' said Emily.

Mr Patterson's face twitched but, as he could find no excuse to deny this perfectly reasonable request, he retrieved the smallest, dirtiest cabbage from the basket behind him and popped it on the counter.

'Thank you,' said Emily trying her best to sound grateful whilst silently wishing all manner of small but painful injuries upon him.

'May I also have half a pound of potatoes?'

Mr Patterson rolled his tongue around the inside of his

mouth as if he was considering her request. Again, he could find nothing to object to and he pushed past her and gathered up a few loose brown spuds into a bag. Emily began to feel faint. Trying to steady herself she placed a hand lightly on the counter. Without warning she felt herself lurch to one side, then the shop was gone and she was standing on what looked like ashes from a fire. She turned around. What was happening? The grocers was nothing more than a burnt-out shell. The haberdashery next door was boarded up, the words 'DANGER! KEEP OUT! STRUCTURE UNSOUND!' were painted sloppily across it in black paint.

Then as quickly as it had appeared it was gone again and Emily was standing at the end of her street. Only it wasn't her street, at least not as she knew it, there was dust everywhere and some of the rooves of the houses were missing slates. It was dusk and the first stars were blinking into view, as if they had come to watch the proceedings. A dark plume of smoke snaked its way up above the houses on the corner. It was coming from the far end of the road. Emily felt her stomach heave.

Mr Thompson, an elderly neighbour, hobbled past with an old blanket thrust under one arm. Emily called out to him but he did not reply; he did not even seem to hear her. She broke into a run and quickly rounded the corner only to stop short in horror. Her house was gone; all that was left was its charred skeleton: the broken bones of her former home. Men in dark blue uniforms and tin hats pumped water onto its smouldering remains. Only two walls remained standing, leaning against each other for support, punch-drunk and swaying like a boxer waiting for the knockout blow.

It took a moment for it to sink in, and then it was as if a switch had been thrown inside her and she sprinted towards where her house had once stood.

'Mum! Celia! Frank!' she screamed. 'Help me someone, help me!'

She got down on her knees and began to claw at the

rubble, desperate to lift as much of it as she possibly could, but as much rubble as she moved the pile never seemed to decrease. A few of the neighbours were standing around, faces so grey they looked as though they had stepped out of a film, even the Baker children from down the road who Emily had never seen stand still for more than a moment were quiet, shuffling behind their mother, the youngest clutching at the hem of her dress for reassurance. Emily shouted at them to help, but no one moved or even acknowledged she was there.

Now she knew with a certainty that burned within her that she was seeing the future. She did not know how it was possible, only that it was true. She wanted to believe it was all a dream but this was different; for the first time she was aware of an energy that was pushing her, controlling her almost. It was like trying to force the positive ends of two magnets together. She knew she was where she was because she had to be there. Somehow this thought calmed her and she began to think. Perhaps they had all managed to get away. Suddenly a cry went up from one of the ARP's who had been digging amongst the rubble.

'We've got one!'

Emily's heart leapt into her throat. The small crowd craned their necks to see what was had been discovered whilst trying to shield the eyes of the children in case it should turn out to be something awful. Emily however could not look away. It was Celia.

'The pulse is very faint. We need to get her to hospital now.'

Two ambulance workers raced across the rubble with a stretcher.

'Are you listening to me?' said a loud, cranky voice, 'what do you want?'

Emily blinked. She was back in the grocer's shop. Mr Patterson loomed over her.

'If you're just going to waste my time then you can get out. Go on, get out of here.'

Barely able to take in her surroundings Emily did as she was told and ran out of the store without picking up her purchases. She ran so quickly she almost collided with Celia who was waiting outside.

'Whoa! What's the matter? What's going on?'

'It happened. It happened again.'

'What happened? What are you talking about? Where's the veg?'

'I... This was gone. It was destroyed. And that,' she said pointing at the haberdashery, 'that had been hit too. The house! The house, it was–'

Emily swayed, almost falling to the ground but she was steadied by Celia.

'What do you mean?'

'I saw it. It happened. It happens. The Germans are going to bomb us, they're going to bomb our street, our house.'

Celia put her hand over her sister's mouth.

'Shhhhh. Don't say that. Not here anyway. Come on, let's get you home. We'll make up some kind of excuse for mum about the shopping, say Mr Patterson had closed for the day or something.'

'Don't you get it?' said Emily breaking free of her sister's grip. 'I don't care about the shopping, I don't care about anything. We're all going to be killed and you're acting like... We've got to go somewhere safe. We must get out of here.'

'Okay, okay,' said Celia, still trying to get Emily to lower her voice. 'Let's just go home. If you're that worried maybe we can talk to mum and see if she'll come to the underground with us next time the sirens go.'

Somewhat placated Emily began to walk home with Celia at her side. All the same she couldn't help but glance skywards every now and again checking for German planes.

'It's going to happen. I'm sure of it,' said Emily, more to herself than Celia.

'But how do you know?'

'I can't explain it. You just have to believe me.'

'What you're saying doesn't make any sense Emily, listen to yourself,' said Celia pleadingly.

'I know, I know it doesn't make sense, but what does it matter? If I'm wrong then you can laugh at me and tease me as much as you like, I won't care. If I'm right then we'll be safe.'

Celia stared into Emily's eyes as if she hoped to see some hint of doubt there, but she found none.

'Come on then,' said Celia with a sigh, 'but you have to explain this to mum and Uncle Frank.'

'Fine.'

By the time they reached home Emily was feeling slightly calmer and she was determined to get her mother's agreement on what to do in the event of another air raid.

'Mum?' she called as she entered the house.

There was no response.

'Mum?' she called again.

'Shhhhh,' said Celia holding her fingers to lips, 'if Uncle Frank is ill in bed and you wake him up I don't even want to know what he'd do to you.'

Emily stalked through the house looking for her mother, but she was nowhere to be found. Eventually she came back into the kitchen to find Celia reading a note.

'It's from mum,' she said, looking up at Emily. 'She says she's taken Uncle Frank to see Doctor McGinley.'

'On a Saturday? It must be serious then. Why didn't she ask Doctor McGinley to come and see Uncle Frank here?'

'You know what Uncle Frank's like, too stubborn by half. He'd have insisted on going down there just to prove he could.'

The feeling of unease she'd carried with her since the vision in the grocers came on all the stronger.

'What if there's a raid whilst they're at the doctors?'

'Then they'll take shelter there. Doctor McGinley isn't going to chuck them out on the street is he?'

'But what if –'

Celia cut her off.

'They'll be okay Emily. If a raid happens when they're out – which it won't – then they can take shelter in the underground. And when they get back here you can tell them what happened alright?'

Emily nodded and started to pack away the groceries, if only to have something to occupy her time. After that she paced the house, moving restlessly from room to room. She wondered what could be keeping them. When she could stand it no longer she stood in the garden on top of the shelter scanning the sky, waiting for the first sign of the planes she was certain were coming, but the sky remained stubbornly, gloriously clear.

On any other day she would have revelled in the warm weather and spent her Saturday playing cricket or perhaps reading in the sun. Every so often Celia joined her in the garden, and though she tried to pretend that everything was normal, Emily caught her shooting glances at the sky when she thought Emily wasn't watching.

Finally they heard voices from inside and they rushed in to greet their mother. As they ran into the hallway they saw Uncle Frank slowly climbing the stairs, looking awfully pale.

'Hello girls,' said their mother wearily, then she called up the stairs after their uncle, 'I'll be up in a minute with your salts Frank, get yourself some rest.'

She hung her gas mask over the banister and made her way through to the kitchen.

'Mum, can we talk to you for a minute?' said Emily nervously.

Their mother was measuring out a couple of spoonsful of white powder from a blue tin into a glass.

'Can it wait? Your uncle needs his liver salts. The doctor says it's heartburn and a touch of the summer flu. He'll be right as rain soon but honestly I've never seen him looking so washed out.'

She topped the glass up with water and the powder began to fizz and bubble. She gave it a quick stir and then shot out of the room to see to their uncle. They waited patiently for her to return, then before she could get distracted with anything else, Emily asked again.

'Mum, I really need to speak to you. Now,' said Emily firmly.

Her mother stopped what she was doing and came to sit with the girls at the table.

'What is it? Is everything alright? You're not feeling poorly too are you?'

'No. No, it's nothing like that.'

Now the time had come to tell her mother, she felt silly. What if she didn't believe her? What if she thought she was cracking up and needed to see a doctor? What if she *was* actually cracking up and needed to see a doctor?

'What's the matter sweetheart?' she asked.

'I've been having these dreams,' Emily began, as matter-of-factly as she could.

'Right...'

'Only they're not really dreams. More like... I don't know what to call them. Visions. I'm in the sky. I'm on a plane and I'm flying over London. And then. Well... well then the plane starts to bomb London, to bomb this street in fact and our house is destroyed.'

'Oh sweetheart, they're just dreams. It's nothing to worry about. With all the talk on the radio and... well it's natural to feel worried,' she said kindly.

'They're not dreams,' said Emily crossly. 'I can't explain it properly. It's different to that. I know what dreams feel like and these... these visions... they didn't feel like dreams. I even have them when I'm awake.'

'Emily, please. I have quite enough on my plate with your uncle already. And your father hasn't written in several... well I just don't need any of your nonsense right now.'

'It's not nonsense,' said Emily feeling her temper rising again. 'It isn't.'

Celia placed a hand on her leg under the table and gave it a gentle squeeze.

'Mum, I don't know what Emily has seen or dreamt, but she almost collapsed at Mr Patterson's and I know she believes what she's saying. She's not having you on. All she wants,' she continued, 'is for us to go down to the shelter next time the sirens go off.'

Her mother looked between the two of them. Emily could tell she was considering what Celia had said.

'Okay. If it makes you happy and it stops all of... well if it helps then we will go down to the shelter next time the sirens go.'

Emily smiled, relieved.

'It has to be the public shelter though,' said Emily.

For a moment it looked as though her mother might argue but instead she shook her head and sighed in acquiescence.

'Fine. But good luck persuading your uncle.'

'He'll go if you go, I know he will,' said Emily and then she ran around the table to give her mother a hug.

She felt as though a huge weight had been lifted from her. She was still frightened about what might happen, but even if their home was destroyed at least they would be safe.

'But if you have any more of these 'visions' as you call them, we're going to the doctor, do you understand?'

Emily nodded. At that moment she'd have agreed to anything if it stopped her mother changing her mind.

'Now get out from under my feet and leave your poor mother in peace.'

The girls did as they were told, returning to the sanctuary of the garden to soak up the mid-afternoon sun. Emily lay in the grass looking up at the sky and wondered what her mother had been about to say about hearing from her father. She hadn't heard from him in several what? Days? Weeks? With all the worrying about the visions she hadn't noticed the absence of his letters on the kitchen table. Besides, surely delays were inevitable. If he was away at the front, it was natural that things didn't arrive with great regularity. It didn't mean the worst had happened. She felt a flush of guilt that he had drifted so far from her thoughts when he was putting himself in such danger.

At that moment the peace was shattered by the cry of the air raid sirens. A chill ran down her spine and turned her blood to ice. It was happening. It was really happening. Emily was sure of it. She sprinted into the house to find her mother and Celia grabbing their coats and their gas masks.

'We've got to get out. Quickly! Quickly!' said Emily hurrying them on.

'We're not going without your uncle, hold your horses. It's probably just another false alarm anyway.'

'But you said—'

'I know what I said, and we will go to the shelter, but we will do it when I'm ready and when your uncle is ready, not before. They'll probably sound the all clear by the time we get him out of bed.'

'I don't think so,' said Celia who was standing with the front door open and whose face had turned the colour of snow.

Over the din of the sirens they could hear the far-off hum of engines. They looked up. In the distance the skies were filling with German aeroplanes. The aerial war that they had all once expected, and then finally dismissed, was upon them. Emily felt a terror strike her deeper than any she had ever known. It rushed through her and made her feel weak, so weak that she feared her legs would give way beneath her. She swallowed hard and summoned up every last ounce of strength she possessed. We can do this, she told herself. Perhaps the visions were a warning, she should have heeded them sooner, but she knew now what she had to do. She would get everyone to safety.

'Come on then' said her mother, 'into the garden. Now.'

'But the underground...' Emily began.

'We're not going out in that, there's no time. Come on, the shelter will be fine.'

Emily wanted to argue but the danger was growing with every second. At least if she could get everyone to the Anderson Shelter they should be safe.

'Go on,' her mother snapped, 'get down the shelter. I'll fetch Uncle Frank.'

'We'll come with you.'

'No, to the shelter. Both of you. We'll be down in a minute.'

Her voice made it clear she would brook no argument. Emily watched her mother turn and go back upstairs. She wanted to call after her, but she knew her mother would never leave without Frank. She wondered why he hadn't come down already. Couldn't he hear the planes? Or was he so stubborn he'd rather die than be proved wrong?

'Come on Emily,' shouted Celia above the din, 'let's go.'

She dragged her by the arm, through the kitchen and into the garden, then rolled aside the sandbags which lay against the door to the shelter.

'EMILY,' she urged her once more.

Throwing a last glance at the house Emily ducked into the shelter. Once inside, they sat in the darkness, neither one daring to speak. Emily kept replaying the terrible visions she had seen in her head, trying to suppress the question that was racing round her brain and refusing to be silenced. What if she really had seen the future and there was nothing she could do? What if everything she had seen was going to happen anyway? She suspected Celia was thinking the same thing.

'Celia?'

'Don't.'

'But–'

'Don't. I don't want to talk about anything. I just want mum and Uncle Frank to be here.'

Then the bombs began to fall. The ground beneath their feet shuddered as each one found its target. Emily pictured the street disappearing in a rain of fire. There was no way of knowing for sure how far away it was all happening. All they knew was that it was gradually coming closer.

How long had it been since their mother had gone after Uncle Frank? Ten minutes? Twenty? Or even more? Time had ceased to exist, there was only one, ever-lasting moment. It was the end of the world. How could they survive this? How could anyone survive this? And yet, even as she had that thought, she felt a sort of desperate hope that despite it all they would come through, that the next day, by some miracle, London would emerge from the fire and the mess, dust itself off, and carry on as before. She wanted to live, she wanted everyone to live.

'Something's wrong. Mum should be down by now,' said Celia finally.

'I know.'

'We've got to go and get them.'

There was a long pause as another bomb exploded. It was the loudest yet and dirt dropped down from the ceiling.

'I know,' said Emily stealing herself to head back into the house.

The girls looked at each other. Even in the darkness they knew the depths of each other's fear, yet somehow knowing how afraid the other was made them both feel slightly better. They had each other. They could do this. Celia pushed open the door to the shelter and climbed out with Emily just behind. They dashed inside without looking up, for Emily suspected that if she saw the planes overhead she might just lose her nerve.

'Mum? Uncle Frank?'

They ran through the kitchen and into the living room. It was deserted.

'Mum? Where are you?'

'Girls?' came a voice from upstairs.

'Mum!' cried Emily.

They ran up the stairs to find their mother sitting on the landing, cradling Uncle Frank's head on her lap.

'Mum? What's wrong?'

'It's Frank. I think he's having a heart attack.'

Frank was taking short, sharp, shallow breaths; his face was ghostly pale and his eyes were shut tight.

'I can't move him. I'll have to stay here. You two get back down to the shelter.'

'I'll get a doctor,' said Celia.

'No doctor's going to come out in this,' she shouted, 'now do what I told you and go back down to the shelter.'

'We're not leaving you,' said Emily as tears began to trickle down her cheeks.

'I'll be okay. This will all be over soon,' said her mother, as calmly as if she were discussing a spot of unexpected rain, but there was a quiver in her voice that told Emily she was frightened too.

A loud explosion rocked the house.

'No! We've got to get out,' insisted Emily. 'Maybe the three of us can get Uncle Frank down to the shelter together.'

'Get... out... get... away...' Uncle Frank had opened his eyes again and spoke between gasps of pain. 'Leave me Joan... I'm here to look after you all, not... the other way round.'

His speech was slurred and unsteady but his meaning was clear.

'You're a stubborn old man Frank Cartwright and you'll see another day yet. Celia, Emily grab those old blankets from the shelter, they're the only ones strong enough.'

'Strong enough for what?' asked Celia.

'We're going to make a stretcher. We'll carry him down on them.'

Emily went to interject but her mother cut her off.

'This is no time to argue. Quick! Quick!'

Uncle Frank took hold of their mother's hand which had been resting on his chest and gave it a gentle squeeze. Reluctantly Emily and Celia turned and raced downstairs, the guns and sirens still blaring in their ears. As she was half way down Emily glanced back to see her mother plant a tender kiss on her uncle's forehead.

Down in the shelter they grabbed all the blankets they could.

'Give them to me quick,' said Celia.

Emily handed over the blankets.

'Let's go.'

'You should stay here,' said Celia.

'No!' cried Emily. 'We've got more chance of getting him out if there are three of us than if there are two. Uncle Frank will be heavy. Stop trying to protect me.'

'Fine,' she said, with a shake of the head.

'Come on, we haven't got long.'

'You're right,' said Celia turning to leave. 'Oh wait, we might need a torch and that first aid kit that's under the bench. Get them as well, just in case.'

There was another huge explosion somewhere close by that bought yet more dirt down from the ceiling. The noise of the planes was growing louder and louder. Emily didn't understand what they'd need a torch for but got down on her knees anyway and rooted around under the bench for the first aid box. It was tricky in the dark but she soon found her fingers scraping on tin. She pulled the kit from beneath the bench. Standing up she saw that Celia had already left. She made to follow but when she pushed at the door of the shelter she found it was shut tight.

'Celia? Celia quick! There's something blocking the door,' she shouted.

'I know,' came a voice from the other side.

Emily threw herself against the door but it wouldn't budge, and she guessed Celia must have pushed the sand bags back against it.

'Celia! Let me out!'

'No. We'll be with you in a minute. Stay there.'

'CELIA!' Emily screamed, but there was no reply.

She rammed her shoulder against the door but it barely moved an inch. There was another loud whoosh and a crash as something fell close by. Emily could hear the whistling of bombs as they tumbled towards the ground.

The dull thud of a distant war had become a deafening roar. She pushed again and again and again, desperate to force the door open, to make any gap that she might crawl through. Then she had an idea. If the sandbags were all against the bottom perhaps she could prize open the top enough to squeeze out. She pushed at the top corner and it moved enough for her to get her fingers through. She couldn't, however, get the rest of herself out. She fell back onto one of the beds. It was useless. All she had succeeded in doing was cutting her fingers. There must be another way, she thought desperately.

'CELIA! MUM! FRANK!' she cried, but to no one answered.

The sound of the planes was even louder now as they drew closer and closer. She looked around the shelter for something she might use to jimmy the door open. Then she saw it, her father's old cricket bat, lying beneath one of the beds. She didn't stop to wonder why he had put it there, instead she slid underneath the bed and grabbed hold.

Emily would never know that it had been this that had saved her life. If she had emerged from beneath the bed, then she would have been killed by the blast that followed seconds later. As it was she was shielded from the falling debris by a combination of the shelter, and the camp bed. Her left ankle was badly sprained, she was severely concussed, and she would be left with a scar on the right-hand side of her stomach caused by a large splinter from one of the struts that supported the shelter roof. She was badly hurt, but she was alive. Come the morning, that would be very small comfort indeed.

Chapter Three

Many times she woke to see someone at the end of her bed, but whenever she tried to gather her thoughts they slipped away from her. She was so tired, she could barely lift her head. Her body was slowly shutting down until she was hardly doing anything more than sleeping. And as she slept she dreamt, she Saw.

She Saw the world on fire, and she heard screams, the desperate cries of people, not even people any more, little more than skeletons crawling through the dirt and filth. Next came the hunger, a gut-wrenching ache that gnawed at her and made her feel sick. She saw thousands of people, people whose eyes burned with a strange fury. She Saw flags and bunting, heard cheering and crying, laughing and shouting but when she awoke she could remember only snatches of these things, tiny fragments that scattered like blossom on the wind. She felt a sort of cold, a deep and biting cold that crept up her spine like a whisper and sat with her for hours. Sometimes the cold had a voice, a snide, nagging voice that ordered her to stop, just to stop.

'This could all be over. No more pain, no more suffering, let go Emily: there is nothing left for you.'

Then one day the voice disappeared without warning. A hand lay upon her head, someone was stroking her hair, ever so slowly and ever so gently. Tobacco and aftershave hung in the air, a scent so thick she could taste it. She felt the cracked dry skin of the hand on her forehead and she knew: her father had come back to her. He had returned. She opened her eyes, hardly daring to believe it.

'You're here,' she whispered.

'I'm here,' he replied.

'Mum, Celia, Uncle Frank…?' her voice quivered and broke.

Her father shook his head. 'I'm so sorry. They… Celia made it to the hospital but her injuries were too severe.'

Emily wanted to tell her father everything. How sorry she was, how she should have done more to stop it, how much she had missed him. Most of all she wanted to ask him if he still loved her, if he could forgive her for surviving when the others had not. She longed to scream with the pain that coursed through her chest, scratching at her ribcage like a wild beast desperate for its freedom. She remembered how, when she was little and she'd hurt herself, he'd haul her up onto his knees and ask her where it hurt, then rub the wound gently until all the pain had disappeared. She wished now he could take her heart in his hands, like some injured bird that had tumbled from its nest, and slowly nurse it back to health until it was strong once more. She longed for him to do something, anything, to make the pain stop.

'Dad…' she said as tears rolled from her eyes.

Just thinking of her family pulled at the jagged hole in her heart they'd left behind, making it rawer, deeper.

'I know…'

Grief had moved them both to a place beyond words. He pulled her to him and she rested her head on his shoulder. She could feel his hot breath and the stubble on his chin. She had never seen her father with stubble before. She began to cry. She cried as she never would again, a loud primal scream that came from a place darker than the blackest night, and she shook as if the grief was trying to escape through her skin.

After sometime, she could not have said how long, she

stopped crying. It was not that she no longer hurt, it was simply that she was empty. Where once she had life, now there was nothing, no feeling remained. She had poured everything into her father and she had nothing left to give. She looked at him properly for the first time. He was older than she remembered, so terribly old and terribly grey. So too was his skin and his hair, all greyer now than before. Even his eyes were dulled, with a ring of tired yellow about them.

She wanted to ask him if he was okay but she didn't know how. There was so much she didn't know about her father and now it seemed wrong to ask. She knew his parents had died some years ago, but he never spoke of them and she wondered if he still missed them, or if the pain of losing someone so close eventually went away? She wanted to ask him if he was angry with her, because she was angry with herself. She had only lived because of her sister. The better daughter had died, the good daughter, the kind and funny daughter, the one who did as she was told and always looked out for others. The wrong girl had survived. And if that was how she felt, how could he feel any different?

Finally, simply to break the oppressive silence that had settled upon the room, she asked, 'How long have I been asleep?'

Her father exhaled slowly. 'You've been sick, very sick. The wound in your chest became infected, I thought I was going to lose you too.'

'But it was... the bombing I mean... it was yesterday...'

'No Emily,' he said gently, 'it was two weeks ago. It's not surprising you don't remember. You had a fever, you were drifting in and out of consciousness. Every time we thought you were on the mend you got worse again. Two nights ago you woke up screaming, you were inconsolable. The doctors thought you might hurt yourself further so they gave you something which knocked you out.'

Two weeks? Emily thought to herself. How could it

have been two weeks?

'I want to wake up,' she said, although she didn't really feel it.

'Soon,' he replied, stroking her hair once more and offering up a small smile that died at the corners of his mouth.

The silence began to grow again until it was so great that Emily feared that if she didn't break it now, she might never find the strength to do so.

'Where've you been? Tell me what's happening. Tell me everything.'

'The Germans are bombing London day and night. It's awful. People are scared out of their minds, though they're trying not to show it. I don't know how long we can last.'

Even through the heavy daze of painkillers and sedatives, Emily could hear the weight of sorrow in his voice.

'I've never seen the city like this. Streets I grew up in, gone. It's all gone Emily... everything's gone...'

He trailed off as he became lost in the things that had passed. Emily needed him to stay talking though. She knew she was being selfish, but in the silence thoughts of her sister and her mother crept back in, and she couldn't bear to think about them just yet.

'When's the funeral? We've so much to do, we've got to get it right...'

She tried to climb out of bed, although even sitting up made her feel dizzy. Her father placed a hand lightly on her shoulder and she lay back down.

'The funeral was two days ago Emily, I'm so sorry. When you're well enough, I'll take you to see them. I'm afraid we couldn't wait any longer, there's nowhere to keep the bodies anymore; the morgues are full.'

Emily nodded. The morgues are full. That one little sentence told her all she needed to know about how the war was going. She shuddered, trying not to picture the image her father's words had called to mind; row upon row of corpses – each of them with her sister's face.

'Dad... Before...'

She broke off. She couldn't bring herself to say 'before the bombing', but he understood. Now there would always be a Before. There would be no need to ever say anything else. It seemed obvious when she thought about it. Their lives had been snapped in two. There was the Before and there was the After and that was that.

'Before,' she said again. 'I saw it happen.'

'I know–' he started but Emily cut him off.

'No. Please. I saw it. I saw it happen *before* it happened. I can't explain. I knew it was going to happen. I saw it all. I... fell... I sort of fell and I saw it all. But I didn't... I didn't realise, I should have tried harder. Mum, Celia, Uncle Frank... I should've made them understand.'

The words tumbled out, chased by the tears that spilled down her cheeks.

'I begged them to go down to the shelter, I... Celia... Celia came with me. I asked her to and she did. Uncle Frank you see, he was sick. Mum had to help him... she sent us away but then Celia... she went back. I wanted to go back but I couldn't, Celia stopped me. Oh, I'm so sorry. She's dead because of me. They're all dead because of me, because I didn't warn them in time, I didn't know what it meant. I should've have forced them, I should've done more. I could've done more...'

She had shaken off her father's embrace and was staring at him, desperate for his forgiveness.

'Emily,' her father voice was barely a croak but he spoke slowly and deliberately, 'it was not your fault. You are not to blame. Celia is not to blame; your mother and your uncle are not to blame. Never think that it was your fault.'

'But–'

'No. No. It wasn't you. You couldn't have done anything.'

'But I could. I saw it all don't you understand? I knew it was going to happen!'

Her father stared at her for what seemed like an

eternity. Finally, he spoke.

'Tell no one what you just said to me. This is important, please it's not safe. If you see anything more don't tell anyone, no one, do you understand?'

'I'm not mad,' said Emily staring fiercely into his eyes.

He met her gaze and held it for a moment, then he seemed to collapse in on himself. 'I'm sorry... I thought I had more time... I should've told you.'

'Told me? Told me what?'

'I meant what I said Emily, it wasn't your fault. Never think that. I should've told you sooner. Can you forgive me?'

'Forgive you? I... I don't understand.'

Emily could feel herself losing control. This wasn't how it was meant to be. She needed her father to be strong for her, what was he doing asking her for forgiveness? What did he need forgiving for?

'You must listen. There are things I never said, things I should've said before now.'

'Dad, please...'

Her father paused as he tried to gather his scattered thoughts.

'I need to tell you about my sister.'

'Your sister?'

'Lottie. She was different, she was special. She had a gift. She could see things others couldn't.'

'What kind of things?'

He paused. He looked so tired, like an old tree in the depths of winter, branches sagging beneath the weight of the snow.

'She could See little snippets, tiny fractions of the future. I didn't believe her when she first told me, who would? But time and again she proved it. Before I found out, we used to play cards and she'd win every time. It made me so cross. Then sometimes she would say things to me, give me advice that would make no sense, but a few days later something would happen and it would all fall into place.'

'Like what?'

'We used to have a vase, a small orangey thing, it was hideous but it was my mother's favourite, so it took pride of place at our dinner table. One evening Lottie leaned over and whispered to me, 'Blame the dog if she asks about the vase.' A few days later I tripped and knocked it off the table. When my mother came in I instantly knew that this was what my sister had meant, so I told her Prince had done it.'

Emily opened her mouth to say something but her father interjected.

'It wasn't just that though, she knew things, things she could not possibly know ordinarily. She was a Seer.'

'A Seer?'

'That's what she called herself. Someone who could see into the future.'

Everything slowly began to fall into place in Emily's head. The visions she'd had. The dreams.

'And you think I'm a Seer?'

'I do, yes,' replied her father, his steady gaze meeting hers.

'But how do you know? How can you be sure?'

'Your Aunt Charlotte – Lottie we called her – was a Seer, and so was my mother. It runs in our family. But listen to me, because this is important; Seeing is a dangerous thing. Lottie died young and my mother is long gone too.'

'But how do you know I'm a Seer? I could have been ill. Maybe I was just dreaming.'

Even though Emily had been certain that she had seen the future, she was waiting, hoping, for someone to tell her she was wrong and to provide her with a better explanation, one that made sense. To find her father suddenly talking about Seeing and visions was disconcerting. He was supposed to make everything all right, but he was making it worse.

'Like I said it runs in families, most of the time at least.'

'What about Celia?'

'Celia wasn't a Seer.'

'How do you know?'

'You can only truly be certain when a Seer comes of age, by which I mean on the day she Sees for the first time. Once that happens they develop a small mark somewhere on their body, like two crescent moons back to back with a tiny orb suspended in the middle of each between the two tips.'

He produced a pen from his pocket and drew the symbol on the back of the chart that hung at the end of her bed.

'But I don't have the mark. I can't be a Seer.'

'Emily, lift up your right sleeve.'

She hesitated.

'Lift up your sleeve, please Emily.'

Emily rolled back her sleeve to reveal the mark, exactly like the one her father had drawn moments before.

'But where did this come from? This wasn't here earlier,' she said, licking her fingers and trying to rub it off, but it didn't budge. She thought back to the first time she had Seen. 'I had a rash for a few days after I had my first vision.'

'It only develops once you've Seen for the first time. It's often found on the forearm, but sometimes on the neck or the small of the back. The Seer's Mark they call it.'

They sat in silence for a while and the full implications of her father's words began to sink in.

'Why didn't you tell me?'

Her father opened his mouth but no words came out.

'If I'd known that I could really see the future, if mum had known...'

He was right, it was not her fault, far from it in fact. He was to blame. If he'd told her the truth she could have saved them. The thought of being able to relieve herself of the guilt, to offload it onto someone else was too glorious to resist.

'Why didn't you tell me?' she said again.

'I thought I would be home by the time you started to See, and that I could help you through it. Most Seers are a little older when they first See. I was worried that if I told you, you might tell someone you shouldn't. I didn't know this would happen–'

'But I did, I knew what would happen, and I couldn't stop it. I could've saved them. If you'd told me I could have done something. But now they're dead and it's your fault.'

'Emily...'

He looked so sad. Grief had carved itself into his features. Part of her hated what she was saying, but she couldn't stop herself from saying it. The guilt and anger surged through her body and just for a few moments she was free from all the pain and the hurt. Then a thought seized her.

'But if I can see the future then I can help can't I?'

'Help?'

'I can stop this, I can stop this happening to someone ever again.'

'NO.'

His voice was fierce.

'No,' he said again, quieter this time. 'I'm sorry but you can't.'

'But–'

'Listen to me Emily, you must never reveal your secret, not to anyone, do you understand?'

He gripped her forearm tightly forcing Emily to look at him.

'You're hurting me.'

'Tell me you understand.'

'I don't understand. You're hurting, let go of me,' she demanded.

He released her arm but didn't look away.

'Why shouldn't I help people? If I can see the future why shouldn't I tell someone? I could predict when the Germans will attack, I could tell... I could tell...'

'Who would you tell?'

'I don't know, someone. I would tell the police, or the army, I could tell them where and when the Germans were going to attack. We could keep people safe.'

'But why should they believe you?'

'Because... because I can see the future.' She felt herself getting frustrated. Why was he being so obtuse? Surely he understood? Surely after all that had happened he wanted to help too?

'So you would tell them you could see the future?'

'Yes, if I had to, of course I would. I could prove it to them, if I'm what you say I am then I could See on command.'

'Go on then.'

'What?'

'See. If you're a Seer, then See.'

'But it doesn't work like that.'

'How does it work then?'

'I don't know do I?'

'Then how will they know you're telling the truth? They'd say it was impossible.'

'Yes but–'

'They'd say you were a liar, or that you were mad. And who's going to believe a little girl like you? They might even lock you up.'

'I'd find a way. It happened before.'

'Okay, let's say you somehow manage to prove to these people you can See, maybe you save a ship full of soldiers, that's fantastic, but what then?'

'What do you mean?'

'What then? Because it won't stop there. You move the ship and it survives and that's great. You think they won't want more from you?'

'More?'

'Troop movements perhaps, or accurate weather reports. You can tell them exactly when would be best to bomb a city, when they could expect fewest casualties for our side, and the most for theirs. Think about it, thousands of people could die and you would be responsible.'

'THEN LET THEM DIE,' screamed Emily. 'AFTER WHAT THEY DID, LET THEM BURN. I DON'T CARE. I DON'T CARE ANYMORE.'

'Of course you do,' replied her father quietly.

'I don't,' she said, but the anger that had raged inside her just moments before had disappeared, and with it all the energy seemed to have drained out of her.

'If you want to go to the authorities then I'm not going to stop you, but remember not every German is a Nazi, and not every Nazi is a German. A lot of the Germans are people just like you. They love like you, they laugh like you, they grieve like you. They read, they sing, they dance and they wanted no part in this bloody war. Maybe they voted for Hitler, maybe they didn't. Maybe they watched in horror as friends and neighbours were beaten and chased from the land of their birth. And now they're cowering in shelters and basements, just like you, hoping they'll see the light of another day. Bombs aren't clever or smart Emily, they don't know where they're going and they don't just kill bad people.'

'I know what bombs do,' said Emily, her voice dropping dangerously low.

'What you See has consequences and you must learn that.'

Once more the rage and frustration swelled up inside her and swept like a wave over her father.

'DON'T LECTURE ME ABOUT CONSEQUENCES,' she shouted. 'I saw them die, I saw it, I watched it happen and I could do nothing about it. I didn't realise and now they're gone. I could've saved them, so don't tell me I don't understand the consequences.'

Emily felt a single hot tear roll down her cheek. She did not wipe it away but continued to stare at her father, the fury burning in her chest.

'I'm sorry,' he said. 'It's natural that you want to use your ability, but you have to use it in the right way. We can't tell people about this. Maybe you're right, maybe people have changed, maybe you'd be safe, but its war time Emily. It's a brutal, bloody war and we're losing, make no mistake about that. Poland, Czechoslovakia, Holland, Belgium, Austria, Hungary, France... All under Nazi rule now. We're alone, the last ones standing – in Europe at least. Give it a year and we could well go the same way as the rest of them. We'll be just another name in a history book, wiped from the map, some colony of the Third Reich that once rebelled against the Fatherland. When times are bad people get desperate, and once that happens they can justify anything, because it's always for the greater good and it'll always go back to normal once the war is over. But war changes what's normal. There's no going back once the secret is out. And what if the Nazis found out? You think they're not going to be interested in someone like you? It's not safe for you Emily. I can't lose you as well. I just couldn't bear that.'

Emily said nothing. What was there to say?

'I need you to listen. I've got to go away for a time and so have you,' he said, his voice full of regret.

'You mean, after all this you're sending me away? Where am I going to live?' Emily said, because it sounded better than the questions she actually wanted to ask, like 'Who's going to look after me?' and 'What could be so important that you have to leave me behind?'

'You'll be evacuated to the countryside. A lot of the children have already gone and since the bombing started people have become even more desperate to get their families out of the cities.'

Her father took her hands in his.

'I'm asking you to be brave. You've already shown more courage than I ever have, and now I have to ask you for more. We will be together again I promise.'

'But where are you going?'

'I can't tell you that. Just know that it's very important. Things are happening, terrible things, and I need to put a stop to them.'

He got up to leave, taking his hat and coat from the stand in the corner.

'I will see you again in the morning, and if the doctors say it's alright, then in a few days we'll go to the cemetery. Now you must get some rest.'

Emily lay back down on her bed, her head swimming with all she had heard.

'I want to see it,' she said after a moment.

'See what?'

'The house,' she replied.

'But there's nothing there to see.'

'I know. I think I just need to see that.'

'I'm not sure it's a very good idea.'

'Just for a few minutes. I want to say goodbye.'

Her father nodded.

'Okay. Sleep tight Emily.'

Emily didn't think she would ever be able to sleep again, not after all she had heard, but the fight with her father had exhausted her and the painkillers were still having an effect. Within moments she had fallen back in to a dark and restless sleep.

Chapter Four

Emily sat in silence as the car wound its way through familiar streets towards the place she still thought of as home. The time since she'd woken was a colourless blur; a combination of the heavy pain killers the doctors had given her, and her own stunned disinterest in everything that was going on had left her unable to distinguish one day from the next. The only emotion she was able to summon with any force was anger. She was barely speaking to her father, and when she did it was only to argue with him further. He'd known that she would one day be able to see the future and he hadn't said anything. If he'd at least confided in her mother, that might have made all the difference. But he hadn't, and now the people she loved most in the whole world were dead, and she would never see them again. No matter how many times she told herself this, she couldn't accept that it was really true. Perhaps that was why she wanted to see the house so much.

Emily knew that it had been destroyed, but she needed to see it for herself. She couldn't quite believe that the place she had grown up in was gone, and right up to the moment they arrived at the spot where her home should have been, a small part of her was still convinced that it would be there.

She climbed out the car and stood in what was once her

front garden, the small square of grass replaced by thousands of tiny pieces of brick and broken concrete. Dust blew around her feet. She had expected to be more upset but somehow it felt right. She couldn't conceive of a home without her mother and her sister in it, and if they were gone then it made sense her home would be too.

She closed her eyes, trying to remember what the house had been like when she was growing up. She began to rebuild it in her mind; walls sprung up out of the rubble, pictures shook off the dust to take their place back on the mantelpiece and the fire flickered into life. She climbed the stairs pausing on the creaky step third from the bottom, then ran to her room, throwing open the door, revelling in the smell, the smell now known only to her, that of wood and old seashells, of cotton and dusty blankets. It smelt of her dreams, of her childhood, of her home. It was the smell of happiness.

She clambered into the tiny recess behind the old wardrobe with three legs, the fourth had been lost long before Emily was born and had been replaced by half a brick and an old newspaper. It was the first place she would look when she and Celia had played hide and seek together as little girls, and it was the first place she would hide too, each time hoping against all logic that she wouldn't be discovered. It was the same place she would run to when she'd been naughty and was going to be told off. Her mother, of course, would always find her in seconds and now Emily hid there again longing to be found just one more time. But no one was looking for her anymore, and no one would ever look for her again. She opened her eyes and the picture vanished. There was no going back.

Other houses on the street were also damaged, but everywhere she looked life seemed to be going on as normal, people struggling by, trying to make the best of it. A few of her neighbours had seen them arrive and were speaking in hushed voices to her father, offering words of comfort and prayers of sorrow, though Emily felt certain they could never comprehend the scale of her loss.

She was just about to return to the car when something small and blue caught her eye. It was a tile from the bathroom, no bigger than her thumb nail. She picked it up and held it tight in her hands. She didn't know why she did this, perhaps it was because she could already feel the past slipping away and this was something real, proof of a life that was now mere dirt and dust. Quietly she slipped the tile into her pocket and headed back to the car where her father was now waiting for her.

'Are you okay?' he asked.

'Fine,' she replied shrugging off the arm he tried to drape round her shoulders.

'Are you ready to go?'

'Yes.'

They drove the short distance to the cemetery. Emily didn't speak to her father but sat in the back of the car staring solemnly out of the window, bidding a silent goodbye to all the places she had played with her sister and friends just a few weeks before. They passed through a pair of black wrought iron gates and parked up. Her father led the way down a narrow path, overgrown with flowers and weeds, past rows of crooked graves and large stone angels whose faces were weather-worn and covered with yellow lichen.

Large parts of the cemetery had fallen into disrepair. Vines, shrubs and grasses crept across every free space reclaiming old pathways, covering graves and vaults and submerging old memorials beneath a slow tide of green. It was as if nature was trying to take back the land for itself. Emily didn't like the idea of her family being buried here, in some forgotten corner of an unloved graveyard, but it was already too late to do anything about it.

Finally they reached a clearing which was better maintained than the rest. The graves were newer and cleaner and as a result they seemed out of place in their dilapidated surroundings, somehow sadder for all their polished splendour. A small bunch of flowers had been laid on each of the graves; lilies, her mother's favourite. Her father picked one of them up, frowning, examining them as if he thought they might be dangerous. Emily had wanted to bring flowers herself but, just like everything else these days, there seemed to be a shortage. She wondered where they had come from. Maybe they were provided by whoever looked after the cemetery. She looked at each of the graves one by one.

FRANK DANIEL CARTWRIGHT (1887 – 1940)
Loyal and loving brother.
He that endureth to the end shall be saved.

JOAN MARY CARTWRIGHT (1903 – 1940)
Darling wife and mother.
The Lord watch between thee and me, while we are absent, one from the other.

CELIA ELIZABETH CARTWRIGHT (1926 – 1940)
Loving daughter and sister.
I thank my God upon every remembrance of you.

Standing there Emily realised for the first time that she missed her uncle. Although they never really got along, she was strangely sad that he was gone. She was sad too for her father who had now lost his parents, his brother and sister, as well as his wife and daughter. He was all alone but for her, and she was all alone but for him. The sorrow welled up in her once more and she fought it back with bitter anger. Her father was responsible for their deaths, she reminded herself. If he'd simply told her sooner, if he'd warned her, she could have done something.

It was hard however, to maintain that anger when she looked at him, standing over their graves, the life and vigour that had once radiated from him, hollowed out. He was a walking, breathing skeleton, just filler for the dark suit that hung from his shoulders. She half-expected that if she stared at him long enough, she might see him fade into nothingness.

He looked across at her and for once she met his gaze with something approaching kindness. He cleared his throat nervously.

'I'll leave you to say... well... I'll let you have a few moments to yourself.'

Emily sat down next to the graves.

'Mum...' she said softly, 'Celia... I...'

Now she was here she was at a loss for what to say. What could she say that could possibly encompass everything she felt at that moment, or express the grief that clutched so tightly at her heart?

'I miss you Cece. Every day, I miss you so much. None of this seems real. You and mum and Uncle Frank... I keep expecting to see you, wherever I am, wherever I go, I'm waiting for you, but you never come. I want to go home, only there is no home now. I guess you knew that...'

She paused, trying to collect her thoughts, she wanted to get this right.

'I'm so sorry, I should have done more... I should have... I just...' words failed her, for all the words she knew no longer seemed adequate. They belonged to some other time, some better time, and now new words would have to be created to serve this hellish world in which they found themselves.

'I wish you were still here, I wish... I'm going away for a while. Dad says I must. I'm going to be an evacuee, dumped with a family in a little village somewhere out in the country I expect. Maybe they'll have cows there.'

She giggled as a memory came to her unbidden. Folding her skirt beneath her she sat down by Celia's grave and began twisting one of the flowers between her fingers.

'Do you remember that time we went to the country for the day and we had a picnic? Dad was in his Sunday suit, mum was in that beautiful dress, the one with the yellow flowers on, and it was sunny, really hot. We went to this field in the middle of nowhere and ate our lunch but then some cows came over and they tried to eat dad's hat...' she giggled again.

'He tried to shoo them away but they wouldn't leave us alone and we were chased by these cows back out of the field, but as we were running dad tripped and fell into a cow pat. We laughed so much and he got cross and shouted at us, but then mum started laughing at how ridiculous he looked! Do you remember? Oh God, I'm going to miss you. And I'm sorry I won't be around to come and see you, but it doesn't mean I've forgotten about you okay? I haven't. I never will. Look after mum, she'll miss dad, and I'll try and look after him. Say hello to Uncle Frank for me, tell him I was right, that'll really annoy him.'

She stopped herself.

'No... don't tell him that. Tell him I miss him too and so does dad.'

Emily waited for a few moments more, wanting to say something about how scared she was and how alone she felt, but she couldn't bring herself to say it, as if by giving voice to the thought it would make it real, so instead she carefully rearranged the flowers, whispered a short prayer, then left to find her father.

At first, she couldn't see anyone, it was as if she was now all alone in the whole world. The silence was broken only by the cawing of the three crows perched upon the tumbledown stone walls. The overhanging trees threw dappled shadow onto an otherwise sunny part of the graveyard.

'Dad?' she called out.

She wondered where he had gone. Was he waiting for her by the car? As she began to walk back in the direction they had come from, she heard voices. Leaving the path she had been following she turned to her left and decided to follow the voices instead. After a hundred yards or so she passed through a large archway and came upon a tall cedar tree which was encircled by what looked like twenty or so stone doorways, all joined onto one another.

Beneath the tree at the centre of this circle was her father. He was talking to someone, a woman, older looking, around sixty if Emily was any judge. She was tall with a bob of short grey hair and she was dressed head to toe in black. She had the look of someone with money; the clothes were a loose cut with swathes of excess fabric that seemed to glimmer in the morning light. She had a string of pearls around her neck and a black hat with a small veil that obscured her eyes.

Emily was about to approach them but there was something in her father's manner that stopped her. She could not hear clearly what he was saying but she was certain that he was angry with this woman, whoever she was. Emily wondered if she was another mourner, but why then was her father so cross with her? How did they know each other? Before the bombing she would have felt excited about the chance to overhear something so secretive: now her interest was minimal. She almost turned to leave but something stopped her. Her father had obviously not wanted to draw attention to himself, other than an occasional raising of his voice, his manner was rather furtive. The last time her father had kept something a secret from Emily people had died. For this reason alone she stayed.

'No. No. You keep away, do I make myself clear?' said her father with quiet ferocity.

'But I can help, David. Let me help.'

The use of her father's name surprised Emily. Clearly this woman was not just some other mourner.

'I don't want your help, you've done more than enough. Or don't you remember what happened?'

'Certainly I remember. I think about it every day, but it wasn't my fault.'

Her father laughed mirthlessly.

'You are unbelievable.'

'David…'

'You're not wanted here; can't you see that? Just stay away,' he said in a coarse whisper.

'Or what? You'll bring me in to your precious Ministry? Is that what you do now?'

Her father said nothing.

'You're making a mistake, if you'd only let me talk to her–'

'Stay away. I won't ask you again.'

With that her father turned and left. Emily took a step back to make sure she could not be seen as he passed close by, then stepped out again to watch the woman. She seemed close to tears and was breathing heavily. She took a few moments to compose herself and then headed towards where Emily had entered. Emily ducked out of sight and waited till she was sure she was gone before slowly walking round and back towards the car where her father was waiting.

'We ought to get going Emily.'

'Okay.'

If Emily had not just seen him arguing she would not have thought there was anything wrong. He held open the car door and she climbed in.

'Who was that woman you were talking to just now?' she asked as they pulled away.

'What woman?'

'The woman at the cemetery.'

'Oh,' he said as though he'd just remembered who Emily was talking about, as if it could have been a long list of people and not the only woman he was having a heated discussion with just five minutes before, 'just another mourner.'

'You seemed upset with her,' said Emily.

'Really? Did you hear what we were talking about?'

'No, but you both looked angry.'

'Well... I shouldn't tell you this really, but I don't suppose you're going to tell anyone. Do you know what a mistress is?'

'A woman who has an affair with a married man,' said

73

Emily nervous about what her father might be about to say next.

'That's about it, yes. Well she is the mistress of a gentleman with whom I worked. He died recently and when I saw her in the graveyard... well I didn't think it was right. His wife doesn't know about the affair and we hardly want her finding out now do we?'

'No,' said Emily, 'I suppose not,' though there was something about it that didn't feel right to her. 'But if she loved him... I mean I know it's wrong to do that, but if she was in love with him and he died, why shouldn't she be able to visit his grave?'

'It's not that straightforward Emily. No one's trying to stop her, I just didn't think it was appropriate so soon afterwards. His wife still comes here most days, what if she saw this woman dressed all in black putting flowers on the grave? What would she think?'

'But if her husband was an adulterer, then wouldn't she deserve to know?'

'What good would it do? Who would gain from that Emily? The poor wife would be devastated, the children too no doubt, and for what? So one woman can mourn in public? Always telling the truth sounds like a wonderful thing, it sounds like you're being honourable and noble, but really you're not. People lie all the time, little lies usually, to make the world run more smoothly, or to spare people's feelings. Sometimes Emily the truth can cause untold damage; some secrets are better buried with the dead,' he said, and there was a finality to his tone that told her the discussion was over.

Chapter Five

Emily said goodbye to her father at the entrance to Paddington Station.

'I'll write to you when I can,' he said. 'Be a good girl. I'll miss you.'

Emily didn't trust herself to say anything so she simply nodded.

'Oh, I almost forgot, I got you this,' he said reaching into his coat pocket, 'hopefully it won't be long before we get to play again.'

Her father pulled out a brand-new cricket ball and tossed it gently to her. Emily caught it and popped it into her suitcase without saying anything.

'We'll see each other soon. I promise.'

'Don't.'

Their eyes met.

'Don't promise. You can't promise that. No one can promise that.'

Her father looked at her for the longest time.

'Yes. You're right. I'm sorry.'

He drew her in for a hug and almost despite herself she found she was wrapping her arms around him. She was still so angry and confused by everything he'd told her, but he was the only family she had left. He'd been called away that morning on a matter of some urgency so could not stay to see her off. Emily actually felt a little relieved, she didn't think she could bear to watch him recede into the distance through the tiny window of a train carriage.

'Somebody will be along shortly to collect you and show you where you need to go.'

He looked around hoping to see someone that would take Emily from him but the station was full of people and it was impossible to pick anyone out. He glanced at his watch.

'Go,' said Emily, 'I'll be ok.'

Her father hesitated.

'I promise. Go on go or you'll be court-martialled.'

Looking as if it was costing him every ounce of strength he possessed, her father turned and walked away, leaving Emily alone once more. She stood with her suitcase at her feet and surveyed the rest of the station. Light poured in through the glass panels of the arched roof and caught the thick white smoke that billowed from the trains below. A few weeks before such a magnificent sight would have captivated Emily, but now it was barely of interest.

People bustled by, the station was busy, groups of children with large tags hanging from their coats were being waved onto packed trains by anxious mothers. Emily was just wondering if she was meant to be on one of those trains when an official looking woman with a clipboard marched up to her.

'Are you one of mine?' she asked.

'I don't know,' replied Emily.

'Name?'

'Emily Cartwright.'

The woman riffled through the papers on her clipboard whilst sucking on the nib of her pencil.

'Ah yes Cartwright, Emily. I'm Miss Pinchman and you're being evacuated. Do you know what that means?'

She continued without waiting for a response.

'It means I'm in charge of making sure you're placed safely out of harm's way and out of London. Though why you were ever allowed back in the first place I don't know.'

Miss Pinchman shook her head crossly as if Emily had been the one to suggest it.

'We spent all that time and money making sure the children were safe and what do the parents go and do? Bring them home again. Anyway, what's done is done. Follow me.'

With that she was off, marching towards the platform and spitting out instructions to other official looking women as she went, cajoling, corralling and controlling everything that moved within the station.

'Keep up,' she snapped as Emily struggled to match her fearsome pace.

'You'll be living in the countryside so I'm sure there'll be lots for you to do. Plenty of fresh air,' Miss Pinchman paused to take a deep theatrical breath before setting off again at top speed.

'Fresh air is good for you,' she declared. 'Little girls should get plenty of fresh air. Any questions? Good,' she said giving Emily no time to answer. 'Little girls shouldn't have a lot of questions.'

'I'm not a little girl,' said Emily finally catching up, suitcase in tow.

'Yes well, let's not make a fuss. Now, let me take a look at you.'

Miss Pinchman studied Emily properly for the first time. The corners of her mouth twitched as she fought to contain her disappointment at what stood in front of her. Emily, swamped beneath a baggy tweed coat that hung limply from her slender frame, stared back resolutely.

'It's important that you make a good first impression. Shoulders back. Head up,' said Miss Pinchman arranging Emily's body with such force that she was sure she would snap in two.

'Well... you'll have to do I suppose. Right hop on, remember don't dawdle, don't slouch and don't speak unless you're spoken to.'

And with that she was off again, back down the

platform leaving Emily to struggle on to the train, hauling her suitcase behind her. Once on board she moved with difficulty down the carriages. She didn't want to be around anyone else, she didn't want the questions about who she was, where she was from, who her family was. She just wasn't ready for that. She managed to find an empty compartment and settled herself in. As she waited for the train to depart she looked out across the station. Mothers and even a few fathers were lined up alongside the train, waving to their children, calling out warnings to behave or reminding brothers and sisters to look after one another. Emily wiped her eyes with the sleeve of her mouldy coat and tried to think about something else.

Just as she turned away however, she caught a glimpse of something out the corner of her eye. Towards the back of the line was a tall man in a long grey coat and trilby hat, beneath which was tucked a familiar streak of blonde hair. It was the man she had seen on her street from her bedroom window, the man she had seen on the day of the bombing. This couldn't possibly be a coincidence. Who was he and why was he following her?

Emily had a sudden urge to confront him but even as she got to her feet, the guard blew his whistle and the train pulled slowly out of the station. For a moment she wondered if he might chase after it and hop on the last carriage like she had seen people do in the pictures; but he remained where he was and seconds later he was lost in the throng of passengers disembarking from a train on the adjacent platform.

Emily thought of the man for some time, but with no idea of who he was or what he might want all she could do was wonder. With everything else that had happened recently, he was the least of her concerns. The rest of the coach was quite busy. Every so often faces would peer in at her, but no one entered. It was as though her grief had taken on physical form and joined her in the compartment, making it seem full when it wasn't. Emily didn't mind, she wanted to be alone.

Desperate not to dwell on the thoughts of her family she began to think about what her father had told her. She really could see the future. Despite what he'd said, Emily was still convinced that she could use her power for good somehow. After all, her father had tried to keep it a secret and look how that had turned out.

Of course, she had not Seen since the day of the bombing, perhaps she would never See again. Maybe it was something that only happened once: you were given an opportunity to make a difference and she had missed hers. Still if this ability did return then she would try to use it, if she could stop other people feeling the way she did then she would; she didn't care what her father thought.

She began to wonder whether it was possible to control the visions, to focus them and see specific events and actions. Then another thought occurred that unsettled her. What if she could See the future but not change it? After all, she had seen the bombing coming and had not been able to prevent what happened. Was it some kind of curse, to have the knowledge of what was to come but to be unable to do anything about it? She thought she remembered a story from school about a Greek goddess with the power of prophecy, but whom no one ever believed. Was that what would happen to her?

She wondered how many others there were like her. She couldn't be the only one after all. Her father said it ran in families so it made sense there would be more. But who were they? Where were they? Why had she never heard of them before? Did they work for the government already? Or did they, like her father, believe it was better to remain hidden?

Before long the shuffling rhythm of the wheels on the tracks, and the gentle rocking of the carriage lulled Emily into a fitful sleep from which she awoke every few minutes as her head dropped on to her chest. Giving herself over to the inevitability of sleep she took one the less irritating jumpers from her suitcase and used it as a pillow against the window before slowly drifting off.

When she next woke a few hours later, she found they had left London long behind. The landscape had changed from grey to green and all that could be seen for miles around were fields of emerald and gold, little parcels of land divided by wild hedges and stone walls. For a short time, the train ran alongside a stream that meandered over rocks and between fields.

Despite the time of year Emily longed to dangle her feet in the icy water. She and her sister would have built stepping stones across that stream, she thought, whilst her mother fussed and fretted at a distance. The further they got from London, the darker the sky became until the clouds finally spilled their heavy load and fat drops of rain hurled themselves against the fragile carriage windows.

Every few miles they would pull in at one of the endless tiny stations that dotted the line to Exeter, though what these stations were called she would never know. Each of the signs bearing the station's name had been blacked out or removed as a precaution should the Nazis invade. The same was true of road signs up and down the country. It was hoped that if their paratroopers ever arrived then this might slow them down, as they would not know where it was they had landed.

The journey seemed to go on forever. At each station a few more people would board and eventually even Emily's compartment became full. Fortunately, one of Miss Pinchman's army of assistants had chosen to sit in hers so it stayed quiet and free from other children. She drifted off to sleep again but was awoken suddenly just a short while later by a sharp rap on the knee.

'We'll be arriving in Exeter in just a few minutes. Grab your belongings and be ready to leave the moment the train stops. No dawdling.'

With an officious nod the assistant stood and left to inform the rest of the children. Emily looked out of the window. A city the colour of sand emerged from beneath the dark clouds as the train settled into its final slow shuffle towards the station. At last, it came to a halt, releasing a long burst of steam that sounded to Emily like a weary sigh, as if it too had been exhausted by the journey. She stepped onto the cold, grey platform. Although it was no longer raining, a storm had clearly just passed through and she had to be careful to avoid the numerous puddles it had left behind.

She clutched her suitcase tightly as if she feared that at any moment someone would try and wrestle it from her. The platform swiftly filled up with the other children who were quieter now than they had been in London. Perhaps they had tired themselves out on the train thought Emily, or perhaps they were just nervous. After all they were about to meet their new families for the first time; the people they were going to live with for the next year or more.

The children were marched across a small footbridge and ushered down into the main entrance of the station where they were met by a sea of brown and grey coats. A large balding man with a moustache so thin and straight it looked as if it had been drawn on with a pen and a ruler, surveyed the group. One by one the coats scuttled forwards, mumbling to each other and occasionally poking, prodding and squeezing the children as though they were fruit on a market stall. With a cough and a nod they would signal to the man with the moustache who promptly made a mark on his clipboard.

At one stage a large coat with a battered looking hat seemed to take great interest in Emily but, upon conferring with the moustache, changed his mind. After a short time all the children had been matched to new homes, all that is except Emily.

'Excuse me,' said Emily to the moustached man who was now making furious notes on a clipboard, 'but where am I staying?'

The moustached man looked at her over the end of his half-moon spectacles as if he was surprised to see her.

'Well didn't I say?' he intoned in a nasal voice.

'Erm... I don't know.'

'Well either I did or I didn't, now come on which is it?' he said sharply, jabbing his clipboard with his pen as he spoke.

'You didn't, no.'

'Let me see now, let me see… Name?'

'Emily Cartwright.'

The moustache consulted his clipboard once more, scrolling through the list of names until he came across Emily's and marked it by jabbing his pen hard into the board again as if to emphasise the precision with which he worked.

'Yes, that's right,' he said confirming a thought as yet unspoken, 'you're staying here.'

Emily looked at him, confused.

'Here?'

'Yes. Here.'

'But this is a station.'

'I know very well what it is young lady,' he replied haughtily, 'but the fact remains you are staying here. You are going to live with Mr Worthington, the Station Master of St. David's. I'm sure he will be along presently. Now if you'll excuse me…'

And with that the man with the world's straightest moustache strode out the entrance leaving Emily alone, still clutching her suitcase.

She waited on the platform, watching the trains pulled in and out of the station, rushing their passengers onto destinations new. The last whispers of light had faded from the sky and Emily was beginning to worry. Mr Worthington had not shown up. Maybe he had forgotten that he was meant to be meeting her, she thought. At that moment she heard the scrape of a key being plunged into a lock. When she turned around there was a tall man in a guard's uniform shielding his face from the chill wind as he endeavoured to light the pipe that struck out from the corner of his mouth.

'Excuse me,' said Emily in a timorous voice.

The man did not look up.

'Excuse me,' she said again, a little louder this time.

Still the man did not reply. Emily edged into his field of vision as he continued to focus all his energies on lighting his pipe.

'Excuse me,' she said once more, 'do you know a Mr Worthington by any chance?'

Finally the man looked at her, yet it was as if he were staring right through her. He sucked deeply on his pipe and exhaled a plume of dusty smoke.

'You're Emily Cartwright.'

It wasn't a question, more a statement of fact.

'Yes,' she replied. 'Are you Mr Worthington?'

'That's right, now let's get you home.'

He paused for a moment as if he were going to say more, then he picked up Emily's luggage and set off at great speed back across the rickety footbridge leaving her struggling to keep up.

'Do you live far away?' she asked as she trailed in his wake.

'No.'

His voice had the rough texture of tree bark. In fact there was something very like the tree about his whole person. He was tall and thin with limbs that jutted off at odd angles and a crooked mouth that revealed a set of jagged, yellow teeth when he spoke. His gnarled and knotted hands clasped Emily's suitcase so tightly that she feared the handle might snap off. Once out of the station they turned left, then right, then left again down a narrow country lane.

It was dark and she could barely see what was in front of her, with only the light of the half-moon to guide them. Mr Worthington walked so fast, despite a pronounced limp, that Emily could not keep up and was forced to follow the smell of tobacco and the occasional dim glow of the pipe. Soon they came to a large cottage. Even in the dark Emily did not like the look of it. It, too, was tall and thin, just like Mr Worthington, and it seemed to lean towards the lane as if straining to hear the murmured secrets of the street beyond. Mr Worthington pushed open the gate which howled in protest at being disturbed at so late an hour.

The path that lead to the front door was overgrown with weeds and thistles and Emily had to be careful that her legs were not cut to pieces. Mr Worthington opened the door and switched on the hallway light which was so dim it seemed only to thicken the darkness.

'D'you know how to make a fire up?' he asked.

'Erm... yes,' she said surprised at the question.

'Good. There's some coal in the scuttle in the front room. I suggest you use it and I'll top it up when I get back.'

'You're going out again?'

'I've not finished my shift. Your room is at the end of the landing upstairs. The electricity works, except for when it doesn't. There's a bit of bread and butter on the kitchen table and a bottle of milk in the larder. Tomorrow you can go shopping and cook a proper meal. I'll be back later,' he said, chewing on his pipe, then without warning he turned on his heels and marched back up the lane at the same speed he had come down it.

Emily stood in the doorway unable to take it all in. She was tired and cold, even once she closed the door she could feel a chill wind rushing around her feet. Although she was wearing a coat she no longer owned a hat or a pair of gloves, and her fingers had frozen on the walk over. She hadn't expected a welcome party but she had hoped her first night in a new home would be slightly more hospitable than this.

Freezing cold and struggling to see more than a few yards in front of her, Emily decided the first thing she needed to do was light a fire. She opened the door to her right which lead through to the front room. The dim glow of the light in the hall illuminated the room just enough for her to be able to make out the shape of an armchair in one corner and a large fireplace in the centre. The wind whistled mournfully down the chimney and rattled the grate.

Emily quickly got to work. Building a fire was something she was good at. Before her father had gone away, he'd taught her how to build one so that it caught quickly and burned for a long time. Back home she'd made the fire up for several months before her uncle had moved in and decided that it wasn't "women's work."

She gathered up a mixture of old newspaper and twigs from the scuttle to use as kindling and, leaving enough space for the air to get through, put a little of the coal on top. Then she struck a match from the box on the mantelpiece. The match fizzed brightly into life and with great care Emily held it to the kindling. The light from the fire bought a warm glow to the cold house. She did not want to add the coal too soon or she might put it out, so instead she sat, her hands turned to the flames, watching the gambolling shadows that were cast by its flickering light. Finally the fire was strong enough, so she popped on the last of the coal before turning her attention to the rest of the room.

In the far corner sat a rocking chair. A crocheted blanket was draped across one of the arms and a well-worn cushion had wedged itself between the elaborately carved wood that made up the back of the chair. Next to it was a tall lamp with a dirty yellow glass shade. She pulled the switch that hung by the side and though it flickered into life for a moment, it didn't stay on. She made a half-hearted attempt to jiggle the bulb but a brief spark of electricity convinced her that she was better off leaving it alone. Emily shrugged, she doubted it would have done much to brighten the room or lift the air of gloom that seemed to seep from the walls. She couldn't help remember something her mother had once told her when she was younger and she had asked why their house made odd noises in the night or when she was alone. 'Houses are living things, they breathe, they sigh, they get restless and bored. That's why you will hear them sometimes moving about. It's nothing to be afraid of.'

Emily tried to put her mother from her mind, thoughts of her bringing, as they always did now, a sharp pain in her heart as if someone had reached into her chest and was slowly squeezing the life from it. Fighting off the rising feeling of despair she decided what was needed was not just warmth and light, but the sound of life too. Something about the way the house creaked and groaned told her that this was a lonely house, crying out for a bit of attention and for some company. She spotted a radio on top of the cabinet next to the armchair so she switched it on and carefully turned the dial until the hiss and whine of the static was replaced by the familiar sound of a jazz troupe.

Emily turned it up so that the sound filled the room, hoping the warm brass would ease the cold isolation of the house. She stood for a few moments with her eyes shut tight, letting the rasping trumpets and the slinking clarinet take hold. The music lifted her up and transported her three years and two hundred miles away until she was back in her old home, in the living room with her mother, father and sister, listening to this very song. Her father was sitting in the corner doing the crossword, her mother was reading the rest of the paper, and Emily and Celia were playing a card game of their own devising called 'Whispers'. They had tried to teach it to their mother but their deliberately elaborate and Byzantine rules had left her exasperated. This was a common reaction in fact, so that the only people who could ever really play it were Emily and Celia themselves. Emily smiled. The memory was so strong she felt as though she could step into it, but when she opened her eyes again she was all alone in the cold and the dark.

Determined not to let her unhappiness take a deeper hold, she decided to explore the rest of the house. Across from the front room was the dining room. A rush of stale air hit her as she entered, and the displaced dust danced a slow waltz in the glow of the light from the hall. Emily got the impression the room had not been used in sometime.

She ran her finger along the edge of the dining table and found it left a clear patch in the dust, like a spot of blue sky on a cloudy day.

On the wall were a few photographs that looked like they too had not seen a duster in rather a long time. One was of a teenage girl in a stripy knitted top, all wild hair and freckles, who was staring solemnly at the camera. Another was of Mr Ferguson on his wedding day, dressed in a smart suit with his beautiful bride standing next to him holding a bunch of flowers and smiling shyly. The final photo was again of Mr Ferguson with ten other men. They were all in army uniform and were huddled together on the steps of a wooden building that resembled the local scout hut. The men were sitting, almost on top of one another, laughing and joking, one had another in a headlock, others had draped their arms off each other's shoulders. She looked at their laughing faces. How happy they appeared. She tried not to think about what might have happened to them, and if any of them, other than Mr Worthington, had made it through the war. At the back of the photo was a young man with a thin moustache, his tin helmet slightly askew, pulling a funny face at one of his friends. He reminded Emily a little of her father, but then everything reminded her of her family at the moment. She felt her thoughts begin to turn to home once more and knew she had to think about something else before got upset. She moved back out into the hallway closing the door behind her.

As she did so Emily felt an unfamiliar rumbling beneath her feet. The house chattered and shook and the crockery in the kitchen clinked like a discordant orchestra warming up. For one horrible moment she thought they were being attacked, that the bombers were back and were flying over the city looking for her. She felt her heart hammering in her chest and sweat began to pour off her. It took several seconds for her to realise it was just a train passing through the nearby station. Was this how she would react to every little sound from now on she wondered?

'Pull yourself together,' she said aloud, letting her words rattle round the empty house.

A brief exploration of the kitchen revealed nothing interesting. Spotting the bread and butter Mr Worthington had mentioned she felt a pang of hunger and remembered that she hadn't eaten since breakfast. She drew up a chair and wolfed down the, by now, slightly stale bread and a cool glass of milk before starting upstairs.

The first floor of the house was even colder than the ground floor. The whole place smelt as if it were dying. She flicked the switch to turn on the lights and was surprised when the landing light actually stuttered on. Emily remembered again what her mother had said about houses being living beings, and she suddenly felt an unexpected kinship with the place. It was clear Mr Worthington did not care about it, just as he did not care about her. The house was cold, forgotten and on its own, and Emily could relate to that only too well.

As Mr Worthington had said, her room was at the end of the landing. It was small with just a bed, a few drawers and a round window, the kind of thing she had only ever seen on boats. There was also a fireplace so Emily swiftly made up another fire to take the chill off the air. Fetching her bag up, she unpacked the few items she had bought with her, then climbed into bed and swiftly fell into an uneasy slumber.

She awoke some time later to the sound of raised voices. Careful to make as little noise as possible she crept down the stairs. Mr Worthington was arguing someone, but before she had even reached the bottom he stopped. Emily wondered who could possibly have upset him at this hour. Standing outside the living room with her ear pressed to the door all she could hear was the sound of deep, heavy breathing. She pushed open the door just a crack to see Mr Worthington, sprawled in the armchair, twitching restlessly in his sleep. Occasionally he would cry out. Whatever he was dreaming about it didn't seem all that pleasant.

Emily heard the quiet whine of the radio and realised she must have forgotten to turn it off. The fire was low and the room was becoming colder. As quietly as she could, she added a few more pieces of coal to the fire and waited for it to catch. Mr Worthington cried out again, frightening Emily half to death.

'No. No. I didn't mean... I'm sorry...' his voice trailed away.

She wondered if she should wake him, but for some reason she didn't think he'd appreciate it. He looked so different when asleep, like a much younger man, more vulnerable too. Emily placed a hand on his arm and, almost without thinking about it, rubbed it gently until he settled down again. Then she took the crocheted blanket from the rocking chair and laid it gently over Mr Worthington's outstretched frame.

Chapter Six

Emily was awoken early the next morning by the sound of the front door slamming shut. Drawing the bedclothes around her she lifted herself up to peer out of the window and saw Mr Worthington disappearing up the garden path. She shivered and lay back down on the bed. The fire had burned itself out during the night and the room was so cold she could see her breath hanging in the air. The wind hammered against the windows, which shook and rattled like chattering teeth.

With some considerable effort, Emily hauled herself out of bed, threw on as many clothes as she could in an attempt to keep warm, then stepped out onto the landing. Despite the light of a new day the house looked as unwelcoming as it had the night before. Layers of dust and grime covered every surface and the smell of decay hung in the air. Moths and spiders hid in the darkest corners, and abandoned cobwebs decorated the ceiling like lace on a wedding dress. The more she thought about it, the more overwhelmed she felt. She'd lost the home she loved with people she loved, and now she was living with a stranger in the middle of nowhere, in a place that was little better than a barn.

She wondered what she was meant to do with her time. Mr Worthington had already gone to work. There was no one to tell her what to do, when to eat, when she had to be home or what time she had to go to bed. Once upon a time all this might have sounded ideal, but now the freedom was frightening. What was she going to do all day? Surely, she would have to go to school at least? But if so, how was she to find it? She didn't know Exeter at all. Without a routine to fall back on she felt lost, adrift in an endless ocean of time.

The one thing she could not do, she decided, was sit idle. The longer she did nothing the more quickly her thoughts returned to recent events. She had to keep busy. If she was going to live here, she thought, she would have to make it somewhere she could live in. Moving from room to room she drew the curtains to let the sunlight pour in, and, despite the cold, she opened the windows too in the hope that the fresh breeze would chase away the stilted, festering air inside. Next she grabbed a broom and began sweeping the accumulated dirt into small piles before attacking the spider's webs with a feather duster she found hidden under the sink.

All her pent-up frustration and rage was focused into these little tasks, and it surprised her how quickly the house started to become more habitable. Emily listened to the radio as she worked. She soon tired of the Home Service with its false bonhomie, its tirelessly positive war reports and its dreary recipes for kitchen scraps. Instead she tuned to the Forces Programme which played popular music – big bands, jazz singers and the like.

After a few hours, she began to feel hungry. Mr Worthington had left a list of the food he expected her to pick up, as well as a few shillings. She wondered how she was supposed to buy anything when her ration book had been destroyed in the bombing and he had not left her his. Emily read over the list again and came to a decision; she would buy those items not covered by the ration – the vegetables and the bread – and leave the rest till she'd had a chance to speak to Mr Worthington about it. She'd noticed an old wicker basket in one of the rooms earlier which would be perfect to carry the food back in.

Emily had only gone a few steps out of the door when she realised she didn't actually know how to get to town, the whole area was new to her and she'd only seen it in the dark. In the distance, she spotted the gleaming spire of Exeter Cathedral so she resolved to head in that direction as the shops would most likely be somewhere nearby.

Twenty minutes later Emily found herself on the high street which was bustling with frazzled-looking shoppers. The street was on a steep slope and, not knowing where any of the shops she needed might be, she decided to walk up the road from bottom to top to familiarise herself with the place, making a mental note of any of the stores she might need in future as none of them were the same as back home. There was Hepworth's the Tailors, Woodley's Shoes, and L.H. Fearis Ltd which sold all sorts of food. Further along the street, there was a Woolworth's which had a sign in the window boasting that nothing they sold cost more than sixpence.

Finally Emily came to Moon & Sons Pianos. She stared in the window of the store for some time and wondered what it would be like to be able to play a musical instrument. She had asked her mother some years ago if she could learn the piano, but her mother said it was too expensive. Thinking of her mother made Emily's stomach clench up and she began to feel sick so she moved on. She had to keep reminding herself not to think about her family; it made her too sad.

She set off again turning left onto Queen Street and found what it was she was searching for. In front of her was a large sandstone building, maybe two hundred feet long. In the middle of the façade were four massive stone columns, either side of which were two small store fronts, then a further two pillars each side of the shops. It looked to Emily as though someone had left a Roman temple behind in the middle of Exeter. A sign declared the building to be 'Exeter Higher Market.'

Stalls lined the edifice, front to back, selling a selection of fruit, vegetables, fish and fresh meat. She had wondered if the food might be better in Exeter, but it was not so different to London; the queues were the same, the vegetables were all on the small side and some of the fruit had seen better days. Despite this she bought a few apples and pears as well as a bunch of carrots, a cabbage and some potatoes.

She had just discovered a stall that sold bread when she heard someone shouting further up the road. Putting her basket down, she looked around for the source of the commotion. A tall, gangly boy was racing down the street closely followed by a large, red-faced man with short hair and an even shorter temper.

'Stop! Come back here you thieving git.'

Something about the man's fearsome rage reminded her of her uncle, and as the boy dashed past Emily gently pushed her basket away from her with her foot and into the path of the red-faced man who went tumbling over it. The goods she had just bought fell out of the basket and rolled down the hill followed by the man.

'Oh! Oh dear!' she exclaimed.

The red-faced man slowly climbed to his feet. Under the pretence of picking up a rather scrawny cabbage which had rolled some yards away, Emily was able to chance a glance behind her and saw the boy step quietly into a tiny side street out of sight.

'I'm so sorry. How clumsy of me...'

The red-faced man was bent double, hands on knees trying to catch his breath.

'Bloody kids,' he said between gulps of air.

'I'm so terribly sorry,' said Emily once more, gathering all of her things back in to her basket and adopting the same sincere voice her sister used if she was ever in trouble at school.

For the first time she spotted that the man was holding a large knife in his right hand and suddenly Emily began to feel a little less guilty about tripping him up, and a little more nervous about what he might do next. The man gave her a cold stare and slowly drew himself up to his full

93

height. From the knife he was holding and the look of his clothes, Emily guessed he was a butcher. At least she hoped he was a butcher. He had on a dark red apron that was stained with blood. She wondered what the boy had done to make this man chase him, strenuous physical activity being something to which he was clearly averse.

'Did you see where he went?' he panted.

'Who?' replied Emily innocently.

'The boy... that bloody boy I was chasing before...' he nodded to indicate the basket Emily was holding.

'Oh no, I'm sorry, I didn't.'

'Right... right...'

The red-faced man stood, not quite knowing what to do with himself. It was clear he wanted to continue the chase, but with no sign of the boy there was no one to chase, so he waited, surveying the street with hands on hips and wheezing like an overweight guard dog. Eventually he seemed to accept that the boy was unlikely to return.

'If you see him,' he said sternly, 'you be sure to let me know alright?'

'Oh yes of course,' replied Emily earnestly.

The red-faced man scanned the scene one final time before deciding he had best return to his shop. Careful not to draw attention to herself Emily walked very slowly down the road before turning left down the same tiny passageway she had seen the boy disappear into.

'Sorry about that,' said a voice from the shadows, 'didn't mean to drag you into it. Nice thinking with the basket though, very quick.'

'Oh, no problem. If you don't mind me asking, why was he chasing you?'

The boy stepped into the light, still looking around to make sure he wasn't about to be chased again.

'Well we had a bit of a disagreement.'

'What about?'

'Chicken.'

'Chicken?'

'Chicken,' he said again this time moving his arms up

94

and down by his side to indicate wings.

'Yes, I know what a chicken is, but why were you running away from a fat man holding a carving knife?'

'It was a cleaver actually.'

'I think you're missing the point.'

'He was trying to sell me some for 4d and I know he sells it for less. He just didn't want me in his shop.'

'And how did that lead to him chasing you with a knife?'

'A cleaver.'

'A cleaver then.'

'I may have taken the chicken and forgotten to give him any money for it.'

'You stole it?'

'That's one way of looking at it.'

'Is there another way of looking at it?'

The boy paused for a moment considering it.

'He was profiteering, he should be in prison. I took a stand for freedom,' he said proudly.

'Yes, you're like Winston Churchill and Charles de Gaulle all rolled into one,' said Emily sarcastically.

'So you think he should be allowed to charge me more just because he doesn't like the look of me?' replied the boy, firing up.

'No, of course not,' said Emily calmly, 'I'm just saying you shouldn't steal.'

They looked at one another for a moment, then the boy shrugged.

'Well, see you then.'

'Wait!'

Emily didn't know why she had said it, perhaps it was the thought of going back to the cold and lonely house, but she was keen to continue chatting to this boy, thief or not.

'I'm Emily, Emily Cartwright,' she offered up a handshake and then felt curiously self-conscious about it and let her hand fall limply by her side.

'Jack.'

'Are you from around here?' she asked.

'Round here? Yeah, I've lived in Exeter all my life. You one of them evacuees?'

Emily noticed he had a Devonshire accent. It was soft and warm, rounding the edges off the words so that they were less sharp and spiky. The 'here' for instance, which Emily pronounced to rhyme with ear, became something more like 'yur', and 'my' became 'moi'.

'Yes, I came down from London yesterday. In fact I…' Emily realised she had lost his attention. Jack was looking straight past her back up the alley.

'I think we're being watched,' he said.

'Who by? Is it the police?' asked Emily alarmed.

Her first trip outside of the house in a new city and she was about to be arrested for aiding and abetting a criminal.

'I don't know,' he replied kneeling down very deliberately to tie his shoe laces.

Emily turned to see who Jack was looking at but he hissed at her to stay looking at him.

'You don't want to look at him now or he'll know we're onto him.'

Keeping his eyes on the mysterious figure, he gestured for Emily to start walking which she did, before he followed on moments later.

'Where are we going?' asked Emily once Jack had caught up.

'The Quayside.'

'Why the Quayside?'

'Dunno,' he shrugged 'but that man was definitely watching us. The Quay is busy, you can lose people in the crowds.'

They walked side by side down the hill towards the Quay.

'What does he look like?'

'Who?'

'You know, the man who is watching us.'

'Smart, proper like, well dressed, a long grey coat, grey trilby…'

And Emily knew what he was going to say next before

he had said it '...blonde hair I reckon, you can just see it poking out from beneath his hat.'

'Is he following us?' she asked sharply.

'I don't know, I can't look back can I? He'd know we'd seen him then.'

Emily said nothing but a few moments later dropped the basket carrying all her shopping onto the floor.

'Oh dear, I am clumsy today,' she said and she began to gather her meagre fruit and vegetable provisions, which were by now rather battered and bruised. As she did this she kept sneaking surreptitious glances back up the street. The man was nowhere to be seen.

'How did you know we were being watched to begin with?' she asked once they had set off again.

Although it no longer appeared as if they were being followed Emily did not tell Jack, he might have decided against a visit to the Quay and she was interested in getting the guided tour.

'You just get a feeling don't you when someone dun't fit?'

'And you think he was following you?'

'Maybe, maybe not, but after the trouble with the butcher I thought I'd best not stick around.'

So, someone really was following her. But why? She thought back to what her father had said about people wanting her for her... what was the word for it? Gift? That didn't seem right given all that had happened. Powers? It sounded ridiculous, and she certainly didn't feel powerful. Abilities? Perhaps that was the closest description: abilities.

Were her abilities the reason he had followed her all the way from London? What was he waiting for? Why didn't he approach her directly instead of lurking in the shadows? And how did he know about her in the first place? The only two people that knew what she could do were her sister and her father. Perhaps her father had sent him to check up on her? But no, that couldn't be it because she had seen him before the bombing and at the train station.

In fact she had seen him too many times for it to be a mere coincidence, but unless he approached her she didn't see what she could do about it. If he wanted to speak to her he seemed to know fairly well where she was, it was up to him. She decided she would keep an eye out from now on and deal with whatever he wanted as the situation arose.

Putting the man from her mind Emily turned her attention to the Quayside which was busy with traders unloading wood, coal and food off their boats. Though it was fairly sunny, the wind was still strong and blew in hard across the water. Despite what Jack had said Emily didn't think that the Quay was the perfect place to lose someone. If anything they looked more conspicuous there than they had in town. The Quay was hardly filled with children. The one advantage that she could see was that if they were being followed by the man in the trilby, he would be far too well dressed for the Quay and would stick out almost as much as they did.

Jack led her down onto the tow path that ran by the riverside and they began to walk out of the city. Emily pulled her coat tightly around her and followed alongside him. Eventually they came to a halt by a small copse where Jack nestled himself up against the trunk of a large oak tree.

'Are we still being followed?' Emily already knew the answer to this but thought it best if it appeared that she was still concerned at the thought of being arrested by the police.

'I don't think so. We must have lost him a while back.'

Emily nodded.

'So where did you say you were from again?'

'London.'

'Oh big city girl are yer?'

'Not really.'

'What's London like then?' asked Jack.

'What's it like?'

'Yeah, I've never been. Never been anywhere outside of Exeter really. I went to the beach at Exmouth a few years ago, but that's about it'

Emily thought for a moment.

'It's busy. Busy and hectic. Everyone's always in a rush. And it's a different colour than it used to be. Everywhere is green and blue. You never used to see a uniform in London now you see them all over, soldiers, sailors, pilots, air raid wardens, ambulance crews. All the buildings are covered with sandbags and at night it goes really dark and really quiet too, or it used to anyway. When war broke out it was almost silent on the streets come nine o' clock, but now with the bombing...' she trailed off not wanting to follow that sentence to its conclusion.

'The people have changed too. There's this weird feeling about the place. Worry, excitement, suspicion – all mixed in together. It's like everyone is slightly giddy. You don't know what tomorrow will bring. All the people you love could be gone, your whole world could change in an instant. How do you prepare for that?' Emily could feel her voice quavering and tears formed at the corner of her eyes. She took a deep breath to calm herself and then in the steadiest voice she could muster she said simply, 'you can't.'

'Have you ever been in an air raid?'

Emily's heart gave a sudden heave.

'What?'

'You know, when they started bombing, where did you go? Was it frightening? We don't get bombed here, I can hear it sometimes when they attack Plymouth but there's nothing in Exeter worth bombing. Where did you stay?'

Emily felt weak and could feel her knees trembling. She started to worry she may fall down.

'I was in the shelter in my garden when the bombing started,' she answered honestly, 'and it was the most scared I've ever been in my life.'

She felt her voice catching but was determined to press on.

'When the war first started we used to go down the

underground when the sirens went. They didn't want to let us at first – the authorities I mean – they said it was dangerous. Only there were too many of us to refuse. There were hundreds of us. It was cramped and sweaty, whole families came down, bringing suitcases with clothes in them in case...' Emily swallowed hard, '...well in case something should happen. There was this one time when it got so full down there that one man had the idea to tie blankets between two sides of the tracks to make hammocks for the children. I know some people liked it down there, or at least they liked being with everyone else, but I didn't. It was uncomfortable, cramped, and noisy. I don't ever want to go underground again.'

Jack eyed her keenly and for a moment she thought he was going to ask her more about it, but he seemed to think better of it. Pretty soon the war had taught even the most curious of children that there are some questions that are better left unasked.

'Have you got any brothers or sisters?'

Emily's stomach gave another lurch. She had known this question was coming sooner or later, but she was still unsure of how to answer it. Part of the problem was that she didn't believe Celia was dead, not truly. She still expected to walk around the corner and bump into her, or hear her mother calling them to come in from the garden. But it wasn't just that. She couldn't bear the pity in people's eyes once they knew.

'Yes,' she answered eventually, 'I have an older sister, Celia.'

'Did she come with you?'

'No.'

'Oh, why not?'

'She's got measles,' said Emily, 'and chicken pox,' she added quickly.

Jack looked at her.

'Can you get both at the same time? That's really unlucky.'

'No,' said Emily, chewing on her top lip as she tried to

correct her excuse. 'I mean she had chicken pox, and now she has the measles. Got them only a few weeks apart, she can't leave London yet, so she's staying at home with my mum. What about you? Have you got any brothers or sisters?' she asked desperate to move the conversation on.

'An older brother, Tommy. He's away too. Merchant Navy,' he said with a forced casualness that couldn't disguise the concern in his voice.

Emily knew all about the Merchant Navy from her neighbour, Mr Willis, whose son was off at sea. They were different to the Royal Navy; they didn't attack other ships or ports; they mainly took cargo from all over the globe across the sea and back to Britain. Mostly they had food on board because food was becoming increasingly scarce. That's why there was rationing, so that everyone got something. Emily recognised the look of worry on Jack's face. The Merchant Navy were sustaining the worst losses of all, not a day passed without more stories of ships being sunk by German U-Boats.

'Do you miss him?' she asked.

Apparently that wasn't a question she could ask a boy. Jack gave her a withering look and made a sort of snorting sound that implied he didn't miss his brother at all.

'I miss Celia,' said Emily defensively.

Jack looked as if he was fighting against himself then finally replied, 'I like it when he's at home. He takes me out. We go to watch Exeter City together. Our house is opposite the ground,' he said proudly.

'Are they good?' asked Emily.

'They're the best football team in the world,' he replied.

'I don't really know much about football. I prefer cricket.'

'You like cricket?' said Jack not bothering to keep the disbelief out of his voice.

'Yes,' replied Emily. 'What's wrong with that?'

'Nothing,' he said. 'It's just...'

'What?' said Emily raising an eyebrow.

'Well... you're a... well...'

'You'd better not be planning to finish that sentence with the word girl.'

Jack grinned.

'Girls can play cricket,' said Emily.

'Girls can't play cricket. Cricket involves throwing and girls can't throw. That's just science or sommit.'

'Go on then,' said Emily coolly.

'Go on what?'

'Prove it.'

'Prove what?'

'Prove that girls can't play cricket.'

'I don't have to. Like I said, science.'

'I bet you I can bowl you out within one over,' said Emily throwing down the challenge.

'You never can.'

'Betcha I can.'

'What's the stakes?' he asked, his eyes narrowing suspiciously as if she were trying to catch him out.

'If I lose I have to admit that girls can't play cricket,' said Emily.

'And if you win?'

'Then you owe me…'

'I don't have any money.'

'Not money. A favour.'

'A favour?'

'Yes. A favour that I can call in at any time.'

'But all you have to do if you lose is say something, I actually have to *do* something' he said as if doing something were the most onerous thing he could think of.

'Don't forget I helped you out with the butcher, you already owe me for that.'

'I guess...'

'Still if you're frightened you'll lose then…'

Jack spat into his hand and offered it to Emily.

'I never lose.'

Emily spat into her hand too and they shook.

'Let's play.'

There was an old cricket bat back at the cottage, and she still had the ball her father had given her at the station, so they made the short walk to the Station Master's house. A few minutes rooting around the garden produced sticks large enough to act as stumps, then they balanced a few twigs precariously on top of them as bails. Jack marked out the crease whilst Emily took twenty-two paces up the garden to create the wicket.

Emily loved cricket. To her it was simple; it made sense. She enjoyed the sounds and smells of it, the leather of the ball striking the willow of the bat, the tinkle of the bails falling from the stumps. She knew some people thought it was a slow and overly complicated game, but she adored it. Her sister always complained about the length of time it took to play a match – 'so long they have to eat tea in the middle of it' she grumbled – but Emily couldn't think of a sport that wouldn't be improved for the taking of tea and cake half way through. Perhaps boxing she conceded, but all others certainly would.

She remembered trying to teach her sister how to play once. It was not an experience she ever repeated.

'How does it work?' asked Celia who had reluctantly agreed to learn something about the game from Emily's expert tutelage.

'I have a ball and I'm going to bowl it at the stumps.'

'What are the stumps?'

'Those three sticks behind you.'

'Right.'

'And you have to try and stop the ball hitting the stumps by using your bat. If you hit it and it doesn't get stopped by a fielder,' she pointed to a watering can and various gardening implements that had taken the place of real people at strategic places around the garden, 'then you should run to my end of the pitch and you'll get what's known as a run. If you hit it straight to the boundary,' here she pointed at the garden fence, 'you get four runs, and if you hit it over the fence you get six, but try not to do that

103

because Mr Thompson won't give me my ball back anymore. Oh and if I catch it before it bounces or if it hits the stumps and knocks the bails off...' her sister looked confused 'those are the sticks on top of your stumps' she added helpfully, 'then you're out.'

'Aren't there usually more people than this?' asked her sister.

'Yes, but there are only two of us. It's fine, I play this way with dad all the time.'

Emily had taken a small run up and launched a slow ball back down the wicket towards the stumps at which point her sister had screamed and held the bat up in front of her face to protect herself. The ball hit the middle stump taking it clean out the ground, and that was the end of Emily's attempts to teach her sister cricket. From now on she either played against her father or on her own.

Jack however looked as if he knew what he was doing. He lightly dug the tip of his bat into the ground in front of middle stump, bent his knees slightly and loosened his shoulders. Emily marked out her run up, took a few paces up to her stumps and sent a slow spinning ball down the twenty-two yards down the wicket only to see Jack heave it effortlessly back over her head.

'That's a six' he shouted, 'gotta be.'

Emily nodded grimly and went to retrieve the ball.

Her next ball she pitched slightly to his right hoping to catch him out with the turn she had put on it. He read it instantly and smacked it away again for another six.

'Come on, I thought you said you could play,' he said grinning.

Emily rubbed the ball on her trousers to get the mud off. She stepped up again and pitched this ball so it would look as though it would stay low but actually bounce up. If she was lucky he would be surprised and mishit his shot so she could catch him out. It did surprise him but he pushed it away well. At least it wasn't a six this time.

'Well that's a bit better I guess,' he crowed, 'you're not so bad really.'

The next two balls he dealt with competently enough. She had pitched them so they too would bounce up and entice him into playing a big shot. It was a risk but she had a plan. She could see him getting cockier and knew he'd want to smash away on her final ball to really rub salt into the wound.

Disguising her grip on the ball she sent it spinning gently down the pitch. Jack thought he'd read it and leaned back to pull it away once more, but this time it stayed much lower and moved far more sharply than he had expected, so that he was left playing at thin air as the ball bounced past him clipping the off stump and sending the bails clattering to the ground. Jack looked furious with himself. He'd got over confident and he knew it; if he'd just stayed cool he could have pushed it away and won the bet. Emily wandered over to him, reminding herself not to gloat, and found Jack still pawing at the ground with his bat, as if hoping to unearth a divot he could blame for his defeat.

'Well bowled,' he said eventually.

'Thanks. Well batted, you really knocked it around well.'

Jack said nothing.

'I'm thirsty,' said Emily, 'how about you?'

'Yeah... yeah me too.'

Emily led the way back inside and Jack followed behind.

'So this is where you live?'

'Yeah.'

'It's sort of... erm...'

'Grim?' suggested Emily.

'Yeah.'

'I know, but it's not so bad really, it's a bit cold and the lights don't always work but other than that...'

'Other than that, it's perfect.'

Emily laughed. 'Come on, I'll show you around.'

She took him from room to room suddenly aware that it had become rather important to her that he like the house.

Why this might be she wasn't sure. Perhaps it was because of how she had identified with it the previous evening, battered and neglected as it was, and to dislike the one was to dislike them both. She conducted the tour quickly not dwelling anywhere for long. Jack to his credit did his best to seem interested.

'And this is my room,' she said feeling slightly embarrassed.

Her mother would certainly not have let her take a boy up to her room, particularly not one she had only just met and with no one else in the house.

'You have to be careful with boys,' her mother had warned her, 'they only have one thing on their minds.'

What it was they had on their minds she never quite explained and it was left to Celia to fill in the details. She had also warned Emily to expect a big talk about the 'facts of life' that her mother would deliver on her fourteenth birthday. Celia called it 'the longest ten minutes of my life.' Apparently their mother had delivered the information about the differences between men and women in the sort of flat monotone normally reserved for announcements about late running trains.

Emily had heard talk of 'the birds and the bees' from friends at school but apparently her mother had confused the metaphor rather by mentioning eggs and honey till, as Celia put it, she thought that sex involved baking a rather sugary cake. It was only when their mother had blurted out the word 'penis' to their mutual embarrassment, that Celia cottoned on to what she was actually trying to explain.

'Mothers,' Celia concluded, 'should not be allowed to say the word 'penis', especially not to their daughters.'

Thinking about Celia bought on a strange ache in her stomach so she tried to think about something else. She pushed open the door to her bedroom. There really wasn't much to show, it was a small room and Emily had no possessions to speak of.

Jack peered out the round window and quickly lost interest wandering back on to the landing.

'What's in there?' he asked pointing to the door at the end of the hall.

'I don't know. It's locked though, I tried it earlier. I'll have to ask Mr Worthington.'

'Mr Worthington?'

'Yes, the man I live with. He's the Station Master at St David's Station. Look, that's him,' she said pointing at a picture that hung on the wall of a much younger looking Mr Worthington stood with a woman and a young girl.

'I'd better go,' said Jack suddenly.

'Oh,' said Emily surprised. 'You don't have to, you're welcome to stay longer if you want.'

'No, I have to erm... I've got something I need to do,' replied Jack already making his way back down the stairs. Emily followed in his wake.

'Well, feel free to come round at any time,' she offered, trying not to sound hurt by his sudden change of heart.

'Yeah, maybe. I'll see you around. Thanks for... you know, the thing with the butcher.'

And with that Jack darted out the back door. He stumbled over one of the stand-in cricket stumps that was sticking out of the ground at an awkward angle. He ripped it up in frustration and then slipped out the gate taking the makeshift stump with him. It was most odd. She wondered if she had said something to upset him but she couldn't think what that might have been. All they had been doing was looking round the house. Jack was the first and only person, other than Mr Worthington, who Emily knew in Exeter. Perhaps she shouldn't have taken him up to her room, maybe she had made him feel uncomfortable in some way. She would have to apologise next time she saw him, although when that might be she couldn't say, she'd only run into him by chance and it didn't seem likely that he would come calling again.

With all that had been going on Emily realised that she hadn't even started preparing dinner for that evening. She hoped the vegetables she'd dropped weren't too damaged to work with. Perhaps she should do a casserole, she thought to herself, something dark to hide the bruising? Emily busied herself in the kitchen. She wanted to cook a nice meal for their first dinner together, it was a way of saying thank you for taking her in, and anything that kept her busy was always to be welcomed.

Mr Worthington arrived home just before seven. They bade each other a cautious welcome before sitting down for dinner. They ate in silence so total that even the clinking of cutlery upon china was almost deafening. Eventually Mr Worthington asked about her day so Emily told him about her trip around the town, visiting all the different shops and seeing Exeter for the first time. She was going to tell him about Jack but she decided against it. She hadn't asked if she could have someone over and she thought perhaps he might be annoyed about it. After dinner Mr Worthington sat back and lit his pipe. He seemed to be studying Emily carefully.

'I think,' he said, 'we ought to talk about how things are going to work whilst you're here. You are a guest in this house. I'm sure we will get on just fine if you stick to one or two simple rules. You work hard and you do as you are told. I don't expect you to make me breakfast or lunch but dinner each evening at seven is essential. You will keep the house clean but you stay out of my room, that is out of bounds to you, is that clear?'

Emily nodded.

'I was tidying earlier and I couldn't open one of the doors upstairs.'

'Oh yes,' said Mr Worthington dismissively, 'it's an old cupboard, nothing in there to speak of. I lost the key a few years back and never bothered having the lock replaced. No need to worry about cleaning in there. Anyway, the days are yours to do with as you please. I will speak to some people I know and we will see about getting you a job, a few afternoons a week, would that be alright?'

'I thought maybe I would be going to school?' said Emily nervously.

'How old are you?'

'Thirteen.'

'But you know how to read, write and count don't you?'

'Yes,' she replied.

'Then work it is. You'd be leaving school within a year anyway, hardly time to even settle in. Any questions?'

Emily thought for a moment.

'The pictures round the house, who are they of?'

'They are my family, my wife and daughter, God rest their souls.'

That explained the dirtiness of the house and his gruff nature, thought Emily. His family were dead too and he wasn't used to talking to anyone anymore. Perhaps he wanted company and that was why he'd allowed her to come and stay.

'What made you take me in?' she asked.

'I got a letter asking if I had any rooms to spare. I gather your father is away and you lost the rest of your family in the first bombing, is that right?'

'Yes.'

'Well I'm sorry to hear that. It's hard isn't it? And don't believe what they say about time being a healer, I think I miss them more today than... well... that sort of talk gets you nowhere. Thank you for dinner,' he said, and with that he stood up and walked out of the room, leaving Emily alone at the table.

Chapter Seven

There was little time to worry about how she might have upset Jack over the coming days and weeks. The bombing directed at the major ports and cities across the country was getting worse. London, Manchester, Liverpool, Coventry, Glasgow had all been hit hard and nowhere now seemed safe. There were some successes, the RAF claimed to have shot down a lot of enemy aircraft, but somehow the Nazis kept on coming.

She wondered what would happen if the Nazis did conquer Britain? Would everyone be forced to work as slaves? And what about the people who had fought against them? Would they all be killed? The knot of worry in her stomach that she had carried around ever since she'd had her first vision of the bombing tightened still further.

Letters from her father arrived weekly but she hardly read them. She missed him terribly, but every time she thought about what he'd done she burned anew with anger and indignation. She knew he wasn't to blame, not really, but she couldn't make herself feel it.

The one positive, if you could call it that, was that since arriving in Exeter Emily hadn't had any visions of the future, or at least no visions like the ones before the bombing. Occasionally she found herself dreaming about a cave, and once she was awoken by a loud bang but whether that had been part of the vision or not she couldn't be sure. Perhaps it was because of how tired she felt. She was working every hour of the day to make the house comfortable to live in. The job Mr Worthington had spoken of had never materialised, but she was so busy planning meals for the next few weeks or altering the clothes she'd been given which were all far too big for her, she hardly had time to do anything else.

Mr Worthington was rarely home so Emily had the house to herself. In some ways she preferred it, she never knew what to say when it was just the two of them, but she did miss the company of others. On a few occasions she had run into Jack in town, but he always seemed to find some excuse not to hang around for very long. Whatever it was she had done to upset him, it seemed the damage was permanent.

One morning, whilst she was sweeping the kitchen, she heard the letter box rattle and the soft flutter of paper falling to the floor. When she got to the front door there were three letters, two brown envelopes addressed to Mr Worthington and one stiff cream envelope marked 'Miss Emily Cartwright' in a curled flowing script Emily did not recognise. Who could be writing to her? The only person who knew where she was living was her father and it didn't look like his handwriting, besides it seemed to have been hand delivered.

Quickly she opened it up. Inside was a letter on headed notepaper from the Imperial, a local hotel. It read:

Dear Emily,

My name is Josephine Alexander and I am a friend of your father's. I gather that you are currently living nearby and I wondered if I might have the pleasure of your company for afternoon tea?

There is no need to reply, I will be at the

Imperial Hotel for the next few days regardless, so simply drop by at around 3pm if you wish.

I look forward to seeing you then,

Yours,

Josephine

Emily was intrigued. Who was this woman? She racked her brains to recall if her father had ever mentioned someone called Josephine. She couldn't remember him doing so, in fact she couldn't remember him ever talking about any of his friends at all, male or female. How had she known that Emily was living in Exeter? Had she spoken to her father? Perhaps he had mentioned her in one of the letters that sat, half read, on the table next to her bed. She ran upstairs and scanned a couple of the most recent ones but there was no mention of someone coming to call on her. In fact, there was little information of any sort in his letters. She understood that he could not give her details about army life, but everything he wrote was so vague she could have crossed out her name at the top, given it to someone else whose father was away and they'd have trouble telling the difference.

Emily was slowly realising that she didn't really know her father. It was strange when she thought about it. She had, after all, lived for years in the same house as him, been tucked up in bed by him, been read stories by him, played cricket with him, laughed with him, and on occasion, been shouted at by him. She'd spent thousands of hours in his company, and yet in some ways she knew him no better than she knew Mr Worthington whom she had only just met. Most of what she knew of her father was mere trivia, facts that anyone could have picked up in a conversation over dinner.

She knew for instance that he loved cricket, and that he was a decent off-spinner, but as to where his love of the game came from, she was none-the-wiser. She knew that he preferred Buster Keaton to Charlie Chaplin, but she had never sat with him in the cinema and watched his face crease with delight as Buster walks out of a river wearing a canoe. When he'd had too much to drink Emily had heard him serenade her mother with a passable version of the Fred Astaire song 'Cheek to Cheek,' but how he'd come to know the lyrics she couldn't say.

She supposed she shouldn't be surprised at all this given that until her mother had mentioned it a few weeks ago, she did not even know her father had once had a sister. How could that be? How could she not have known that? How could he not have told her? Did she mean so little to him that she'd just faded from his life? Emily felt with a burning conviction that there would never be a single day she didn't think about Celia. The idea that she wouldn't talk about her to someone she loved was inconceivable.

It seemed there was so much she didn't know about him. She didn't know where he'd grown up, or how he and her mother had met. She didn't know what he'd been like as a boy, or anything about his parents. He'd always danced around the subject and she had been too self-involved to notice.

Again her mind returned the questions that had been troubling her since their talk in the hospital. Why hadn't he told her about what she could do? Why hadn't he prepared her for what might come? She'd thought she was losing her mind, if only she'd known, if she'd only had some hint of what was going on maybe she could have done something. And now there was a woman who claimed to be a friend of his, asking to see her. Well who was she? Why was she staying in a hotel in Exeter? And how exactly did she know her father?

She read through the letter once more. The Imperial Hotel was not far from the cottage, a fifteen-minute walk at most. For the first time since she had arrived in Exeter, Emily felt the tiniest change in her mood. Curiosity had, for a short while at least, displaced a little of the grief that so weighed on her. It was time to get some answers.

Emily spent a great deal of time choosing what to wear. She had only been out for afternoon tea once some years before. It was her tenth birthday and her mother had taken her to the Lyon's Corner House in Piccadilly as a surprise. She remembered it vividly. She asked for a slice of the Lemon Drizzle Cake she'd seen in the window. She'd never had any before and she could still recall the way the sponge seemed to melt in her mouth and how the lemon icing had tingled on her tongue. It was the most delicious thing she had ever eaten.

Perhaps this was why she wanted to look her best, maybe she wanted to impress this Josephine Alexander, whoever she was, or maybe she just wanted to look nice for once. She had spent so long in ugly hospital gowns or in huge baggy clothes that made her look like she was wearing a sack, that for once she was going to try and look like some of the other girls she saw around town.

This was easier said than done. All her clothes had been destroyed in the bombing, the few she had bought with her were donated by neighbours and charities. Generous though they had been, her father had been the one to choose from the various proffered items and was apparently under the impression that Emily was some sort of giant, so big were the clothes he had picked. Still, with the alterations she had made she now had one or two nice dresses. She selected the least threadbare of these, a pale green, knee-length dress with white spots, which she paired with a blue woollen cardigan that she felt matched her eyes.

She then spent several minutes painfully pulling a brush through her unruly hair. She had hardly brushed it since she'd arrived in Exeter. Most of her time was spent on her own in the house, she so rarely saw anyone she had almost stopped bothering. She only had one pair of shoes, a pair of black sandals. They didn't compliment her outfit in the way she'd have liked but there was nothing to be done about it.

Before she knew it, it was 3 o' clock and she was stepping nervously into the grand-looking foyer of the Imperial Hotel. She was greeted by a man dressed in a sharply-pressed blue jacket with thin gold trim and sparkling gold buttons. He looked so smart, it was intimidating. Suddenly Emily felt as if all the effort she had put into her appearance had been in vain. This man could see her for what she was, a child with no home and with nothing of any value to her name.

'How can I help you young lady?' said the man running his eyes over, what Emily was now certain, was a clumsily-altered dress that should never have seen the light of another day.

She tugged nervously at the new stitching and felt it begin to fray at her hips. She hadn't even bought any money with her. What had she been thinking?

'I'm here to see Mrs Alexander,' she said quietly, her cheeks glowing with shame.

Emily was surprised at how embarrassed she felt. If she'd been asked just a few months before she'd have said she wasn't bothered about what she wore or how she looked; in fact Celia had often teased her about her habit of wearing her favourite jumper until it was more holes than jumper, so why was she suddenly so concerned about her appearance? Perhaps it was because for first time she understood that what she looked like to other people might actually be important. She had no one to protect her or stand up for her, and there was power in the clothes people wore. Right now she was scruffy looking and easy to dismiss, and she was certain that this was exactly what the man would do at any moment. So certain was she in fact that she had to ask him to repeat himself when he asked her a question.

'Are you Miss Cartwright?' he said again.

'Yes,' replied Emily somewhat taken aback.

'Tea is being served in the Orangery. Mrs Alexander is expecting you, please go on through.'

Emily thanked the man, now feeling slightly less self-conscious than before. She had no idea what an Orangery was but didn't want to ask the attendant in case he changed his mind about letting her in. She walked down the corridor, doing her best to look as if she belonged, and quickly found herself standing at the entrance to one of the most beautiful rooms she had ever seen. It was made almost entirely from glass and was shaped like a beer barrel that had been cut in half lengthways then turned on its side. Dark metal arches spanned from floor to ceiling and down again, and at the far end of the room was a huge semi-circular window that reminded Emily of a peacock's tail.

As she stood looking out over the glorious room Emily couldn't help but think of the ballroom of a steam liner she had read about. The amber light of the sinking winter sun poured in through the glass and gave the room a warm glow. The Orangery was on two levels. The entrance served as a waiting area, with a few tables scattered here and there, though none of them were currently occupied. Just beyond them was a set of white stone steps lined with thick red carpet that led down into the main dining area.

It was certainly busy, the waiters in their black suits and bow ties scuttled between tables taking orders, obsequious smiles plastered to their faces. She counted fourteen tables in all, each resplendent with crisp white tablecloths. Emily wondered how she was going to spot Mrs Alexander and decided to ask the next waiter who passed. In the meantime she scanned the room looking for a familiar face, perhaps they'd met when she was younger, even if her name was unfamiliar. She scanned the room twice before she noticed a tall, grey-haired woman talking to a young man at a nearby table. She was wearing a light blue jacket that was cut wide at the shoulders before it swept sharply inwards as if by the stroke of an artist's pen, and was held tight at the waist by a thick black belt.

Beneath she had a long pleated skirt that hugged her figure closely right down to her ankles stopping just short enough to reveal a pair of white high heels. Emily had a strange feeling of recognition, but where did she know her from?

At that moment the woman looked up from her conversation with the young man and broke into a wide smile as she caught Emily's eye. Emily hesitated wondering whether or not she should introduce herself, but seconds later the woman had ended her chat and was beckoning for Emily to join her. She made her way down the steps and as she approached the table the woman stood up to welcome her.

'Emily my dear, a pleasure to meet you at last.'

She held out a thin, delicate hand. A cloud of perfume hung over her, sweet but not overpowering.

'Pleased to meet you too Mrs Alexander.'

'My friends call me Josie, so that is what you should call me too, for I think you and I will soon be firm friends.'

She had a curious way of speaking; it was crisp and quick, with a clipped, staccato rhythm. Though at first she sounded English there was the hint of something else there too, her slightly elongated vowels made Emily wonder if she'd ever lived in America.

'You're wondering who I am aren't you?' she said with a smile playing around her lips.

'I was rather, yes,' Emily admitted.

'There'll be plenty of time for explanations, in the meantime sit, sit. We must have tea. You'd like that wouldn't you? That's what we do in Britain isn't it? Drink tea? Tea must be bought before Hitler can be fought isn't that right?'

She laughed at her own little joke and summoned a waiter who appeared at their table as quickly as if she had conjured him from thin air.

'May we have a pot of tea for two and a cream scone each if you please?'

The waiter nodded and left without a word.

'Yes, tea and scones. That's what the British do when faced with adversity.'

Mrs Alexander stopped talking and fixed Emily with a piercing look. A silence descended on the table. Emily wasn't sure what to say.

'I must confess you're not quite how I imagined you would be.'

'And how did you imagine I would be?' asked Emily conscious again of the ragged nature of her dress, particularly when compared to Mrs Alexander's far more glamorous outfit.

'Younger, of course, much younger. But I'm afraid that's the curse of age child, people become locked in time. Even I don't look how I think I should. I'm constantly surprised whenever I glance in the mirror – and I confess I do that much more often than I should – to see an old woman starring back at me. Still, it happens to us all,' she added with a theatrical sigh.

Emily was confused. Why had this woman imagined her to be younger than she was? Why did she think of her at all? And they were supposed to become friends? Emily didn't have many friends anymore and she'd never had any adult friends.

'So, how are you finding Exeter?' asked Mrs Alexander.

'Oh erm... it's...lovely,' replied Emily, unsure how honest she should be.

'It has a certain charm about it doesn't it? One of the prettiest cities in England. Have you visited the Cathedral?'

'Erm... no.'

'No, of course not. Why would you? It's adults that are obsessed with the past, children just care about the future. We have that in common.'

Mrs Alexander was asking questions, but Emily had the impression she wasn't terribly interested in the answers.

'And you're staying with a family here are you? Are they treating you well?'

'I'm staying with Mr Worthington, he's the Station Master at St. David's. He's very... nice,' said Emily casting around for the right word.

'Nice? I see,' she replied but did not illuminate Emily as to exactly what it was she saw.

'I don't see him all that much; he's very hard working,' said Emily suddenly feeling the need to defend him in the face of her implied criticism.

'Well of course, everyone's so busy these days.'

'Except you it seems,' said Emily, the words slipping out before she had a chance to stop them.

If Mrs Alexander was offended then she didn't show it.

'Oh I'm busy child, but I know how to relax too. That's vitally important.'

Another pause. Emily wasn't certain she liked this woman and was about to ask how she knew her father when the waiter arrived with their tea.

'The one thing I miss whenever I am away is a good cup of tea, nobody makes tea like the British,' she said taking a satisfied sip.

'Do you travel often?' enquired Emily.

'All over, or at least I used to before the war, it's a lot harder now' she replied with one eye on the young waiter who was now moving off to serve at another table.

Emily opened her mouth to speak, but the woman cut her off.

'Do you really not know who I am?'

Emily shook her head.

'I see. I thought... maybe once you saw me... I didn't want to introduce myself in a letter, what with us never having spoken before, so formal, but still...'

Emily was lost.

'I don't want to appear rude,' she said, 'but I have no idea what you're talking about. Who are you?'

Mrs Alexander smiled.

'I'm your grandmother dear, and I must say it's lovely to see you again.'

'My grandmother?' repeated Emily incredulously. 'I'm

sorry, I think you've made a mistake. My grandmother is dead.'

For a moment Mrs Alexander looked hurt, then she shrugged it off.

'That's what he told you is it? Wishful thinking on his part I'm afraid. I suppose I should have guessed. Frank and David didn't agree on much but they were of one mind when it came to me and my capability as a mother. I was, in their opinion, somewhat... lacking I suppose you would say.'

Emily suddenly realised where she had seen this woman before.

'Wait, you were at the cemetery. You were arguing about something with my father.'

'Oh you saw us did you?' Far from being annoyed, she appeared delighted. 'I'm glad to see you've inherited my tendency to overhear things you shouldn't. But then we were arguing quite fiercely, I imagine it would have been harder not to hear us.'

She took out a cigarette from a silver cigarette case, lit it, and took a long drag. Emily was still confused.

'If you're my grandmother then –'

'Why does your father want you to have nothing to do with me?' she said, correctly anticipating Emily's question. 'It's a long story for another time.'

She blew the smoke over Emily's head and eyed her eagerly.

'I have to say he did a very good job of hiding you.'

'Hiding me?'

'Yes, quite extraordinary. It's taken weeks for me to track you down, and between you and me that's really saying something.'

Emily was more confused than ever.

'What do you mean hiding me? He hasn't hidden me, I'm right here.'

'Don't be obtuse child, of course he's not hidden *you*, he has hidden all the records of you, your paper trail, mentions of you in the newspapers, that sort of thing. Even the people that bought you here have no documentation of your journey and clam up if they're asked about you.'

'Why would he do that?'

'Many reasons, not least among them he didn't want the two of us to speak.'

Emily was struggling to process everything she was being told. It all seemed too unlikely.

'How do I know you're my grandmother? You could be anyone.'

'Surely not anyone dear,' she said with a sly smile and Emily was struck by an idea. If this woman was really her grandmother, then she must be a Seer too. That's what her father had said hadn't he? That the ability ran in her family, and that his sister and his mother had both been Seers. But what if this was some sort of trick? Maybe someone was trying to lure her out. Her father had warned against telling anyone about her abilities, what if someone had found out and was testing her for some reason? She needed to find a way to ask if Josephine was a Seer but without speaking plainly. Then she remembered the Seer's Mark.

'Dad said that his mother had a birth mark in a funny shape on her arm.'

Mrs Alexander's mouth twitched at the corners.

'Do you mean this?' she said casually rolling up her sleeve to reveal a familiar mark on her left forearm. She smiled, looking very pleased with herself, then rolled her sleeve back down.

Emily took a sip of her tea, trying to work everything out for herself. This woman claimed to be her grandmother, but her father had told her she was dead. Why would he lie about something like that? Then she thought back to their conversation at the hospital. The word 'dead' had actually never passed his lips. He'd always used a euphemism. His sister Lottie had died yes, but his mother was 'long gone.'

Then she remembered what she had seen at the cemetery. When he and Josephine were arguing, she had sensed real feeling between them. He had seemed too upset by their confrontation for it to be about the mistress of a colleague or whatever that ridiculous story was that he'd told her. When was she going to realise, her father was a liar? He had lied to her time and time again. The realisation that she could not trust her own father left her feeling tired and hurt.

'Are you really my grandmother?' she asked quietly.

'I am,' replied Mrs Alexander quietly, 'and I'm a Seer too; the best there is. I've been waiting a long time to meet you again Emily Cartwright. You're a very important person, more so than you realise and I'm here to help you.'

'Help me? With what?'

'With Seeing of course. Unless you've figured out how to do it on your own.'

'Well no, but...'

'Then it's settled. I will help you to master your abilities. Who better to do it than your own grandmother? What?' she asked sharply, seeing the look on Emily's face.

'Dad... he told me I shouldn't.'

'Shouldn't what?'

'Use my... abilities,' she finished quietly.

'Don't be ridiculous child, it's a gift don't you understand?'

'A gift? I watched my family die and I could do nothing to prevent it. It doesn't seem like much of a gift to me.'

Josephine's face fell.

'I know. I Saw it too.'

'You Saw it?'

'Of course. And it broke my heart.'

'Then why didn't you call dad or send a telegram or... or... something?'

'I did. I did all of those things, but it was only a matter of hours before those terrible events took place. Emily, I know how you feel. I watched my son die and I was powerless to stop it.'

The energy that seemed to radiate from Mrs Alexander

disappeared all of a sudden. For a moment Emily wondered if she might cry, but she merely paused to take a long, deep breath.

'Just because you saw what you did, doesn't mean you should give up. If anything the opposite is true. If you could go back and change what happened would you?'

Emily nodded reluctantly. She spent most of her waking hours trying to block out what had happened and didn't like this woman – somehow she couldn't quite bring herself to think of her as her grandmother just yet – bringing it up. Mrs Alexander did not seem to notice her hesitancy however and seized on Emily's agreement enthusiastically.

'Of course you would, but you can't. All you can do is learn from what happened and use your powers to keep others you love safe.'

'But what if I see something terrible?'

'Then at least you'll have a chance to fix it. Trust me Emily, I can teach you. You have more natural talent and power than I ever had.'

'How do you know?'

'I'm a Seer dear, it's my job to know.'

They fell into silence for a while. Mrs Alexander seemed happy to let Emily try and work through what she had told her, and instead of trying to persuade her further, she sat contentedly smoking her cigarette. Eventually Emily had to break the silence.

'How did you find me if my father had hidden me so well?'

'Money can buy you just about anything providing you know where to shop. Fortunately I do.'

'But where did you get all your money from? We're not rich.'

'You ask the right questions child I'm impressed. What you must understand about me is that my powers are not particularly strong.'

'But you said you were the best there is.'

'And I am. A few Seers can See further than me, but

none Sees better. I may only be able to see a few days or weeks ahead but I'm excellent at interpreting and understanding what it is I've Seen, then doing what needs to be done. Anyway, some years ago I began to use my powers. I began to invest in the stock market – not directly you understand, it's frowned upon for a woman do such things, but through various outside parties. I looked in to the future and invested what little money I had in certain businesses, checking on them all the time, looking just far enough ahead to make sure my investments would be sound, then I sold my shares at the right time and made substantial profits. I even foresaw the Wall Street Crash. You know what that was?'

'Sort of,' said Emily struggling to remember what she had been told about it in school.

'It was the stock market crash of 1929, a lot of people invested with the hope of getting rich quick, some businesses weren't as successful as they'd made out and the whole thing began to unravel. People pulled their money out to try and stem their losses but that only made it worse. It was a terrible thing Emily, but there was nothing I could do about it. I had to watch as friends lost their money while I sold my shares at the right time and put it into companies that had a future. I made a fortune.'

'Couldn't you have warned people about what was going to happen? Especially if they were your friends.'

'I couldn't risk exposing myself. I didn't make them put their money into these companies, they wanted to get rich quick. Sometimes we have to suffer the consequences of our actions.'

Emily frowned. It was all very well saying people had to suffer the consequences when without her abilities Mrs Alexander would surely have been in the same situation. She didn't think she'd be able to keep quiet if she knew something bad was going to happen to someone she cared about.

'I came back to England when I Saw what was going to happen to our family. I wanted to help if I could, but your father sent me away again.'

'Don't people ask where you got your money from?'

'No, people are very sweet like that, especially the British. You see dear, there are only three things of interest to anyone in life, money, power and sex, and yet it's considered terribly bad form to ask about any of them. The situation really is very tedious but it suits me down to the ground. I don't want people asking too many questions about my wealth, and the more of it I have, the less they talk about it. You say you inherited it from a distant relative, adopt a suitably grand sounding name and that's all there is to it. The Americans in particular lap it up. You buy the right piece of land and get yourself a title and you're made for life. But it's an act, all of it.'

Josephine leaned in conspiratorially and suddenly her accent changed completely. Gone was her well-to-do voice with its gentle American lilt, and in its place was a rough cockney dialect that took Emily by surprise.

'You play a part see? And if you play it well enough then no-one'll ever believe that your mother was a seamstress from Cheapside, and your father was a lace warehouseman who gambled away every last penny he 'ad then drank 'imself into an early grave.'

Moments later her – for want of a better word – normal accent returned.

'You see?' she said with a smile, 'It's an act. And I act better than anyone. Oh I have so much to teach you Emily. You could be great, truly wonderful.'

'Then why doesn't my father want you to see me?'

'He thinks I'm a terribly bad influence,' she said, swatting away her father's objections like the last traces of cigarette smoke. 'I tried to talk him out of it, but it only made him more determined. He blames me for his Lottie's death, so does Frank. I miss her every day Emily, really I do, and I miss my boys too, David and Frank. Maybe if I hadn't lived so far away, maybe in time we'd have worked things out… I don't know. Perhaps I was to blame… I was her mother, I should have kept her safe, I should have kept

Frank safe... You know what it's like I'm sure, to miss people so much, to feel that crack in your heart that will never heal? I'm a failure Emily, I am. I have failed to keep my family safe. I've been terribly foolish and terribly selfish, but I'm older now. What I've learned has come at a dreadful cost, but I have lived and I have learned. I can help you.'

She looked upset, but Emily couldn't work out if this was just another part of her act.

'Your father thinks I'm dangerous,' she continued, 'but he's wrong. I'm the only one who understands what you're feeling right now, who knows that grief you carry with you. David doesn't like our abilities, I'm sure he's made that clear to you. He's scared of them, but they are perfectly natural. Asking us not to See is like asking a bird not to fly. It's a gift and if you use it well you could achieve incredible things.'

'Why have we never met before? Why didn't you try and find us sooner?'

'I stayed away at your father's request, but that was before, things are different now. The moment I Saw what was to happen I flew straight over, but that's not as easy as it once was. I've been keeping as close an eye on you as I could given the circumstances.'

'Have you been having me followed?' asked Emily thinking of the man she had seen at the station and outside the grocers.

'Nothing so crude no.'

Emily's head was swimming with questions.

'You said you were the best, you mean there are other Seers?'

'Yes. Not many, and they don't make themselves known for obvious reasons.'

'Then how do you find them?'

'You learn to spot the patterns, people who have sudden unexplained wealth, smart women with dumb husbands. You've heard the saying "Behind every successful man stands a woman?" Sometimes that's truer than you might think. I've met hugely successful men whose talents don't extend beyond playing a good round of golf, and yet they have a curious knack for making money. It's a perfect disguise. You play the good housewife while gently guiding your partner towards the right deals.'

'So you want me to make money?'

'No, I want you to make a difference. We're fighting for our lives here Emily, the country could be invaded by the Nazis in a matter of weeks. You might be the greatest weapon we possess.'

'I'm not a weapon,' she insisted angrily. 'I won't kill anyone.'

'Good grief child, I'm not asking you to, no, no, no. But you do owe it to yourself to develop your powers, if for no other reason that you are a danger to yourself like you are.'

'What do you mean?'

'It's a terribly long story my dear. I'm not trying to deceive you, I will explain I promise, but not today.'

Emily leaned back in her chair. She hated not knowing the full story and she suspected that Mrs Alexander was only withholding it in order to make sure she visited again.

'Are we agreed?' asked Mrs Alexander as she opened her cigarette case.

'Agreed?'

'That I will teach you to See. You will come here let's say… twice a week?' Though it sounded like a question, it felt more like an instruction. 'Yes that works nicely doesn't it? Meet me here and I will show you everything you need to know about Seeing.'

Emily hesitated for a moment. Her father's words were still fresh in her mind, but this woman was family wasn't she? Surely she could trust her? Besides, her father had lied to her time and again, so who was he to talk about trust? Josephine was right, it was natural for her to want to use her powers. If she'd been able to See properly she might have been able to prevent what happened to her mother and sister.

'Agreed Grandma,' she replied.

'Oh goodness no child, do not, whatever you do, call me Grandma. It makes me feel terribly old. Call me Josie or Josephine.'

'Ok... Josie,' she said unsteadily. She had never called an adult by their first name before. 'When do we start?'

'Thursday at 2 o' clock. Be here on time, I really can't abide lateness, it's a terrible habit,' she said taking another long drag on her cigarette.

Chapter Eight

On Thursday afternoon at precisely 2pm Emily found herself knocking on the door of Room 104 of the Imperial Hotel.

'Come in,' called a voice from inside.

Emily pushed open the door to find her grandmother standing at a full-length mirror holding two long dresses, one of purple silk, the other of red velvet, up against herself.

'What you think? The purple or the red?'

'I prefer the purple,' said Emily cautiously.

'Then purple it is,' she said throwing the red one over a chair.

'It's a big room,' said Emily.

'Yes,' said Mrs Alexander dreamily, still holding the purple dress up to herself. 'I've got all the rooms on this floor, they all lead on to one another you see. It pays to be careful, I don't want us to be overheard and I can always do with the extra wardrobe space.'

'Just how rich are you?' said Emily looking around the room for the first time and taking in the variety of trinkets and ornaments that were scattered across shelves and tables.

Her grandmother smiled slyly and picked up a letter from her dresser.

'You've heard of JD Rockefeller?'

Emily let out a little gasp. JD Rockefeller was an American businessman and the richest person to ever live.

'Well I'm nowhere near as rich as him,' she said enjoying the expression on Emily's face, 'but these hands won't ever scrub another floor, believe me.'

Emily surveyed the room again. She had never seen so much paraphernalia. There were numerous perfume bottles, several ornate vases bursting with freshly-cut flowers, a silver drinks cabinet that overflowed with liquors and spirits of various kinds, and a golden carriage clock that Emily suspected was made of real gold. She looked over at her grandmother who was toying with a gaudy, jewel-encrusted object while reading a letter.

'Is that a knife?' asked Emily.

'Don't be foolish child, it's a letter-opener for unsealing correspondence from my army of not-so-secret admirers,' she said, before casually tossing it onto the bedside table, toppling the substantial pile of letters, leaving it buried somewhere beneath them.

'And what's this?' said Emily holding up a small, but surprisingly heavy, bronze box with the figure of a nude woman on top of it.

'It's a cigar box. Honestly, I don't even know why I still have it, I hate cigars. It was given to me by my second husband, Gerald, when he made his first million so I suppose I've come to think of it as a lucky charm.'

'His first million?' said Emily, her eyes widening in disbelief, 'you mean there were more after that?'

'Well of course,' replied her grandmother, as if it was the most natural thing in the world, 'but you're not here to learn about the past, you're here to learn about the future, so let's get down to business. I'm guessing that up till now you've had a few visions but nothing you could control, nothing you chose to see, am I correct?'

Emily thought of flying in the plane, watching the airman jump, and seeing her house in ruins, then nodded.

'What I want to do is help put you in charge of your powers, rather than letting your powers be in charge of you. Of course, that's not possible 100% of the time, but that's for another lesson.'

'No, please tell me, what if I need to know?'

Josephine looked at her, her eyes racing over Emily's face as if searching for something only she could see.

'Perhaps you're right,' she said eventually, 'perhaps you should know.'

She sat down at her dressing table and indicated to Emily to take a seat on the chaise longue by the window.

'Sometimes, not very often mind, there is an event so big that it overrides everything else.'

'Like what?'

'Well there have been very few in my lifetime, there was one a dozen or so years ago that the Sisters all saw.'

'You have sisters?' said Emily, suddenly alarmed that her father had hidden more family from her.

'In a manner of speaking. It's the name we've given ourselves. It was meant as a joke but somehow it stuck. As I said, there are more Seers in the world than just you and me. How many I couldn't say for sure, it's not as though we all get together for Christmas, but if we get a strong vision, one that we have no control over, then we will meet up to discuss it. You have to understand most Seers have very little power at all, sometimes it's less of a power than it is a party trick. You'll often find Seers make their living as fortune tellers or magician's assistants, that sort of thing. Only a few have a true gift, and there are plenty of charlatans out there.'

'Then how come I can See the future?'

'I don't know for sure. It tends to run in families, down the female line, but I think everyone has little insights and glimpses into the future, we just call it déjà vu.'

'I thought it was only women who could See?'

'It is, but everyone has some trace within them. Well, I think so anyway, but of course it's not easy to study these matters. It's something I've discussed with the Sisters on a number of occasions. But more on them another time, for now let's concentrate on the matter in hand. As I was saying sometimes a great event may be foreshadowed, that means that all the Sisters will See the same thing. This war with Nazi Germany was one of them. Of course, just because we all See the same thing doesn't mean we always know or even agree on what it means. Anyway, such events are rare, you don't need to worry yourself about them, your whole life may pass without another one happening. What's more important is that you learn to control what you can See, but before we start there's a few things you need to know.'

Emily leaned in, intrigued as to what Josephine might tell her.

'Firstly, you cannot See along your own timeline. By that I mean you can't See your future directly, you can only See where your future intersects with the lives – or deaths – of others. Secondly there is nothing that says you will like what you See, so be very careful before looking along someone else's line. You'll spoil the story if you go skipping to the final page every time. Allow yourself to live in the moment, if you know what everyone will do and say every time you meet them your days will be very dull indeed.'

Emily nodded, eager to hear more.

'Thirdly and most importantly, tell no one about your gift. I don't think you realise how dangerous your powers can be and how much others would dearly love to have them. Keep them secret. Don't show off, don't draw attention to yourself, don't get noticed. Do you understand?'

At this Emily found herself getting annoyed.

'But you said I should learn how to use them, and you're hardly shy and retiring, hiring a whole floor of a hotel just for yourself.'

She was half-expecting to be admonished for this outburst, her mother certainly wouldn't have stood for it, but Josephine just smiled.

'Of course you should learn how to use them, that's why I'm here isn't it? But that's different to telling everyone that you have them. Whilst I may disagree with your father about *using* your gift, he's not wrong about keeping it a secret. The most talented Seers don't tend to live to a grand old age; most end up dead.'

'Why?'

'People want what we have, and if they can't possess the knowledge then they want to possess the carrier of the knowledge. That's why it's important that I'm here, it's not just that I want to teach you to use your ability, it's that I can also help you hide it and keep you safe. I draw attention to my wealth because, as I have already explained, it is helpful for me to do so. It stops people looking into other areas of my life. It's a sort of distraction, although I will not deny that it also allows me to live in a manner that I find most enjoyable.'

'But people don't know about Seers?'

'Wrong. Most people don't know about Seers, but the few that do are often dangerous.'

Emily nodded. She thought about what Josephine had said and her mind wandered to the man with the blonde hair, the one who appeared to be following her. She wondered if she should ask about him, but then he couldn't know about her abilities could he?

'Now, to the lessons. Let's start with something simple,' said Josephine picking up a large silver coin from the dressing table. 'A game of heads or tails.'

The disappointment must have shown on Emily's face, because Josephine burst out laughing.

'Dear child, you didn't think you'd be the Oracle of Delphi by a quarter past two did you? First, you need to learn to see something with a clear outcome; humans are much more complicated, much more difficult to predict. You need to understand that what we do is an art, not a science. Even the best of us can get things wrong. The future is not set in stone, all you are doing is divining the most likely outcome. With heads and tails it's relatively simple, it has to be one or the other. So, close your eyes, clear your mind, and relax.'

'Close my eyes? Don't I need to gaze into a crystal ball or something?' and as she said these words Emily saw Josephine bristle.

'You most certainly do not. I know a few of my sisters use them, but really, a crystal ball has no special properties at all. They are not mystical artefacts with the power to channel visions, whatever certain people may claim. No, the focus that you require is found within you, not in some tawdry prop meant for a third-rate carnival act. Now close your eyes and concentrate.'

Emily did as she was told.

'Think of me tossing the coin,' said Josephine. 'Can you see it?'

'Yes.'

'Picture it in your mind. Focus on the moment of the throw. See the coin in the air turning over and over. Now watch as it lands.'

'Heads,' said Emily confidently opening her eyes.

'Tails,' corrected Josephine with a stern expression. 'Try again. Focus only on the coin. See it. Feel it.'

Emily tried again though she wondered how on earth she was meant to "feel" a coin in her mind.

'Heads,' she called.

'Tails,' said her grandmother. 'Try again. Stop thinking about the result, focus on the coin, focus on the spin, *see* the moment it lands. You need to be in the room, in the instant it happens.'

Emily closed her eyes and once again imagined the coin turning in the air. But no matter what she did, it didn't feel like the times she had Seen before. On those occasions she was convinced she had been there, she had experienced it as if it had happened to her for real, now she was merely picturing it.

'I can't do it,' she sulked.

'You can do it. Now relax, shake out your body, think about this moment and only this moment.'

Emily did as she was told and tried to hold the coin in her mind's eye. Suddenly her world shifted. She could taste something metallic in her mouth and hear the ring of her Grandmother's nails flicking against the coin. When she opened her eyes, it was as if time had slowed almost to a standstill. The coin rotated in the air, glinting in the light that poured through the window. It landed on –

'Heads,' she called out.

'Correct. Was that a guess or was that you?'

'No, I saw it this time. The second it landed I knew I was right.'

'Okay,' said her grandmother with a smile, 'let's try again. Focus. See the coin.'

Emily tried again, now she had done it once she was sure it would be easy to do it again, but despite all her efforts, she couldn't make herself feel the way she had before.

'No. No it's gone again,' she complained, opening her eyes.

'That's okay. It happens. Tell me, have you ever tried sawing through a piece of wood?'

Emily shook her head.

'It might look like the best way is to use force, to power your way through, but actually the opposite is true. It's the teeth of the saw that cut the wood, not the force you yield the saw with. Does that make sense?'

'I think so,' said Emily hesitantly. 'It's like in cricket, if you hit the ball with the right part of the bat you can send it much further than if you hit it with another part, even if you're swinging harder.'

'If you say so dear.'

Emily looked at her grandmother dressed in her fine silks. 'When was the last time you sawed a piece of wood?'

Her grandmother laughed.

'You'd be surprised at the things I've done. Now let's try again.'

Emily closed her eyes. For a moment she heard the ringing in her ears again, as if every sound in the world had become amplified. She saw the coin spinning in the air but in her excitement she lost focus and the vision disappeared.

'Almost. I had it and then I lost it.'

'You're still trying to force it. Focus not force is what you need. Breathe deeply, clear your mind.'

She did as she was instructed, trying to shake the feeling of frustration that was growing inside her. Mrs Alexander flicked the coin and Emily found herself watching it turn over in her head before landing on –

'Tails,' she cried.

'Good,' said her grandmother. 'Now clear your mind and we'll give it another go.'

Again Emily Saw the coin and again she called it correctly.

'Very good. You have a talent for this child.'

Emily beamed.

'Okay, let's try again.'

She tossed the coin in the air and Emily closed her eyes. She watched it turning when she spotted something.

'It's a different coin. Both sides have heads on them.'

'Remarkable,' said her grandmother slowly. 'You not only Saw correctly, you found something else, you weren't put off by the change of coin, you read it anyway.'

Josephine's voice had changed. It was only a subtle thing but it was as if she was slightly wary of Emily now.

'That's enough for today I think,' she said brusquely.

'Oh but–'

'No,' she replied raising a stern finger, 'what we do is not easy, it takes a great deal out of you. In a short while you will begin to feel tired, extremely tired. Go to bed, get some rest. You may not realise it but you've run a marathon, you'll be exhausted later.'

'But I feel–'

'Trust me child,' she said, her voice softening. 'Besides I have to get ready for this evening.'

'What's happening this evening?'

'A fine young gentleman has promised to take me out to dinner. He'll be here at eight.'

'That's not for another five hours.'

'Five hours? Is that all? When you get to my age child it takes a great deal more effort to look effortless. Go,' she said shooing her out of the door, 'I'm done with you now. Be here Saturday at ten sharp.'

The door closed firmly shut behind her. Once again Josephine had not checked with Emily if the time she had proposed suited her. She wondered if perhaps she had looked down her timeline and Seen she would be free, or if she just assumed Emily would have nothing better to do. She knew she shouldn't complain, but her dismissive attitude annoyed her a little.

It was barely a ten-minute walk back to Mr Worthington's house, but by the time she got there she was exhausted, her joints were stiff and even her bones ached. The chill seeped through her jacket and wrapped itself around her skin until she felt she would never be warm again. Although her grandmother had warned her she would feel tired, Emily was unprepared for just how drained she felt, she could barely keep her eyes open. She settled down in front of the fire and pulled an old blanket up over her. In just one hour her whole world had been turned on its head again. For the first time in a long time she didn't feel so alone, she had someone to talk to, someone who would look out for her.

Her thoughts wandered once more to her father, and she felt another stab of anger towards him for his deception. He had sent her to live with Mr Worthington, a complete stranger, rather than with his own mother. Josephine said that he blamed her for his sister's death, but did that justify his actions? What else might he be lying about? Once upon a time she had idolised him, but ever since his admission at the hospital she had done her best to shut out all memory of him. He had let her down. He had lied. He was responsible for her living in this cold, dark house. He was the reason she had to leave all her friends behind. He was the reason she had no family. The list of charges against him grew longer and longer as she repeated them to herself.

From time to time a small voice inside piped up to ask her if she really thought he was trying to hurt her, and if perhaps he was acting in her best interests. But she smothered that voice with the full weight of her fury. He had betrayed her, she was not interested in what he thought was for the best. It was time for her to make her own decisions. She hadn't realised quite how lonely she was before, and now that weight had lifted a little. The fire crackled and spat in the grate. Emily felt her eye lids drooping and before she knew it, she was asleep.

She awoke some hours later to a loud cry. The fire was almost out, the warmth had fled from the room. She tried to gather her thoughts. What had woken her up? Some sort of shout or call, perhaps an owl or a fox, she wasn't sure. The countryside and all its attendant sounds were still new to her. She glanced at the clock on the mantelpiece, it was just after six thirty. She ought to put the dinner on. Outside a cold winter wind threw itself against the windows and whistled down the chimney. Drawing the blanket around her, Emily made her way over to the fire and stabbed at the embers with a poker before adding a few pieces of kindling to try and spark it back into life. Suddenly she heard a sound, a loud thump from upstairs like someone falling over.

'Hello?' she called out.

There was no reply.

'Hello? Mr Worthington?'

Still there was nothing. Emily was used to the house making odd noises but this was different. Keeping hold of the poker she prepared to investigate. There was another thump, quieter this time, but audible nonetheless in the stillness of the house. The hairs on the back of her neck prickled.

'Is anyone there?' she called out again.

Now all the sounds of the house were amplified, its little creaks and cracks sounded like explosions as she waited for whoever might be upstairs to show themselves. She tried to swallow the fear that was slowly rising in her throat.

'I'm coming up,' she called.

She made her way cautiously up the twisting staircase. The first floor of the house was colder than the ground floor and she could see her breath rising in front of her. Outside, the gentle applause of the falling rain grew to a crescendo and the wind billowed in the trees. The landing light cast jagged shadows in front of her and it felt again as though the house too was listening, waiting. There was a long, slow creak as the door to Mr Worthington's room crept open a few inches and then began to close again. Emily's heart leapt.

'Who's there?' she said, although by now her throat felt so tight the words were little more than a whisper. 'I've got a poker. I'll hit you with it, I will. Come out right now.'

The door creaked open again, just an inch or two, and then drifted shut. It was probably the wind she told herself, but she clutched the poker tighter still. Reluctantly Emily took the final step onto the landing then pushed open the door to Mr Worthington's room as fast as she could. She stood back, half expecting some figure in the darkness to rush through.

Crack!

Emily jumped. Outside, the front gate had caught in the wind and was being slammed against its post. It was like the house was making fun of her. No one emerged from the gloom of Mr Worthington's room so she inched inside. She could hear a gentle shuffling, scuffling sound, though where it was coming from she did not know. It might simply have been leaves rustling against the windows, or the mice that scuttled around under the floorboards, but she didn't think so.

She had not been in Mr Worthington's room since the first morning; he had told her that she was not to go in there, not even to clean it, so she had obeyed. She switched on the light to the room and it flickered into life. She told herself she was only going to have a quick look, make sure everything was all right, then get out of there. He didn't have to know. The room was large and sparsely furnished. In the corner was a wardrobe with a full-length mirror attached to one of the doors. Emily tried not to look at it, somehow seeing her own anxiety reflected back at her made it worse.

In the centre of the room there was a rug, one corner of which was turned over. Emily went to put it back in place but noticed that one of the floorboards the rug would normally hide was sticking up slightly. She pulled at the board and it came away with surprising ease, as if it were removed often. Wondering what might be down there, she peered into the hole but was unable to see anything in the darkness. With some trepidation she reached in, half expecting a rat or a mouse to rush out. She shuddered, but her curiosity overcame her fear. Slowly she pushed her hand along the space until she touched something cold and hard, and instantly she pulled back. Her heart pounding, she examined her hand closely but, finding no injury, she tried again, this time grabbing hold of the mysterious object and pulling it out into the light.

What she discovered was most unexpected; it was an ornate silver jewellery box. Very carefully she opened the lid to see what was inside. To her surprise the only thing it contained was a rusty key about four inches long. Emily picked it up and examined it, wondering why anyone would keep a key in an old jewellery box underneath the floorboards. What was it for? What did it unlock? It didn't look like any of the keys she had to the house, and if it was a spare key why keep it hidden inside?

She took the key and tried it in the lock to the room, but it didn't work. The gate outside slammed shut again making her jump once more. Other than the jewellery box there was little to see, nothing looked as though it had been disturbed, the window was open a fraction and a cold breeze toyed with the creaking door. She pulled it shut and carried on looking around the room. The bed was made, the drawing table's drawers were all closed. It did not look like the house had been burgled. Perhaps the box was valuable and Mr Worthington had hidden it beneath the floorboards for safekeeping. Maybe he had just put the key in there and forgotten about it. Now she thought about it, the jewellery box was as strange as the key. Why did he have a jewellery box? Who did it belong to? Perhaps it had been his wife's, but if so, why hide it?

The questions circled in Emily's head and then a thought struck her. There was only one door in the house that she could think of that was locked all the time, the door to the old storage cupboard at the top of the stairs. Mr Worthington had said he'd lost the key, but as there was nothing in there and he had no need to store anything, he had never got around to having the lock replaced.

Climbing to her feet she crept out of the room and along the landing until she was standing in front of the cupboard door. She thought for a moment about what she was doing, after all Mr Worthington had asked her to stay out of his room. It didn't matter that the rug was out of place, he hadn't intended her to find this key. Besides, maybe he had good reasons for locking the door. Still, he would never know and Emily had never been able to resist a mystery. There was another bang from outside and the shuffling noise from above her started up again. She slipped in the key and then twisted it to the right. The lock clunked, giving way with surprising ease and the door swung open.

To Emily's astonishment, what she found was not a cupboard at all, but a set of stairs. She stepped back. If Mr Worthington hadn't wanted her to find this key, then he had definitely not intended her to find these stairs, nor whatever lay at the end of them. She couldn't help wondering though, where did they lead and why had Mr Worthington told her this was just a cupboard? She looked around for a light switch but there was nothing and she really didn't want to go up the stairs in the darkness.

Suddenly she remembered an old oil lamp Mr Worthington kept by the back door and she decided to fetch it before going any further.

She ran down to the kitchen and took the lamp from its place by the door. There was another thud from upstairs. Emily felt a strange combination of fear and excitement rising in her chest. She twisted the little silver knob on the lamp to make the flame as bright as possible. Why had Mr Worthington lied? He must have known what was behind the cupboard door, so why didn't he want her to see it? What was he hiding? Emily figured that she owed it to her herself to find out. She didn't know Mr Worthington that well after all. What if he was dangerous?

The door to the hidden staircase had swung shut whilst she had been away, and ever so cautiously she pulled it open again. A waft of stale air drifted down from whatever lay beyond. Slowly she began to climb the stairs, holding the lamp high above her head to light the way, but she stopped in her tracks when she heard more rustling coming from above.

'Hello?' she called out again taking a small step backwards and holding the poker in front of herself.

'I'm coming up,' she said again.

There was another rustling and rattling. She crept up the dusty wooden stairs. Though she trod as softly as she could, the stairs groaned in protest at her every step. The darkness closed behind her, when she turned around her could barely see the landing anymore. She carried on climbing the twisting stairs until she came to another door.

'Hello?' she said again.

All was quiet.

'I'm coming in now,' she called, trying to fill her voice with a boldness and confidence she did not feel.

She pushed open the door and stood back. What lay before her was most surprising. It was simply a bedroom, but a bedroom that had not been lived in for many years. It was a like a ghostly exhibit from a museum. She guessed the room must have belonged to a girl, for there was a pretty hairbrush lying on the dressing table and an old doll on the bed. Tucked in the corner of the room was wardrobe.

Emily almost dropped the lamp as she turned around to see a girl standing behind her.

'AAAHHHHH,' she screamed, before realising it was her own dim reflection in the dusty mirror that hung from the wardrobe door.

She took several deep breaths to calm herself. Really there was nothing to be scared of; it was just a bedroom. The room was quite small with a sloping ceiling on one side, and a window that would have looked out over the garden had the boards not been shut. Emily realised she could see the room from outside but had always assumed it was just an attic and had thought no more of it.

Why had Mr Worthington locked this room away? Why did he lie to her? The place gave her the creeps. It was as if it was suspended in time, like the occupant had only just left and could return at any moment. The bed was half made and the curtains hung limply from their rails serving no purpose, and their faded colour gave the impression of a room that was slowly disappearing.

There was another rattle and flutter, closer this time. Emily jumped. It was coming from the fireplace. The grate had been boarded up, but whatever was making that noise was behind it. It must be a bird she thought, a pigeon perhaps that had somehow become trapped in there. She pulled at the boards but they wouldn't come loose, so she slid the poker down a small gap between the brick work and the wood and began to lever the boards away. There was more banging and scuttling. Emily hoped she was right; if she opened it and hundreds of mice ran out then she thought she might be sick.

Finally, the boards began to shift until, with a puff of brick dust they were free and the fireplace was open once more. The noise had stopped. Emily peered into the black, lantern in hand. All of a sudden a large bird flew out the fire place and into the room. Emily fell backwards. It had almost hit her in the face. The bird fluttered round the room and landed on top of the wardrobe. She could barely make it out in the darkness, she could just see two white eyes staring at her through the gloom.

'CRRAAWWW', it cried.

Outside, the wind continued to howl and the gate screeched as it swung in the breeze. The house moaned and creaked, though to Emily's ears it sounded more like mocking laughter. She wondered how on earth she was going to get the bird out of there. The window was boarded up so she couldn't just open it and let it fly out. Perhaps it was best to shut it in the room overnight, then in the morning she could come up again and open the door so it could find its own way downstairs. In the meantime if Mr Worthington heard shuffling, he could come and deal with it himself, and that way he would never know she had discovered the room.

As she stood up to leave, she noticed that the wardrobe was slightly ajar. Inside hung some neat white blouses, a few woollen cardigans, a jacket with a matching skirt made from some heavy, coarse material that felt like sandpaper to the touch, and one beautiful, long blue dress that, hidden in the dark of the cupboard, had retained its vivid colour. She ran a hand down the length of it and found it wonderfully soft to the touch. Finally, she closed the doors to the wardrobe. The mirror on the front swung gently and in its reflection she saw the figure of a large man standing right behind her.

Chapter Nine

'Found anything interesting have you?'

'M... Mr Worthington,' stuttered Emily, 'I'm sorry, I...
I was...'

'Why are you up here? What are you looking for?
Money? Jewellery? I haven't got anything worth stealing
you know.'

'I heard a noise, there was... I came upstairs and then I
saw...'

'You saw what?'

A slow feeling of shame began to creep through her.
She could feel her cheeks turning red and now she wished
she had just left well alone.

'I saw the rug in your room was up.'

'And of course you put it back into place...'

'No,' said Emily looking at the floor. 'I... I noticed that
a board was loose too, so I lifted it up.'

'I don't remember asking you to come into my room
and go through my things. In fact, I remember very clearly
asking you – no, telling you – to keep out.'

'I'm sorry.'

'I wouldn't have had you down as a thief, but it just
goes to show you can never tell.'

'You think I was trying to rob you?' she asked
incredulously.

'Then what were you doing up here? Or were you just

having a good nose around, is that it?'

The accusation of theft stung Emily into defending herself. What she had done was wrong, she knew that, but she wasn't a thief.

'I heard a noise, a thump, I thought someone was upstairs. I found the box and it had a key in it...'

'So you heard a noise, found a key and thought, this key must be making an awful racket, I'd best pick it up.'

'No of course not, but I... I thought it might open the cupboard door, that maybe there were mice in the cupboard.'

'Oh you were looking for mice now were you? Overweight mice? Mice wearing heavy boots, clomping around on the staircase? Well that explains it then,' he said in a mock-friendly tone, 'of course you had to go snooping around my room and unlocking doors that are supposed to remain locked.'

Even in the dark of the room she could see his face was turning a deep shade of red.

'I know I shouldn't have taken the key, I know I should have left it alone,' said Emily, doing her best to curtail her own temper, 'but then I heard the noise again, and when I found the key I thought about the cupboard, and I unlocked it. Only it isn't a cupboard.'

'No. It isn't.'

'Anyway there was this bird, it got stuck down the chimney...'

Emily looked around the room in search of the bird that had been perched on top of the wardrobe only a few minutes before, but there was no sign of it. It must have found its way downstairs already.

'I think it's best you go to bed,' said Mr Worthington in a studiously, even manner. 'In the morning I will call Miss Pinchman and ask her to find you somewhere else to live.'

Emily stayed where she was.

'You're throwing me out?'

'You're either a thief or a liar. Maybe both.'

'I'm not a thief or a liar,' insisted Emily.

Mr Worthington's voice was quivering with barely supressed rage.

'Did I or did I not ask you to stay out of my room? Hmmm?'

Emily opened her mouth to respond but no words came out.

'I made myself very clear. I said that my room was out of bounds if you wanted to stay in this house and you agreed to that, you gave me your word. Well a person's word has to mean something, it has to be worth something. But you broke yours and that makes you a liar. You know, when I first met you, you reminded me of Clara, but you're nothing like her. Nothing.'

Emily didn't know who Clara was but she didn't ask either. She could feel the bitter frustration building up inside her.

'I can't believe... all I've done since I've got here is try to be good, to tidy the house, keep it clean, to do your washing and cook your meals. I haven't once complained about the cold or the darkness, about not seeing anyone else, about how much I miss my family and friends. I've tried, I've really tried to make the best of it and now you're calling me a thief and you're going to throw me out? Search me if you like. Look in my drawers, go through my pockets; you'll soon see I haven't taken anything.'

'You took the key.'

'Yes. Alright. And I know I shouldn't have taken it, but you can't send me away. You can't. Where will I even go?'

'That's not my problem,' sneered Mr Worthington. 'Now I want you to get out of this room right away.'

'No,' said Emily.

'Get out,' repeated Mr Worthington in a low growl.

'Whose room is this?' said Emily meeting his fearsome stare.

'Get out,' he said again.

'No.'

'Get out of this room, do you hear me? You shouldn't be here, you don't belong here. GET OUT, GET OUT, GET OUT,' he roared and thumped one great hulking fist against the wardrobe, causing the mirror that hung from it to splinter and crack.

Emily dashed past him, down the stairs and straight to her room slamming the door behind her, and immediately began packing up the few possessions she had. She pulled her coat from the cupboard and laid it out in front of her. If he wanted her gone, she would go, and she wasn't going to wait for Miss Pinchman to come and collect her. The moment Mr Worthington went to bed she would sneak out of the house and leave the dirty old cottage behind.

She sat on her bed turning over what had happened again and again in her head. She could feel the anger pulsing through her and it felt good; she nurtured it and nursed it until it smothered everything else, the hurt and the guilt, how scared she was and how lonely. She had no plan for what to do next, once she left the station master's cottage where would she go? The only person she knew in the whole of Exeter was Jack, but she didn't exactly know where he lived and she doubted he would let her stay. Then a thought struck her, she did know someone else. She had a grandmother. What's more she knew where she was currently staying and that she had a bed available, a whole floor of a hotel in fact. Her problems were solved. Once Mr Worthington was asleep she would creep over to her grandmother's and explain to her what had happened.

Unfortunately this plan had several flaws, not least of which was getting around Exeter in the blackout. For one thing she could get seriously hurt; there were reports every day of people being killed in the blackout, falling over, getting hit by cars, wandering onto train lines. Did she really know the city well enough to find her way to the hotel in the pitch darkness? She could get lost and end up wandering around the city for hours. She could be stopped by one of the wardens. If she was found out and about they were bound to take her to Miss Pinchman, and then who knows where she would end up and how long it might take her grandmother to find her again. She tried to push these thoughts from her mind and focus on planning the route in her head; it was only a fifteen-minute walk after all, she would just have to be extra careful.

She changed out of her dress; if she was going out into the night she would need something warmer, so she picked out a vest, blouse and woollen cardigan. Next, she packed a bag with a few extra items of clothes in case she had to disappear with her grandmother quickly. She stayed awake for several hours listening, waiting for Mr Worthington to turn in. Once Emily heard his bedroom door click firmly shut she waited for a few minutes more until she felt the rumbling of his snores through the walls, then she snuck silently down the stairs and out of the front door. She walked quickly keeping close to the hedge, pausing every few metres or so to listen for the sound of footsteps that would warn her that someone was coming, but it was hard to hear anything over the wind which continued to billow and blow. Occasionally some moonlight would sneak through the dark clouds but otherwise there was no light to be seen. She could hardly see her own hands in front of her face.

She made it across the first road without a problem, slipping through the hedge on the other side to continue her walk along the field. The slightest sound bought her to a halt, the snapping of a twig or the rustling of the few remaining leaves on the otherwise barren trees.

Once she reached the end of the field she crept carefully through another gap in the hedgerow and sat, listening. She could hear no footsteps or voices. She scanned the dark beyond looking for anything that might reveal that there was someone out there, the faint glow of a cigarette for example, the brief flare of a match. Still she waited. When she was convinced that she was alone, she crawled out of the ditch and walked along the road. She knew she wasn't far from the railway crossing now and that she would have to be extra careful there as it was bound to be manned. Ideally, she would have avoided it entirely but she didn't know of any other route to the hotel.

Emily approached the crossing as quickly as she dared. If a car came past, even with its headlights dipped, she would be spotted in an instant, but she couldn't risk running or making too much noise. She hoped that the guard at the crossing might be asleep or at least engrossed in a book so as not to notice her, but her luck was out, as he was standing diligently at his post starring out into the night. Every few minutes he would take a short walk around the crossing, probably to keep warm. She was pretty cold herself and it hadn't been long since she had left the cottage.

She kept waiting for him to go inside and warm up; it would give her the best chance to make a run for it, but he didn't. So Emily was forced to stay where she was, crouched down in the field, fifty yards from the crossing, whilst every few minutes trains rolled in and out of the station. Then she had an idea. Seeing a long freight train crawling towards them, she waited until the last possible moment and then made a dash for it. With the train between her and the guard post, she could no longer be seen. She leapt onto the side of the last carriage and held on to the flimsy wooden handle then pulled herself round onto the back of it. After a few moments she leapt off the other side and rolled down into the ditch. The noise of the train completely covered her exertions and while the guard at the crossing continued to look out into the fields she had just come from, she sneaked onto the footpath behind his back and quietly made her way towards the hotel.

Finally she arrived at the hotel only to be faced with a whole new problem: namely how was she going to get up to her grandmother's room? At first she thought she could climb up onto the roof, but it was too risky. If she was caught she would look like a thief and who knew what might happen then? Also there didn't seem to be any easy way up; the drain pipe bent alarmingly beneath the lightest of touches. She stalked the building, looking for a door left slightly ajar, or maybe an open window, anything to get her inside, but there was nothing. In the end it seemed like the simplest thing might be just to ask. It was a hotel after all, someone would be up all night. If she knocked and told them that she needed to see Mrs Alexander then at least she would be inside the building. At worst she could always make a run for it, get to her room and bang on the door. Her grandmother was bound to answer before she could be dragged away. Not feeling confident about her plan, but tired and eager to be in the warm, Emily twisted the ornate handle to the front door and stepped into the lobby.

A large balding man in an ill-fitting uniform was sitting reading a newspaper. Hearing someone enter the building he tried, unsuccessfully, to hide this fact, leaping to his feet, clearly annoyed at being disturbed.

'Excuse me, I would like to speak to Mrs Alexander in Room 104,' said Emily with a confidence that she did not feel.

The man frowned at her.

'It is rather late to be calling don't you think?'

'It's a family matter,' said Emily. She had thought about this, it seemed best not to be too specific. 'It's important. I need to speak to her right away. I'm her granddaughter.'

'I'm afraid Mrs Alexander is... out at the moment,' he said with a glance at the keys behind him.

'Do you know when she'll be back?'

'No m'dear, I don't.'

Emily wondered what she would do now. She hadn't really considered that her grandmother might not be there and she still didn't have anywhere else to go.

'I don't suppose she mentioned where she was going did she?'

'Sorry my love, not a word. Here, you're a little young to be out all on your own at this time of night aren't you?'

'I had to come. It's rather important I speak to her.'

'Won't your ma and pa be worried about you?'

'No. They know I'm here. In fact, they sent me,' she lied.

'Tha' right is it?'

'Yes. It's important you see, a family matter.'

She thought about expanding further, but she'd always been a hopeless liar and was worried she'd be caught out.

'Oh aye, a family matter, you said. Well as long as they know you're safe and well.'

Emily looked about her, in the day the hotel had a certain grandeur to it, but at night with its windows shuttered up, most of the lights off, and the guests all in their rooms it was eerie.

'Would it be okay if I waited?' she asked.

'Well...' the man looked as though he was trying to do a complicated sum in his head, 'it's most unusual but I suppose that would be okay. What's your name?'

Emily replied with the first name that popped into her head. 'Clara. Clara Verity.'

'Nice to meet your Clara Verity, my name's Ralf Ferguson. Take a seat, I'm sure your gramma' will be home soon.'

Relieved Emily sat on a tall green chair opposite the front desk, leaning her bag up against the wall behind.

'Thank you,' she said.

Mr Ferguson went back to reading his paper. In the silence of the dark Emily found herself drifting off to sleep, waking with a start each time as her head lolled on to her chest.

'You must be very tired young Clara,' said Mr Ferguson.

Emily managed a weak smile.

'I'm okay. I don't think she'll be much longer now.'

In truth she had not expected her grandmother to be out for so long.

'I tell you what,' said Mr Ferguson, 'I'm not supposed to do this, so don't go telling anyone, but perhaps you could wait for your gramma' in her room? Seems silly you falling asleep down here when she's got rooms a plenty

152

upstairs. You should get some rest, and when she comes back I'll let her know you're in there. I'm sure she won't mind, you bein' her grand-daughter an' all.'

'That would be wonderful. Thank you.'

'Follow me Clara my love, but this'll be our little secret all right, or I could get into big trouble.'

Emily assured him she wouldn't say a word.

'Good, good.'

He unhooked the key to Room 104 from the rack behind him and slipped it into his jacket pocket before leading Emily up the stairs. Emily was so tired she could hardly wait to crawl into bed.

'There we are,' said Mr Ferguson opening the door to the room. 'Now you get yourself into bed.'

He switched on the lights which sparkled in the chandelier. After the gloom of the rest of the hotel it dazzled Emily's eyes.

'Thank you, Mr Ferguson,' said Emily, blinking as she struggled to adjust.

'Please, call me Ralf,' he said standing in the door way.

Emily smiled at him and turned to face the rest of the room. She was looking forward to getting some sleep, then in a little while her grandmother would return and she could talk to her about what had happened at the cottage and try and sort things out.

'Goodnight then Ralf,' said Emily.

Mr Ferguson was still stood in the doorway as if he was waiting for something.

'I'm afraid we don't have any night clothes for you, guests normally bring their own luggage.'

'It's fine, you've been so kind, thank you' said Emily touching him on the arm. 'Oh! Luggage! Of course, I left my bag downstairs.'

'Not to worry,' said Ralf, 'I'll fetch it for you.'

With that he was gone. Emily kicked off her shoes and lay down on the bed, struggling to keep her eyes open. A door closed somewhere close by and she jerked awake, hoping to see her grandmother standing there.

'Your bag my love,' said Mr Ferguson.

'Oh,' said Emily distracted, 'thank you Mr Ferguson.'

'I told you, call me Ralf.'

He continued to hover at the edge of the room.

'Thank you, Ralf.'

Emily wondered what he was waiting for. Was he expecting a tip? She didn't have money, if that's what he was after, he'd have to wait until her grandmother returned.

'You look tired,' he said.

'I am. Very,' she replied, hoping he would take the hint.

'I bought you some night clothes,' he said suddenly, producing a white robe from behind his back.

'Oh…' said Emily surprised, 'that's kind, but I don't think… I'm sure my grandmother will be back soon and then we'll have to go straight away.'

'Aye, but who's to say how long Mrs Alexander might be? Off with one of her gentlemen I expect, maybe she won't be back tonight at all.'

The fog of tiredness that had engulfed Emily's brain began to clear as a shot of fear passed straight through her. Something had changed in his tone of voice. She couldn't say quite what, but there was a menace to it that hadn't been there before.

'You do look very tired, my love. Maybe you should just get changed into these lovely clothes and then lie down on that bed.'

'That's very nice of you,' said Emily, struggling to keep her voice level, 'but I think on second thoughts I'd better go.'

'Oh? I thought this was urgent family business? Why else would you be out on your own so late at night?'

'My mother and father will be getting worried about me.'

'Your ma an' pa don't know you're 'ere. No folks I know would send their child out alone in the blackout. Ain't no one who knows you're 'ere Clara.'

The horrible truth dawned on Emily; he was right: she was all alone.

'There's no need to rush off. We've got all these rooms to ourselves. There are no other guests on this floor, your gramma' – if she really is your gramma' – booked them all out. So, what was the plan? Were you going to rob her? Must say it's a bit risky showing your face like that. Or are you working with someone? You go round the front to distract me and they go round the back? 'Cos you should know they've left you swingin' in the breeze my love. I went an' checked. There's no one out there, and all the doors are locked, including the front door.'

'I don't know what you mean,' she replied, 'I think I'd better go.'

'You won't find a way in or out of this building. I made sure of that. And you can't scam me 'cos I know all there is to know about scammin'.'

Emily edged around towards the door that led into the next room. Mr Ferguson turned and locked the door to room 104 behind him, dropping the key back into his jacket pocket.

'There, now there's no chance we'll be disturbed.'

Emily's whole body ran cold. Why had she been so foolish? Why hadn't she just waited until morning? Why had she come up here with this stranger? Mr Ferguson smiled and moved slowly towards her.

'I think you're very pretty. Has anyone ever told you that before?'

His voice made her feel sick. It suggested tenderness and caring, though what he had in mind was anything but.

'Stay away from me. Let me out of here. Please. I'm begging you.'

'But you look so tired, wouldn't you prefer to rest here with me?'

'No, I want to go.'

Emily tried to push past him but he caught her by the wrist.

'Let go of me.'

'Come on Clara, don't be like that. Come and lie down here with me.'

His voice was perfectly friendly but Emily could see a fire in his eyes that was terrifying.

'Get off me,' she shouted.

He grabbed her round the shoulders now and held her tight.

'Listen to me, you're going to stay here with me. We're going to stay together. We'll have a lovely evening you and me. You're so pretty Clara, don't make this difficult.'

Emily tried to hit him but he grabbed her arm with sickening ease. As he did so, the sleeve to her cardigan was pushed back to reveal the Seer's Mark.

'Well now, what have we here?'

He held her arm tightly, examining it, then he looked her straight in the eye and grinned.

'The good news is I'm going to let you live… when he sees what I've brought him he'll be very happy indeed. He won't even care if I've taken my payment upfront.'

Emily had no idea what he was talking about.

'I'll scream if you don't let go of me,' she said.

'I wouldn't do that my love, you'll only get hurt. 'Sides it won't help, there's no one to hear you.'

'HELP!' Emily yelled.

Mr Ferguson smothered her mouth with his hand so she bit it as hard as she could.

'Argh, you little bitch,' he said, and he let go.

Emily seized her chance and ran for the door to the next room, hoping it wasn't locked. She twisted the handle but the door stayed closed. Mr Ferguson moved closer.

'That was a silly thing to do. I don't want to get rough with you, but I will if I have to.'

Emily felt the terror growing inside her. She looked around for something she could throw at him or hit him with but there was nothing to hand.

'Please just let me go. Please.'

'You don't need to be scared. I don't want to hurt you Clara my love. I knew a Clara once, pretty girl, bit older than you though. She cried a lot. I wouldn't want you doing the same.'

The tears began to roll down Emily's cheeks.

'Please. Please, let me go,' she begged.

'You don't understand, you have to stay now. I can't let you go now. You'd tell people and I can't have that. Besides, I need you.'

'I wouldn't tell anyone. I wouldn't say anything,' she insisted.

He began advancing towards her again, Emily backed away.

'Don't make this more difficult Clara, come and sit beside me on the bed.'

Emily backed off further and prepared to launch at him with all her might if he came any closer. He took another step forwards and Emily flung her full body weight at him, hoping somehow to get past him and out of the door. She did knock him to one side, scratching his face with her nails but he didn't fall down and soon he was on her. He lifted her off her feet as easily as he would a rag doll and threw her down onto the bed. He began clawing at her cardigan desperate to undo the buttons on it. Emily struggled and managed to get a leg free to kick him, but he shifted his body and soon he was back on top.

'Stop it, please stop.'

She wriggled desperately and tried to free herself but to no avail. He began to kiss her neck, his horrid spittle-flecked lips on her skin, his fat body crushing her ribs. Her insides had frozen, every part of her felt soiled and sullied. He tried to kiss her on the lips but Emily wiggled a hand free and punched him.

'Why are you being like this Clara? You'll like it if you just stop struggling, I promise.'

She closed her eyes. The sight of his reddening face made her feel sick. Up close she could taste the pungent cologne with which he had doused himself in a failed attempt to cover the oozing stench of stale sweat. She managed to get a hand free once more and grasped for the lamp that was next to the bed, the base was just inches from her fingers, perhaps if she could reach it she could hit him with it. It had to be worth a try. She stretched out a little further and managed to touch it with the tips of her fingers, but she couldn't bring it any nearer. Instead her hand landed on her grandmother's pile of letters, knocking them to the floor. Something remained however, something cold and hard in her palm. The letter opener. She grasped it tight, waiting for one chance, just one moment when he might loosen his grip. By this time he had ripped open her cardigan and was pawing at the blouse underneath. He made another attempt to kiss her and Emily spat in his face. He roared with fury and released her long enough for him to wipe away the dripping saliva. Emily seized her chance and with all the force she could summon she rammed the letter-opener into the spot between his neck and his shoulder.

Mr Ferguson roared again, this time in pain. He rolled off her and Emily managed to crawl away, desperate to reach the door before he recovered. She clambered to her feet and sprinted across the room but was bought crashing back down when a giant hand wrapped itself around her ankle. Slowly he pulled her towards him, shifting his considerable weight on top of her slender frame. She had never been more frightened, not even during the bombing. The bombing was terrifying but impersonal, a sort of careless annihilation. She hadn't been chosen, the bombers couldn't see the people they killed. This was different. This was about power. This was about control. He was revelling in her helplessness, relishing her struggle, watching her as she fought for life.

Emily was exhausted. She couldn't fight much longer. She had the oddest sensation as if her mind had detached itself from her body. She started to drift away, if what she thought was about to happen was going to happen she didn't want to be there when it did. She began to think about her sister and mother, about her old home and her old friends. She remembered building a snowman with

Celia in the back garden, and her mother baking her a cake for her birthday. Then she recalled the story of her mother hitting the school bully. This thought seemed to send a surge of energy through her body. She gave one final kick with her free foot just as Mr Ferguson pulled her other leg towards him and she connected fully. There was a cracking sound and Mr Ferguson let out an almighty scream.

Emily scrambled to her feet. He lay on the floor a few feet away, awash in a pool of his own blood. He had let go of her and was in a foetal position, breathing heavily and whimpering. She knew she had to get away but she needed the keys. Luckily he had thrown his jacket off onto the floor close by so she reached into the pockets and grabbed everything she could, then ran to the door. She kept glancing behind her as she struggled with the lock, but eventually she pressed down on the handle and could have cried with relief when the door swung open.

Emily dashed down the stairs and out of the front door, pulling her blouse and cardigan back on as she ran. She didn't dare look behind her in case he was following. Rain had started to fall and the wind was still fierce but Emily didn't care. She ran. She ran as hard as she could, harder than she ever had in her life, as if by running she could turn back the clock on everything that had happened in the past few months. She didn't care who might hear her or if she might be seen. She didn't even know where she was running to, she just ran, letting the rain stream down her face hoping it might somehow wash her clean.

'Whoa there young lady.'

She hadn't noticed the direction she was going and had run straight into an air raid warden who was patrolling the streets in the centre of the city.

'GET OFF!' she screamed, 'Don't touch me, don't touch...'

But that was all she could manage and she vomited on the man's shoes. He cursed and let her go but Emily was too tired to run any further. She could barely move.

'What's the matter eh? What are you doing out at this time of night? It's dangerous, you could get killed.'

Emily didn't say anything.

'What's your name?' asked the warden.

Emily said nothing.

'Come on, come inside' he said gesturing to the Guildhall which was close by, 'we'll get you a nice cup of tea.'

Emily didn't move.

'You're hurt,' he said shining a torch at the cuts on her face. 'What's happened? Are you all right?'

Emily decided she wouldn't say anything, she was still scared of being sent away before she could talk to her grandmother. Besides the world belonged to adults, as a child it didn't matter what you said, they would do as they pleased.

'Julie? Get over here.'

'Keep your voice down John Kitson.'

'Get over here, there's a little girl needs some help.'

'A girl? At this time of night?'

A woman in a dark blue uniform appeared.

'Whassup my love?'

Emily flinched at being called "my love." It's what *he* had called her.

'Quiet one eh? Well let's have a look at you then.'

Emily backed away.

'Now I'm not gonna 'urt you, but I need to 'ave a look at those cuts alright, and I can do that better inside. Come on, come with me.'

Emily allowed herself to be led inside to the warmth and light of the Guildhall. There was something about the woman that made Emily trust her, but even so she remained on her guard. Despite the hour there were a number of people busy working away inside the building. Emily was seated on an old wooden chair and a blanket was wrapped round her.

'Now do you want to tell us why a young girl like yourself is out roaming the streets of Exeter at three in the morning covered in cuts and scratches?'

Emily didn't speak.

'You're not in any trouble, we just wanna help you,' continued the woman, 'at least tell me your name. Mine's Julie and this fella 'ere is John, and you'll have to speak up when you talk to him, cos he's old and he don't hear so good no more.'

'I heard that though,' said John with a smile.

He kneeled next to Julie and passed Emily a cup of sweet tea.

'My goodness,' said Julie pointing at the Seer's Mark on Emily's forearm, 'is that a bruise?'

'No, it's a birthmark' replied Emily quickly pulling at the sleeves on her cardigan till they covered her wrists, but she saw Julie and John exchange a look.

Emily took a sip of the tea and some of the warmth began to return to her body.

'My name's Emily,' she said quietly.

'Nice to meet you Emily,' said Julie. 'Now would you like to tell us what happened?'

Emily shook her head and drew the blanket tight around herself.

'John, maybe you could give us a few minutes alone?'

John looked momentarily put out but then he smiled at Julie. 'Of course, I'll be with Mary if you need me for anything.'

'Okay,' said Julie briskly, 'let's get you patched up shall we? Now this might sting a bit.'

She dabbed some antiseptic lotion onto the cuts and some warm water was bought over to wash her face. Emily barely noticed.

'Brave girl. Now are you hurt anywhere else?' she said gently placing her hand on her collar bone. 'Perhaps you've got some scratches you don't want anyone to see?' she asked quietly.

Emily nodded and Julie looked into her eyes, holding her gaze for a moment.

'John,' she called out, 'have we got a screen I can

borrow? Young Emily here needs to get changed out of her wet clothes.'

'Certainly,' said John and sure enough a screen was found.

Julie helped Emily out of her soggy clothes and even produced some overalls for her to put on.

'Sorry we haven't got much in your size,' she said. 'Do you feel like you could tell me what happened Emily? Where did this blood on your hands come from eh? And why are you out so late all on your own?'

Emily didn't reply.

'Was it your dad who did this Emily?'

Emily shook her head.

'Because you can tell me if it was. Or maybe a boyfriend? Pretty girl like you, maybe you met a fellah and he got a bit physical?'

Emily shook her head again.

'Could I sleep here for now?' she asked quietly.

The woman looked like she was about to say no, but then changed her mind.

'You can stay here until the morning; we can sort things out then. You know, if you've been hurt, if someone's hurt you it would be best if you went to the police.'

'No police,' said Emily firmly.

She had to speak to her grandmother first. Everything else could wait.

'Ok. Let's talk more in the morning. I'm sorry we can't make you more comfortable.'

'I'll manage,' she replied and began to make herself a bed on the floor out of blankets.

Julie offered her a sympathetic smile and left. Emily lay listening to the noises around her, people talking, gossiping, swapping stories about their day. Somehow the mundanity of their chatter was comforting; it was a link to a world she had forgotten, a world where the price of fish or what one neighbour had said about another was still important. She wished she could live in that world again.

If Emily could have looked into her own future at that moment she would have done, so desperate was she for reassurance that things would get better, but sadly for her she could not. Instead she began to plan for the morning. How would find her grandmother to tell her what happened? She could hardly go back to the hotel. She was confident that Mr Ferguson wouldn't say anything about what had happened but she didn't want to risk running into him, who knew what he might try and do?

She tried to clear her head and think logically. The only people she knew in Exeter were her grandmother, Mr Worthington and Jack. Her grandmother was who knows where and Mr Worthington thought she was a thief and wanted to send her away. Her only option was Jack. She would have to find him and hope that he could help. Maybe he could take a letter to her grandmother? She would need money and food before then though, and a place to sleep where she wouldn't be found.

She hoped Julie wouldn't call the police. She thought she could be trusted but if she had learnt one thing over the last few months it was that adults rarely told the truth. She would have to slip out early, maybe at the change of shifts. In the meantime she desperately needed some rest. She pulled her knees up to her chest and wrapped the blanket around herself as tightly as she could and promptly fell asleep.

She was awoken a few hours later by Julie with another mug of tea.

'How are you feeling?'

'I'm fine,' lied Emily.

'Still not going to tell me what happened last night?'

When Emily said nothing she continued.

'I'm worried about you. What are you going to do? Where are you going to go? Whatever's happened we can put it right.'

Emily allowed herself a small smile.

'I appreciate what you're trying to do,' she said, 'but believe me no one can put this right. I'll be okay. Please don't call the police. Nothing happened, not really, I'll be fine. I'll deal with it in my own way. They can't help me.'

Julie eyed her with concern.

'I think your clothes have mostly dried out, they might still be a little bit damp, we had to stick them in front of the paraffin heater. Oh, and I sewed some buttons onto your blouse for you, you seemed to be missing a few.'

'Thank you,' said Emily as Julie handed over her clothes. 'Is there a toilet round here?'

'Yes, it's down the corridor, second on your right.'

Emily made to go but Julie called her back.

'Just in case you were thinking of leaving via the back door you might want to know that the police station is out there. We're normally swarming with bobbies this time of day. They must have had a busy night. I hear a lot of them were sent over to Plymouth to help clear up the mess the Germans have made over there. Anyway, if someone were looking to make a quiet exit there's a side door that doesn't lock properly. It'd lead them down a small path and out onto Queen Street. You know, if someone were lookin' to get away.'

Emily nodded and gathered together the few bits and pieces she had left. She'd only just realised that in her rush to escape she had left her bag at the hotel. All she had now were the clothes on her back. Still she did not have time to think about it yet; she had to get out of there. She would try and come up with a plan later.

'I'm here most nights,' said Julie with a kind smile, 'if you ever feel you need help again, you come and find me okay?'

Emily simply nodded as she didn't trust herself to say anything. Julie's kindness was somewhat overwhelming. Following her instructions, she slipped out of the side door as quietly as possible and followed the path to Queen Street.

Chapter Ten

She hadn't really thought about it before, it was only now she was in a different city that she appreciated the community she'd grown up in. Not so long ago Emily had been known wherever she had gone. Everywhere she'd played, everywhere she walked; every shop she went into, she was recognised. She was Joan and David's girl. It was like there was an invisible thread that tied everyone to one another. Everybody knew everyone else and kept an eye out for them. Here it was different for her. Here she was unknown, and unknown was bad, unknown drew looks and it drew suspicion.

Emily's clothes were a mess, dirty and torn. Her hair was tangled and matted, and though the scratching on her face was mild, she felt as if the marks were glowing, inviting further investigation. The first thing she had to do, she thought, was to get off the main roads and on to the quieter back streets. The fewer people noticed her, the better. She didn't yet know if Mr Worthington had discovered that she had run away, but she decided it would be best to stay out of sight regardless.

Now she had to find Jack. He was the only person left in the city that she knew, and she hoped she could persuade him to help. Not that she was even certain he would actually speak to her. The first time they'd met he'd left very suddenly and he hadn't been that keen to be seen with her since. That was a problem for later however, first she had to find out where he lived. She remembered he'd mentioned something about the football ground, so she set off in that direction hoping to bump into him.

Once she arrived at the ground she took a walk around looking for the best place to wait. If she was too conspicuous she would be seen and someone would want to know what she was up to, but if she kept completely out of sight there was a chance Jack could walk right by her and she wouldn't see him. Eventually she found a small spot towards the back of the football ground nearest the road that led to town. If he went into the city today he would have to pass by, she was sure of it. She settled herself down close to one of the turnstiles and waited.

Without meaning to she began to think back to the previous evening. She was grateful to have escaped relatively unscathed but every time she thought about Mr Ferguson looming over her, her insides froze and she felt sick. She wasn't sure if it was her imagination or not but she thought she could still smell him on her, that awful mixture of sweat and cheap cologne.

A thought that had been quietly nagging at her since the attack pushed its way to the front of her mind. It was perhaps the thing that worried her above all else. He had gone back downstairs and locked the front door. When the opportunity had presented itself he'd had the presence of mind to ensure that they would not be disturbed, he had not rushed into it, he had thought it through. Somehow she doubted that she had been the first girl he'd attacked. How many more had there been she wondered? And what had been the fate of the others?

Something else troubled her too. The attack had happened quickly and she had been so frightened that she couldn't be absolutely certain, but she thought he had recognised the Seer's Mark on her arm. She remembered how he'd stopped when he'd spotted it, and that he'd said something like, "when he sees what I've brought him he'll be happy." Who had he been talking about? And why would this person be happy? In all the confusion it was possible she'd misheard him, but she didn't think so.

She tried to not to dwell on it, but with nothing else to occupy her time, it was difficult. She rummaged round in her pocket and found a small silver sixpence. At least she could use the wait to practice her Seeing. She began to flip the coin and try to predict which way up it would land. She found it helped her to block out the previous night's events. She was careful not to do too much however, remembering how tired she had felt after an hour's lesson with her grandmother.

It was mid-morning when she first saw Jack. Unfortunately he was with a woman Emily guessed was his mother, so she couldn't approach him. Still she had seen where he had come from so at least she now knew where he lived. If she got really desperate she would just have to walk up to the front door and knock, but for now she waited. By the afternoon she was thoroughly bored. She had given up hiding for a while and took a stroll up and down the street just to keep her body from becoming too stiff. She was cold and hungry, not having eaten since lunchtime the previous day, and now she was beginning to feel faint.

Finally, at almost two o' clock, Jack appeared on his own and began walking down the street. Emily was waiting for him down a side alley, and when he passed she slipped out and followed him as fast as her aching limbs would allow.

'Jack,' she called.

He turned around, smiling when he saw her, but as she got closer his expression changed.

'What happened to your face? Did you fall over?' he asked as she approached.

'It's a long story,' she replied. 'Listen, I need your help.'

'To do what?'

Emily sighed. She didn't know where to begin.

'Gimme your coat, I'm freezing.'

For a moment she thought he might argue with her, but

then he looked her up and down again and reluctantly handed it over. They walked around the other side of the football ground where it was less windy and Emily began to recount the story of the night before; how Mr Worthington had threatened to chuck her out; how she had gone to the hotel and been attacked and spent the night at the Guildhall. She surprised herself at how calm she managed to remain whilst telling him what had happened, but as she came to the end of her story she felt herself welling up.

'I'm not going to the police,' she said before Jack had a chance to speak.

'I never said you should.'

'I don't know what to do, but someone needs to stop that evil man before he does anything else.'

'Emily–'

'And what was Mr Worthington thinking? I know I shouldn't have been up there, but he went crazy Jack, you should have seen him. I was scared: he looked so angry.'

Jack rubbed his face as if he hoped it would make everything she had told him disappear.

'I think I know why Mr Worthington was so cross,' said Jack quietly.

'Really? Why?'

He opened his mouth to speak but then changed his mind.

'Come on, come back to mine. It's bitter out here.'

Emily nodded appreciatively and followed Jack back up the road to his house.

'I don't know what sort of places you're used to,' he said as they reached the door of a rather shabby looking two storey building, 'but this is my home.'

'It's great,' she said giving him the most reassuring smile she could manage.

'I'm sure London folk all live in grand houses, but this ain't London.'

'It's a home Jack. My house back in London… well it's definitely not as nice as this,' she replied truthfully

168

thinking of the rubble she had left behind.

Looking a little more reassured he slipped the key into the lock and went inside. Jack put the kettle on and made up a fire, then they sat down at the kitchen table whilst Emily warmed her fingers round her mug.

'Come on then, what made Mr Worthington so cross? And how come you know about it anyway?'

Jack poured himself a mug of tea too and sat down opposite Emily, brow furrowed as he tried to work out what to say.

'Everything I'm about to tell you... well it happened a while ago most of it, some of it years ago before I was born, and some of it when I was just a little boy, so I didn't understand most of what was going on.'

Emily nodded, encouragingly.

'Mr Worthington was married to a woman, Elsie I think her name was, and they had a daughter called Clara. He went to fight in the Great War whilst she was quite young, but he took a bullet in the leg during the Battle of the Somme and was sent home.'

Emily now understood why Mr Worthington walked with a limp, though in truth she had suspected it might be something like that. It wasn't that unusual to see people around London with limbs missing from the Great War.

'When he came back from the war Clara would have barely recognised him, but they quickly grew close and she helped her mother nurse him back to health. She was a beautiful girl, long auburn hair and sparkling eyes, and as she got older there was more than a few men who took a keen interest in her. Mr Worthington was very protective though and he didn't like the look of any of them, so he sent them packing. However unknown to him Clara had already met the man she wanted to marry, a local boy called Thomas. Now, Thomas didn't have the best of reputations it's fair to say, bit of a drinker, liked to gamble when he could afford it, and just as often when he couldn't. He had a temper on him too, he lost his first job for fighting, but with Clara he was kind and gentle. They really were in love. Eventually he came and asked Mr Worthington for Clara's hand in marriage. Mr Worthington refused but Clara begged him to reconsider. Mr Worthington told them that they would have his blessing if, and only if, Thomas straightened up, got a proper job and stopped drinking every night and getting into fights. Thomas did as he was told and got a job on the railway working alongside Mr Worthington. He quit drinking and tried his best to be the kind of man Mr Worthington would choose as a son. After a few months Mr Worthington relented, finally giving his blessing for them to marry. As soon as he could, Thomas asked Clara to marry him.'

'She said yes I take it?'

'It depends who you ask.'

'What do you mean?' asked Emily, intrigued.

'The night he proposed to her she disappeared, and the next day her body was found in some nearby woods. Her throat had been cut.'

'By Thomas?'

'That's what the police thought. He was arrested and sent for trial pretty quickly, found guilty and sentenced to life in prison.'

'They didn't hang him?'

'No, the judge took pity on him, on account of his age he said, but others say it was because he disagreed with the verdict.'

'He was innocent?'

'The police said that he'd asked her to marry him, but when she'd told him no he lost his temper and lashed out, forced himself on her and then killed her.'

Emily tied to push the image of Mr Ferguson from her mind.

'He liked a drink, that was well known, and as it happened he had been seen drinking earlier in the local pub. Now Thomas claimed it was just a few shots of Dutch courage, you know, so that he could ask Clara to marry him, but when they found him the next morning he stank of whiskey. Anyway, they say he was angry when she rejected him, that they argued and he'd hit her, that maybe he hadn't meant for it to get so out of hand but that he'd killed her.'

'And what did Thomas say?'

'He said he proposed to her and that she'd said yes, then they'd gone their separate ways for the evening.'

'He didn't walk her home?'

'He was on duty late that night, so he walked with her as far as the station and then they'd parted.'

Emily nodded, thinking things over.

'When they found her… did she have the ring on her?'

'No, the ring was missing. Thomas claimed whoever attacked her must have taken it, but the police insisted he'd panicked and thrown it away.'

'What else?'

'When they arrested him they searched his room and found her hanky with blood all over it in the pocket of the jacket he'd been wearing that night. Of course, he denied ever having seen it before. That was what did for him. He said he was attacked on his way home from work, but he couldn't say why or by who, just that someone had snuck up on him that night and attacked him and that they must have left the hanky on him to frame him. It just looked like the story of a drunk. The ring was key. If she said yes to him why was there no ring on her finger? It came down to who the jury believed most. Mr Worthington was well liked in the town, a war hero, and Thomas was nothing. People wanted to find him guilty from the start.'

Emily nodded again but she wasn't certain she agreed with Jack's interpretation.

'It does sound pretty… odd,' she said carefully.

A shadow of anger flashed across Jack's face, but it lasted only a moment.

'I know. I know it does, you're right, but I swear to you that he didn't do it. Thomas is innocent.'

'How do you know? How can you be sure?'

'Because Thomas is my brother.'

171

At last Emily understood. She wondered how many other people knew about this. Probably a fair few, Exeter was a small city and gossip travelled fast. She thought again of how she was known everywhere she had once gone, that thread that had bound her to the community, and how it would have felt if someone had cut that thread and turned her loose. She thought about how people must look at him, how they must treat him, the boy whose brother murdered a vibrant young woman; the daughter of a war hero.

'Jack;' she said softly.

'And there's another thing,' Jack continued, seemingly afraid to stop. How often must his brother's story have ended a potential friendship, Emily wondered? He was the brother of a murderer and that was a stain that could never be washed out.

'That same night another girl went missing – Annie Blatchford – and she has never been seen since.'

'You think Clara was killed by this other girl, Annie?'

'It's possible I suppose, but I doubt it, you see there have been more missing girls since. I've kept track; girls who went out one day and never came home again. Sally Roberts, Irene Brown, Claire Stewart, Molly Gordon. The police suspected Tommy of killing Annie Blatchford too but with no body, no sign she had even been hurt, they couldn't do anything. It's possible it's just a coincidence and she ran away on the same night, but maybe not, maybe she saw something and was too scared to report it.'

It all sounded a little vague to Emily, and she prepared to ask the question she didn't want to ask.

'Jack, how can you be sure that Thomas is innocent?'

'You've got a sister right?' asked Jack.

Emily nodded. It was not the time to tell Jack about what had happened.

'If she was accused of murder, could you ever believe it? With no witnesses? Just on a flimsy piece of evidence? If she said she didn't do it, you would trust her, because you'd know if she was lying, you'd feel it, deep down inside right?'

Emily thought about it for a moment. She couldn't imagine that sort of thing ever happening to Celia, but she knew that if it had she would have trusted her completely. After all, when she had started having visions of the future Celia had believed her, or at the very least she had not disbelieved her.

'Thomas didn't do it,' insisted Jack. 'He has never confessed, which is something that almost cost him his life. He risked being hanged because he wouldn't show remorse for what he was supposed to have done. He loved her. He still talks about her all the time. He's not a killer Emily.'

Jack stared into Emily's eyes, daring her to disagree, but she couldn't. He was right. If the circumstances had been reversed she would never have doubted her sister's word.

'What happened to Mr Worthington's wife? What happened to Elsie?'

'She passed away a few years later I think. She just couldn't cope with it all.'

Emily thought of the house and how when she had arrived it seemed to have been frozen in time, the shawl on the rocking chair, the room that had once belonged to Clara preserved as she had left it. She wondered why Mr Worthington had ever agreed to take her in. Perhaps he was lonely and wanted a little bit of company in his life, or perhaps he was just doing his duty. Perhaps Emily was just part of the war effort to him. Whatever it was she found her anger towards him begin to ebb away.

'I should go back and talk to him.'

'But you told me how angry he was. And how are you going to tell him what you found out? You can't tell him you heard it from me, he wouldn't like to know that you've been talking to me of all people.'

'I suppose so. But where am I going to stay?' she asked desperately.

'I'd let you stay here but my ma doesn't want anything

to do with him. If he found out you were staying here…
well it could all get very complicated. He'd probably tell
everyone we'd kidnapped you.'

'It only needs to be a few nights. The reason I went to
the hotel last night was to see my grandmother, only she
wasn't there. I'm due to see her again in two days, I just
need somewhere until then.'

'If you've got a grandmother here why aren't you
staying with her instead of Mr Worthington?'

'It's a story for another time,' she replied wearily.

Jack nodded, still thinking.

'You could always hide out in an air raid shelter.'

'What?' said Emily, trying to keep the panic from her
voice.

'You know, one of the Anderson shelters. Loads of
them were built round here, but we never use them
because there are no raids on Exeter. We should find a
garden that's easy to access, then wait till dark. You could
sleep in there for the night and then get up early before
anyone sees you. There'll probably be blankets and a few
candles lying about, maybe even some food.'

Whilst this idea might have appealed to her once, there
was no way she could bring herself to go back down into a
shelter like that. Even the thought of it made her feel like
she was going to be sick. The colour must have drained
from her face because Jack asked if she was okay.

'Yeah, I'm fine,' she lied, 'but I can't hide in a shelter.
What if I get caught? They might think I'm a spy and lock
me up.'

'You could–' Jack insisted.

'NO,' said Emily more forcefully than she had
intended. 'Not the shelters. I'm sorry, I just can't.'

Jack fell silent, deep in thought.

'Wait, I know the perfect place,' he said, a look of
excitement in his eyes.

'Where?'

'Underneath us.'

'What are you on about?'

174

'The passages! There are passages that run beneath the streets of Exeter.'

'Why? What are they for?'

'I don't know, that's all history isn't it? My old teacher used to talk about them. No one goes down there now though. I think they carried water into the city in Mid Evil times.'

'Medieval times.'

'That's what I said. Anyway, he was always saying they should restore them but no one has the money. I reckon they could be used as air raid shelters if needed.'

'How come no one knows about them?'

'They're not unknown, just unused, they're not much good for anything anymore. Anyway it's perfect, no one will find you no matter how long they look for you, they're safe and you'll be close to town. I've been down there a few times, they're not so bad. I mean, I've never spent the night in one but how bad can it be?'

He could see the doubt on Emily's face.

'Come on. Have a look at least. You'll be dry and out of the wind. You can spend the days at mine, then you just pop down to the passages in the evening.'

'What'll I do for food, or warmth for that matter, I don't have any more clothes with me.'

'Leave that to me,' he said with a grin.

He looked as though he were enjoying himself.

'So where are they? How do we get in?'

'Follow me,' Jack said mysteriously, rising from the table.

Emily trailed Jack until they reached the Cathedral. Checking to make sure no one was watching them, he led her into a small courtyard and pointed to the corner where there was a gap in the cobbled paving.

'Isn't it a bit small?' asked Emily sceptically.

'It's a squeeze, but you'll be fine,' replied Jack with confidence.

'Is it far down?'

'Nah, a few feet at most, you'll see. I'll go first if you like.'

Having already rejected the idea of the air raid shelters without being able to tell Jack why, Emily refused this offer. She didn't want him to think she was a sissy. She glanced around to make sure they weren't being watched and then squeezed down the gap into the dark beneath. Jack was right. The opening sloped down a few feet before there was a longer drop from which Emily was able to lower herself down slowly. Moments later she was joined by the tumbling figure of Jack who landed right on top of her.

'Oops. Sorry,' he said blowing his hair out of his eyes and rolling away.

Emily brushed herself down and got to her feet. She found herself in a sort-of hollow area with two narrow passages at either end that led off into the darkness. The room, if she could call it that, was no more than ten feet wide. It was small but it would be big enough for her purposes. At least she could stand up without hitting her head. It was dark but for the thin shaft of light that came in from the courtyard. The walls were built from large chalky bricks that curved up over her head, and a steady trickle of water ran down one side of the passage, a tiny stream that followed a path carved out over hundreds of years.

'This is amazing,' whispered Emily. 'Sort of spooky though.'

'Yeah,' said Jack with glee creeping into his voice.

'How often do you come down here?'

'Not often. It's no fun on your own.'

The way in which he said it, with a total lack of self-pity, broke Emily's heart. She knew he wouldn't want her sympathy but he had it all the same. He was an outsider in his own world.

'Have you explored all of the passageways?' she asked.

'I've been up and down them all a few times, but not recently. Some of them are easier than others. A couple are really cramped; you have to get down on your hands and knees and crawl half the way. One of them is caved in too.'

'Caved in?' said Emily alarmed.

'Don't worry, this part is perfectly strong enough,' he said and to prove his point hit his hand slightly too hard against the wall. 'Argh, bugger it.'

Emily laughed.

'Like I was saying,' he continued shaking his hand to relieve the pain, 'these passageways go all over the city, trouble is it's so dark and wet you wouldn't want to use them most of the time. I used to cut across the town this way until I realised it was a lot quicker to go above ground than below it.'

Jack made to climb back out of the passage.

'Stay here, I'll be right back.'

'Where are you going?'

'Supplies. You've gotta eat, you've gotta be warm right?'

'Try not to get caught this time,' she called after him, 'I won't be there to trip up the butcher if he decides he wants another go at making sausage meat out of you.'

After what seemed like an age Emily heard a noise from outside. Suddenly the light from the gap was blocked out and a bag came tumbling through. Emily stepped back, startled. It was followed by a grotty blanket, a pair of feet and finally Jack, skidding down the slope and landing hard at the bottom.

'My bag!' said Emily shocked and relieved at the same time. 'How did you get that?'

'I thought I'd pay a quick visit to the hotel. It was quiet up there. I asked after Mr Ferguson, claimed I was from the bookies and that I wanted to give him his winnings. They said he was unwell, that a friend had taken him home early that morning and that they weren't expecting him in for a few days.'

'But how did you get the bag?'

'It was being kept behind the counter. I said I was

177

going to pop round his house, take him his winnings to cheer him up, offered to take his bag too and they agreed.'

'Thank you Jack,' she said.

She might not have much in the way of possessions but at least she had a few items of clothing now.

'You haven't heard the best bit.'

'What's that?'

'I paid a quick visit to their kitchens and managed to acquire a few rations for later.'

He pulled from his pockets some cuts of ham, a few pieces of cheese, some biscuits and a couple of apples.

'Nothing special I'm afraid, I couldn't steal too much, I had to be quick. Besides we can't cook anything down here, we'd either choke on the smoke or be spotted when the smoke disappeared out of that hole. Still it'll do. I've lived on less.'

'Jack?' said Emily cautiously. 'What would you have done if he had been there? What would you have said?'

Jack paused.

'I don't know,' he said eventually. 'I was angry. I just wanted to get a look at him, make him real y'know? I expect I'd have made something up, I'm quick on my feet. People shouldn't be able to get away with stuff like that.'

'No,' said Emily, 'no they shouldn't.'

'Now, what are we going to do for the rest of the day? We can't stay down here the whole time.'

'Well we can't go into town; Mr Worthington might be out looking for me.'

'Okay then, follow me.'

With that Jack scrambled halfway up the gap that was the entrance to the passage. He stuck his head slowly out the top to check no one was watching and then heaved himself clear. Emily followed immediately after.

'Where are we going then?' she said once she'd dusted herself down.

'The park.'

So the pair of them set off towards the local playing field.

'It's not as big as it was,' Jack informed her, 'they've dug a lot of it up to plant food, but there's still a nice patch near the bandstand.'

'Can I ask you something?' said Emily, who had been struck by the realisation that they were the only two children she had seen out and about.

'Course.'

'Why don't you go to school?'

'I dropped out the moment I turned fourteen. Too stupid.'

'You're not stupid, said Emily frowning, 'you're pretty bright I'd say, but probably too cheeky. I bet you got caned a lot.'

'All the time,' he agreed. 'I didn't like school, I wasn't very good at it; except woodwork, I was okay at that. Ma says it's in my blood. Why aren't you at school though?'

'I went when I lived in London,' Emily continued, 'but Mr Worthington seemed to want to find me a job instead.'

'Isn't that illegal? I mean, how old are you?'

'Thirteen,' said Emily, 'but I doubt anyone's going to come looking for me and force me to go back to school,' she said remembering what her grandmother had said about her being missing from the official records.

'Anyway, why did you drop out really? And don't try and tell me it's because you're too stupid,' said Emily sternly.

Jack looked away.

'My ma says she took me out of school to educate me herself. Says she can do as good a job as any teacher. But the real reason is that no one would have me. I got into too many fights, no school would take me back.'

'What were the fights about?' she asked.

Jack gave her a look.

'Oh yeah. Right. Sorry.'

'It can't have been easy.'

'Everyone knows the story of my brother, or thinks they do. So half the kids are scared of me and the other half want to fight me, so they can say they beat up the

179

brother of the murderer.'

'But you didn't murder anyone.'

'Some people don't draw a line between me and my brother. Maybe if I acted like I was ashamed of him they'd have left me alone. But that's the way it goes, you have to stand up for what you believe in.'

The park was quiet. It was a cold day and those that weren't at work or at school would most likely prefer to be inside in the warm. Jack had found a football from somewhere and was practising keep ups.

'You don't play football at all do you?' he asked.

'No,' replied Emily.

'I could teach you,' he said, rather optimistically in Emily's opinion.

'Do you think so?'

'Certainly. You can play cricket, and that's a boy's game so I'm sure you won't be too girly to play football.'

Emily looked at Jack. He had a sly expression on his face as if he knew exactly what to say to get her to join in.

'I'm insulted Jack. You think I'll play just because you called it a boy's game.'

'No,' said Jack innocently, 'I'm just saying that football is a tough sport, but maybe I'm wrong, maybe you wouldn't be cut out for it after all...'

He allowed his sentence to trail off and dropped the ball at Emily's feet.

'Okay,' she said reluctantly, 'what do I do?'

'Great, I'll go in goal, you just try and shoot between these two trees here,' he said pointing at a couple of saplings that looked as if it would take only the slightest breeze to uproot them.

Jack rolled the ball to her and then ran back to the goal fifteen or so yards away. Emily looked at the ball in much the same way that a dog might eye a suspicious parcel. The ball was dark brown and held together with a thick, leather lace. Taking a few steps back she ran at it and threw a hefty kick in its general direction. The ball shot high into the air and was comfortably caught by Jack. The momentum took Emily head over feet however and she landed in front of Jack in a heap.

'ARGH! What is that thing made of?' she asked pointing accusingly at the football under Jack's arm.

'It's leather obviously. Just leather and-'

'Stone?' offered Emily.

'It's not that hard.'

'I think I've broken my foot, or maybe my whole leg,' she said rubbing it gingerly.

Jack helped her to her feet.

'You get used to it. At least it's not too wet. When this thing gets wet then it really is a nightmare, especially if you have to head it.'

'Head it?' said Emily her voice strained with incredulity. 'Head it? How can you head that? It's so heavy, and there's a lace on it. Don't you cut yourself ever?'

'Oh sure sometimes, but most of the time you just get a bit of a headache.'

Emily said nothing but decided that cricket was definitely more her sport. Still, Jack had helped her and she didn't want to let him down so she made willing for a short while at least, doing her best to ignore the throbbing in her foot. By the end she could at least kick it without wincing and once or twice she even made Jack dive to stop the ball.

After one particularly hopeful punt that saw the ball disappear into the bushes Emily persuaded Jack that they should go back to town as it was getting dark. It was then she realised that they were no longer alone. Over the far side of the park was a tall man wearing a long grey coat and a trilby hat.

'Don't look now but I think we're being watched.'

'What? Who by?'

'There's that man again; the one we saw the first time we met.'

Jack chanced a glance over his shoulder. Sure enough there he was, at the far side of the park, sitting, smoking a cigarette on the park bench.

'What's he doing?' she asked.

'I don't know,' replied Jack, 'nothing much by the look of things.'

'Is he watching us? Following us?'

'No, I'm not even sure he knows we're here.'

'I'm going to go and talk to him,' said Emily, summoning a bravery she did not truly feel.

'Don't be silly,' said Jack, 'he's just sitting on a bench smoking, that's not against the law. And I thought you were trying to stay away from the police?'

'You think he's a policeman?'

'I don't know what he is, but he's definitely got power.'

'How do you know?'

'You get a sense for these things. Come on, let's get out of here.'

As discreetly as possible they began to back away until they were almost out of sight when at the last moment the man stood, turned, looked at them and smiled tipping the brim of his hat in their direction before swiftly leaving the park by the white gates.

'He saw us!' said Emily.

'Of course he saw us, he was watching us. But why? Why is he here?'

Emily shifted guiltily certain he was there because of her, but the question still remained, who was he? What did he know? Why had he made himself so visible? Was he trying to intimidate her? Or was it some sort of signal? If so she had no clue as to what it was supposed to mean.

They made their way back to the passages taking a longer route in case they were being followed. In the passages Jack immediately started tucking into the supplies he had stolen from the hotel. Emily lit a few candles and placed them around the passage to give them some light. They chatted for a while about nothing in particular, games of cricket they'd seen or played in, films they'd watched. They both, it turned out, enjoyed the movies of Errol Flynn, particularly The Adventures of Robin Hood. Jack revealed that after seeing the film for the third time he had made himself a bow and arrow, but his mother had snapped it two when she'd caught him trying to shoot an apple off their dog's head. In the end he had given up, partly because he broke his arm falling out of a tree and partly because of a lack of Merry Men to fight with.

'Not to mention no Maid Marian,' said Emily but Jack did not appear too bothered about that.

'She just gets in the way,' he said.

Privately Emily agreed. It seemed a woman's role in an adventure film was just to scream and faint a lot then wait to be rescued. If she was in a film like that she'd want to be off fighting with the men. When she made the mistake of mentioning this in front of her uncle he'd laughed at her, but she didn't see why it was so ridiculous. Across the country women had begun doing work that was previously the preserve of men; now there were female mechanics, engineers, pilots, air raid wardens and ambulance drivers. Perhaps one day they would be equal in everything.

They chatted some more and Emily was surprised to find it was nearly seven o' clock.

'I'd better get going,' said Jack, 'not that anyone will notice if I don't go home, mum works all hours these days; by the time she gets home I'm normally asleep.'

Emily had forgotten she would be sleeping in the passages alone. The candles had burned right down and were flickering on the edge of extinction; in a few more minutes she would be left in darkness till the following morning. Suddenly it seemed too much, she didn't want to wait down in the cold and dark on her own.

'Jack... remember the cricket game we played?' she asked delicately.

'Yes,' said Jack shooting her a sideways glance.

'Remember the deal we made?'

'What deal?'

'If I won then you would owe me a favour, one that I

183

could call in at any time?'

'Yes,' he replied in a voice that suggested he didn't much like to be reminded of it.

Emily swallowed hard.

'Stay.'

'Pardon?'

'With me. Here. Tonight, I mean. I don't want to sleep down here alone. I'm not scared,' she added hastily and then stopped herself. 'No... I don't care anymore. I lied, I am scared. I've been bombed, I've been sent away from my family to a place I don't know, and to live with a man who hates me, I've been attacked and now I'm sleeping in a dark cave and I feel a million miles from anyone and anything I love. I'm frightened. I don't care if you think that's stupid or girly. I don't want to sleep here alone tonight. Will you do that for me? Will you stay?'

Jack shrugged.

'Alright, you don't need to go on about it. Course I'll stay. You can't welch on a bet.'

'Thank you,' said Emily suddenly feeling rather embarrassed about her outburst.

Jack threw her some blankets and Emily hastily made herself up a bed. One by one the lights from the candles spluttered and died and they were left in pitch darkness. The silence between them was a peculiar sort, it hung in the air like a balloon waiting to be popped. Eventually Jack spoke.

'What did you mean when you said you'd been bombed?'

Emily didn't reply immediately, instead she wondered what she should tell him, how much did he need to know?

'I haven't been completely honest with you Jack. You told me about your family and I think it's only right that I should tell you about mine.'

'Your sister isn't sick is she?'

'How did you know?'

'Chicken pox and the measles?'

Emily allowed herself a small smile.

'You're a terrible liar Emily Cartwright,' he said gently, 'what happened?'

Emily took a deep breath. She had rehearsed this in her head. No dramatics, no tears, just the facts which she delivered in a voice barely louder than a whisper.

'It was the first day of the Blitz. Our house was hit. My mother, my uncle and my sister all died.'

She heard Jack swear under his breath.

'I'm so sorry Emily, that's awful. How come you survived?'

'My uncle, he had a heart attack I think, and mum stayed with him inside the house. The sirens were going off but she stayed with him and sent us to the shelter in the garden to grab some blankets. We were going to make a stretcher and carry him out. Only once we got to our shelter my sister shut me in and went back for them. That's when the bomb hit. It's why we're staying down here instead of in someone's shelter. I can't go into one of those things again. I just couldn't take it, it's hard enough down here.'

'I'm so sorry Emily. I just… that's terrible.'

'Yes,' said Emily simply, 'it is.'

The darkness gave them cover to talk freely and without embarrassment. Jack began to tell her all he knew about his brother, how he even had trouble finding a job in Exeter because of what his brother was supposed to have done. Emily told Jack about her sister and did an impression of her uncle that made him laugh out loud. It felt good to be sharing memories of Celia again. She remembered the promise she'd made at her sister's graveside, never to forget her, and she felt a stab of guilt that it had taken so long to talk about her.

As the evening wore on it grew gradually colder, far colder in fact than Jack had thought it would be. Each of them lay beneath their thin, moth eaten blankets quietly shivering, neither one wanting to complain. Emily felt particularly bad about forcing Jack from the warmth of his bed to come and sleep in some dank cavern in the freezing cold. She was just about to tell Jack that he should go home when he spoke.

'Emily?'

'Yes?'

'Are you awake?'

'Well obviously.'

'Are you cold?'

'Very.'

'Me too.'

Without another word Jack quietly climbed under the blanket with Emily and threw his blanket on top. Huddled together in the darkness, neither spoke. She thought about Mr Ferguson and how he had forced himself on her. This was different. Jack only wanted to share heat, he did not pull her in or touch her in any way. Perhaps he was embarrassed or perhaps he too was thinking about Mr Ferguson and didn't want Emily to misconstrue his actions.

Now Emily became aware of every part of her body, worried that she might come into contact with him. Even as they moved closer for warmth they still kept a fraction of an inch of space between themselves as if they were being pushed apart by some invisible force, like there was some unspoken agreement that their bodies should not touch. After a few minutes, though she could not truly say she was warm, she was at least less cold than she had been earlier, and gradually she drifted off to sleep. When she awoke a few hours later she found their unspoken agreement had been breached, they were wrapped tight in each other's arms, the cold outweighing any sense of shame or embarrassment. In the dark you could cling to whatever got you through the night.

Emily drew closer still as the cold continued to bite. She closed her eyes and tried to fall back to sleep. Jack stirred briefly then drifted off once more. The dark was so deep Emily could not even make out his features so instead she pictured them in her mind's eye, his bright blue eyes, his floppy fringe and his dark red hair. She breathed in the scent of his skin, sweat and soap and something else she could not place all mingled together so that she could almost taste it on her tongue. She was glad he was here, glad that she had asked him to stay.

Suddenly she felt that all too familiar pull, the stretching of the moment that meant she was about to See again. She fought against it, she didn't want to See, not now, but it was too late.

Emily was standing in darkness, but she knew immediately where she was. She was in the passages beneath the city, perhaps not far from where she was lying right at that moment. She knew the smell and recognised the stones.

'Stay back. I really don't have the time for this.'

A man's voice echoed through the passages and suddenly she could hear the pounding beat of footsteps. Someone was running and running hard by the sound of it. There was a loud bang and from the gloom came Jack. He was sprinting as fast as he could. He chanced a glance over his shoulder but stumbled in the wet and lost his footing falling to the ground. Emily heard a shout. Someone was chasing him. A gunshot ricocheted off the wall of the passageway. Jack scrambled desperately to his feet and ran on. Emily followed. Another shot was fired and Jack dodged it with speed and grace.

Then out of the darkness came two more gun shots and when she turned back Jack was lying on the floor of the cave, his blue eyes open wide in horror. A steady trickle of blood was already spreading out beneath his body, mixing with the small stream of water that ran beneath her feet. A man stepped out of the shadows. He was tall with a long grey coat that was ripped at the seams. His blonde hair fell roughly across his face. The man knelt down beside Jack, placed his gun on the floor of the passage, and felt for a pulse. Seemingly satisfied he stood up and ran back down the dark tunnel.

Emily sat up straight, waking Jack.

'What is it? What's going on?'

Emily looked around. Was it safe? She felt as if the blonde man could appear at any moment. Should they run for it? Flee?

'Are you okay? Did you have a nightmare?'

She sat still for a moment, trying to compose herself. What could she say? How could she make him understand? And what good would it do?

'It was nothing,' she said eventually, 'just a bad dream. Sorry.'

Jack lay back down and promptly fell asleep, Emily though stayed wide awake. In the morning, she decided, she would have to tell him what she was. It was time for the truth between them.

Chapter Eleven

Jack woke at first light and immediately started pulling on his boots.

'Come on, I need to get back to mine before my ma notices I'm missing.'

Emily, who had barely slept, took little persuading. They slipped out of the Cathedral courtyard unnoticed and continued their way across town as quickly as possible, leaving their blankets behind them in the passages. Emily hoped her grandmother would be back soon so she wouldn't have to spend another night down there.

Jack persuaded her to wait for him outside his house whilst he went in and made his excuses. Emily was pleased to get a few minutes to herself, as she needed to work out what she was going to say to him. He was sure to think she was crazy, or that she was making fun of him. It all sounded so unbelievable, even to her, but she couldn't just do nothing. She had to warn him. She wasn't going be like her father and put his life in danger by keeping what she knew a secret. After a few minutes Jack emerged smiling.

'Come on, ma says you've got to come in.'

'What do you mean?' she said, surprised that Jack had told his mother about her.

'She wants to meet you.'

'Meet me?'

'Yeah well, she sort of caught me coming in, so I had to make up a story for why I'd gone out so early. That's when I decided to tell her about you. I said that you're an evacuee who's only recently arrived in Exeter, and that the family you're staying with chuck you out first thing every morning. She thinks that's a disgrace and says you can come here for the day. I mean, it's almost the truth isn't it? I told her we met yesterday in the park. To be honest I wasn't sure she would buy it, but I think she's just so happy I've made a friend she doesn't want to ask too many questions.'

Emily made her way up the steps of the house and was met at the door by a tiny woman with a mess of curly red hair. She was barely as tall as Emily, thin and slight but with an abundance of energy that seemed to spark from her.

'You must be Emily, Jack's new friend,' she said with a significant look at Jack. 'Come on in.'

She ushered Emily into the hall before giving her an appraising look.

'You're freezin', poor thing. Come through to the kitchen, I've just put the kettle on.'

She led the way and Jack followed.

'Sit yourself down by the fire and don't mind him,' she said giving the large Irish Wolfhound that was sleeping in front of the flames a gentle kick. The Wolfhound lifted its head off the floor looking around for the source of the disturbance before promptly falling back to sleep.

'Great lazy bugger. Surrounded by 'em I am Emily, and I don't know which of 'em is lazier, the dog or this one 'ere,' she said taking the mug of tea out of Jack's hands, giving it to Emily instead. 'Still, at least the dog has manners. Ladies first Jack or she'll think I taught you nothin'.'

Jack rolled his eyes at Emily.

'Thank you for the tea Mrs...'

'No Mrs anything, you call me Rosie or you call me nothing at all you understand?' said Jack's mother with a smile.

Emily nodded and took a grateful sip from the mug, enjoying the feeling of the warm tea trickling down her throat. After a long, cold night it was exactly what she needed.

'So tell me about yourself Emily, where are you from?'

Emily recounted what felt like her whole life story, only skipping over a couple of crucial details, spinning Rosie the same lie she'd told Jack about her sister's illness, this time making sure to give Celia just the chicken pox. Jack understood and did not correct her.

'You must miss them terribly,' said Rosie.

'I do,' replied Emily who was shocked to find that she had tears rolling down her cheeks. She wasn't sure what had set her off; the exhaustion; the visions; the attack; finding herself homeless or talking about her family, but once the tears started there was nothing she could do to stop them.

'Hey there my dear, don't cry. I shouldn't have gone meddling in your business.'

Emily smiled weakly and was rewarded with a cloth to wipe her nose with.

'Sorry,' she sniffed.

'And don't apologise neither, it's me wants knocking round the head with a stale loaf, making you all upset like that. Never learned to keep my trap shut have I Jackie? Don't go getting yourself too down, you'll see them again soon.'

Emily smiled weakly and blew her nose again on the cloth.

'Listen to me now, you're welcome round here any time,' Rosie continued. 'Fact, I've a mind to give this family you're staying with what for, chucking you out each day, poor thing like you. You tell them from me they should treat you with a bit more respect.'

Emily wiped away the tears and tried to change the subject, feeling embarrassed to have cried in front of them.

'What's the news today? Anything good?' she asked

spying a copy of that morning's *Express and Echo* on the table.

'Have a read for yourself if you like,' replied Rosie passing it over. 'Now, can I get you some breakfast?'

Despite her hunger Emily really didn't feel like she could say yes. She knew how tight things must be for Jack's family without having an extra mouth to feed on top of it all.

'Oh no, that's really okay, I'm not very hungry,' she replied, just as her stomach gave a low growl of disagreement.

'Nonsense, girls gotta eat, same as anyone else. You'll have some porridge won't you?'

Emily decided that perhaps that wasn't such a bad idea. The feeble meal they had eaten the night before seemed a long time ago now.

'Only if it's no bother.'

'No bother at all my love. You catch up on the news.'

Rosie turned on the radio and the voice of Vera Lynn drifted through the room, Rosie hummed along, sometimes with the music, sometimes to a tune of her own creation that occasionally intersected with the original.

Emily leafed through the paper Rosie had left for her, the front page of which announced, 'MUSSOLINI'S FORCES ROUTED IN AFRICA'. According to the story, British and Australian troops were having great success in driving out the Italians from Libya. It was a rare piece of good news from the front.

She carried on flicking through the rest of the paper, not that there was all that much of it. With ink and paper being rationed the newspapers had fewer and fewer pages in them, although people joked that this was more to do with the fact that there was so little positive news to report. She skimmed over a couple of recipes for soups that could be made from kitchen scraps and a story about the 'War Weapons Week' that was to be held in Exeter in February, when something caught her eye.

'Jack, have a look at this will you?'

Jack perched himself on the arm of the chair and read the article over Emily's shoulder.

'MAN DROWNS IN RIVER EXE' ran the headline.

There has been another call to review the current blackout procedures after local man, Mr Ralf Ferguson, was found dead in the River Exe yesterday. It is believed he was on his way to his job as a doorman at the Imperial Hotel when he slipped and fell into the water due to the extreme darkness. Police have again advised that the public stay home after dark, and if they must venture on to the streets, then to use the upmost caution. It is suggested that pedestrians carry a newspaper or a white handkerchief to make themselves more visible.

This latest incident takes blackout-related deaths in the UK to more than three thousand in the last eighteen months. Campaigners say more must be done to protect those who have no choice but to leave their homes after lights out. Mr Ferguson of Howell Road was a bachelor and lifelong Exeter resident. He is survived by his brother, Albert Ferguson, of Salisbury Road, Plymouth. Their mother, Mrs Muriel Ferguson, passed away last year at the age of 68.'

'No wonder I couldn't find him when I went looking yesterday.'

'Yes...' said Emily unsure. 'Very odd though isn't it?'

'What?'

'He attacks me, then a day later he's dead.'

'It's war time Emily, and like the article says, there's lots been killed in the blackout.'

'I guess you're right,' Emily agreed reluctantly.

It was certainly the most probable explanation, but since when was the most probable answer the right one in her life? Something about it sat uneasily with her: it was too much of a coincidence. She thought back to the man who was following her, had he got something to do with it? Had he somehow found out about Mr Ferguson attacking her at the hotel and then gone back later to kill him? But why would he do that? He didn't know Emily, and so far he hadn't done anything other than follow her at a distance. Then another thought stuck her. Maybe her father had sent him to keep her safe, but what power did he have to do that? And hadn't she Seen this man, whoever he was, shoot Jack? It made no sense.

'Aren't you glad he's dead?' asked Jack.

Emily thought again about what had happened, replaying it for what felt like the hundredth time in her mind, Mr Ferguson holding her down, making her feel dirty and scared for her life. Did she want him dead?

'No,' she answered eventually. 'I wanted him caught, maybe I even wanted a little bit of revenge for what he tried to do, but I didn't want him to die. I wanted him to understand, to feel the terror I felt. He had to be punished, but I wanted him to know why he was being punished, and to know that I had somehow bought it about. I wanted to turn that feeling of helplessness that I felt back on him.'

She thought about it for a moment longer before adding, 'and I wanted to be sure that there were no more.'

'No more what?'

Emily lowered her voice to make sure Rosie couldn't hear her.

'No more like me Jack, no more girls. What do you think would have happened to me after he'd... had his way?'

But before Jack could reply they were interrupted by Rosie.

'Pop the paper away you two, breakfast's ready.'

Two steaming bowls of porridge were laid down in front of them, putting an end to their conversation for the moment. After breakfast Emily washed the dishes, insisting that Rosie put her feet up. In truth Rosie looked exhausted, she had been at the munitions factory all night.

'You can come round more often,' she said nodding approvingly at Jack.

Jack offered to help dry, but really he was looking for an opportunity to talk to Emily some more.

'I was thinking about what you said,' he whispered,

'about Mr Ferguson.'

'Yes?'

'You really think he'd have killed you?'

'I don't know. He said something... something strange, like there was someone else involved.'

'Involved how?'

'I'm not sure. It was so confusing.'

Emily didn't think she could explain about the Seer's Mark without inviting more questions.

'He couldn't have risked me reporting what he'd done, that's for sure.'

Jack nodded, mulling things over.

'I was just thinking about my brother. If... if Mr Ferguson lived here his whole life...'

'Yes?'

'Well, isn't it possible that he attacked Clara Worthington?'

That thought had occurred to Emily too, but the trouble was she didn't know how on earth they could prove it. When she didn't dismiss the idea Jack continued.

'What if they met somehow after my brother left her? What if he saw her and attacked her?'

'I suppose it could've happened.'

'You don't sound very convinced,' he said moodily.

'Well we don't have any evidence – *not* that I'm saying your brother did it,' she added hastily.

'How many killers do you think this little city has? If my brother didn't do it, then someone else did. We know he was violent, you said yourself you don't think you were the first. I doubt he's just been waiting all these years for a young girl to walk into the hotel late at night.'

'But then why haven't there been more deaths since then?'

'Maybe there have been, don't you remember? Another girl went missing that same night and there have been more over the years, not always in Exeter, but close by. Not murders though, missing children, girls and boys of around your age; sometimes a little older, but no bodies, no proof of wrong doing. Perhaps it was him all along.'

'When he attacked me... he said something, it might be nothing of course, but he said he knew a girl called Clara once. I lied about my name when I came in, I said the first one that came into my head, Clara.'

'It must have been him then.'

'I don't know. He only said he knew her; he didn't say he'd killed her,' said Emily trying to keep Jack from getting carried away, 'it's not exactly proof is it? He could have been talking about any Clara, or he could have been making it up, trying to scare me.'

Emily knew that Jack was hoping he could prove his brother's innocence, and now that looked less likely than ever. If Mr Ferguson had really killed Clara then the proof had died with him. Just as they finished the washing up, Rosie announced she was going to bed for a few hours.

'Will you join us for dinner?' she asked Emily.

Emily politely declined but Rosie waved away her objections.

'Of course you will, don't be silly. I'm making hotpot. I'm afraid it'll be more hot than pot but that's rationing for you. Now, I'm going to get some rest so keep the noise down and stay out of trouble okay?'

Jack grinned.

'When am I ever in trouble?'

'Honestly Emily, he has all the brains of a feather duster. I'm counting on you to make sure he doesn't get up to anything silly.'

Emily smiled.

'I'll do my best.'

The door swung shut leaving Jack and Emily alone in the kitchen.

'You know, I think ma would adopt you right now if she could. She always wanted a daughter and instead she got two sons. When everything happened with my brother... well you can imagine. Clara was like one of the family and then suddenly the world came crashing down around her head. A girl she loved just as much as she loved me or Tommy was brutally murdered, and her boy got the blame for it. It was devastating. I was quite young, I don't remember all that much, just that she was crying an awful lot and I couldn't make it stop.'

Emily could imagine it only too well. Even if Rosie knew her boy was innocent, she had still lost someone she cared for deeply. Her whole life had been overturned by this one event. Her son was in prison for life, and she had to watch him suffer, had to bear his sorrow and pain as her own.

It was then Emily knew that she could put it off no longer. She would have to tell Jack about her abilities, and about what she had Seen in her vision the night before. He had been so good to her, and she would miss him, he was her only friend in all of Exeter, but she was putting him in danger. She was certain now that Mr Ferguson's death had not been an accident. Something was going on that she didn't understand. She was being followed, that much was clear. But why would the man who was following her shoot Jack? She must be the cause somehow, it was the only explanation. It wasn't fair on Jack to pretend everything was okay, and it wasn't fair on Rosie either. She had to find a way to explain; to make him understand. She thought for a moment or two, then put her hand in her pocket and pulled out a silver sixpence.

Chapter Twelve

'Jack,' said Emily nervously, 'I need to show you something.'

'What is it?'

Emily opened her palm to reveal the coin.

'Sixpence? Thanks Em but I'm not that poor, I have seen sixpence before.'

'It's not the sixpence, it's what I can do with it,' she replied, giving him a withering look.

'Are you going to do a magic trick?' he asked.

'Something like that. Just… please don't say anything for a few minutes, okay?'

'Okay.'

'I need you to toss this coin, but don't show it to me or tell me what's on it until I ask.'

'You really are doing a magic trick aren't you?'

'Jack!'

'Sorry. Not talking.'

Jack flicked the coin into the air. Emily focused on the moment exactly as her grandmother had shown her. If Jack was going to believe her then it was vital that she get this right. She focused on the coin turning over in her mind, heard the familiar ringing, then felt the strange force pulling her until she was in the room watching it all unfold.

'Heads,' said Emily.

Jack checked under his hand.

'Heads it is.'

'Okay, do it again, but do it three times in a row and remember what comes up. I'll tell you exactly what you got.'

Again Jack carried out her instructions to the letter, and Emily got each one right.

'Not bad,' said Jack, 'how are you doing that?'

Emily ignored the question.

'Please, just do it again, five more this time.'

Jack looked puzzled by the request but did it anyway. Emily correctly called all five.

'You should go to a casino or something,' he joked. 'So aside from being really good at this game, is there a point to this?'

'I just had to show you I could do it. In fact we could do it all day and I doubt I'd get one wrong. Listen to me now, I know what I'm about to say will sound crazy, but on my life, on my sister's grave, I promise you that it's the truth.'

Jack became more serious, he knew she wouldn't make that sort of promise lightly.

'Back in September I started having these dreams, not even dreams really as I wasn't always asleep, it was like...' She let out a frustrated sigh. It all sounded so unreal when she explained it out loud.

'The things I saw were different to dreams... they felt like they were really happening. It was as if I was actually there. They were visions of the future Jack. I began to see danger, planes coming to London. I saw the bombs falling. I didn't know that the visions were real until it was too late, but I saw the future. I can *see* the future. That's how I was able to tell you which way up the coin would land, and it's how I knew about the Blitz before it had even started.'

Jack stared at her. He looked as though he wanted to laugh, but he didn't.

'But how is that possible? I mean... it's not possible is

it? It must be something else. Maybe you dreamed it and it felt really real, and then it happened. It's a coincidence, it's not... I mean what you're talking about... well it does sound crazy,' he said eventually.

'I know. I'm not sure how I can prove it to you. I'm still just starting out. My abilities... well I can't control them properly yet. I need to learn, but it's complicated. I'm not supposed to tell anyone, you understand? It's a rare ability and it could put me in danger. I'm told that once I develop it I'll be able to See down a person's life line, like skipping forward a chapter in a book. I'm not very good at it yet. I can only do little things, seeing the outcome of a coin toss for example.'

'Then how come you saw the bombing if you can only do coin tosses now?'

Emily considered this for a moment.

'When you first started playing cricket, you couldn't bat straight away could you?'

'Not really.'

'Exactly when you start out, sometimes you manage to hit the ball well, but it's a fluke really. Most of the time you'd miss, or you'd catch it on the wrong part of the bat and it would hardly go anywhere. You're not able to do it whenever you need to, it takes practice. It's the same with Seeing. It's a sort of muscle that needs to be built up over time. I can only choose to see very small things at the moment, but occasionally something big overrides everything else. My grandmother is meant to be teaching me.'

'Your grandmother can do it too?'

'Apparently it runs in families.'

Jack sat in silence and Emily waited nervously for him to respond.

'What are you thinking?' she asked eventually.

'My grandma can't even knit.'

'Jack!'

'What? Your grandma can see the future, while mine can't even make me a decent jumper. The last one she knitted she forgot to leave a hole for the head.'

'I think you're missing the point,' said Emily.

'I still had to wear it on Christmas day.'

'Jack, I'm serious,' she said with a despairing laugh. 'Look, in some ways it's just another ability. Certain people can run really fast or jump the highest; I can see the future.'

This time it was Jack's turn to laugh.

'It's nothing like being able to run the fastest. Everyone can run, but some people are better at it than others. I can't see one minute into the future, let alone a day or a week.'

'But you can.'

'I think I'd have noticed that.'

'My grandmother was telling me, we all have this sort of vision. Have you ever had a feeling of déjà vu, when you have the strangest sensation that what's happening now has happened before? It's like that. You've already seen something happen but you only remember it once it's happening. Everyone sort of has it, but mostly it's useless, 'cos it doesn't stay with them.'

'So if I worked on it, I could become a Seer too?'

'No, because you don't know you're doing it. It's sort of like an instinct to you, something that is uncontrollable, like the beating of your heart. You can't tell your heart to stop beating, you can try but it won't do anything right? Whereas Seers, we have the ability to control this muscle. Does that make sense?'

'Of course it doesn't make sense Em, it's crazy…'

Emily's heart fell into her stomach. If she couldn't make Jack understand then how would she be able to protect him?

'…but I believe you.'

'You do?'

'I don't think you'd lie to me. After everything, I don't think you'd lie. So, how far can you see into the future? Can you tell me who I'm going to marry and what it is I'm having for dinner tonight?'

'Hotpot,' answered Emily instantly.

'Wow. I've always dreamed of meeting a girl named Hotpot. What's she like?'

'You're an idiot Jack Copleston,' said Emily with a smile.

He grinned.

'So hotpot for dinner then?'

'Yes, your mother told us before she went to bed; remember?'

'Oh yeah.'

'I can't See on demand. At the moment I'm more like you; I can't control this muscle, I just know it exists. I'm not a proper Seer yet. I can't choose much of what I want to See. But like I said, big things, really important things, they sort of take over my brain and I can See what's going to happen without meaning to. That's the reason I'm telling you about it now. Last night I had another vision that I couldn't control, like the ones I had before my family… before the bombing started.'

Emily took a deep breath. It was one thing to get Jack to believe that she could see the future. It would be another to get him to accept what she was about to tell him.

'I had a dream or a vision or whatever you want to call it, I Saw. I Saw you running through the passageways and you were being chased by that man we spotted at the park, do you remember? The man with the blonde hair and the trilby hat. He turned up on the day I first met you too. You thought we were being followed. Well you were almost right, *we* weren't being followed, *I* was. That man has been following me for months. I saw him a few days before the bombing, I saw him at Paddington Station as I was leaving on the train and now I've seen him in Exeter. I don't know who he is or what he wants, but it's definitely something to do with me. It has to be.'

She paused and her throat went dry. She feared that what she was about to say would drive him away from her forever. If he didn't believe her then she wouldn't be able to keep him alive, and now that was all she wanted. If she could keep Jack alive then maybe some good could come from her abilities after all.

'You must listen to me, and you must believe me. I saw him shoot you, Jack. That's why I'm telling you all of this. You're in danger if you stay near me. I've put you in danger. I'm sorry.'

Jack sat in a sort of stunned silence. Emily remained quiet.

'You're joking right? This is a joke.'

'This isn't a joke, I'm sorry.'

'But who'd want to shoot me? I'm great!'

'Oh Jack…'

'It can't be real. If there were people with the ability to see the future we'd know about it.'

'Why would we know about it?'

'Well if I could see the future I'd tell everyone.'

'Would you? And if you saw someone you loved die, or get their heartbroken, would you tell them? Would you always want to be the bearer of bad news? And wouldn't those powers be useful to other people? To criminals perhaps? How long would it be before they came looking for you?'

It was only now that she was saying this to Jack that she fully understood why her father had wanted her to keep her abilities a secret. She was beginning to scare herself.

'What happens to you then?' said Jack.

'Sorry?'

'What happens to you? You say this man is following you but he shoots me, so what happens to you?'

'I don't know. You can't see along your own timeline, except where it crosses with other people's. Maybe I wasn't there? Maybe I'd already been shot? I'm not sure.'

'Could you ask your grandmother to See?'

'She wouldn't do it. She doesn't like to look along the line of someone she loves, even if it's for their own safety. It's not like reading a book; you don't get the narrative leading up to the action, just the action itself. You can't judge the causes properly. You could end up making it happen instead of preventing it. She says Seeing is more of an art than a science, and its why she sticks to making money rather than meddling in other people's affairs. She described it to me like this. When you have a painting, everything the artist wants you to see sits within the frame, nothing outside that frame matters, all the artist is trying to tell you is right there. When you See, the opposite is true. Seeing is more like a photograph taken at random. It hasn't been composed, it just is. This photo might show you everything you need to know but it might not. It might show one man punching another, but it can't show you the words that sparked it off, or the friend he was protecting. That's what Seeing is like. You get that brief moment. You can learn to focus the image a little, make it sharper, make it try and tell you more of the story. But the truth is that the world doesn't fit within a frame; we're part of it and we can only See what's around us. That's why you have to stay away from me. Do you understand?'

'No.'

Emily felt all her hopes slowly deflating.

'I don't know how else to explain it.'

'Oh I understand alright,' said Jack. 'What I mean is no, I won't stay away from you, I won't leave you. If I'm in danger from this man then you are too. We have to stick together. We're friends and friends look out for one another. If I agreed to stay away from you then I'd be abandoning you Emily and I won't do that. As I see it though, there is another way. We simply make a promise. We promise that we will never go back to the passages. Never. If we are never down there, then I won't get shot and we've changed the future.'

'I suppose...'

'No suppose about it Em. We agree then, we shall never step foot in the passages again?'

He spat into his hand and offered it to Emily. Surely it couldn't be that simple to cheat fate, she thought? She wanted to argue with him, but the look of hope and optimism in Jack's eyes, not to mention the loyalty and kindness he had already shown her, allowed her to push aside those feelings. Besides, how did she know that this wasn't the right answer? After all, if she had persuaded her family to leave the house they would still be alive. Maybe this man, whoever he was, would still go down to the passages, but now they wouldn't be there to disturb him.

Emily spat into her hand too and they shook on it, then, looking at the trail of spittle left on their palms, swiftly wiped them on their clothes.

Emily spent much of the rest of the day helping out around the house, cleaning, polishing, any household task she could find to do to repay Jack's mother for her kindness. Jack disappeared in the late afternoon without saying a word to anyone.

'He's always doing that,' said Rosie trying not to seem concerned. 'I just hope he keeps out of trouble.'

'I'm sure he does,' said Emily, ignoring the fact that the first time she met Jack he was being chased by a butcher wielding a meat cleaver.

When he finally returned he signalled to Emily that he wanted to talk to her somewhere private.

'What's going on? Where did you go?' she asked.

'I was thinking about what we were discussing earlier, about Ferguson. If he really is responsible for Clara Worthington's death then we need to know.'

'I agree, but how can we hope to find anything out? He's dead.'

'But what if there was some evidence somewhere that would prove it?'

'That would be great but unless you know of anything new then nothing has changed.'

'There's one thing we didn't think of. We can't talk to Ferguson, but we could take a look around his house.'

'Is that where you were this afternoon?'

'When I went to the hotel the other night I said I had his winnings for him and they gave me his address, so I thought I would stop by and check it out. I couldn't go in, 'cos it's a busy road, there was a chance I'd be seen, but I thought we could go there once it gets dark.'

'I don't know...'

'Come on, it'll be okay. There's no one home; this is the perfect opportunity, in fact it may be our only opportunity. In a few days someone will probably be around to clear the house, and if there's anything in there it will be gone, and Tommy will be stuck in prison for the rest of his life. Besides you haven't had any visions about his house have you?'

'Well no…' conceded Emily.

'Exactly. And you said you See the big things, the important things.

'I'm not sure that's how it…'

'This is important Emily. This is our only chance.'

'How do we do it?'

'We leave at sundown and wait till it's dark enough to break in.'

'What are we even looking for?'

'I don't know. Something, anything that may prove that we're right. I just hope we know it when we see it.'

Emily still had her reservations about the plan, but she could see it was important to Jack. After everything he had done for her, she didn't have the heart to disagree.

'All right then,' she said finally.

'Great, I'll get together a few things and we'll leave in an hour or so.'

The last of the light was fading from the sky as Emily and Jack strolled up Howell Road. People along the street were drawing their blackout curtains across their windows. The sun was melting into the horizon and dusk was settling in. Taking pains not to be noticed, they found a small gap in a hedge near the Mr Ferguson's old house and hid themselves from view.

Once it was dark and they were as certain as they could be that they wouldn't be spotted, they set about breaking in. They decided they had best try the back door first as they were least likely to be seen there. Jack gave Emily a boost so she could climb over the side gate, then she undid the bolt and let Jack though.

The back door was locked, as they had expected. They tried all the windows too but they were firmly shut and locked. The last window however felt flimsier than the rest. Even pulling at it gently saw the wood warp, and great chunks of the rotting frame came away in their hands. Eventually they were able to get enough space beneath it so that they could get a firmer grip and have a go at pulling the window open. This they did but with limited success. As they pulled at the frame, the glass in the window cracked, splitting in several places, though it did not smash. Very gently Emily pushed at one of the pieces, moving it backwards and forwards like a loose tooth. She hoped the rest of the glass wouldn't fall down and smash; if it did they would have to make a run for it. The wood was so rotten around the window pane however, that she felt confident she could remove this one shard. Finally it came off in her hands. Emily placed it on the ground, slipped her hand in through the gap it had left, and unlocked the window. As quietly as they could, they slid up the heavy sash and climbed inside.

Once in, Emily pulled the curtain closed behind them. She didn't want anyone spotting the lights and coming to investigate.

'Now what?' whispered Emily.

'Now we look around.'

Jack reached for a switch and turned on the light. They were in the kitchen. There was not likely to be anything of interest there, so they moved through to the next room, turning the light off after them. The blackout curtains were still in place in the living room, so they were able to turn on the lights without risk of being seen.

The room was small and neat. Emily's eye was caught by a photograph of Ralph Ferguson and his mother, dressed in their finest clothes, at some sort of wedding. The photo hung in a frame of polished oak. She shuddered.

Seeing his face again made her feel a little sick. There was another picture by the radio of Mrs Ferguson and someone she presumed was Ralph's brother. He had very similar features but was a little taller and with slightly more hair. Mrs Ferguson was in a long dress and stared intently at the camera in a manner Emily found unsettling. She put the photo back. The living room was unremarkable. The cabinet in the corner revealed nothing more than a few trinkets: a silver spoon, a delicate china tea-set and a small glass vase. There was nothing much of interest to them, so they decided to try upstairs.

Pushing open the door to the first room they found themselves confronted by a messy sprawl of papers. They were everywhere, on the floor, on the bed, on the desk. It was a stark contrast to the rest of the house which had been extremely tidy.

'Someone's been here,' said Jack.

'Maybe it was Mr Ferguson. His mother died recently, perhaps he was sorting through her things. Most likely he didn't know what to do with all of this stuff. Neither do I. Where are we even going to start?' she asked hopelessly.

'I don't know do I?' snapped Jack.

Emily said nothing. She knew all his hopes of getting his brother free rested on the discovery of some incontrovertible piece of evidence which – even if it existed – did not look like it would be easily uncovered. If Mr Ferguson was responsible for the disappearances then he was hardly likely to have left a signed confession. Jack sat on the bed looking utterly deflated. Emily suspected his earlier optimism had got the better of him.

'Come on,' she said taking his hands in hers and pulling him up off the bed, 'we'll stay all night if we have to. You look over there' she pointed to a roller desk in the corner, 'and I'll go through this little lot. Anything that might be useful we put on the bed. Agreed?'

'Agreed,' said Jack, looking a little ashamed of how easily he had been put off.

They both set to work but after an hour or so reading

old correspondence from the bank, sifting through bills and receipts from the cobblers, the coalman and the grocers, Emily found she had a headache. The tiny smudged writing, faded with age, was difficult to read on the gossamer paper, and none of it seemed relevant to what they were looking for.

'Did he throw anything away?' she asked, almost to herself.

'I know, look at this,' said Jack, 'there are newspapers here from five, ten... fifteen years ago.'

He picked a pile of them up and moved them to one side to better concentrate on what was left. After another hour of fruitless searching, Emily decided that she was done.

'If there's anything here I'm not going to find it and I'm going blind with tiredness. Let's have a look in another room.'

Jack agreed and the pair of them traipsed next door to what appeared to be Mrs Ferguson's old room. In contrast to Ralph's room, his mother's was pristine. Jack immediately started to root through the drawers of her dressing table. Emily wandered through the gloom feeling out of place, like she was intruding on something. She picked up a large picture that stood on the windowsill of Ralph, his brother and his mother, posed in front of the house, looking adoringly at one another. It was strange to see him like that, so kind and loving when she knew what he was really like. She remembered his voice, the smell of his breath as he'd crawled on top of her. She felt her heart begin to race and she put the photo down. She never wanted to see his face again.

'Look at this!' said Jack holding up a pretty wooden box.

'What?'

'All these,' he said lifting up the lid to reveal several bracelets, necklaces, rings and broaches.

'It looks as though he wasn't the only one to hoard things. I wonder if these are worth anything?'

'We're not here to steal, we're here to find evidence.'

'I know, but she's not going to need it now is she?'

'Jack, don't you dare.'

Jack sheepishly put the jewellery back in its box and continued going through the dresser. Despite herself, Emily picked up the photo again. The elderly Mrs Ferguson and her sons, dressed in their Sunday best, standing side by side. There was something about the photo that bothered Emily, but she couldn't say what it was. There was a second photo on the dresser of the three of them from some years earlier. She examined it carefully. They were all smartly dressed, Mrs Ferguson wore a large hat and a long dress, while the brothers were in matching dark suits. They were standing in front of a plush, velvet curtain backdrop. Both of the photos were in expensive looking frames, but that was not so unusual. Emily just couldn't shake that feeling she was missing something obvious.

'Are there any more photos around?' she asked Jack.

'Just the two we saw downstairs,' he replied.

Emily made her way back down the darkened staircase and into the sitting room to retrieve the pictures. What was she not seeing? She stared at them, willing them to give up their secret. Something was out of place but she was too tired to see it, she couldn't think straight. She headed back upstairs, taking the photos with her to show them to Jack, hoping he might spot what it was that was troubling her.

'Jack', she said as he rummaged around underneath the bed, 'take a look at these.'

'What is it?' he said emerging from the other side.

'It's more photos, but there's something that's bothering me about them. What do you think?'

Jack studied each of them in turn but couldn't say what it was that might be wrong.

'Sorry,' he said with a shrug of his shoulders.

Emily gave up and popped them down on the dresser.

'Jack do you think–?'

Jack held his finger up to his lips and beckoned for

Emily to listen. There was a noise coming from downstairs. Someone else was in the house. Jack quickly switched off the bedroom light.

'Burglars?' whispered Emily.

'I don't know. Could be.'

They listened intently but the house had fallen quiet.

'We should get out of here?' urged Jack

'How? They're downstairs, we'd be seen.'

There was a loud creak and the sound of footsteps on the stairs. They had to hide, but where? Under the bed was too obvious but the cupboard was too risky.

'The window!' she whispered excitedly. 'They're not going to look out the window are they? It's still dark out. If we climb onto the sill and pull the blackout curtains back across...'

Jack made a face.

'Have you got a better idea?'

They rushed over to the window, climbed up and forced themselves as deep into the alcove as they could. Silently, Emily drew the curtains. There they waited, backs pressed up to the glass, hardly daring to breathe. Their fingertips brushed against each other, then their hands interlinked. Jack squeezed hers gently. Emily looked across at him and he whispered to her, 'If they open the curtains, run.'

Emily wasn't about to argue as she heard the door open. They were no longer alone.

Chapter Thirteen

Emily glanced at Jack whose body was pushed so tightly against the window it was as if he thought he could disappear through it by force of will. Neither of them dared to move. It seemed incredible to her that the intruder could not hear her heart clattering against her ribcage. She took a long, slow breath and tried to calm herself. She wished that she could pull back the curtain just a little bit and catch a glimpse of whoever was in the room, but she couldn't chance it. If she leaned forwards even a fraction she would likely slip off the window sill and then they would be in serious trouble.

Time seemed to slow; five minutes felt like five hours. Whoever had broken in didn't seem like an ordinary thief. They were looking for something, slowly and methodically, opening drawers and closing them again, rifling through papers and documents. Just like Emily and Jack, they clearly thought there was no chance of being discovered. Then a thought struck her. What if the intruder wasn't really an intruder at all? What if it was someone connected to the house? A friend or a neighbour checking in? It would certainly explain why they hadn't heard them until they were on the stairs, as they would have let themselves in with a key.

Emily's legs and back began to ache from standing so straight for so long. She looked again at Jack who had a similarly pained expression on his face, and with his free arm he clutched the jewellery box to his chest. Suddenly the intruder gave a grunt and she guessed that he – she was almost certain it was a male voice – was looking under the bed. He was only a foot away now. The floorboards creaked beneath him. Jack and Emily both held their breath. What if it was the jewellery box looking he was looking for, thought Emily? What if he wouldn't leave until he had found it?

The floorboards creaked again and the man let out another grunt as he climbed to his feet. Emily could feel Jack looking at her. She knew what he was asking. Are you ready to run? She looked back at him and nodded. If the curtains so much as twitched they would sprint out of the room and head for the back door. They had the element of surprise. They might just make it out before he caught them.

She heard footsteps and the metallic clink of the lights going off. He was moving away from them. The door clicked shut and the noise of his footsteps grew fainter. He was heading downstairs. Slowly, Emily drew the curtain and let out the breath she had been holding in. For several moments neither of them spoke in case the intruder hadn't gone as far as they thought. Emily pressed her ear to the door, listening for any hint he might still be in the house, but she could hear nothing. He had gone.

'I'm sorry I got you into this,' whispered Jack.

'It's not your fault. I made my choice,' replied Emily firmly.

The clock at the bottom of the stairs struck one startling them both.

'Who do you think that was?'

'I don't know, but whoever they are they're not just an ordinary burglar. They were looking for something specific.'

'How d'you know that?'

'If they had wanted to burgle the place they could have been in and out in minutes. Why take your time and risk

213

being discovered?'

'Maybe they thought they wouldn't be, not at this time of the morning in an empty house anyway.'

Emily wasn't convinced.

'There's a cabinet with the family heirlooms in it downstairs. They could have taken them and been away; I'm sure that tea set would fetch a decent price. And why go to the trouble of leaving the place tidy? Look at this room, it's exactly as we found it earlier. Why not just rummage around, grab whatever you can carry, and go? Whoever it was either didn't want anyone to know they'd been here or didn't want to mess up the room for another reason.'

'Like what?'

Emily had been giving more thought as to who might have been able to let themselves into the house with a key.

'Well, Ralph Ferguson had a brother right?'

'That's what the newspaper said.'

'So it could have been him couldn't it?'

'I suppose.'

'I mean it explains why he wouldn't want to mess up the room, why he's left it as he found it. It was his mother's room. He was definitely looking for something, I wonder what it was?'

'Maybe it was this,' Jack said excitedly holding up the jewellery box.

'Shhhh, keep your voice down,' Emily hissed.

'Sorry,' he replied, lowering his voice, 'still perhaps this little lot is worth something after all.'

But Emily wasn't listening. Something Jack had said had set off an avalanche of thoughts in her head. The answer was in this room, she was sure of it. She began examining the framed pictures again.

'That's it. That's what's missing,' she cried.

'What is?' said Jack, gesturing for her to lower her voice.

'The jewellery. In all of these photos Mrs Ferguson is in her best clothes, but not once is she wearing any jewellery. Don't you think that's odd?'

'I suppose,' said Jack but she could tell he wasn't convinced.

'You don't think if she owned all this jewellery she wouldn't wear at least one piece? And these photos are the ones she was proudest of; they're in expensive frames, they were important to her. She's dressed up in her finest clothes for these pictures, I'm sure she'd have worn some of her jewellery too if she'd had it. And how can she afford all of this anyway?' she said taking the box from Jack and holding up some of the finer pieces. 'Mr Ferguson was a night porter at a hotel, he couldn't have bought it for her, so whose is it?'

'Maybe her husband got them for her? Or the brother, what was his name? Albert? Maybe that's why he was here, looking for the jewellery, they were things he'd bought and now he wants to sell them. Or maybe it was stolen, if Ralph Ferguson attacked people maybe he was also a thief?'

'A thief? Oh God...' Another thought hit her and she threw the box down onto the bed in disgust. 'The ring, Jack. The ring your brother gave to Clara; it could be in here.'

Jack stared at the box which had disgorged its contents over the bed.

'You mean you think this is all jewellery from...' he couldn't bring himself to finish the thought

'From the missing girls. Yes,' said Emily, equally appalled.

She touched him gently on the arm.

'You should have a look, if the ring is in there it might be the piece of evidence we need.'

Jack began reluctantly picking through the jewellery on the bed. Emily wondered what other horrors the house might hold. Not that they'd be able to find anything under all the mess in Mr Ferguson's room. Now something else was bothering her. The mess. Why was his room so untidy and his mother's so clean? Why had he kept so much rubbish? What if it was for the same reason?

'How old did you say those newspapers were Jack?'

'I don't know. A mixture I think. Some were pretty old though, ten, fifteen years or more,' said Jack still examining the jewellery.

'So around the time your brother was put in prison?'

Jack looked up and was about to say something when Emily stopped him.

'Can you smell something?' she asked.

Jack sniffed the air.

'Yes...'

They looked at one another.

'Fire,' they said in unison.

Emily opened the door a fraction. A cloud of black smoke was creeping up the stairs like a malevolent spirit.

'Bloody hell, let's get out of here.'

'Wait!' Emily grabbed Jack by the shoulder. 'We don't know if he's gone.'

'Emily, the house is on fire, he's not likely to have stuck around is he? We'll just have to take our chances and hope no one sees us.'

'Well we can't go without the papers, they might be part of the proof we need.'

'Okay, but be quick we haven't got long.'

Jack was right, the fire had spread rapidly. The living room had been engulfed and the flames were already sneaking up the walls at the bottom of the stairs. The fumes were making it difficult to breathe. Covering her mouth with her cardigan Emily ran into Mr Ferguson's room and grabbed as many of the newspapers as she could. From the street Emily could hear the furious clanging of a bell that told her the fire brigade were on their way. She began to panic. The smoke had filled the room in such a short space of time.

'Jack!' she cried.

'I'm out here. Come on.'

Emily stayed as low as she could, crawling towards the sound of Jack's voice.

'Emily, come on.'

'Keep talking,' she coughed, 'I'm coming.'

She wouldn't have expected fire to be so loud and yet it seemed to roar through the house. The smoke stung her eyes till she could no longer see. They hurt so much she shut them tight and called out again.

'Jack!'

A hand grabbed her and pulled her down the stairs. The heat was intense. Jack had found a blanket from somewhere and held it up as a flimsy barrier against the flames. Together they ran into the kitchen and pushed open the window they had come through. The night air flooded in, causing the fire to surge towards them once more.

'Quickly.'

The street was filling up with people. They had to get away without being seen or they would both be in trouble, Jack in particular. If he got spotted running away from a mysterious fire he would almost certainly end up joining his brother in prison. The garden gate lead out onto a narrow passageway between the two rows of houses. They simply had to hope no one would be out there. They couldn't risk leaving any other way or they'd be spotted for sure. She undid the bolt and together they raced down the alley and slipped out into an adjoining street.

'Were we seen?' she asked.

'How should I know?' spluttered Jack between coughs.

'Come on, if anyone catches us we'll be for it.'

'Turn that light off,' someone called from nearby.

'There's a bleedin' fire mate,' came another voice. 'You think the German's are gonna spot my light when there's a fire three doors down? Do me a favour.'

Emily and Jack stuck close to the shadows watching the chaos unfold.

'What now?' asked Jack.

They were both surprised by how quickly the fire had taken hold. The flames had engulfed the building despite the best efforts of the fire brigade who were battling hard to keep it from spreading.

'Have you got the box?' she asked.

Jack took the jewellery box from beneath his jacket.

'Give it to me,' Emily insisted.

'Why?'

'Because if we do get caught it's better it's found on me than you. I think we ought to split up and meet again tomorrow.'

'But where will you sleep?'

'I'll go back to the passages,' said Emily though she didn't much like the idea.

'But we agreed we'd stay away remember?'

'That's why we have to split up. I'll sleep down there for the night and if you're not with me there's no way you can be shot is there?'

'Be careful,' he said and squeezed Emily's hand.

'You know me Jack, I like a quiet life.'

Emily moved through the streets like a breath of wind, constantly checking over her shoulder to make sure no one was watching her. Eventually when was convinced she hadn't been followed, she slowed her pace and double backed towards the cathedral. She couldn't stop thinking about what had just happened. Somebody had deliberately set the Ferguson's house on fire. But why? Did they know something about the murder of Clara Worthington or of Ralph Ferguson for that matter? And if so what else did they know?

She remembered the attack by Ralph and what he'd said to her in the hotel room, "When he sees what I've bought him, he'll be very happy indeed." Could the 'he' have been his brother? And if so, why would his brother have been happy?

Perhaps the two of them worked together, and Albert knew that there was some evidence lying around the house that he needed to dispose of. When he hadn't found it, he'd decided to burn the whole place to the ground to be on the safe side. She wondered where he had gone to after he'd set the fire. Had he waited to make sure it caught, and if so had he spotted her and Jack coming out of the house? She hoped he hadn't been close enough to see their faces or they could be in trouble.

Emily felt the frustration rising inside her. She was close to an answer, she was sure of it, but something still troubled her. What could be worth the risk of burning down a house? And if it was Ralph's brother in there, why wait not wait till morning, then do the search in a more methodical manner? So distracted was she by these thoughts that she didn't notice as a long black saloon car drew up alongside her.

'You're out late aren't you?' came a languorous voice from inside.

Emily jumped. The car drew to a halt and a tall man in a long grey coat climbed out. He had on a trilby hat which he removed in greeting to reveal a slicked back streak of blonde hair. She thought about running, but where could she go to? She didn't know the streets of Exeter well enough in the light let alone at night, and besides how could she outrun a car?

'I think it would be best if you came with me,' said the man.

'I'm not going anywhere with you,' said Emily firmly.

'Well that is your choice to make, but it's late and you're running through the streets of a strange city alone, perhaps you'd be safer with me.'

'Why are you following me?'

'Get in the car and we'll discuss it. I'll drive you back to Mr Worthington's. I am really not what you should be afraid of right now.'

Emily still didn't move.

'You can get in or not, it's entirely up to you, but officially you're a missing person, your clothes reek of smoke, and not far from here there is, what looks to me at least, like quite a large fire. If you think that other people, people a lot less sympathetic to your situation that I am, won't start asking questions when you turn up stinking of smoke and unable to account for your whereabouts for the past two days, then you're not as smart as I'd thought. Now, are you getting in or would you prefer we hang around here all night?'

Reluctantly Emily climbed into the front passenger seat of the car. The car was warm and smelt of leather and cigarettes. They began to drive slowly round the empty streets of Exeter towards the Station Master's Cottage.

'Who are you?' asked Emily, 'and why have you been following me?'

'My name is Peterhouse, and I am your Ministry appointed Shadow Guardian.'

'My what?'

'Your Shadow Guardian. I am supposed to look out for you, protect you.'

Emily let out a derisive snort.

'Well you've done a spiffing job so far,' she said. 'And what do you mean Ministry appointed? What Ministry?'

'I work for His Majesty's Government. I was appointed as your Guardian, but unfortunately for both of us your father intervened.'

'I don't understand. Intervened in what? How? My father doesn't work for the government.'

'Oh Miss Cartwright,' said Peterhouse with an amused expression on his face, 'do you truly believe that?'

'My father's a soldier.'

'Once maybe, but not now. Now he is many things, but he is not a soldier.'

Emily felt something twist in her heart. Another secret. Another thing he hadn't told her. But why should she believe this man? This man whom she had Seen shoot Jack. He could be lying to her, trying to get her to drop her guard.

'What's a Shadow Guardian?' she asked.

'When someone with – skills like yours shall we say? – first starts to use their abilities, the Ministry appoints a Shadow Guardian to watch over them. Mostly we work in the background, making sure they don't hurt themselves or others with their gifts, occasionally recruiting them if we think they could help us. And sometimes we must intervene directly. You see, we are part Shadow and part Guardian.'

But Emily had stopped listening. He knows, she thought, he knows. She tried not to let her surprise show. She had guessed his arrival must have had some connection with her abilities, but how did he know about them to begin with? Only three people alive knew about her powers, Jack, her father and her grandmother. Had one of them told this – what had he called it – Ministry?

'Why are you here?'

'I've told you, I'm your Shadow Guardian, I am here to protect you.'

'I don't need protecting.'

'You have no idea how wrong you are. This is not a game Miss Cartwright. This is not like one of your little adventures with your friend Jack: this is real. You are in danger of the gravest kind.'

Emily bristled at his patronising tone and had to work hard to control her temper.

'I've been bombed and I survived. I've been attacked and I survived. And just now, just a few minutes ago whilst I was supposedly under your protection, I escaped from a burning building. So what is it you're protecting me from exactly? Because so far you've not done a very good job.'

'Believe me this was not that way I would have gone about things,' replied Peterhouse, 'if I'd had my way–'

'No,' said Emily cutting him off, 'I've Seen your way. Feels good does it, to shoot an unarmed boy?'

'What? What are you talking about?'

'You shot Jack, or you're going to shoot him. I've Seen it. We're in the passages under the city and you shoot him.'

Peterhouse looked troubled by the news, but whether he was genuinely upset by it or just annoyed that Emily knew something he didn't it was hard to tell.

'That is… unfortunate,' he said finally.

'Unfortunate? Is that all you have to say? You shoot a boy and it's unfortunate?'

'I haven't shot anyone yet,' he said with a hint of menace.

'But I've Seen it.'

'And have you Seen why I shoot him? Have you ever stopped to wonder that? Why do you think Jack would go down to those passages? Why would I? I have no interest in Jack Copleston, he isn't special. If we're down there, it will be because of you.'

'So now you're blaming me?'

'I'm not blaming you, I'm trying to explain that some things are more complicated than your simplified world view can possibly allow.'

Emily chewed her lip, biting back the abuse she wanted to hurl at him. Here he was claiming to be her protector, yet she had almost died three times. And now he wanted to blame her for Jack getting shot, or even killed?

'Why now?' she said shortly.

'I'm sorry?'

'Why now? Why are you here now, in the middle of the night? Someone from the Ministry, whatever that is, doesn't just come to Exeter in the middle of the night to see a young girl and tell her he is her Shadow Guardian. Something's happened. Something's changed. What is it?'

He eyed her, seemingly impressed by her reasoning.

'Ah, not so stupid after all then. You're right, it is unusual but there's been a lot of chatter in the last forty-eight hours, messages we have intercepted about a weapon that the Nazis are trying to obtain, then earlier this evening the chatter stopped and I got word that you had gone missing. Of course, I was fairly certain you were still in the city having seen you only the day before, however this was still a concern to us. Now, the Nazis may not know about you yet, this weapon they've been talking about could be something else entirely, but we can't take the risk of you falling into their hands.'

'What do you want with me?' asked Emily.

'I want you to come to London.'

'Why?'

'We can protect you better in London than we can here.'

'I've seen your protection, and I think I'm better off without it.'

Peterhouse stopped the car and turned on her.

'You have no idea how dangerous you are,' he said in quiet voice. 'No idea, no idea at all. You could bring the world to its knees. Imagine that, humanities fate in the hands of a child. They are coming for us and we are this close,' he said holding his thumb and finger up a fraction apart, 'from losing everything. And if we lose, that's it. Five hundred years of progress is finished. We'll be dwellers in a new dark age, an unending darkness the likes of which we have never known. We will lose every freedom we have fought so hard for. Freedom of speech, freedom to worship, the right to vote, the right to marry whomsoever we please. They will usher in a new era, an era of fear and cruelty. Whatever you think you have Seen me do, remember that. Think about that.'

Emily shook her head disbelievingly. 'I tell you that you will kill a boy and you call it unfortunate? What kind of person does that make you? You talk of a new dark age, but you're a creature of the dark, you're as bad as they are.'

'Oh Miss Cartwright,' he sighed, 'maybe I am – as you would put it – a creature of the dark, but I'm still half in the light I think, a devil on the side of the angels. And you don't want to see what those devils who aren't on our side are like. I'm trying to help you, I'm trying to make this right. That is why I'm here.'

'Why not just arrest me then? Or take me away?'

'That's not what we want. We want you to help us. It's taken us this long even to be allowed to approach you. Your father saw to that,' he added bitterly. 'The Nazis know something is here, some sort of weapon. If they truly knew how powerful you could become they'd invade, they'd be half way across the channel right now. It's time for you to choose your side Emily.'

'I know my side,' she replied firmly.

'I'm glad to hear it. There are a lot of advantages to coming to London. First of all, you wouldn't be stuck doing housework all day, every day. Secondly, you could see people your own age, receive a proper education, and we could help you to master your undoubted abilities,' he said.

Emily had to admit that the offer appealed to her. Even so, she was reluctant to leave Exeter. After what Jack had done for her didn't she owe it to him to stay and help him get his brother released? will Peterhouse pressed on.

'What if I could offer you something in return for your help?'

'I don't want anything.'

'You haven't heard what I have to offer yet,' he said slyly.

'I don't care, all I want is to be back with my mother and my sister. Can this Ministry of yours give me that?'

'Of course not, I'm sorry…' he said quietly, 'but if we can't reunite your family, perhaps we could reunite someone else's. I've been taking a lot of interest in Thomas Copleston's case. It seems there are a number of inconsistencies that could form grounds for appeal. I think if the family were to get the assistance of a top class legal expert, one from His Majesty's government for instance, they would stand a very good chance of seeing their boy free again.'

'You'd get him out?'

'We'd certainly do everything in our power to accommodate his appeal.'

'Those are some weasel words aren't they?' said Emily shrewdly. 'You'll do everything in your power to accommodate his appeal? Not good enough. If he isn't free then I'm going nowhere.'

'His Majesty's government doesn't do deals with

murderers.'

'I must remember to let the people of Czechoslovakia know, I think they'll be somewhat surprised to hear that.'

Peterhouse flushed.

'Don't lecture me girl, you think you have all the answers don't you? "Peace in our time" wasn't pleasant, but it bought us some breathing room, it bought us three hundred Spitfires and countless bombers. Munich gave us a year to prepare, and that year might be the difference between winning and losing this war. You can sneer and make your little jokes, but that's the truth of it.'

Emily ignored him.

'If you get him a re-trial I'll come with you to London.'

'It's not as easy as that, for us to get him a re-trial we need new evidence. No matter how good your legal team is they still need something to work with.'

'We've got evidence,' said Emily and she began to explain about the jewellery they had found in Mr Ferguson's home, and about her suspicions of Mr Ferguson's brother. Despite himself, Peterhouse looked impressed.

'And these other items of jewellery, you think they belong to other victims?'

'To the missing girls, yes. We don't know for sure but we think so.'

'Give them to me and I will ensure it's investigated.'

'How do I know I can trust you?'

'You can't trust me, you can't trust anyone. You'd do well to remember that. Still, we both have something the other wants and that's normally enough isn't it?'

Emily looked at him thoughtfully.

'Why are you so sure that I am this all-powerful weapon the Nazis are after? All I can do is tell you which way up a coin is going to land; you'd be better off taking me to a casino than to a military briefing.'

'You'll have to trust me on this.'

'You just said I couldn't trust you.'

Peterhouse smiled. 'Ok then, you'll have to believe me.

There are some things I can't tell you, but remember this if you remember anything, the one thing you have going for you is that if the Nazis do want you, then they want you alive, at least for the moment; they want the intelligence that you could give them.'

'I wouldn't help them.'

'Really? What if they took your loved ones and threatened to slit their throats right in front of you? What would you do then?'

'I...'

'You don't have to like me; you don't have to trust me, but you might have to accept that my motives are good, even if my methods seem questionable.'

'Half in the light?' said Emily.

'Half in the light,' agreed Peterhouse.

He started the car again and they crawled along the narrow county lane towards the cottage. Something he had said bothered her.

'Wait, you said the Nazis want me alive for the moment?'

'Yes.'

'Meaning that perhaps they wouldn't at some other time? Why would they want to kill me if they invaded? If I could tell them the plans of the Allied Forces, why would they want me dead?'

'You know you are not the only Seer in the world don't you?'

She was about to say that her grandmother was one too, but then she thought better of it. Hadn't he told her not to trust him? If he didn't already know about Josephine then Emily wasn't going to be the one to tell him.

'I figured as much,' she replied.

'We think there might be a way. If you had enough of people like you, you could make your predictions more powerful, almost fool proof; you'd be the ultimate weapon. No one could launch a surprise attack, you'd already know about it. You'd know what was in people's souls Emily. Think about that. You'd know their truest

226

intentions. Does that sound like a power you'd like the Nazis to have?'

Emily shook her head.

'That's why we want to keep you safe.'

Emily looked at Peterhouse. Perhaps he was right, perhaps she would be better off in London. Despite everything though she kept coming back to the words of her father in the hospital: "When times are bad people get desperate, and once that happens they can justify anything, because it's always for the greater good and it'll always go back to normal once the war is over." What if the British government decided that she was a weapon they'd like for themselves? Did anyone really deserve that power? Once again she wished she could talk to her father, there was so much he hadn't told her, so much she needed to know and understand.

They pulled up outside the Station Master's Cottage.

'Wait,' said Emily suddenly remembering, 'why have you brought me here? Mr Worthington threw me out. I can't stay here.'

'I think you'll find Mr Worthington has had a change of heart.'

'But why?'

'That's for him to explain.'

Emily was, by now, so tired that all she wanted to do was crawl into a nice, warm bed. If Mr Worthington was happy enough to let her sleep back at the cottage for the night, she wasn't going to argue.

'So you'll look into the evidence I've given you?' she asked.

'As a matter of urgency, yes. And if we get Jack's brother a retrial you'll come to London?'

Emily paused. What other choice did she have?

'Yes, I'll come.'

She opened the car door and stepped out. Just as she about to close it a thought hit her.

'You said you came to find me when you heard I'd gone missing. How did you find me?'

Peterhouse gave Emily a tired smile.

'Generally speaking where you're concerned Miss Cartwright, I look for trouble and there you are. Go and get some rest. I expect Mr Worthington will want a word with you.'

Emily watched as the car pulled away and she opened the front door of the cottage to see Mr Worthington slumped in his chair in the living room fast asleep. She closed the door behind her and he started.

'Emily? Is that you?'

Emily entered the room.

'It's me.'

'Where have you been? I've been worried sick.'

Emily almost laughed. Hadn't he told her he wanted her gone?

'I ran away. I –'

But Mr Worthington cut her off.

'You look exhausted,' he said, then he paused and sniffed the air. 'I suppose I shouldn't ask why you smell like a bonfire?'

Emily went to speak but he held up his hand to stop her.

'Say nothing for now, we'll talk properly in the morning. Get yourself to bed.'

Emily was grateful for this small mercy. She didn't think she could stay awake any longer and sure enough she was asleep almost before her head hit the pillow.

Chapter Fourteen

The next morning Emily awoke to the smell of sausage, eggs and bacon sizzling on the stove. She made her way into the kitchen to find Mr Worthington shaking the pan, trying to dislodge the bacon that had welded itself to the bottom.

'Morning,' he said over the crackling of hot fat.

A high-pitched whistling sound signalled that the kettle was coming to the boil, so Emily lifted it off the hob and started to make them both a cup of tea.

'Sit down, sit down,' he said dropping a lump of two-day old bread into the pan to fry along with a few shrivelled mushrooms.

Emily did as she was told.

'I haven't had a fry-up since the war started but I thought we deserved a little treat. We'll just have to get creative the rest of the month as this is all we're likely to get in the way of bacon and fresh eggs.'

Emily could tell he had gone to a huge effort. The kitchen was cleaner and tidier than she had ever seen it, and she had never before witnessed Mr Worthington pick up a pan, let alone cook with one.

'Sorry,' he said, placing her plate down in front of her, 'the bacon might be a little on the crispy side, I don't cook very often.'

Emily didn't know what to make of it all and was still

half-expecting Miss Pinchman to appear at any moment.

'Tuck in,' said Mr Worthington, mistaking Emily's bewildered expression for politeness. She was too hungry to argue. She had almost forgotten how little she had eaten lately and her stomach growled happily as she wolfed down the sausages. After she'd finished eating Emily got up to turn on the wireless. She knew Mr Worthington normally liked to keep up with the latest news from the front, but he called her back.

'Sit down girl,' he said taking a large sip of tea. 'There'll be plenty of time for that later. The war ain't gonna stop anytime soon more's the pity. Let's just enjoy a bit of peace and quiet.'

Mr Worthington mopped up the last of the juices from his plate with a small slice of stale bread, then moved it to one side and began to fill his pipe with tobacco. Emily wondered what was going on. Of all the reactions she had anticipated, him making her breakfast was not at the top of the list. Eventually he turned to her, tapping his pipe on his knee and frowning to himself. Just when Emily was about to ask if anything was wrong, he spoke.

'I don't like to talk much. It's never been my way. Everybody has their own troubles, no point me blathering on about mine if it just adds to someone else's. My wife Elsie, God rest her soul, was always on at me. "What's going on in that head of yours Arthur Worthington?" she'd ask. And I'd smile and say anything but what was really on my mind. See, I always thought she knew, deep down, and that her asking was all for larks. Let me tell you Emily, there's no distance so great as the distance between people who love each other and can't find a way to say so.'

He sighed and re-lit his pipe which had burned out.

'I am not an educated man. There are some things I simply don't have the words for, and the ones I do have seem awful small. Brittle words, frail words, words that would fall down if you put too much of a burden on them. Grief. Sorrow. Love. All too weak for the weight they carry. That's what I thought anyway. Only, something happens to those words when they're said out loud, when they're spoken to someone you care for. They get stronger, and they give you strength in turn. That was something I learned far too late.'

Though he was addressing her she felt as if he was really talking to himself, like this was a conversation he'd been having in his head for many years.

'I lost my little girl. Did you know that?'

'Yes, I erm... I heard. I'm so sorry.'

'Well, people like to talk don't they? Clara was killed ten years ago. That was her room you were in the other day.'

'I'm sorry Mr Worthington, I know I shouldn't have—'

'No you shouldn't,' he interjected. 'If someone asks you for a bit of privacy then that is what you should give them.'

'I know, I just heard a noise and I was worried, but it was also wrong of me.'

He nodded, saying nothing either way.

'Can I ask,' said Emily carefully, 'why you keep it locked?'

Mr Worthington shifted in his seat and started tapping his pipe against his knee again.

'It was because of Elsie. When someone you love dies, they leave a massive hole in your life, and that's a hole that can never be filled. You know that as well as I do. Clara was young, she had a grand life ahead of her, and that was brutally snatched away. She was ripped from our world and it left us both lost. Elsie... well... Perhaps if I'd had the words I could've talked to her, I could've helped her, but I didn't even know how to help myself. So I let her drift away from me. I was angry at her you see?'

'Why were you angry with her?'

'I was angry at everyone Emily, I just didn't realise it. I was angry at myself, at Elsie, at Clara and at the boy who killed her. Elsie's grief was so strong, so overpowering that it made mine feel small by comparison. Like I didn't

231

love my daughter as much as she did. Elsie always said that I was quieter when I came back from the Great War, but it was the words again. I couldn't tell her about all that had happened. I didn't want to tell her. She was my island, safe away from it all. She hadn't lived through it or seen the things I'd seen. I didn't talk about it, because I couldn't. How can you talk about something you can't understand? After Clara died I saw the same change in Elsie. She began to spend time away from me. She would wander down to the river where Clara liked to play, or she'd go out to the fields and call for her like she thought she could still bring her home. Then when she didn't come, Elsie would drag herself back to the cottage and spend the rest of the day sitting on Clara's bed, weeping. And instead of saying, "my dear, I'm so sorry," and sitting with her until perhaps she had found the words to explain everything she was feeling, I lost patience. I told her she needed to get over it.'

Just recalling these words seemed to cost Mr Worthington a great deal.

'Get over it,' he said again, shaking his head in disbelief. 'I never in my life raised a hand to Elsie, but when I spoke those words it was like I'd slapped her hard across the face. She shrank away from me. I can still see the look in her eyes. Watching her image of me crumble into dust, seeing her hurt and disappointment at the person I'd become, that's the hardest thing I've ever had to face. Harder than France, harder than the trenches. I'd run through a storm of bullets before I'd see that look again.'

He rubbed his chin thoughtfully. He was yet to shave that morning and there was the shadow of stubble around his mouth.

'Each day Elsie would go up to Clara's room, sit on the bed and stare out of the window like she was expecting to see her coming up the garden path. I couldn't take it. Day after day, night after night, waiting in that room, wasting away in front of me. In the end I sealed it up, put boards over the windows and locked the door. I hoped by forcing her out of there she'd come back to me, but she didn't. I'd taken away the one place she still had left, the one place she still felt connected to our daughter and after that she faded away quicker than ever. She hardly ate, rarely spoke and slept most of the day, only to lie awake all night. That winter she caught pneumonia and died.'

Mr Worthington paused to compose himself. Emily could see his eyes glistening with tears, but he blinked them away and cleared his throat before continuing.

'Anyway, once the room was locked I couldn't bring myself to unlock it again. I felt that to do so would make what I'd done even more foolish, sorta like admitting that I'd made a mistake. Easier to leave it and pretend there was nothing behind that door and nothing I could do. I was scared to go up there. Can you believe that? I couldn't step inside without being reminded of what I'd done, of what I'd said. But when you arrived something in me changed. I started thinking about that room again. I even took the key out a few times, trying to summon the courage to go back up to her room. Then when I found you standing there... I just... for a moment I thought Clara was back, that there she was, looking through her wardrobe just like before. It was only for a few seconds, but a few seconds can sometimes feel like forever.'

He stared off into the distance, lost again in the memories of his family. Emily wanted to tell him that she understood, that she knew the pain of loss and to reassure him that she didn't hold what he had done against him, but he still had more to say.

'I'm sorry Emily, I shouldn't have behaved in the way I did, but they were my world. If you are to live here again we need to come to an understanding that some places really are out of bounds to you. You remind me so much of Clara, and that's not easy, it makes me remember all the things I've missed about her, but I have to say it's been good having you around. You may not know it but you've changed me. Just having life about the place for once is refreshing, and I have to say the house is cleaner and tidier than it has been in years. I'm sorry I haven't been a better host. I wouldn't have taken you in at all, but when I heard about your family, about what you'd lost... well I just thought perhaps that two damaged souls might be good for one another. You've been good for me no doubt, but I haven't been so good for you. Things are going to be different from now on, I promise.'

'Mr Worthington–'

'Let me finish. You're welcome to stay here, if you want. If you'd prefer to live elsewhere I will call Miss Pinchman right now, tell her it's not working out, no hard feelings. But I'd appreciate it a great deal if you'd stay.'

Emily didn't know what to say. She felt a stab of guilt in her chest. How could she tell him that she might be returning to London soon in order to secure the release of the very man he believed killed his daughter? On the one hand she didn't want to repay his honesty with lies, but on the other she didn't yet know where the new evidence might lead, so surely it was better to wait and see? If the evidence was worthless then she wouldn't be going anywhere and he would never have to know about any of it. Her father's face floated to the front of her mind. Perhaps this was how his lies to her had started, with the best of intentions, but in the end they had proved disastrous. This was different though, Emily assured herself, for the truth would be far too complicated and hurtful to explain at that moment.

'Of course I'll stay. I am sorry for what I did, and for running out; it was wrong. Can we start again?'

He looked at her thoughtfully, eyes running over her face.

'I'd like that. I'd like that a lot,' he said breaking into a wide smile. 'A new start for the both of us. Now I'd better give the police a ring, let them know you're safe and well.'

He raised himself off his chair and limped through into the hallway to make his call. Perhaps it would be okay, she thought. Mr Worthington was a reasonable man, and once the evidence was known he would see that it was wrong for Jack's brother to be locked up. And it might even help. He'd been fond of Tommy hadn't he? He wouldn't want to see him suffer, especially if they could catch the real killer.

Mr Worthington returned from his call.

'All sorted,' he said clapping his hands together. 'Now I must get to work, I'll try and get home on time tonight. Have a good day.'

Emily set to work cleaning the house. Despite Mr Worthington's insistence that the war could wait, she turned on the radio for the latest news and caught the last few minutes of '*Children's Hour*'. The familiar theme tune began to play and Emily found herself transported back seven years. She was sitting on her mother's lap, enchanted by the story of 'How the Leopard Got His Spots'. Her sister was there too, listening but pretending not to, being almost two years older than Emily, she felt herself far too mature for such tales, though secretly she adored them as much as Emily did.

Emily took a long, deep breath and wiped away a tear from the corner of her eye. Grief, she had discovered, was always lurking, and could sneak up on her when she least expected it. She fought hard not to think of her family very often, as it hurt so much, but then she would find herself feeling guilty for not thinking of them more, because if *she* didn't take time to remember them, then who would? Besides her mother and sister had both given up their lives for people that they loved. They were acts of heroism so great that Emily could hardly comprehend them. They had known the danger and carried on regardless. The courage they had shown still astounded her. So what could she do in the face of such bravery but try to be as courageous as them, and bear the hurt and the pain that remembering them bought her?

Still, she found it tiring, always struggling to hold herself together. Sometimes all she wanted was for someone to put their arms around her, to take the weight from her chest and carry it for a while so that she could rest. She didn't want to remember everything all of the time if remembering always meant feeling such sadness, such guilt.

The title music ended and a newsreader solemnly announced that Hull been bombed most severely the previous night, but that Berlin had also been attacked with great success. Emily wondered what constituted success? Lives lost? Buildings destroyed? Families torn apart? Suddenly she felt sick, sick of anything and everything to do with the war. She twisted the dial searching for something else to listen to until she stumbled upon the Forces Programme and found to her delight that it was playing one of her favourite songs, '*I'll Be Seeing You*'.

'I'll be seeing you in all the old familiar places,
That this heart of mine embraces all day through...'

It was a slow, lolling tune, and for a few moments she found she was able to lose herself in the warm swirl of the clarinets and the muted wail of the trumpets. Everything else, Mr Worthington, Mr Ferguson, her father, her mother and sister, all faded away, just for a minute.

'I'll find you in the morning sun and when the night is new,
I'll be looking at the moon but I'll be seeing you...'

She was pulled from her reverie by a knock at the door. When she opened it, she was surprised to see Jack standing on the step looking agitated.

'Jack, what are you doing here?'

He came straight in.

'It's the ring. It's my grandma's ring Em, no doubt about it.'

'You're certain?' said Emily.

'Absolutely,' he said twisting the ring in his fingers. 'Once I got it home into the light it was obvious. I just needed to be sure, so I compared it to the photo of my

236

grandparents that my mum has in the sitting room. It's identical.'

'So that means–'

Jack cut her off.

'That means that it was Ralph Ferguson who killed Clara Worthington; not my brother.'

He sat down at the kitchen table, stunned into silence.

'Jack?'

'I just... I've always known Tommy didn't do it, but this is the first time I've had proof, something definite...'

'If it comes to trial though, they could say he found the ring, or bought it off someone else, couldn't they? After all the ring was never found,' said Emily, not wanting Jack to get carried away just yet.

'That's where the rest of the jewellery comes in,' he said excitedly, 'buying one piece might be understandable, but having the jewellery of several missing girls, that's a lot harder to explain.'

'Assuming that it belongs to the girls. We'd have to find the families and have them confirm that.'

'It's gotta be, I know it. And I've got a plan. What have you done with the box by the way?'

Emily realised that she hadn't yet told Jack about running into Peterhouse the previous night. She filled him in on the details. To her surprise Jack was furious.

'You mean you've given away the only evidence we have?'

'No, it's not like that Jack; he's from the government; he's going to look into it. He promised me he would get a retrial for your brother but he said he needed the jewellery as proof.'

'And what if he doesn't do what he promised Emily? Did you think of that? My brother's best chance of getting released will be gone forever.'

'He will do as he promised,' said Emily, although without any of her former certainty. 'I'll make sure he does.'

'And how are you going to do that? He's not to be

trusted, you said it yourself; you had a vision of him shooting me for God's sake.'

'I know, but this is different,' she insisted lamely. Had she made a mistake? Had she been tricked and cost Tommy his one chance of freedom?

'He shoots me Emily, or does that not bother you?'

'Of course it bothers me, I don't want you to get hurt. It just seemed like the right thing to do.'

'The right thing to do? To hand over all the evidence to a potential murderer? What if he was in on it? What if it was him in the house? What if he started the fire?'

Emily shifted uneasily in her seat. She hadn't thought of that.

'Don't you think it's a bit suspicious that you ran into him by chance, somewhere in Exeter in the middle of the night?'

'You think he followed me?'

'Well obviously. How else could he have found you?'

Emily thought on this a moment.

'He can't have done. I was careful. I kept an eye out, I took several detours through the back streets. He couldn't possibly have followed me in the car. Anyway...'

Emily hesitated. She hadn't yet told him about the deal she had struck.

'I think he's telling the truth about helping your brother. After all, he could just have snatched the box off me, but we both have something the other wants.'

'And what does he want from you?' asked Jack.

'He wants me to come and work for him, for this Ministry he works for. He knows all about the Seers, he wants to give me training.'

'Ah so that's it. You wanted training on how to be a real Seer and so you just gave up the evidence.'

'No,' said Emily stung by the accusation, 'it wasn't like that. I don't care about Seer training and I don't want to go back to London. I did it because it seemed like the right thing to do. I did it because I didn't know how we were going to get anyone to take our side on this. We had evidence, but what could we do with it? We're not the police, we can't investigate it all ourselves, we can't interview the families of the missing girls or interrogate Mr Ferguson's brother. I did it because I thought it was the best chance we had of getting your brother out of prison. I did it for you and for your family. I told him I would only leave Exeter to go to London if he could guarantee a re-trial for Tommy, and that I definitely wouldn't go unless that happened.'

There was a long pause as Jack took on board this new piece of information.

'You're leaving?'

'Maybe. I mean, I suppose I am once Peterhouse has looked into the jewellery and matched it to the missing girls.'

'Oh,' was all he could manage in response. 'Well, I suppose I should go home, not point in staying is there? Let me know if Peterhouse ever gets in touch.'

With that Jack turned and left, letting the front door slam behind him. Emily thought about running after him but what good would it do? Besides, he would understand soon enough. She had done what was best for both of them, hadn't she? Emily searched deep down inside herself to see if it were true. Were her motives as pure as she claimed? Had she really just wanted to help Jack, or was she also helping herself? Hadn't she been a tiny bit tempted by the offer of proper Seer training? The thought of using her abilities to help win the war appealed to her, as did the idea of disobeying her father. He had begged her not to make herself known, but it turned out everything he had told her about his life, about his job, about her family even, was a lie. He didn't deserve her obedience. If what Peterhouse had said was true, then her father was not even a soldier like he'd always claimed. She wondered if her mother had known? Had she been in on the pretence? Emily thought not. She hadn't known about Emily's ability to see the future after all. And if she hadn't known about that, then he'd probably told her the same lies he'd told Emily.

Of course, Peterhouse could have been lying too, about her father, about helping her and about helping Jack. What if she had given over the jewellery needlessly? What if she really had cost Jack's brother his one chance of freedom? But that didn't make sense, why would he have followed her all that time? And how would he have known about her abilities if he was not part of this Ministry like he claimed?

Still the thought continued to eat at her. Her father never talked much about his work, even before the war. Maybe he wasn't allowed to. Then she remembered something her grandmother said, about him hiding the records of her. She had never thought about it before. How was he able to hide her existence? Who were these powerful allies that Peterhouse spoke of?

At that moment the letter box coughed out a small cream envelope. The handwriting on the front was familiar. It was from her Grandmother. Quickly she tore it open. Inside was a note that read simply:

Deller's Cafe, the High Street, 2pm.

Time seemed to crawl for the rest of the morning and Emily did everything she could to distract herself from all that was worrying her. Finally it was time to leave and she began her walk into town. She had heard all about Deller's, though she had never been in before, for it was a favourite meeting place for people in Exeter. Once inside it was easy to see why; it was an oasis of opulence in a time of austerity. On the ground floor was a huge ballroom filled with tables, above which were two levels of ornately decorated balconies with scenes of Roman goddesses painted in vibrant blues, yellows and golds.

The cafe was busy but not full. Emily knew that money was tight for most people, and she noticed a lot of the customers were carefully nursing a pot of tea whilst looking longingly up at the balconies where others sat enjoying cakes and sweet desserts. On the far side of the room there was a small raised stage where the band played. It didn't take Emily long to locate her grandmother, even in all the bustle. She was in the top balcony smoking a cigarette and drawing scandalised glances from those around her. It was unusual to see a woman smoking in public. Emily suspected that was why her grandmother did it, just to upset people and to amuse herself.

'Dear child, it's so good to see you.'

She held Emily at a distance and then leaned in to kiss her once on either cheek.

'It's good to see you too,' replied Emily truthfully.

'I'm so glad you're alright, I was worried about you. I did wonder what kind of state I might find you in to be honest. I thought it best we not meet in the hotel after what happened.'

'You know about that?'

'I became aware something was wrong late that evening. I had a feeling of unease that I could not shake, and so I did something I rarely do and looked down the path of a loved one. It's not easy to do, and as you know I don't like doing it, but I was worried about you.'

'You Saw what happened?' said Emily appalled. 'Then why have you only come back now?'

'I came back the moment I Saw obviously, but you were already gone. I knew you were okay, and really it is better if one learns to deal with these things oneself. Anyway, what could I do to help you? I had Seen that you would return to Mr Worthington eventually.'

Emily was stunned.

'You could have offered me somewhere to sleep for the night, that would have been something.'

'I didn't think you'd want to stay at the hotel after... well you know...'

'You could have put me somewhere else, there are other hotels in Exeter.'

'But by then you were a missing person, I can't afford

to draw attention to myself Emily,' she said lighting another cigarette. 'Besides I saw you were with a boy, a nice young boy.'

'Jack.'

'Jack is it? Well I didn't want to interfere.'

Emily shook her head.

'I was just looking out for your best interests.'

'My interests? What about my safety?'

'You're here aren't you? You're alive?'

'Yes but–'

'Well then your general wellbeing is the least of our concerns.'

The words were like a punch to her stomach and her disgust must have shown on her face for her grandmother continued.

'You were attacked, and I'm sorry about that, truly I am; rest assured I will be taking my business elsewhere in future, but I can't help what happened. I can only try and make sure it doesn't happen again. You could have been killed but you weren't, I don't know how you got away but you did, we got lucky. That's three times now, so someone up there obviously likes you. You're a tough girl, you've come through so much already; you want a shoulder to cry on and a bit of sympathy, I understand–'

Emily felt the fury that had been simmering inside her burst forth.

'You don't understand, you don't understand one bit. I'm not looking for anyone's sympathy, I hate people knowing what happened, I hate the way they look at me, but I wouldn't mind if you were concerned about me, if I had some sense that you were genuinely upset about what went on, but you're not. This is just a game to you. No wonder dad wanted nothing to do with you. I couldn't understand why he went to such lengths to keep me hidden from you, but now I do. You're poison. What does it say about you that even when he had no one else to turn to, he still didn't want your help?'

Her grandmother appeared unmoved by Emily's tirade.

'Are you quite finished?'

Emily nodded: she felt empty now. That was the thing with rage; it was unsustainable, like a fuel that could power you along at a hundred miles an hour but burned out just as fast.

'I am concerned, very concerned believe me. Emily, you are my grandchild, and I would go to the ends of the earth to protect you. Didn't I just say that the reason I looked down your path is that I was worried about you? I just have a different way of doing things. I'm sorry if you don't like it, your father was always dismissive of my parenting skills, but look at him, he turned out wonderfully.'

Emily snorted derisively.

'Oh yes, wonderfully. If you ignore the fact that he wouldn't talk to you for years, and he won't let you see his family.'

Josephine let out a long sigh and stubbed out her cigarette.

'I always thought I'd make a better grandmother than a mother, but perhaps not. Still I am doing my best. I am sorry I didn't come to your aid, but I Saw you were safe and that felt like the most important thing. Besides as I have already mentioned, I Saw you return to Mr Worthington. This is important. I do not like to challenge the fates unless I absolutely have to.'

'What does that mean?'

'I can see into the future, I can learn from it before it has happened, but I do not seek to change it. I profit from it yes, but I have rarely tried to stop something I have Seen from happening.'

'You mean you can never change the future?'

'I didn't say never, so let's assume that I did not mean never,' she said irritably. 'What I am trying to make you understand is that it is an exceptionally hard thing to do well. As I have told you, I prefer to interpret events, not to challenge them. After all, how do we know for certain that the actions we take won't *cause* the thing we wish to avoid? Hmmm? What if I had taken you in and it stopped you from making up with Mr Worthington? Who knows what sort of long term damage that could do. Maybe he saves your life one day, maybe you save his, but maybe none of it happens because I intervened out of concern for your welfare. I can't foresee all the consequences of an intervention Emily, which is why I am so cautious about meddling when I don't absolutely have to. The Greeks understood this. You like to read don't you? I'm sure the library must have a copy of Oedipus you can borrow. Very instructive. So come now child, let's not quarrel.'

Emily had begun to regain her composure. She was a little worried by her grandmother's insistence that it was hard to change the future. Wasn't she trying to do just that with Jack? They had agreed not to go back to the passages together in order to avoid what she had Seen happen to him. She wondered if she should ask her grandmother about that, but first she had some things that had been playing on her mind, and her grandmother was the only one who could help.

'What does my father do?'

'I'm sorry dear?'

'What does dad do? I thought he worked for the foreign office, and that when war broke out he signed up to become a soldier again, but that's not true is it?'

'Who told you that?'

'Does he work for the government, maybe in a different capacity?'

'Emily?'

'I was being followed by a man, he says he works for the Ministry.'

'The Ministry? Puffed up popinjays the lot of them.'

'You know about them?'

'Of course, they are well known to anyone with our abilities. Always sniffing around, hoping that we'll help them with whatever grand scheme they've come up with this time.'

'The man I spoke to, he said that my father had gone to

great lengths to protect me, to stop anyone from talking to me. And when we first met you said he'd done a good job at hiding me. What did you mean?'

'If your father hasn't told you what it is he does then, I don't believe it's my responsibility to tell you.'

'But you do know,' said Emily.

'Emily it really isn't my place to–'

'It wasn't your place to come and find me either. It wasn't your place to start teaching me to See but you did. Besides, grandmothers are meant to spoil their granddaughters.'

Her grandmother laughed and shook her head.

'Ah so now you want me to be your grandmother?' she said raising an eyebrow. 'Here I was thinking I was a terrible failure. Poison I believe the word was.'

Emily blushed but pressed on regardless, sensing that her grandmother wanted to tell her.

'What is it that dad does?' she asked again.

'Your father isn't a soldier, you're correct. He works for the Ministry, or at least he did. In peacetime the Ministry is a department of government that tracks those with such gifts, it makes sure they're not a danger to themselves or to the public and offers them work. However in wartime their role changes. In wartime they are responsible for chasing down those with gifts, particularly those who may seek to help the enemy, whether they're from this country or from abroad. The people who do this are known as...' she paused to think for a moment, 'Shadow Catchers, I think it is. You see, this is the problem I have with the Ministry. Why must they insist on giving themselves such ridiculous job titles? Shadow Guardians. Shadow Catchers. I think it's because most of them don't have abilities of their own, so they try to make themselves sound more important. Anyway, their job is to ensure those with special powers are not a threat to Great Britain and her Empire.'

'And father is a Shadow Catcher?'

'Yes.'

'What's the difference between a Shadow Catcher and a Shadow Guardian?'

'A Guardian is on your side, they would never be allowed to harm you, or at least that's what they say. A Shadow Catcher is something different, they will go after anything or anyone they perceive to be a threat.'

'Will they kill them?'

'I would be surprised if they didn't, though I don't think that's their aim,' she added seeing the look of horror on Emily's face.

Emily didn't know why she was so shocked. Before, she had thought her father was a soldier, so she had known he must be killing people, but this was different. A soldier had signed up to fight. These people he was catching, what were they like? Were they just like her? People who wouldn't cooperate and wanted nothing to do with it all? Or were they a threat? Were they feeding information to the Nazis to help them win the war? Perhaps they had even told them the best time to bomb London on the day her family had been killed.

'But dad wouldn't kill someone would he?'

'Your father survived the Great War. All those years in some muddy ditch in France, people shooting at him day and night; he almost certainly killed someone then.'

'But that's different.'

'How is it different?'

'It's on the field of battle. It's… I don't know… it's allowed I suppose. Both sides knew what they were getting themselves into, it's what they signed up for.'

'Did they? A lot of men were conscripted into the army. They had no choice. It was that or face prison, possibly even death. And not to join up brought shame upon a family, people became outcasts in their own towns. Shame is a powerful tool Emily; some people would literally rather die than live with the humiliation of being branded a coward. Besides many men saw it as their duty to protect their country and the ones they loved.'

'Okay, but killing like that, at a distance, you don't

know who it is you're killing. You're just shooting. This, this is personal. This is hunting.'

'I'm not sure that distinction matters very much to the person who gets killed.'

'My mother and sister didn't agree to go to war, they weren't on the front line with a gun in their hands. They weren't making munitions or building planes. It's not fair. They didn't agree to that but they were killed. That's murder.'

Emily had never stopped to think about it before. She hated what the Nazis had done to her family and the thought that her father was doing something, albeit on a smaller scale, ate at her.

'There's an old phrase that springs to mind at this particular moment,' said Josephine seriously. "All that is necessary for the triumph of evil is that good men do nothing." Your father is a good man, and he won't stand by and do nothing whilst the Nazis spread their evil creed across the globe. Sometimes, we must do things we don't want to do in order to make the world a better place. I'm sure your father does all he can to avoid bloodshed, but if he has to kill one person to save ten or twenty, isn't that the right thing to do? And what if taking just one life, no matter how innocent they may be, then saves the lives of hundreds or maybe even thousands? I'd say that was a fair exchange. It would be lovely if we could all remain purer than pure, but this is war my child. Your father is a brilliant man. I know what he does must weigh on him, but knowing that the Nazis might win would trouble him far more.'

Emily took a sip from her tea that was languishing on the table, growing ever colder. The band had returned from their break and were currently halfway through an upbeat number called '*Painting the Clouds with Sunshine*'.

'Why did dad lie to me? He lied about his job, he lied about you, he didn't tell me about my abilities. How do I know what to believe if I can't even believe him?'

'Your father's job is incredibly dangerous, he is in and

out of the country all of the time, and he has to lie for a living. Perhaps it's a habit, perhaps he was simply doing what he thought was best.'

Her grandmother lit another cigarette but, getting no pleasure from it, immediately extinguished it.

'I think it's time for another lesson, don't you?' she said.

'What here?'

'Why not? We'll be quiet and it won't be anything too difficult. Have you been practising?'

'Of course,' replied Emily.

'Show me,' said Josephine pulling a coin from her purse.

Emily closed her eyes and felt her way into the frame of mind she needed and began to picture the coin. Suddenly she was watching it spin, landing neatly on heads.

'Heads,' she said without opening her eyes.

'Good, very good.'

They did this few more times before her grandmother called it to a halt.

'Okay, well you've got that mastered. That's the easy part. Let's try something a little trickier,' she adjusted her seat slightly so that she was facing the entrance.

'I want you to picture the entrance to the cafe in your mind's eye, can you do that?'

Emily studied the entrance carefully, trying to capture the look and feel of it, trying to See it in her head.

'Yes,' she said finally.

'Good. Now tell me who the next person will be to walk through that door will be. Describe them to me.'

Emily closed her eyes and tried to focus on the door but she couldn't do it.

'You're concentrating too much on the idea of it all. Just let it happen,' said her grandmother.

It was a difficult skill, much harder envisioning the coin had been, trying to be in the moment, trying not to imagine the moment but to See it instead.

'Can you do it?' asked Emily after several failed attempts.

'Of course,' replied Josephine.

'Show me.'

Her grandmother closed her eyes and remained silent for such a long time Emily wondered if she had fallen asleep. Suddenly she spoke.

'Tall woman, hat, small dog, long blue skirt, dark green coat. Trips on the entrance mat.'

She opened her eyes.

'How did I do?'

They waited eagerly for the next customer to arrive. It felt like an age to Emily but finally the door swung open and in walked a tall woman in a green coat exactly as her grandmother had described. She had only taken a couple of steps inside when she stumbled over the upturned corner of the doormat.

'Brilliant,' said Emily, 'but where's the…?'

At that moment she heard barking and a small dog poked its head around the frame of the door. Her grandmother raised an eyebrow as if to say, "how could you ever doubt me?"

'Now you try,' she said.

Emily shut her eyes once more and let the image of the entrance settle in her mind. Finally she felt a sort of tugging on her skin and when she opened her eyes she was Seeing the entrance properly. Slowly the doors opened and in walked a young boy carrying a box of some sort. He was stopped by the man at the door and given quiet but very firm instructions to go elsewhere.

'A delivery boy I think,' said Emily piecing the scene together. 'He's come to the wrong entrance and is being told to go to the back.'

She opened her eyes and the image was gone. Together they waited for the door to open again. Sure enough moments later a young boy arrived and was swiftly sent packing.

'Very good,' said her grandmother clearly impressed. 'I

hadn't expected you to pick that up quite so quickly. Let's try another one.'

They passed the next hour Seeing who would come through the doors next and predicting the set list of the band. Finally Josephine called a halt to proceedings.

'I think we'll end it there for today.'

Emily felt the first signs of tiredness already creeping up on her, something she couldn't hide from her grandmother.

'Come on, I'll take you home,' she said firmly.

Leaving plenty of money on the table for the tea and cake, they stepped outside into the late afternoon sun. They had barely been standing there twenty seconds when a car drew up.

'In you get,' she said with a smile.

Emily climbed in. The car was long and thin; the seats were covered in a plush red material and she suddenly felt very aware of how dirty she must be, for despite washing her clothes and hair she still smelt of smoke from the fire. Her grandmother sat in the back next to her and knocked on the small glass window in front of them through which Emily could see a man in a dark grey uniform drumming his fingers on the steering wheel.

'The Station Master's Cottage,' Josephine instructed, before turning to Emily. 'Now let's have a little drink shall we?'

She tapped on the wooden panel in front of her which opened up to reveal a small built-in drinks cabinet. She pulled out a decanter of sparkling glass and poured herself some of the clear liquid into one of the glasses from the cabinet. Then she revealed another decanter which had a similarly clear liquid and filled the glass to the brim.

'Here, get this down you.'

'What is it?' said Emily.

'Something to help you sleep,' she replied.

Emily took a large gulp. It was dry and bitter; it tasted horrible, like water gone sour. If she could have spat it out she would have done. Her grandmother was already fixing herself a glass of the same substance.

'I think there's something wrong with your drink,' rasped Emily.

Her grandmother gave her a thin smile.

'Quite the opposite. I make an exquisite gin and tonic. You'll get used to the taste.'

'How come,' said Emily, struggling to keep down the gin, 'how come you have a car? I thought petrol was rationed.'

'Everything is rationed dear, but everything is available too, if you know where to look.'

'But couldn't you get sent to jail for buying from the black market?'

'Only if I get caught, and I don't plan to. You forget I'm pretty good at staying one step ahead.'

They arrived at the cottage in just a few minutes. Emily handed back her glass which was still full of gin, much to her grandmother's displeasure.

'Get some sleep dear child, practise what I taught you. Remember focus only on things with a definite outcome for now. The tricky part comes later. And try not to worry about your father.'

'How do I do that?' asked Emily hopelessly.

Josephine gave a weary laugh, 'I don't know, but if you find out do tell me won't you?'

Emily climbed from the car and watched as it pulled away at speed. She hauled herself to her bedroom and fell asleep with her shoes still on.

Chapter Fifteen

Although she had been certain that she was doing the right thing when she had handed over the jewellery to Peterhouse, Emily was starting to have second thoughts. She desperately wanted to believe that he would help her, but what if he didn't? Then where would they be? And what power did Peterhouse really have to find out the truth, and to set things right? He was a Shadow Guardian working for a secret branch of the government. The Ministry sounded impressive, but did they have power over the police?

What they needed, she thought, was some definitive proof that Tommy was innocent, not just speculation and circumstantial evidence. They were close to something, she was sure of it. Someone had been worried enough about whatever was in Mr Ferguson's house to burn it down. That was a huge risk to take and it told Emily one thing for certain: somebody else knew what Ralph Ferguson was up to.

Did he perhaps have a partner in this awful business? Had they been the one to kill him? She didn't believe for a moment that he'd fallen into the river; it was far too much of a coincidence. Emily was left wondering what had spooked them so much that they felt they had to do such a thing. An uneasy feeling began to creep over her, her skin prickled and her stomach started to churn. If this person, whoever they were, was willing to go to such reckless lengths, what did that mean for her and Jack?

No matter how many times she ran it over in her head, she always came back to the same name: Albert Ferguson, Ralph's brother. She thought again about the night of the fire. Neither she nor Jack had heard anyone break into the house, which surely meant that whoever it was must have had a key. They had come in the dead of night, but they were surely not a thief for they had gone straight upstairs. They hadn't spent time looking around the living room where there were a few valuable objects on display. They had taken their time, they had been measured, and Emily was sure then that this person had been looking for something specific.

She wondered what she should do. She had no proof Albert Ferguson was involved, and she had no way of contacting Peterhouse to inform him of her suspicions. It could be weeks before she got the chance to tell him about her theory, and the more time that passed, the more chance there was of someone else getting hurt, or of whatever evidence remained being destroyed.

Emily had never been blessed with a great deal of patience. She always wanted things immediately. It was why her father had always said she was a better bowler than a batsman. If things weren't going her way she became rash and impulsive, liable to swing for balls that weren't there to be to hit. 'And that's how you get out,' he told her.

In this instance however it wasn't just her natural impatience at play. She badly wanted to make things right with Jack, to prove to him that trusting in her hadn't been a mistake. The germ of an idea planted itself in her head, and Emily began to water it with rash confidence and wild speculation, spurring herself on in the face of all doubts. The newspaper had said that Albert Ferguson lived in Plymouth, so why not go and see him in the flesh? It wasn't far after all and she wouldn't get into any trouble, she wouldn't try and speak to him, she would just follow him, watch his house, and get an idea of what his life was like, for what *he* was like.

At first she dismissed it. What could she hope to learn just watching after all? But the idea of doing nothing, of just sitting around and waiting for Peterhouse to come back, was too much for her. She kept picturing the hurt in Jack's eyes when she'd told him she had given Peterhouse the jewellery. This was her way of proving how much his friendship meant to her.

She would have to take the train to Plymouth, but of course she couldn't leave from St. David's as Mr Worthington might spot her. Instead she would get the 6.15am from Exminster, four miles away. She had to make sure she reached Plymouth early. If she arrived too late then he would already have left for work, she would miss him, and the entire trip would be pointless.

The newspaper hadn't given an exact address, just that he lived on Salisbury Road. It wasn't a lot to go on, but Emily hoped it would be enough. The other problem she faced was that she didn't have much money so she took the week's housekeeping and hoped that her grandmother would lend her the money to replace it.

There was no time to lose in Emily's view, so the following day she rose at dawn and sneaked out of the house before Mr Worthington was awake. He had been up late the previous evening manning one of the checkpoints near the airfield as part of his Home Guard duties, so subsequently he was still sound asleep when she left.

The journey to Exminster was difficult, not because of the distance involved, but because she did not know the way, so had to stop frequently to check the old map that she had found in the cottage. This was made more difficult by the fact it was quite dark at that time in the morning. Still, she made it to Exminster Station with ten minutes to spare and proceeded to purchase a ticket, thought even this proved more trouble than she had thought it would be. The ticket seller seemed very interested in why she was travelling on her own so early in the day. Emily parried his questions as best she could, telling him that her grandmother – who lived in Plymouth – was sick and she was taking her to the doctor. She could see he didn't entirely believe her, but she wasn't going to let it deter her. She fixed him with the most sincere look she could and smiled sweetly.

'Is everything all right?' she asked innocently. 'I have got the right train, haven't I? I'm sure my father told me to get the 6.15.'

The other passengers who were queueing behind her began to grumble about the delay, and finally the ticket seller issued her with a return ticket to Plymouth. As she waited on the busy platform she spotted a man she thought she recognised. His face seemed familiar but she couldn't place it. He was in his fifties and his hair was greying at the temples, but other than that there was little about him that stood out. He was pushed from her thoughts when the train to Plymouth pulled in just a few minutes later. Emily was grateful to find a seat, having already walked a fair distance that morning she knew she would need her strength if she was going to spend the day on her feet too.

She sat on the hard-wooden bench feeling quite self-conscious, aware that she was the only child on the train. There were a few women on board, but not many. It was mainly full up with men, men too old or too crippled to join the fighting. She didn't belong here, this was their world and they weren't happy to find a girl in it, even if she wasn't doing anything to cause them any bother.

Emily ignored their querying looks, clutching her ticket like a shield, and slowly they lost interest. Once or twice she thought the man she had spotted on the platform at Exminster was watching her, but when she looked up at him he was engrossed in his newspaper. After all she had been through, she realised it was natural to feel this way. She had been followed by Peterhouse for so long it wasn't a surprise that she was a little paranoid. It was even possible that he'd been sent by Peterhouse to keep an eye on her whilst he was back in London. However, when the train drew into Plymouth just before 8am, the man rudely pushed past her in his eagerness to reach the carriage door first and marched off down the platform without giving Emily so much as a second glance.

Now she had arrived, the flaws in her plan began to reveal themselves to her. She was worried she might not even spot Albert Ferguson. What if he had left early for work? She could be standing on his street all day and never see him. In fact, he might not even work in Plymouth itself. She had already spent most of the money she had with her ticket, so if he got on a train to go somewhere else she would have to hop on too and hope there were no inspectors on board.

She had studied an old map of Plymouth before she'd left and was confident she knew where Salisbury Road was. She found it quickly and was at the end of the street nearest to town by 8.00am. She took a short stroll up the road, keeping an eye out in case anyone should emerge from one of the houses. She had a funny feeling, not for the first time that day, that someone was watching her. She half-expected to see the man from the train standing beneath a lamppost, looking across at her, but, as far as she could tell, no one was paying her any attention at all.

She had been there almost half an hour and was beginning to lose hope of tracking down Albert Ferguson when she saw a man emerging from a small house several doors down. This man was taller and a little thinner than Ralph Ferguson had been, but he had a similar gait, and the same thinning hair. He was dressed in a dark blue boiler suit, a black jacket and flat cap which he placed on his head as he closed the front gate behind him. He also had a canvas duffel bag which he carried over his shoulder.

Was it him? The man began walking towards her, causing Emily to panic. It took her a moment to remember that he didn't know her and would therefore have no interest in her. As he drew nearer she recognised him from the photos at Mr Ferguson's house. She had found him. She felt a small surge of triumph and once he had passed her she followed at a safe distance. She didn't need to get too close, she could tell by his clothes where he was heading; the docks.

Of course, this presented its own challenge. The Plymouth docks were bigger and busier than the Exeter docks. At the Exeter docks she had looked out of place, but at least she could pretend she was passing through on her way to somewhere else. That wasn't the case here. She began to regret coming alone. If she'd had Jack with her they might have been able to take it in turns to keep watch. Emily hung around near the entrance but she couldn't really go down there as she drew too much attention.

She was beginning to feel as if the whole day was a waste of her time and money. Really, what had she thought he would be doing? He was hardly going to be wandering around with a sign saying, 'I killed my brother,' was he? Still there was just a chance she might rescue something from the whole experience. After a fruitless hour trying to keep watch on Albert, Emily decided she would be better off going back to his house. If no one was in she might just be able to find a way inside and have a look around. Then she could come back at lunchtime and see what, if anything, Albert got up to. It wasn't much of a plan, but it was better than nothing.

Of course, it wasn't as easy as it had been before. Without the cover of darkness it was tricky to get near enough to tell if anyone was home. She couldn't risk breaking in and finding his wife – if he had a wife – sitting in the kitchen. Eventually she concluded that the best way of finding out who, if anyone, was inside, was also the simplest. If she knocked on the door and no one answered, then she knew no one was home, and she might just be able to find a way in round the back. If someone did answer then she would claim to be looking for another house entirely, a simple mistake.

Emily strode confidently up the garden path and

banged hard on the front door. There was no response. She tried again, just to be on the safe side, but there was still no reply. There was a window to her right with only a thin pair of net curtains dangling inside. She pressed her face up against it, trying to see in. The curtains obscured much of her view but not all of it. She could just make out a sofa, a radio and a fireplace. All perfectly ordinary. There was a door at the far end that lead through to the kitchen and for a moment she thought she saw movement inside. She stepped back from the window. Was someone in there? And if so why weren't they answering the door?

She knocked gently on the window. Perhaps they were a night worker and had only just gone to bed, in which case she was braced to receive a stern telling-off.

'Can I help you?' said a voice to her left.

A woman in a floral pinafore with her hair up in rollers was looking at her over the crumbling garden wall.

'I was looking for Mrs... Verity, is she in?'

The woman eyed her suspiciously.

'No Mrs Verity round here girl. You from London?'

'Yes.'

The woman pursed her lips disapprovingly.

'What address you need?'

'This is Beaumont Road isn't it?' replied Emily remembering a street she had passed along earlier.

The woman rolled her eyes.

'Nay child, this is Salisbury Road. Beaumont is four over,' she said pointing back down the road. 'Go to the crossroads, turn left on to Gwyn Road, keep walking and you can't miss it.'

'Excellent, thank you,' said Emily beating a hasty retreat in the direction the woman had given her.

Emily returned to the docks just in time to see many of the men going on their lunch break. With so many of them taking their break at the same time she almost missed him. Once again it was his gait that gave him away. He walked in a slightly lopsided manner, as if one leg worked better than the other. Whilst the others headed towards the pubs not far from the docks, Albert turned in the opposite direction.

Emily followed him, still keeping her distance. She felt exposed being on her own and thought again that she should have told Jack what she was up to. Even her grandmother might have been of some use, though she supposed an elderly lady dressed in an evening gown might have stuck out somewhat in the surroundings of the docks.

She wondered where Albert was going. He wasn't heading back towards his house for lunch, neither did he seem keen on spending time in the pub with the others, and he kept glancing over his shoulder as if to check he wasn't being followed. Emily was careful never to get too close, hanging back as far as she could. After about ten minutes he turned down a narrow side street. Emily longed to follow, but stayed where she was. It was too risky to trail him down an alley. What if it was a dead end? She could find herself in serious trouble. She should just go back to the docks and wait for him there she thought, but she couldn't bring herself to give up quite yet. She had come to Plymouth to learn about Albert Ferguson, but what had she learnt so far? He worked on the docks and he lived in a house, probably by himself. That wasn't going to get Tommy out of prison any time soon. Maybe she wouldn't find anything out by following him, but she couldn't hope to learn more by doing nothing. She had to decide quickly. She could feel her chance slipping way, every second she waited increased the risk of losing him.

Against her better judgement, she crossed the road and moved stealthily up the cobbled alley. It was narrow, too narrow to fit a car, and high above her head hung a chain of washing lines with sheets strung from them. They billowed in the breeze that whistled its way down the street. The buildings on either side were several stories tall and cast a shadow which fell like silence over the whole lane. Not a soul stirred and she felt with absolute certainty that he had chosen the lane for that very reason. It was the perfect place to meet with someone if your intention was not to be seen.

Emily also did not want to be seen. Fortunately there were a number of sets of small concrete steps that jutted out into the alley behind which she could hide if she needed to. As long as no one came out of any of the houses she would not be seen by Albert, who was standing at the end of passage about forty yards away, smoking a cigarette and staring off down the adjoining path. He appeared to be waiting for someone; he had already checked his watch three times in the past few minutes.

Emily decided to get a little closer. She waited for him to turn his back to her then she shot silently across the alley until she was just twenty yards away, her position concealed by another set of steps which were just large enough to crouch behind. She chanced a glance over them and saw Albert throw his cigarette to the floor and stamp down hard on it.

He picked up his bag, seemingly about to leave, when suddenly he stopped. Emily thought she could hear footsteps. She stayed low, waiting until she heard voices then, very carefully, she peered over the steps once more. Albert was talking to a young man with a sharp suit and a sharper smile. The man was short and his dark hair was slicked back over his head. He was holding a bag identical to the one Albert had on his shoulder.

'How much did you get?' said the man, though it sounded more like an accusation than a question.

'As much as I could,' replied Albert.

The short man peered into the bag Albert had given him and shook his head.

'That's not enough for what we're paying you.'

'I couldn't get anymore, they've clamped down. It was hard enough getting this little lot out. You've got a thousand packs of ciggies there.'

'We were promised two.'

'Well one's all I've got.'

A silence fell between them, a silence that crackled

with the unstated threat of violence. The two men eyed each other fiercely. Emily could tell that Albert was frightened despite having several inches over his adversary, and in the end it was Albert who broke the silence first.

'I can maybe try and get some more tomorrow. It's not easy though. I'm telling you they've started watching us like bleedin' hawks. I get caught and I could end up doing five years in prison.'

'Then don't get caught,' said the other man slowly.

He opened the bag he was carrying and took from it more money than Emily had seen in her entire life. He placed half of it in the bag with the cigarettes, which he kept, then put the rest in the other bag and handed it to Albert.

'Half the goods, half the price. You'll get the rest when we get the rest. Tomorrow. Same time.'

'That... that seems fair,' said Albert, trying to sound casual, though his voice, shrunken with fear, betrayed him.

'More than fair. It's a bloody steal,' said the man flashing his knife-like smile.

'Tomorrow then, same time' said Albert sternly, as if to show that he was the one in charge.

The short man nodded and headed back down the passage the way he had come. Albert waited for him to go. As he did so he fiddled with the collar of his boiler suit and drew himself up to his full height, somehow during their exchange he seemed to have shrunk by several inches. Apparently feeling a better he adjusted the cap on his head, then picked up his canvas bag and began to walk back down the passageway.

To Emily's horror she realised he was coming towards her and there was no way for her to get out without her being spotted. She wondered what he would do if he saw her. He was bound to be cross, she certainly wasn't meant to have seen what she had. What if he was like his brother? Fear bubbled up inside her.

She pressed her body against the steps, praying he

would simply walk by. She heard his footsteps drawing nearer and had to fight the urge to close her eyes. Then all of a sudden the footsteps stopped. Perhaps, she thought crossing her fingers, he had decided to go the other way, but she didn't dare peer round the steps to see. The quiet was broken by the familiar rasp of a match being struck and Emily realised he was lighting another a cigarette. She could smell the burning tobacco. There was a horrible, acrid tang to it, it wasn't sweet like her father's. Albert coughed. Apparently the cigarettes he had stolen weren't very good.

Emily knew she would not get a better opportunity, she had to run for it. If she could just reach the main road she would surely be safe. Without another thought she burst out from behind the steps and sprinted down the alley towards the street. Though she wasn't the fastest she had the element of surprise and it took a few seconds for Albert to realise what was happening.

'Hey!' he shouted after her.

Unfortunately for Emily, Albert was quicker of mind than he was of body, and he hurled the canvas bag at her. Whether by luck or judgement it sailed over her head and landed just in front of her. Before she could get out of the way her feet were tangled up in the handles. She only made it one more step before she lost her balance and went flying head over feet, landing hard on the cobbles, scraping her knees and hands badly. With his long stride he was on her in an instant. He hauled her to her feet, dragging her back down the alley and up against the steps she had been hiding behind. Now there was no chance of anyone seeing them unless they walked right past. He placed his hand over her mouth, smothering her cry for help before it could escape her lips. Emily began to panic and tried to kick at his shins, but he put one of his long legs across hers, which acted like a clamp, pinning her to the wall.

'Whoa there little girl, where are you runnin' off to?'

Emily couldn't reply as he still had his hand over her

mouth.

'What were you up to eh? Little girls shouldn't be playing in dark alleys, they're dangerous.'

He smiled to himself as if he'd just made a particularly funny joke. His breath reeked, a disgusting combination of the cigarettes and the boiled egg he'd eaten for breakfast, tiny bits of which were still visible in his moustache.

'Now I don't know what you saw, or rather what you think you saw, but I don't think it'd be wise to mention it to anyone, do you?'

Emily shook her head. Her heart thumped in her chest and she began to feel faint.

'I'm going to let go and you're not going to scream are you?'

Emily shook her head. Slowly Albert removed his hand from her mouth. Emily did not make a sound.

'Good. Now I meant what I said. I don't want to hurt you, but if you say anything to anyone, things will end very badly for you. Do I make myself clear?' he asked, and from his pocket he produced a sharp flick knife, bringing the blade up to Emily's eyes, a manic grin, creeping across his face.

'What were you doing down here anyway?' he asked her.

'I... I... live here,' she said, indicating the building behind her.

'Oh I very much doubt that,' he said, his smile suddenly falling away. 'Do you want to try again?'

Emily knew she had to think quickly and did her best to look ashamed of herself.

'I... I was meant to be meeting my boyfriend down here.'

Albert smiled knowingly.

'Sailor is he? On leave? You're a bit young for that I'd have thought, still some people like that sort of thing I guess. Well, I won't keep you from lover boy, but remember, if you say just one word I will cut your tongue out of your snitching little mouth. See how your sailor friend likes you then won't we?' he growled.

Suddenly there came a voice from the end of the lane.

'What's going on here?'

At the sound of the voice Albert stepped away from Emily and slipped the blade into his pocket just as a policeman appeared.

'Afternoon officer,' he said with a smile.

'Everything all right miss?' asked the policeman.

Emily nodded, not quite trusting herself to speak yet, worried she might cry. Her whole body was shaking and she couldn't stop it no matter how hard she tried.

'I was just giving this young girl directions to the train station,' said Albert obsequiously.

'I see,' said the policeman, unconvinced. 'Well perhaps it would be best if I escorted the young lady to the station myself.'

'Most kind of you sir,' replied Albert in a voice so greasy Emily was surprised the policeman didn't end up with oil on his uniform.

'Nice to meet you miss,' said Albert, doffing his cap to her before sauntering back up the street.

'And what's your name then young lady?' asked the policeman kindly.

'Emily Verity,' she replied.

'And where do you live?'

'Exeter.'

'I see. What are you doing in Plymouth then? Where's your family?'

'I'm an evacuee, I just got myself a bit lost.'

'Hmmm, very lost I'd say. These streets are no place for a girl such as yourself. You're just lucky a gentleman happened to be passing who saw the two of you together. He asked me to take a look as he thought you appeared somewhat distressed.'

'I'm fine,' Emily managed.

The policeman raised an eyebrow but did not contradict her.

'If I take you to the station will you be able to find your

way back to Exeter okay? Have you got a ticket?'

Emily nodded eagerly. She wanted to get back to the cottage as soon as possible. The kindly policeman led the way and Emily followed, deep in thought. Why had she been so foolish? How did she think she would get away without being seen? It was stupid of her, and it could have been a lot worse if the policeman hadn't arrived when he did. She shuddered at the thought. Would Albert really have stabbed her over some illicit cigarettes? She wasn't sure, but she had put herself in a position where she might have found out.

At the station the policeman bade her farewell. Emily saw a small group of women waiting for the train back to Exeter and she stood as near to them as possible. She didn't want to be on her own for a little while. She was still shaken up, and it was several hours before she began to feel calm again.

At least her trip hadn't been a total waste of time, though what she had learnt had cost her more than she was willing to admit. Albert Ferguson was making money on the black market, stealing cigarettes and selling them on. Of course, this didn't prove he had anything to do with the girls going missing, or that he knew about what his brother had been up to, but it was something. After all, if he was involved in black-marketeering, what else might he be involved in? The brothers were a nasty pair that was for sure.

So deep in thought was she that she almost missed the stop at Exminster, reaching the doors just as the guard was shutting them. She hopped off, offering a garbled apology, and then walked the four miles home under a slowly darkening sky. It was almost 5 o' clock when she got in. She was tired and miserable, but she couldn't let it show. She didn't want Mr Worthington asking too many questions. She switched on the radio and turned up the volume, hoping to drown out the thoughts in her head with the sound of song.

Chapter Sixteen

Emily had not seen Jack since she had told him she had given away the jewellery, so she was a little surprised to find him knocking at her door a few days later, standing there with a bag slung across his shoulders.

'Come on,' he said without so much as a hello, 'we've got an appointment.'

'An appointment with who?' she asked.

'A solicitor.'

'What have you done now?'

'It's not about me. It's about Tommy, and it's with the man who worked on his case. I thought we should talk to him. I tried to see him two days ago, but he was away on business. He always told my ma that if there was ever anything he could do he'd be happy to help, so I made us an appointment.'

'But Peterhouse is dealing with this.'

Jack gave her a look which summed up precisely how he felt about any help Peterhouse might be able to offer.

'In case you've forgotten he's going to shoot me, so excuse me if I don't do summersaults.'

Emily wasn't sure if they could trust Peterhouse either, but she still felt on the whole that he was their best chance of freeing Tommy. The ring they'd found was a vital piece of evidence, but their hope lay in proving that the rest of the jewellery belonged to the other young women who had disappeared long after Jack's brother was sent to prison. If they were going to find out what really happened to them they would need the help of the police.

'So why are we going to see Tommy's solicitor?'

'I'm going to present him with the evidence. The newspapers were a clue; they all have one thing in common, they all contain stories about the missing girls. And then of course there's the ring. You might have given away the other pieces,' he said not bothering to keep the annoyance out of his voice, 'but the ring is the most important one.'

Emily bit her lip.

'You disagree?'

'No I–'

'Don't lie to me Emily, you're a terrible liar.'

'How did you know I was lying?'

'You always bite your lip when you disagree with something but don't want to say so. It's like not saying what you really think for just one second makes you eat your own face.'

Emily laughed and punched him on the arm.

'Shut up.'

He flashed her his familiar lopsided grin, some of their old easiness returning.

'It'll be strange not having you around,' he said. 'I've kinda got used to you.'

'Why Jack, you charmer. I guess I've kinda got used to you too. Still, don't get carried away, I'm not going anywhere just yet.'

'I suppose.'

'And maybe you could come and visit?'

'I don't think they'll let me come to this top-secret Ministry of yours Emily.'

Emily hadn't really thought about that but decided not to dwell on the matter.

'Do you think once this is over you'll go back to school? If your brother is found innocent people will have to leave you alone won't they.'

'I'm done with school. Besides there's no one left that would have me.'

'You could get a job though?'

'I haven't thought much about what'll happen afterwards. We've not really lived together as a family. I mean, we've barely seen each other these last ten years.'

'You've seen your brother though, on visits and the like.'

'Once a month. I was trying to work it out the other day, I think I've seen him for a total of five days in ten years. Five days Emily. I've spent more time with you than I have with him.'

'But he used to take you to football matches...'

Jack's cheeks reddened and Emily's voice trailed away as she realised he'd been lying. He'd never been to the matches with him. It was a fantasy concocted at the start of their friendship, something to make him appear more normal, a brother away in the Merchant Navy who returned home to take him to football matches, because he feared the truth might have driven her away.

She began to reconsider her own life. Before the bombing she'd been pretty lucky. She'd had two parents who loved her, an older sister whom she adored, a good home, nice friends, and Uncle Frank... who meant well at least. And what did Jack have? A brother who was locked up for a crime he didn't commit, the shadow of which hung over every part of his life. He had few friends, little education, and a mother who had to spend most of her time working just to make ends meet.

'Jack, can I ask you something?'

'What?'

'It's personal. You don't have to answer if you don't want to.'

'Okay...' he said warily.

'You never speak about your father. What happened to him?'

'Don't know. Never knew him. He ran out when I was little.'

'Ran out? Where did he go?'

'I don't know and I don't care. The only thing he ever gave me were his carpenter's tools, and that was only because he couldn't be bothered to take them with him. Mum and I look out for each other. We've done alright.'

Emily thought about this last statement. She knew some people would disagree. He'd been thrown out of school, he didn't have a job and his brother was in jail, but somehow he had remained kind and open hearted. That in itself was an achievement. Or at least it was to Emily.

'More than alright I'd say, you're a bloody marvel,' she said with a smile, taking his hand in hers and giving it a squeeze.

Jack's face flushed and their eyes met. Emily felt an unfamiliar rush in her stomach. She let go of his hand as casually as she could, suddenly aware of how awkward her body felt.

'Where is this place anyway?' she asked in an unnaturally loud voice.

'The office is just off Fore Street, near the bank,' replied Jack.

'And what time is the meeting?' she said.

'Eleven.'

'We'd better get a move on then, we don't want to be late.'

She marched up the road almost doubling their speed. On the way she filled him in about her trip to Plymouth and was surprised by Jack's reaction.

'Why didn't you tell me you were going to see his brother?' he snapped.

'I needed to leave early, so there wasn't much time,' she replied, careful not to bite her lip this time, for though what she had told him was the truth, it was not the whole truth. She didn't want to admit that she had been worried at how angry he'd been with her, or that she'd felt the need to do something, anything, to regain his trust. 'Anyway,' she continued, 'the important thing is that now we know more about Albert Ferguson.'

'You could've been killed Em.' He shook his head wearily. 'I thought I was supposed to be the stupid one. You're lucky a policeman came along.'

'I don't need looking after Jack, I'm doing fine.'

'I'm not saying you need looking after, I'm saying you need a friend. You and I, we've got to stick together on this. I could've helped you.'

As much as she hated to admit it, Emily knew that Jack had a point.

'You're right,' she said finally, 'I won't do it again. From now on we're a team.'

'Good.'

'So do you think the brothers were working together?' she asked him, keen to finally discuss her findings.

'I dunno, could be, but just 'cos your brother does something doesn't mean you're automatically the same.'

'I know.'

'In fact, I hope they weren't. I mean, what if Albert tries to claim the jewellery we found was stolen? Better to get a few months in prison for handling stolen goods than get locked up for life isn't it?'

'I hadn't thought of that.'

'He could say he was trying to sell it on the black market on behalf of Ralph and that he hadn't known where he got the jewellery from.'

They continued to speculate until they arrived at a shabby looking set of offices just off Fore Street. Inside was cramped and dimly lit, the window from the street did not offer much in the way of light, and the brown and beige interior swallowed the little it did. Closing the door behind them they were met by a severe looking woman in a long brown dress. She sat at a sturdy wooden desk and was typing at some speed on an ancient typewriter. If it were not for the movement of her hands over the keys it would have been easy for her to blend in with her surroundings. She did not acknowledge their presence and after a few moments Emily cleared her throat loud enough to be heard over the chatter of the machine. The woman looked up and appeared surprised to find anyone else present. She peered at them through her spectacles as if trying to ascertain whether or not they were some sort of illusion. Apparently convinced of their existence, she finally spoke.

'Can I help you?'

'We're here to see Mr Kitson.'

The woman blinked. The thick glasses she was wearing had the effect of making her eyes appear like two giant marbles rattling around inside her head.

'And who are you?'

'We have an appointment,' added Jack quickly.

'I'm sure that you do, but in order for me to confirm this I must first know who you are,' she croaked.

'Copleston. It's Jack Copleston and I have an appointment to see Mr Kitson at 11 o' clock.'

As he said these words a small clock rang out in a discordant impression of the Big Ben chimes.

'You know he really is quite busy, I'm not sure that…'

The door behind her swung open, and a man in a crumpled tweed suit stepped through holding a thin paper file in his hand.

'Mrs Whitelaw I'm expecting a visit from the police shortly, please come and find me, it's important I speak to them.'

'Certainly Mr Kitson. This is Jack Copleston, he says he has an appointment with you,' she said surveying her appointments diary suspiciously, as if Jack had somehow tricked her into putting him in there.

'I've bought my cousin Emily Verity, she needs to come too,' said Jack.

They had discussed this beforehand. They thought it best that people should think they were family in case Mr Kitson objected to discussing the matter of Jack's brother in front of a stranger.

'Of course,' said Mr Kitson, his eyes alighting on Emily for the first time. 'Well, please won't you come on through?'

Mr Kitson was a tall, thin man, wiry, like a pipe cleaner that had been bent out of shape. His wispy brown hair was showing the first touches of grey at the temples and he had a thick moustache, which was also greying. Emily thought his face seemed familiar, but she couldn't quite place him. He closed the door behind them and told them to take a seat whilst he sat back in his worn leather chair, placed the file on top of the tower of papers that were taking over his desk then began to fill his pipe.

'How can I be of assistance?' he said not looking up.

'I'm here about my brother, Thomas Copleston. You dealt with his case several years ago.'

'I'm sorry, you'll have to speak up,' he said, 'I'm a little deaf in my right ear. A little present from the German's last time around.'

'Oh err…' Jack cleared his throat and increased his volume. 'I'm here about my brother, Thomas Copleston. You represented him some years ago.'

Mr Kitson glanced up from studying his pipe and considered Jack for a moment.

'Ah yes, I remember, the murder of the Worthington girl. Terrible business.'

'He didn't do it. Thomas is not guilty Mr Kitson.'

'I see,' said Mr Kitson evenly, 'unfortunately the jury disagreed.'

Emily could tell he was already losing interest, she understood how it must look. A family member comes to him and tells him that their loved one is innocent and should be set free. He must see it so often. For a moment she thought Jack might try and persuade him of the merits of his case, but he knew what he had to do.

'Tell me, is your mother joining us Mr Copleston?'

'No. She doesn't know about this yet.'

'I see,' said Mr Kitson again, frowning this time.

'She's been through so much. I would really appreciate it if we kept it between ourselves until we are certain there is something to report.'

Mr Kitson's mouth twitched at the corners, then he let

out a weary sigh.

'I suppose there is no harm in hearing you out. But I warn you, if you're wasting my time I will have no hesitation in showing you the door.'

'We have new evidence that proves Thomas is innocent,' Jack stated simply.

Mr Kitson leaned forwards, his interest piqued.

'Before we go any further I have to tell you that any new evidence would need to be very strong to force a re-trial.'

'I know,' said Jack, 'I wouldn't have come to you if I didn't think... I wouldn't waste your time if it was something trivial.'

Mr Kitson lit his pipe and leaned back in his chair. They had his full attention now.

'We think we know who really killed Clara Worthington.'

'I see. And you say you have evidence to support your claim?'

'Yes.'

'Very well. May I ask what it is?'

Emily waited for Jack to produce the ring but he seemed to be hesitating, she looked at him.

'Mr Copleston,' said Mr Kitson in an agitated manner, 'I don't wish to appear rude, I know you must have been through an awful lot but I have a great deal of work to be getting on with so if we could perhaps hurry this along?'

Emily could see the doubts beginning to settle in Jack's mind. Suddenly he was in the world of adults, his eloquence had deserted him. She knew he was smart, smarter than he believed anyway, but his confidence was low. He was too afraid of letting his brother down.

'There was a man, he worked at the Imperial Hotel in Exeter as a porter and he attacked me,' said Emily taking the lead in the hope that Jack would follow.

'He attacked you?'

'Yes, at the hotel, he tried to force himself on me. I'm thirteen years old. I was there to see someone who was

273

staying at the hotel but she had gone out. He offered to let me stay in her room as it was very late, then he attacked me.'

'I see. And when did this happen?'

'A few weeks ago.'

'Did you inform the police?'

'No. No I didn't tell anyone.'

'May I ask why not?'

'It's complicated,' said Emily.

Mr Kitson chewed his pipe thoughtfully.

'Ah yes. I thought I knew your face. You were the girl who vomited on my shoes as I recall. My colleague Julie looked after you.'

That whole night was such a muddle in her head that it came as no surprise to her that she hadn't recognised him sooner.

'I'm sorry about your shoes,' said Emily, at a loss for what else to say.

'I think, given the circumstances, that's quite all right. Still, taking what you've said to be true, what does that have to do with Thomas Copleston?'

'A few days after Emily was attacked,' began Jack, but before he could say more he was interrupted by a knock at the door.

'Mr Kitson,' said the secretary poking her head around the door, 'the police are here to see you regarding the Ferguson case.'

'Thank you, Mrs Whitelaw. Would you excuse me a moment?' he said to Jack and Emily and left the room.

'Did she just say the police were here about the Ferguson case?' said Jack, getting up out of his seat and starting to pace around the room. He always fidgeted when he was nervous, Emily had noticed.

'Ferguson is a common name though, it could easily be someone else,' she replied. But Jack wasn't listening, he was look over the files that were piled up on Mr Kitson's desk.

'Perhaps we should find out for ourselves,' he said

leaning forwards and plucking the file from the top of the pile.

The file was only thin, it had various notes and memos within, but on top was a letter from the Exeter Police Force that must have been delivered that very morning.

Dear Mr Kitson,

I am writing to you in relation to the last will and testament of Mr Ralph Ferguson who was declared dead on 21/02/1941. Due to a severe administrative error, the previous report and its findings must be immediately discarded. We no longer believe that the body found in the River Exe was that of Ralph Ferguson, and as a result I must instruct you not to proceed with the division of his estate until this matter can be adequately resolved.

If you have any information that may be of use to us in our ongoing inquiries regarding Mr Ferguson's whereabouts, or if any persons claiming to be Mr Ferguson contacts you, then please let me or my officers know presently.

Thank you for your cooperation in this matter,

Chief Inspector Rowsell
Exeter City Police

There was another knock at the door and the secretary scuttled in. Jack hid the file behind his back.

'Mr Kitson is sorry about the delay,' she informed them, 'and asks if you would like anything to drink whilst you wait?'

Emily and Jack assured her that they didn't, though this just seemed to upset her. Perhaps, she felt, when offered a drink by a man such as Mr Kitson, one should always accept. She closed the door behind her and Jack put the file back on the desk.

'What do you make of that?' asked Jack.

'It's very odd,' said Emily, picking up the file Jack had just discarded. "If you have any information regarding Mr Ferguson's possible whereabouts..." Does that mean he isn't dead?'

'I don't know. I'm not sure if they even know, but it looks that way.'

'And that's a heck of an "administrative error" don't you think?' said Emily, her mind racing now. 'Hey, do you think maybe Ralph Ferguson burnt down his own house?'

Jack opened his mouth to reply but Emily cut him off.

'Why do that though? What was he afraid of? And why did he wait till he was "dead" to look for it?'

'He must have been really worried about something I guess. Why else would you fake your own death?' said Jack catching up with her. 'Perhaps he was scared you would tell someone about what happened.'

'No, I don't think it was that, and even if it was, why burn the house down? If you've died already, why do that? The only evidence in that house that we found were the newspapers and the jewellery. If he was worried about someone finding them he could have got rid of them ages ago.'

'Maybe there was something else then, something we missed.'

'Like what?'

'I don't know, something that needed destroying.'

Emily shook her head. They were clutching at straws.

'Maybe he needed the money?' she said.

'Is there a will in there?' asked Jack pointing to the file. Emily flicked through.

'No. Nothing. Why would you fake your own death, then return to your house to burn it down and risk being seen? It doesn't make sense. Even if he needed the money, burning the house down wouldn't help would it? He could hardly claim the insurance if he was dead.'

'So maybe it wasn't him. I don't know. Maybe... maybe the brothers had a falling out. Maybe that was

276

actually Albert Ferguson who they found in the river?' he said excitedly.

'No, you're forgetting, I saw him up close yesterday. It was definitely Albert I met, not Ralph.'

'Oh... oh yeah.'

Silence fell between them as they chewed over this new information.

'Do you think,' said Jack finally, 'that you should tell Mr Kitson about meeting Albert? Y'know, about what he was up to?'

'No, I don't think so. I already told him about Ralph Ferguson attacking me, if I mention the theft and black-marketeering that his brother gets up to, he might think I've got it in for the family. Besides he'd only have my word for it, I don't have any proof.'

There was a noise from outside and Emily quickly shoved the letter back in the file and chucked it onto the desk. Mr Kitson returned still puffing on his pipe, and eased into his chair with a small groan.

'It's only 11.15 and I'm already exhausted. Sorry about the delay, I trust Mrs Whitelaw offered you something to drink?'

'Yes, thank you.'

'Right, you were saying about your brother's case?'

'The person who attacked Emily was Ralph Ferguson,' said Jack.

The name clearly registered with Mr Kitson because he frowned and leaned forwards again, tugging gently at his ear.

'Forgive me, did I hear you correctly? Ralph Ferguson? I'm struggling to see what this has to do with your broth–'

'We think Mr Ferguson was responsible for the murder of Clara Worthington and the disappearances of several other girls over the years.'

'And what brings you do this conclusion?'

'I know it wasn't my brother,' said Jack quickly 'and how many murderers do you think Exeter is hiding?'

Mr Kitson looked as if he were trying to contain his

frustration.

'I'm asking you for evidence and you're giving me accusations. I'm afraid if you don't have anything then I will have to cut this meeting short.'

'We have evidence,' replied Emily firmly.

'So you've said, but all you've bought me so far are unsubstantiated allegations. Little more than rumour and tittle-tattle.'

Jack spoke up.

'When I heard that he had died I realised the only hope of clearing my brother's name was to see if we could find something, anything, at his house.'

Mr Kitson looked alarmed.

'I must warn you, you are not my clients, so if you have anything to do with the fire on Howell Road the other evening I would be required by law to report that to the police.'

'We didn't burn his house down, but we did break into it, replied Jack, 'and whilst we were there we found a box of jewellery which included the ring that my brother gave to Clara Worthington on their engagement, the missing ring.'

'Jack, I can see you desperately want to get your brother out of prison and that is very commendable, but you're in real danger of landing yourself in trouble. I think we should stop this discussion right now.'

'No,' said Jack in a panicked voice, 'that's not the only thing. The jewellery, Emily tell him about the jewellery.'

There were tears in his eyes. He was watching his one chance of freeing Tommy disappear.

'There was other jewellery in the box. We believe it belongs to the other girls that have disappeared.'

'And do you have any proof of this?'

'There were also newspapers from years ago,' Emily continued, retrieving a few of the papers from Jack's bag, 'the only ones that were kept were the ones reporting on the disappearances of the girls.'

Mr Kitson frowned as he looked over them.

'That is a little… odd I grant you, but I'm sure he would argue he just had an interest in those cases. It might be distasteful, but not illegal.'

'But if the police investigate the jewellery and find it has come from the missing girls?'

'If they find out you took the jewellery from this gentleman's house, then you'll just get yourself in trouble and your evidence will likely be disregarded, after all who's to say that you didn't plant it there yourselves?'

'But we didn't,' said Jack indignant at the idea of it.

'Surely,' said Emily intervening 'the police could take the pieces to the families and find out if they belonged to them or not.'

'I suppose they could do that, but as unlikely as it sounds they could just say you had bought the pieces yourselves. It isn't strong enough to get your brother released I'm afraid, and with Mr Ferguson dead there is no chance of getting a confession out of him.'

'But Mr Ferguson isn't really dead is he?' said Emily.

Mr Kitson paused and his eyes flicked towards the file on his desk. Emily made sure to keep her gaze steady and focused on Mr Kitson's face.

'Who told you that?' he asked sharply.

'No one. We saw him for ourselves,' she lied.

Out of the corner of her eye she saw Jack open his mouth as if he was about to say something, then change his mind.

'You saw him?'

'The night of the fire, the night we broke into his house. He was looking for something. I think it was the jewellery box.'

Jack shifted nervously in his seat next to her.

'So you were in the house on the night of the fire?'

'Yes but we didn't have anything to do with it I promise.'

Mr Kitson took his pipe from his mouth and laid it on the desk in front of him.

'I am the executor of his estate, I suppose… you're

certain you saw him?'

'Absolutely,' replied Emily meeting his gaze.

'Then we need to tell the police.'

'No,' said Emily 'that can't happen. If it comes to light how we found these items they would never believe us, you said it yourself.'

'Perhaps... no that's not right...'

'What?' said Jack and Emily in unison.

'Perhaps you could leave the jewellery with me. I will make my own discreet enquiries and, *if* what you say is true, then I suppose I could make them part of his estate and "discover" them for myself, then bring them to the attention of the police.'

He grimaced, clearly having second thoughts.

'This is highly irregular you know? But I always believed in your brother's innocence.'

'Please Mr Kitson,' said Emily fixing him with a stare, 'I know this is difficult, but isn't this what we are fighting for? For the right to be free? And Jack's brother has had that right taken from him. We are begging you for a chance, however slight, of proving his innocence.'

Mr Kitson did not reply but took up his pipe again and lit it.

'He has never changed his story. That would work in his favour, a lot of men faced with the gallows suddenly find God and repent their sins, your brother has never wavered. I think the judge believed he was innocent too. He should have hanged for what he was convicted of, that he didn't was purely down to the judge. As it stands this won't be enough to prove his innocence, but it could at least open the door to the crime being reinvestigated.'

'But–' Jack started to speak but Mr Kitson cut him off.

'He has been found guilty by a court of law Mr Copleston. This isn't proof of his innocence but it does cast in to doubt certain facts about the case. He still can't remember what happened that night?'

'No.'

'That's a pity. The jury held that against him.'

'But if Mr Ferguson's still alive, then there's still a chance isn't there?'

'If he is still alive, and I am not saying that he is, but *if* he is still alive that could have some bearing on this case.'

'Thank you, Mr Kitson,' said Jack.

'Don't thank me yet, we've still a long road ahead of us,' he said with a weary smile.

But Emily could tell that Jack wasn't listening. He was already picturing the day his brother would walk through the gates of Exeter prison a free man.

'Have you the items we discussed with you?'

Emily glanced at Jack.

'No, the jewellery is with a friend for safe keeping.'

'Miss Verity, if I'm going to help you're going to have to give me the jewellery. Without it I have nothing to go on.'

'I have my grandmother's ring,' said Jack retrieving it from his jacket pocket.

'Well, that's something at least. In the meantime I shall make some enquiries, but please don't get your hopes up. Bring me the rest of the pieces as soon as you can. Given that your mother doesn't know about this, how would you like me to contact you if the need arises?'

'You should talk to Emily first,' said Jack. 'I don't want my ma to hear about this until we're certain. She's been through too much already. If this doesn't work there's no need that she ever know.'

Emily jotted down her address and was relieved to see Mr Kitson lock the ring in his office safe.

'We can't...' Jack began, looking slightly ashamed. 'I can't pay you anything for this, at least not yet...'

'That's not a problem,' said Mr Kitson. 'In this instance perhaps we can settle on a fee further down the line, once I've seen where my investigations lead me.'

'Thank you,' said Jack eagerly.

'Now, if you don't mind, I really have to be getting on.'

Emily and Jack let themselves out under the watchful eye of Mrs Whitelaw. Emily glanced back and saw her sneaking a look at them between a gap in the blinds, only to pull them shut the moment she was spotted. Emily smiled to herself, for the first time since she had come to Exeter she felt like she was making a difference. If they could get Tommy out of prison then she could leave Exeter having achieved something wonderful, and it would mean so much to Jack. She could never reunite her own family, but perhaps she could reunite someone else's.

Chapter Seventeen

Emily was undertaking her least favourite of all the chores, washing hers and Mr Worthington's clothes, when a note was pushed through the letter box. Normally it was only her grandmother who sent her notes, but this was written in a hand she did not recognise. She opened it up and started reading.

Dear Verity,

Please be at the phone box on Exwick Hill at four p.m. precisely.

Yours,

Bradman

At first, she thought it must have been delivered to her by mistake. She opened the front door looking for whoever had brought it, but there was no one to be seen. The address on the front of the envelope was neatly written and stated clearly that it was for Verity at the Station Master's Cottage. Emily wandered back into the living room and settled down in Mr Worthington's old armchair to read the note again. Verity? She didn't know any girls called Verity did she? She hardly knew anyone in Exeter other than Jack and her grandmother. Perhaps it was for Mr Worthington's wife? But no, her name was Elsie, and she died several years before.

The note was from someone called Bradman. The only Bradman she knew was... and then it hit her. Verity and Bradman. Why had she not thought of it before? Hedley Verity was her favourite cricketer, and Donald Bradman was the batsman she always pretended to bowl against. There was only one other person in the world who knew that. The note must be from her father. She frowned and read it again, a bubble of worry forming in the pit of her stomach. If the note was from her father then why didn't he just say so? Was it meant to be a joke? No, she decided, it wasn't a joke; it was a code. But why? The bubble grew a little larger. If her father felt the need to communicate in code then it meant he was in trouble. She glanced at the clock that hung next to the back door. It was 3.47 already. Without further delay she ran out of the house and arrived at the red phone box on Exwick Hill just as a shrill ringing started up inside. Emily opened the door and lifted the receiver.

'A call for a Miss E. Verity from a Mr D. Bradman,' said the operator.

A mixture of fear and panic flooded her body, why was he calling her now? And why all the subterfuge? She had only ever received letters from him before, never a phone call, not in all the time he had been in Exeter.

'Shall I connect him?' asked the operator.

'Oh yes, of course, sorry,' said Emily.

With a click the operator was gone.

'Emily?'

'Dad?'

'I'm so glad you're okay,' his relief rushed down the telephone line in the form of a sigh, as if he had been holding his breath until she picked up the receiver.

'What's going on?' she asked, the little thrill she had at hearing his voice again giving way to concern. 'Are you alright? Is everything okay?'

'I'm fine. I just needed to speak to you.'

There was a long silence broken only by the crackle on the line. Her father's voice sounded dim and distant. She wondered where he was calling from.

'Dad?'

'Sorry, I'm still here.'

'What did you want to speak to me about? Why are you sending me coded messages?'

'It was just a precaution.'

'But why not call the house? We have a telephone there.'

'Which is bugged I expect. This will probably be the nearest telephone box to you that isn't.'

'Bugged? Who by?'

'The Ministry of course.'

'Oh. Them.'

Emily didn't know what else to say. At once she was reminded of all of his lies, of everything he had kept from her, and she felt her grip tighten on the receiver.

'I know you've had a visit from a man calling himself Peterhouse,' said her father.

'Yes.'

'He told you some things, didn't he? Some things about me.'

'He told me some things you should have told me yourself.'

'Believe me when I say this, I have only been trying to keep you safe.'

The worry that had been building in Emily's stomach disappeared beneath the hot flame of her anger.

'You *keep* saying that, but so far you've only made things worse, and you haven't stopped me getting hurt.'

'I know that, I know,' his voice was quiet, almost confessional, 'please you must understand, I never meant for any of this to happen.'

'Tell me the truth then,' said Emily, who in contrast to her father was practically shouting, 'that's the only way you can keep me safe. Trust me to make up my own mind.'

There was another long pause before her father finally spoke.

'What do you want to know?'

Emily thought for a moment.

'Why did you lie about Grandma Josephine being dead?'

'She found you?'

'Why didn't you want me to live with her?'

'It's difficult Emily. It always is with families.'

'That's not an answer.'

Her father sighed.

'Your grandmother is a great woman, truly she is. But she is a terrible mother. I didn't trust her to look after you, or to look out for your best interests.'

'I like her,' said Emily stubbornly.

'Of course you do, she's very likeable, and you share certain... characteristics.'

'You mean our abilities?'

'No, it's more than that. I mean both of you are inclined to speak your mind –'

'But you –'

'Regardless of whether it is the wisest course of action,' he said before she could interrupt. 'Money will only have made her worse. It insulates you from consequences. People will excuse all kinds of behaviour in a rich person that they wouldn't tolerate from someone poorer. If you can pay enough then all of life's little difficulties and complications disappear. The cooker is broken? Buy a new one. You don't like cleaning? Have someone else do it. You need petrol? Someone will find it for you. You begin to exist in a painless bubble and you forget how life takes its toll on others. You are kind Emily, you have a good heart. My mother... well she's not unkind, but she doesn't empathise with others in the way you do. I don't wish to sound cruel, but if you didn't have the gifts you do, then I think it's unlikely she would have come looking for you. You wouldn't have been interesting enough. After all, she had thirteen years already, and she never visited, rang or wrote.'

'She said that was because you forbade it.'

'You've met her, do you really think that would have stopped her? She's always done as she pleased and I didn't want you to live with her because I was worried that she would put you at risk.'

'You mean you'd rather send me to a stranger?'

'Mr Worthington's not a stranger, at least not to me. We were in the same regiment during the Great War. We fought side-by-side in the trenches. I hope I don't sound like I'm boasting, but I saved his life at Mametz. He's an honourable and decent man. I knew his daughter had died a few years ago, and I thought that you might do each other some good.'

Emily thought back to the photo which hung on the dining room wall, the one of Mr Worthington dressed in his uniform, surrounded by his fellow soldiers. The boy at the back of the group who was pulling a face at his friend. Had that really been her father? She had not thought on it since the first night she came to Exeter because the photo had made her so sad, but she made a note to look at it again the second she got back.

'Why didn't you tell him about me? Or tell me about him? We had something in common all along and I never knew.'

'I haven't spoken to him in years, but I was looking through the list of families who had offered homes to evacuees and his name stood out. I thought it was a happy accident, but I didn't contact him because I didn't want anyone to make that link between us, just in case word got out to the Ministry. It seems as if all my precautions were useless anyway. Peterhouse must've been following you since before the bombing. Let me tell you though, you're safer with a man like Arthur Worthington than you are with the Ministry or your grandmother.'

'But why?'

'Your grandmother is reckless. She is obsessed by her

ability, it is the only thing that really means anything to her and I feared she would push you to make the most of your powers, whether you wanted to or not. She wouldn't think twice about putting you in danger if it was interesting to her. She was no mother to any of us. She resented us, can you believe that? Her own children. You don't know what that's like Emily, to grow up in a house where your presence is accepted only begrudgingly.'

Emily's mind immediately turned to Uncle Frank and she wondered how she would have coped if he had been her father instead. But Grandma Josephine was as far from Uncle Frank as it was possible to be wasn't she?

'She'd always been free-spirited,' her father continued, 'but then we came along and we stopped her from doing whatever she wanted, whenever she wanted. The biggest crime you can commit in my mother's eyes is to be dull, and Frank and I just weren't fun enough for her. But my sister was different. Through Charlotte my mother could relive her youth. She pushed her to explore her powers before she was ready and it ended in disaster. Lottie began to believe that her abilities would protect her no matter what, that she could never be caught unprepared. In a way I think mother did too. But a Seer cannot always understand everything she Sees. Lottie became complacent, arrogant even, everyday life was boring to her, so she started seeking out risk and adventure.'

'What happened to Lottie?'

'There is still so much you don't know yet about Seeing. There is more to it than simply looking into the future, there are other factors at play. Did you know that you can be tricked into seeing things that aren't really there?'

'How can I be made to see something that doesn't exist?' said Emily, confused.

'The world is not made up of Seers and normal people. There are others with special abilities, all sorts of abilities in fact. In the same way that you can See, others can Project. That is, they can force people to see what they want them to see. It doesn't just work on Seers, it works on everyone. A person with that power could stand in front of you one moment as one person, then return minutes later as someone else and you would never know.'

'But what do they do exactly? They change their faces, their bodies?'

'No, they simply change how you view them, your perception of them. By doing this they can implant false memories and, in Seers cases, false visions. If you were on your own with a Projector they could show you a whole scene that only existed in your head. A powerful Projector could convince you that you were drowning on dry land.'

'How do you know all this?'

'Because I'm one of them.'

It took a moment for his words to register with Emily.

'You're… a Projector?'

'Yes.'

Once again her father had withheld an important piece of information from her. He'd kept her at a distance. Her rage and frustration began to simmer up again.

'Why didn't you tell me this before?'

'What difference would it have made?'

'I… I… It might have kept me safer,' said Emily although she did not know how.

'Forgive me Emily, I'm trying my best, I don't know how to handle all of this any better than you do. I've made so many mistakes in my life. I didn't think I would be away from you for so long, I thought I should give you time to adjust to all that has happened before piling on with even more.'

'What happened to Lottie?'

'There is a view – it's not one I have ever seen any evidence for – but there is a view that powers can be consumed. By killing another person with power you can increase your own.'

'Kill a Seer and become a Seer?'

'Not quite. More like it amplifies the ability you have. As I've said there's no proof for this, but some of the old texts talk about it. Lottie was unfortunate enough to run into someone who believed this nonsense whole-heartedly.'

'And he killed her?'

'Yes. She shouldn't have had to go through what she did, she should have been warned, but that was mother, she never stopped to think. In all your time together has she ever mentioned Projectors?'

'No, but then neither had you until now.'

'I know. And maybe I should have done back in the hospital, I just... it was so much for you to take in. But your grandmother has had time and she hasn't changed. She hasn't learned, because she is still too interested in the powers themselves and not the people who hold them. That's why I didn't trust her with you. I've only ever tried to protect you, and I know it hasn't been enough. There's still more I need to tell you but I can't be on here for much longer.'

'Then I have to ask you something and you have to promise to answer truthfully. Do you promise that?'

'Emily...'

'Do you promise?'

'I promise.'

'Are you a Shadow Catcher?'

'How did you know about them?'

'Just answer the question.'

'Yes. It is my job to track down those with abilities like yours and mine and bring them over to our side.'

'What are they like?'

'What are who like?'

'The people... the ones with abilities?'

'They're all different.'

'Have you ever had to kill one of them?'

'Emily...'

'Have you?'

'No.'

Emily nodded to herself. It was some conciliation she supposed. Her father continued.

'I know you must have a thousand questions for me, and I will come home as soon as I can, but right now you have to trust me. What did Peterhouse want from you? What did he offer in return?'

'The Ministry want to bring me back to London. They are frightened the Nazis might find me. They think I could be a weapon.'

'You mustn't go with them.'

'But –'

'No Emily. Things are happening there, things I can't explain. The Ministry isn't what it once was, the war has changed them. There are a few good men left, Peterhouse might be one of them for all I know. And he may think what he is doing is for the best but once you're in their clutches they will never let you go. You can't trust them. You can't trust anyone.'

'But don't you work for the Ministry?'

He gave a short, bitter laugh.

'I created the Ministry. This is all my doing in a way. I thought if I built a place that people with abilities could come together and work together for a common goal, that we could do wonderful things. But it's changed, I no longer have the influence I once did.'

'Why not?'

'Many reasons, not the least of which is that I traded it to keep you safe, to keep you from their clutches. But now it makes no difference, they found you anyway.'

Then a thought occurred to Emily, then another and another. A cascade of thoughts and realisations which hit her like a series of blows to the stomach.

'Mum… she didn't know about me being a Seer did she? You never told her.'

'No.'

'And you couldn't tell her could you?'

'No.'

'Because if you told her about that, you'd have to come clean about everything else.'

There was no reply.

'Dad?'

'I'm still here.'

His voice sounded so small.

'Mum didn't know about you, did she? She didn't know you were a Projector. That's why you didn't tell her about me, because you would have had to tell her about what you could do too.'

'I wanted to tell her so much.'

'Then why didn't you?'

The line fell silent again but she could hear her father breathing. Finally he spoke, slowly and carefully.

'When you love someone Emily, you want them to accept you as you are, warts and all. You are so vulnerable. When you're courting, sometimes you hide those parts of yourself you worry about the most, the bits that make you seem different or odd. But there comes a point where you have to reveal them or stay silent, because to admit you've been hiding a side of yourself, to admit that you have – in effect – been lying all that time, becomes a problem of its own. I kept quiet for too long, and by the time I realised that I should have said something, it was already too late. It became easier to say nothing. And it did no harm, or at least it didn't to start with. I had a wonderful family, a wonderful life, and I was able to keep pushing the decision to tell her about my ability – our abilities – further and further back.'

Emily heard what sounded like a muffled gun shot from the other end of the line, followed by shouting in a language she didn't recognise.

'Dad, is everything okay?'

'I... I must go. I'm sorry, I wish I had more time. Listen to me, if you get in any trouble, any trouble at all, find Mr Worthington. He had his suspicions about me, about my abilities and about what I could do. I used them with the men, when they were at their lowest I gave them the happiest dreams of home they could ever have wished for. He'll remember. I saved his life. Tell him that you are the daughter of Captain David Cartwright of the 8th

Devonshire Regiment and that the time has come to repay the debt that he owes me. If all else fails Emily, go to your grandmother, her money should be good for something, but don't let her lure you in. Remember she cares more about your powers than about you. And remember one other thing above all others, and that is that I love you.'

The line went dead and Emily placed the phone slowly back on the hook. Once again her world had been turned on its head. Emily felt more lost than ever. Her father had finally told her the truth, or what he claimed was the truth, and things were murkier than they had been before. He had never shared his secret with her mother – his own wife! She could hardly believe it. She thought back to all those times she had seen them together laughing and joking, so in love, and yet she had never known this whole other side to him.

And what about her grandmother? Was he right? Was she the terrible mother he thought she was? Or was that his grief talking? Was she truly responsible for his sister's death, or was he just lashing out, looking for someone to blame? Emily remembered how angry she'd been with her grandmother when she hadn't come back to Exeter after she was attacked. She could never imagine her mother behaving like that.

She thought again about her father's newly revealed ability. It made her uncomfortable. The idea that someone could control her mind was quite terrifying. Projectors could look like anyone, but you would never know if they were really themselves or if what you were seeing was true, you could no longer believe your own senses.

She felt so confused she wanted to scream. She needed to talk to someone and the only person she could talk to was Jack. She raced across town but was surprised when she arrived at his house to find the front door wide open. She could hear voices inside.

'Hello?' Emily called out.

The door to the kitchen swung open to reveal Rosie standing with an expectant look upon her face.

'Oh,' she said when she saw Emily, 'hello Emily love, I thought you might be Jack. You haven't seen him have you? Only no one has seen him since yesterday afternoon and he didn't come home last night.'

'No, I'm sorry,' said Emily.

'When did you last see him?' asked Rosie.

'Erm... yesterday morning.'

'You need to call the police,' came another woman's voice.

Rosie ushered Emily through into the kitchen which was packed with the women from the street. Apparently the neighbours had all been summoned in the hunt for Jack. Tea was being consumed in an endless cycle as each woman took their turn at keeping Rosie calm.

'I'm not calling the police, I've already lost one of my boys to those buggers... what'll they say when I tell them he's missing? Try and fix him up for something he hasn't done I shouldn't wonder.'

'Don't upset yourself Rosie, boys 'll be boys. He'll probably turn up sometime this afternoon wondering what all the fuss is about and asking after his dinner,' said another woman and the council of neighbours nodded their heads in agreement.

Rosie made a half-hearted attempt to smile.

'Ron's out looking for him, so are Bill and Jim. I'm sure they'll find him.'

Emily wondered where Jack might be. They had agreed, they were a team. She was sure if he was doing something like investigating the Fergusons then he'd have come and found her first. A feeling nagged at her. The Fergusons. What if they'd somehow found out what she and Jack were up to? If Ralph was still alive and had seen them at his house, maybe he had gone after Jack. Or what about Mr Kitson? They had told him what they suspected only the day before and suddenly Jack had disappeared, was that just a coincidence? After all, how much did they really know about him? Perhaps he was in league with them, or maybe they had been watching his offices for some reason? Jack trusted Mr Kitson, he had lived in Exeter for years and had defended his brother in court, but maybe he was involved in some way, though how she couldn't say. It was all just speculation. She had not a shred of proof for any of her theories. Suddenly Emily knew what she had to do.

'Rosie, if you don't mind, I think I'll go and look for him. You never know, I might be able to help,' she shrugged.

Rosie wasn't really listening but gave her a gentle squeeze of her arm. Emily tiptoed upstairs to Jack's room. It was small, barely big enough to fit a bed and some drawers and it was made all the smaller by the clothes and shoes he left scattered around the place, like his dirty football boots which were strewn across the floor, one at each end.

Emily wasn't really sure how, or even if, she could See in the way that a true Seer like her grandmother could. Her visions so far were either involuntary or very simple, easy things with definitive outcomes. It was possible she wouldn't be able to See anything useful at all. Still, the last time she had Seen the future properly had been down in the passages when she was lying next to Jack. Perhaps recreating that moment would allow her to See again. She had to try at least, she owed Jack that much.

She closed the door behind her so that she wouldn't be disturbed, and from his drawer she pulled a dirty looking shirt. She held it up to her face and breathed it in deeply. She closed her eyes and breathed in again, even deeper this time, trying to capture every last scent, the mixture of sweat, soap, grass, sausages, mud and butter.

She felt a familiar stretching but then nothing. What did this mean? Was he dead? Or had she simply not done it right? She tried again and this time she was met by a new smell, a damp, mouldy sort of smell but seconds later it was gone. She sat down on his bed and tried to remember the techniques her grandmother had taught her, to focus only on the moment, not what comes after or before, just be in the place, live it. She closed her eyes, shutting her mind to everything else.

Suddenly she was back in the dark of the passages.

Her surprise at succeeding knocked her out of the vision. They had agreed, neither of them would go back to the passages. Why would he be there? She tried again, and once more she found herself in the passages, the cloying darkness, the narrow walls and scent of stagnant water. She could hear footsteps nearby and she was sure there was a figure, just beyond her in the darkness. Someone was running towards her, she was sure of it.

The vision disappeared. Emily tried twice more but with no luck. She wanted to keep trying but she was wary of the tiredness that followed. She would be no good to Jack if she couldn't go and find him. Another thought began to trouble her. How could she be sure she was getting it right? What if she had looked weeks into the future and not minutes? Still at least he was still alive, that was something. And what else did she have to go on? She ripped the pocket off the shirt and pushed it up her sleeve in case she needed to See some more, she wouldn't be able to do it without help.

Emily headed downstairs and then sprinted back to the cottage to fetch a torch. Knowing how dark it was down in the passages she felt certain she would need it. She grabbed the one that hung by the back door and was just about to leave when the phone began to ring. Her first instinct was to ignore it, but then she thought it might be her father again. If he was ringing a phone that he suspected of being bugged then it would be a real emergency.

'Hello?'

'Emily?' came a voice at the other end.

Expecting it to be her father, it took her a few seconds to recognise the speaker.

'Peterhouse?' said Emily.

'Yes, it's me. I've got some important news.'

Emily was barely listening, she was too worried about Jack to be bothered by anything that Peterhouse considered important news.

'I'm quite busy right now Peterhouse, Jack's gone missing.'

'I know.'

Emily was taken aback, and her mistrust of Peterhouse began to rise to the surface once more. How did he know? Was he responsible for his disappearance somehow?

'That's why I'm calling,' he continued. 'I've been a fool. I thought the danger was from without, but really it was from within.'

'You're not making any sense Peterhouse, what has this got to do with Jack?'

'Forgive me, I'm getting ahead of myself. As you know I've been investigating Tommy Copleston's conviction since we spoke a few nights ago and I discovered something. I can't believe… anyway it doesn't matter right now. What's important is that we get you somewhere safe.'

'Like London you mean? Look, if this is all just –'

'No, not like London,' he snapped, 'you have to believe me, you're in real danger.'

'So you've said for the past… I don't know how long. What is it this time?'

She was losing patience with him, Jack could be in trouble and he was wasting her time. Suddenly there was a knocking at the door.

'Hold on a moment,' she said, hoping it might be Jack, 'I'll be right back.'

Emily placed the receiver down on the table next to the cradle and rushed to open the door. To her surprise an agitated Mr Kitson was standing on the doorstep.

'Ah Emily, I'm glad you're here, I bring news and Jack said to update you if I found out anything important.'

'Oh hello,' she said, 'if you wouldn't mind waiting here a moment, I won't be long. I'm just on the phone.'

In truth he had come at a bad time, but he had information about Jack's brother and there was a chance it could be related to Jack's disappearance, even if he didn't realise it. Mr Kitson did as he was asked, and Emily picked up the phone again to speak to Peterhouse.

'Are you still there?'

'Who was that at the door?'

'Just Tommy's solicitor. Jack got in touch with him after we found the jewellery box.'

'Emily listen to me you're in the most terrible danger. It's Kitson, it's all to do with Kitson. You must get out of there right now. Meet me at the cathedral as soon as you can, I'm not far away.'

'But –'

'No buts. Run, run as fast as you can and don't talk to anyone. Stick to the main roads, stay where you can be seen by as many people as possible at all times. You need to get away from Kitson. Get out now. Run!' he urged her down the crackle of the phone.

Emily placed the receiver back on the cradle and readied herself to run, but when she looked round she found her path blocked by Mr Kitson who was standing in the doorway, and from the look on his face he knew what she had just been told.

'You're finished,' he said with a smile that was more of a grimace, 'excellent. Now we can talk.'

Chapter Eighteen

Emily dropped the torch that she was holding. It clattered to the ground, bursting open, spilling out its batteries which rolled slowly across the stone floor.

'Sorry I didn't mean to startle you,' said Mr Kitson.

'Oh erm… no problem… I was err… I was…' Emily could barely get her words out. She couldn't let him know there was a problem. She had to get away.

'Who were you talking to?'

'When?'

'Just now on the telephone.'

'No one.'

'No one?'

'No, not no one. What I mean is erm… it was…' she was hit by a flash of inspiration, 'it was Mr Worthington calling from the station to say he'd be coming home soon for lunch.'

'I see,' Kitson said, bending down to pick up the batteries which had come to a halt at his feet. 'Anyway, I have news for you.'

'Good news?'

'I think so,' he said handing back the batteries to Emily and closing the distance between them to just a few feet.

'What's that then?' asked Emily, wanting to appear interested whilst desperately plotting her best way out of the cottage.

'It's regarding Jack.'

'What about Jack?' she said sharply.

'Why don't we go through to the front room where we can discuss this properly?'

Emily hesitated.

'Is there a problem?'

'No. Not at all,' she said.

'These old bones of mine are creaking a little today Miss Cartwright,' said Mr Kitson with a warm smile, 'maybe if we sit down then I can explain everything.'

He held out an arm gesturing to the front room, but Emily still didn't move. If she went into the front room she would be trapped. At least where she was she might be able to make a dash for the door. Mr Kitson's expression remained unchanged and just for a moment Emily wondered if Peterhouse had got it wrong, or if he was actually trying to stop her listening to what Mr Kitson had to say. Perhaps Peterhouse was the real danger.

'Miss Cartwright?'

Emily didn't know what to do. Was Mr Kitson really a threat to her? Was he working with the Fergusons? She was so confused. Then the words of her father popped into her head. If she was in trouble, he'd said, the two people she should put her faith in were Mr Worthington and her grandmother. If she made a run for it maybe she could reach the station before she was caught.

'Who was really on the phone Miss Cartwright?' he asked again.

A cold certainty settled upon her.

'How did you know my surname was Cartwright?' said Emily calmly. 'I told you it was Verity.'

Mr Kitson smiled but now the warmth had vanished. Their eyes met, and in that moment they each knew what the other was about to do. With nothing to lose Emily ripped the phone from its socket and hurled it at Mr Kitson, then spun on her heels and raced towards the front door. Her fingers were already on the handle when she felt an arm wrap itself around her waist and she was yanked backwards into the air.

'Oh dear. I had hoped to do this differently.'

Emily screamed and he smacked her head hard against the wall.

'Scream all you like, there's no one to hear you, but believe me you're only making things worse for yourself. The people I work for don't want you dead, but they'd rather that than the alternative,' he said, taking a gun from his jacket pocket and putting it to her forehead.

Emily stopped struggling and he let her go, but he did not remove the pistol from her temple.

'What do you want with me?' said Emily.

'There will be plenty of time for explanations later,' he replied, 'right now we need to leave. My car is parked outside, you will climb into the passenger seat and you will say nothing. You will do nothing. If you try and hurt me or disrupt me in anyway, Jack will die.'

'You've got Jack?'

'Yes. And unless you follow my instructions to the letter you will never see him again. Do I make myself clear?'

Emily nodded. He nudged her out of the front door and into his car, then they drove to his office in town. There he gathered up a large number of files and placed them in his bag. Next he doused the room in petrol and set a fire going in one corner before opening a door to a small set of stairs that led down into the basement.

'Down. Keep walking, don't turn around, don't run. I want to be very clear about this I will shoot you if you disobey me.'

'Where are we going?' Emily demanded, trying to keep the fear from her voice.

'Never you mind,' came the response.

The basement was a musty old storage room that looked as though it had not been used in years. He ushered Emily into the room and shut the door behind them.

'What do you want with me?' asked Emily.

'That's not important,' he replied.

He was standing in front of a large cabinet. With tremendous effort he pulled the cabinet away from the wall to reveal a small, rusted metal door. Taking a similarly rusty key from his pocket he unlocked the door and tugged it open. The basement, it turned out, was right above the underground passages.

'Where are we going?' she asked for a second time.

'Still not important.'

'Well I'm not going anywhere until I know.'

He cocked the gun.

'I really don't think that's your decision, do you?'

'I just want to know where I'm going, that's all.'

Kitson shrugged.

'Germany.'

Emily laughed, but the look on Mr Kitson's face made her stop.

'Germany?'

'Yes. We leave tonight. These passages will take us to the edge of town where I have a car waiting. After that we head to Exmouth. We have an important meeting to get to and it's vital that we not be late.'

'I don't understand. How are you going to get to Germany from Exeter?'

'It's not important that you understand, it's important that you follow my instructions.'

'What if I don't want to?'

'Well, in the best-case scenario I shoot Jack. In the worst-case I shoot you and then Jack. I don't want to do it like that, but I will if you force me.'

'What have you done with him? Where is he?'

'He is waiting for us further along. I bought him down here, away from prying eyes.'

'But –'

'No more questions. Now put your arms behind your back so I can tie them. We don't want you doing anything silly now do we?'

Emily did as she was instructed, though she wanted to disobey, she couldn't risk anything bad happening to Jack.

Kitson gave Emily a push, forcing her into the passages, which seemed to stretch on forever, at times becoming so narrow that it was hard even for her to squeeze through them. Now she understood why Jack had said it was quicker to go above ground. Still, she had to admit that it was perfect for travelling undetected across the city. With every step she took the fear gripped tighter, sapping the strength from her. A feeling of hopelessness that she hadn't experienced since the dark days of the hospital began to envelop her so she tried to stave it off by talking.

'Why are you doing this?' she asked, sounding braver than she felt.

'For the good of my country,' he replied.

'But you're English,' said Emily confused.

He laughed derisively. Now he was underground he seemed happier to talk.

'I'm half-English. My father was English, my mother was German. I grew up in Germany until the age of nine, then I was packed off to boarding school here. I fought for Germany in the Great War. I was injured days before the end of the fighting and by chance I ended up in a British field hospital. When I heard that Germany had surrendered, I couldn't believe it. We were winning. We still occupied half of France for goodness sake.'

'But how did you end up in Britain? Why didn't you just go back to Germany?'

'I thought about it. No doubt if I had declared who I really was they would have made me a prisoner of war and shipped me back once the treaty was signed, but I was angry, too angry to just accept what had happened as so many others had done. Instead I waited, and then in the chaos of the newly declared peace, I slipped away on a boat to England. If you were smart enough you could claim to be anyone you wanted to be, no one would challenge it. I became John Kitson.'

'So you came to Britain looking for revenge?'

'Exactly. I hoped to kill the king.' He laughed again. 'I can see now I wasn't in my right mind. I had hoped to reignite the war between our two countries by killing your beloved leader, but that was never going to work and as I got better I realised my mistake. Nothing would have changed. "The King is dead. Long live The King." That's how it goes isn't it? I thought again about going back to Germany, but what was left for me there but shame and devastation? Our soldiers returned to a land with no jobs to offer us and no homes to shelter us. I heard stories from friends who were turned out on the streets whilst the criminals who signed the treaty slept soundly in their beds. I decided to stay in England. I'm not ashamed of it. But when Hitler came to power I knew it was finally time to go home. I would do anything in service of the Reich, I would gladly fight in this war and I told Hitler just that, but he had other plans for me. I would be of more use to him in England, he said. I was to recruit those with abilities the Reich might be able to use.'

'You're a Shadow Hunter?'

'That is what your Ministry calls them I believe, yes.'

'But why Exeter? Why not London or Birmingham?'

'Oh we have people everywhere Miss Cartwright, don't worry about that. But Exeter is different. Exeter is important.'

Emily could tell that he was proud of whatever it was he had been singled out to do. She was sure she could keep him talking, and if she did he might just say something that would help her.

'What's so important about Exeter?'

'It was foretold.'

'What was foretold?'

'This. You. You were foretold Emily Cartwright. On the day of your birth you created a *Voraussagen* like no other we have ever seen.'

'A Vor Ow Sargen?'

'A Foretelling. A monumental psychic event. All the Seers we had at our disposal knew something would happen here.'

'A foretelling of what? I'm not special.'

'I'm inclined to agree,' he sneered, 'but then I am not a Seer. Hitler wanted someone he could trust in place to find you when the time was right. He's a great man. It has been an honour to serve him. He knows that Britain and Germany should be allies in the war against the Communists and the Jews. This great country has been led astray by a bloodthirsty drunk and his coterie of effete and feeble toffs. But Britain's time is almost at an end. Germany is rising. Soon there will be three great powers, Germany, Russia and America and in a few years only two, the German Reich and the United States. With your help finally there will be just one. The whole world united and at peace under the German flag.'

Emily felt sick with fear. It was a future she never wanted to see. She tried to clear her head. She needed to stay focused on the present. How long had they been walking now? Had they left the city yet?

'Are you meeting the Fergusons?' she asked. 'Is that where we're going? Have you been working with them this whole time?'

'Ralph Ferguson is dead and his brother is nothing more than a nasty spiv.'

'But the letter–'

'A forgery. I wrote it and left it where I knew you could not resist reading it.'

'But why?'

'I didn't know what sort of evidence you had. It's why I followed you to Plymouth. I've been keeping an eye on your ever since you ran into me outside the Guildhall. It's a good job too, someone had to alert the police to your little altercation with Albert Ferguson.'

'That was you?'

'It was foolish of you to go wandering off down darkened alleyways after dangerous men. Still I couldn't risk you being killed now could I? But it worked out even better than I could have imagined. After what you saw, you returned even more certain of the Fergusons' guilt.'

'Did you kill Ralph Ferguson?'

'Of course I killed him. He had outlived his usefulness, he might have killed you before we had even met. But destiny was on my side, you escaped from his clutches and ran straight into mine. From the moment I met you I had a feeling about you, and then I saw the Seer's Mark on your arm. Of course, Julie who looked after you believed your cock and bull story about a birth mark, but I knew better. And once you'd made your escape I asked her about you. She said she thought you'd been attacked, maybe by a boyfriend or your father. She wanted to go to the police but I managed to talk her out of it. I had a suspicion Ferguson was behind it so I confronted him, and I was right. He threatened me, told me he could expose me so I ought to be nicer to him. I waited until he was on his way to work and then I killed him.'

Everything began to fall into place in Emily's mind.

'It was you in Mr Ferguson's house that night.'

'I was looking for anything he could expose me with. Though it turns out I needn't have bothered as you ended up bringing me everything I needed.'

He laughed to himself.

'And Clara's death, that was you too?'

'Who? The Worthington girl? Yes.'

'But why?'

'We were recruiting.'

'You mean Clara was a Seer?'

'No, not that worthless child. Ralph had tipped me off about a girl... what was her name? Blatchford, that was it. Anna – no Annie Blatchford. Ralph used to get wind of things that I never would. Whispers and rumours, gossip and old wives' tales. He'd heard talk about an odd girl; people said she was psychic, her father was a gambler who had suddenly hit a suspiciously long winning streak. Given where she lived I thought she might be the one I'd been waiting for. She certainly had talent and I was sure I could persuade her to join our side. Unfortunately she proved less malleable than I had hoped, then Clara Worthington stumbled into what was happening and I was left with no choice; I had to kill her, so I did, and then I framed her new fiancé Tommy. I knew all about him and his life, I had already represented him in court for brawling or some such nonsense. Clara was out where she shouldn't have been and she saw us so she had to be dealt with. There was nothing else for it. We hid the body as best we could, then I went to see him. I knew he couldn't resist a drink, I found him in the pub, bought him a drink, drugged him and took him home. Once he passed out I made it look as though he had been in a fight, poured whiskey all over his clothes, and put a hanky with her blood on it into his jacket pocket. Then to top it off I offered to represent him in court. I told the family I would take on his case as I believed in his innocence. I made sure no evidence could emerge that would contradict the story the prosecution told. I even tried to get him hanged but that fool judge let him off.'

'You're sick. No, you're evil.'

'All I want is peace. It's all Hitler wants too. That's his gift to the world, peace for a thousand years.'

'Funny kind of peace,' said Emily.

'You're an ignorant child with a loud mouth; it's not a pleasing combination,' he snarled. 'I was in the trenches, I saw fighting up close, good men dying right in front of me and for what? What did we get out of it? When the war was over, our country forgot about us. They were embarrassed, ashamed even. Can you believe it? They were ashamed of the men who had risked their lives day after day for four years. We were betrayed and left with nothing. No jobs, no food, and homes more suited for animals than people.'

Emily ignored his ranting.

'What happened to the other girls? Were they all Ferguson's doing?'

'We had an arrangement. He would help me get the girls I needed. If they didn't cooperate they were Ferguson's to do with as he pleased. I never liked the man but he was useful to me. I am not a violent person, not unless I have to be. I left that to him, he had a taste for it, but then his appetites got the better of him.'

'Why did you want the girls?'

'I've told you, you're not the only one with special abilities. They had a variety of skills. Some were Seers, though most could barely look minutes into the future, so we disposed of them. Others were Healers or Projectors. Most came willingly. After all a lot of these girls had nothing else to live for, no money, no future, little work. There was no great outcry. They were poor, no one paid much attention, they were missed only by their families. If they came voluntarily then we allowed them to say goodbye to their loved ones, told them that they had been picked for some great adventure in the Empire. If they played along then the families got a little money. If they didn't they got nothing. Those that didn't want to come... well Ferguson took care of them. It's... distasteful but he served a purpose.'

'You killed them?'

'We made them disappear. What happened to the bodies I don't know, like I said, that was down to Ferguson. I just provided an escape route, a way in and out of the town without being seen.'

Finally the darkness up ahead was broken by the faint glow of candlelight. As she drew closer she realised there was a body propped against the wall of the tunnel. It was Jack. He wasn't moving. Emily tried not to panic. Please don't be dead, she whispered under her breath.

'What have you done to him?'

'He's okay, for now at least. I've given him a little something to put him to sleep.'

'Why?'

'To ensure your cooperation. Normally we use family members but with your father away and no one else left alive I had to be a little creative and I wasn't sure Arthur Worthington would be enough.'

'What do you want?'

'You, Emily Cartwright, I want you. But first I need

you to understand that you are in my power, totally and utterly. Anything you do to disturb my progress will result in more harm befalling poor Jack here.'

He checked his watch.

'Not long now.'

In the corner was what looked like a suitcase. Kitson looked his watch again then opened the case. Inside was some sort of radio device. He flicked a switched and it sparked into life, gently humming to itself. As the minutes ticked by Emily could see him growing more and more agitated; he frequently checked his watch, sometimes glaring at it as if it might be lying to him. Hope sprang from the pit of her stomach. Perhaps Peterhouse had intervened, perhaps he had found whoever Kitson was waiting to hear from. She saw him doing calculations in his head. Suddenly the radio started to beep. Kitson grinned and pulled a notepad and pen from his inside pocket.

'Better late than never,' he muttered.

When the beeping stopped he called to Emily.

'You. Come here.'

Emily stayed sat by Jack who, unnoticed by Mr Kitson, had begun to stir.

'Get up,' said Kitson gesturing with the gun for her to come to him.

Reluctantly she stood up and walked over. Kitson produced some more rope and began to tie her feet together in addition to her hands which were already tightly bound. The light of the lamp flickered, casting long shadows on the wall.

'I'll be back in a moment. If you move, if you try and run, you'll both die. Don't be a fool.'

With that he disappeared in to the darkness. Emily wondered how long he would be gone. Long enough to escape perhaps? But even if he was gone for hours what hope did she have?

'Jack. Jack, wake up,' said Emily urgently.

Jack made a noise but did not open his eyes.

'Jack. You've got to wake up. Please. I need you.'

Emily dragged herself slowly across the floor to be next to him.

'Jack. We're in real trouble. Come on, please wake up.'

Though her hands were tied tightly at the wrist, she was able to take Jack's hands within hers and squeeze them gently.

'Jack please, please wake up. I need you. You have to help me.'

Jack began to stir.

'Emily is that you? Where are we?'

'Jack listen, we're in the passages, there's no time for questions. Can you stand?'

'What?'

'Can you stand?'

Jack tried to stand but immediately fell over, cutting his lip on the floor. He tried again but with similar results.

'He gave me something to drink. I think it was… I'm so tired.'

'Jack, you've got to focus. It's Mr Kitson, he's going to kill you. He's going to take me to Germany and kill you. You must get that lantern and bring it to me,' she whispered, unsure how close Kitson might still be.

Jack forced himself onto his knees then slowly raised himself up to his full height. Though his hands were bound, Kitson had not tied them behind his back as he had with Emily's. Perhaps he had thought it not worth the effort as Jack was still supposed to be out cold. They were clearly running behind schedule. It wasn't much, but Emily felt the tiny flickering hope begin to grow.

Jack took down the lamp, opened the little window and removed the candle from inside. Then he placed the candle on the floor and began to burn through the ropes that tied his hands together. Once that was done he hurried over to Emily to do the same. They hadn't quite finished hers when they heard footsteps. Jack put the lamp back on the wall, grabbed the remnants of his ropes, placed them over his wrists, and pretended he was still unconsciousness.

310

Emily stayed by Jack's side hoping to distract Kitson from the gently swaying lamp and the smell of burnt rope by making him believe she was trying to rouse Jack.

'Jack, wake up, please wake up,' she pleaded loudly.

'He can't hear you,' said Kitson dismissively as he re-entered the chamber. 'It's here. Come on, let's go.'

'Am I supposed to hop all the way there?'

Kitson untied her feet. There was a moment, just a moment, when Emily thought she might have been able to kick him, knock him backwards and take his gun, but he was not stupid, he had read her intentions.

'Don't even think about it,' he said tapping the gun that stuck out the top of his trousers. 'You try and run, I will shoot you. A bullet doesn't have to be fatal to do an awful lot of damage you know?'

'What about Jack?'

'He stays here as insurance. Once he wakes up I think he'll just about be able to make it back to town, but by then we'll be long gone. And if you fail to cooperate I'll come back here and shoot him.'

With a last glance back at Jack she saw his eyes follow them out the room and she knew he would soon be tailing them. She hoped he had the good sense to do so quietly but she feared that quietly wasn't Jack's style. Then a thought hit her. She had seen this happen. In her vision she had seen Jack running through the passages. She had always assumed he was being chased by Peterhouse, but what if the pair of them were following Kitson? She knew then that Jack was about to make a terrible mistake, but there was nothing she could do. If tried to stop him she would give the game away and he would shoot Jack anyway. She had to think quickly.

'You know you're right about me,' she said suddenly.

'What do you mean?'

'I mean, I am a Seer, a powerful Seer. I've Seen what is about to happen. It was weeks ago but I've only just understood it.'

'There we are,' he said with a ghoulish smile, 'the

311

Führer is never wrong. You are going to be a wonderful asset for Germany. Think of all the lives you can save. German lives. British lives.'

'But not your life,' goaded Emily.

Kitson said nothing.

'I've seen you die. I didn't realise it was you before, but now I know it for sure. It happens tonight. Did you think when you got up this morning that today would be the very last day of your life?'

'If that is what the Führer wants then that is what has to happen,' he replied evenly.

'You aren't upset? Not even a little bothered that you won't get to share in this glorious future of yours?'

'You think I did this for personal gain?' he said, and to Emily's great surprise he seemed genuinely hurt. 'I did it for the love of my country. I did it for Germany and for her people who have been humiliated for too long. Well not anymore. Now we stand up. If I am not there to see it then that is... sad... of course it is, but if that is what it takes then–'

'Don't you want to know how it happens?' asked Emily innocently.

'I think I've heard enough from you.'

'It's probably for the best. It's not a good way to go.'

'Keep walking.'

Her head was spinning and her mouth was dry with fear, but she had to keep talking, force him into a mistake. Despite what he had said, she didn't think he was as calm about the prospect of death as he claimed.

'You don't win you know?'

'Be quiet,' he snarled.

Emily allowed herself a small smile. It was working.

'I've Seen it all. You don't win. Germany is devastated. Hitler is a mad man and he ends up destroying his own nation. You don't even manage to get me out of England.'

'I said be quiet.'

'It won't be long now. You'll see I'm right.'

'Another word from you and I'll blow your head off.'

'I don't think so. What would you tell your beloved Adolf then? You lost your temper and shot me? If I'm so important then I think you'll do everything in your power to keep me alive.'

'Maybe so but that doesn't mean I have to put up with your insolence.'

Emily felt a dull thudding pain on the back of her head as Kitson hit her with the handle of his gun, and her legs gave way beneath her.

'Stay right there. Don't move or I will shoot.'

Emily recognised the voice. It was Peterhouse. Kitson swung round, pulling Emily in front him.

'You should've shot me while my back was turned. Oh no, don't tell me, an Englishman could never shoot a man in the back. Most ungentlemanly. So instead the girl will die.'

'The girl's not going to die, you're going to give her back to me.'

'Why would I do that?'

'Because the game's up. You're not going to get away. I have men waiting for you at every exit.'

'No, you don't,' replied Kitson slowly. 'Before now you didn't even know this section of the passages existed. Like everyone else you thought they'd caved in centuries ago. Well they had, but Ferguson and I dug them out again. It gave us the perfect way to get in and out of the city unnoticed. Even the door in the basement of my office is meant to be locked, and the only key kept by the city council, but again Ferguson had his uses and now I have a copy. So, no, I don't think anyone is waiting for us. And even if it were true, in a few minutes an air raid will begin on Plymouth the likes of which they have never known. Oh, and that fire in my office should be burning beautifully by now. Yes, I think that will be more than enough to distract everyone. You see? I've thought it all through. Survival of the fittest old boy, Britain needs an injection of new blood. You're an old power on the wane, Germany is on the rise. We select and breed the best of the best whilst England is still ruled by handshakes and old school ties. Who cares how clever you are so long as you played rugby for the right college. Your time is at an end, and Emily here is going to help us whether she likes it or not. We're breeding a race of supermen. She will give us the most powerful Seers in the history of the world. Nothing will be beyond our grasp.'

Emily felt a wave of revulsion sweep over her. They didn't want her just for her powers: they wanted *her*. They wanted her body. They were going to use her to breed children with the gift of second sight. No wonder Kitson had been so concerned by Ferguson's actions; he didn't want his precious bounty damaged. She had to be whole: pure.

'But I'm not even of age. I can't–' she spluttered.

'It won't be long now,' replied Kitson indifferently. 'Besides the Führer is a patient man, he will wait for you to produce his army of Seers.'

Peterhouse edged closer. Their guns were still pointed at each other.

'Stay back,' warned Kitson, 'I really don't have the time for this.'

He took aim in an instant and fired a volley of shots off towards Peterhouse who ducked out of sight, back down the passageway. Heaving Emily over his shoulder Kitson began to run, occasionally stopping to let off a round of gunfire which prevented Peterhouse from following them too closely.

Jack however would not be deterred; she could hear his footsteps pounding on the stone floor. Then they emerged into another larger chamber that Emily recognised only too well, and suddenly she knew what was going to happen. There wasn't even the time to call out as Jack emerged from the darkness. Kitson dropped her to the ground and she watched helplessly as Peterhouse fired several rounds at Kitson who pulled himself into a nearby alcove, before replying with two quick shots of his own. It was then that Jack made a break for it. Like a dancer in a blood-soaked ballet, he ran, pirouetting around Kitson's first shot, and leaping towards him, only to be cut down by a second bullet which ripped through his shoulder and sent him sprawling to the floor.

Chapter Nineteen

Emily could not see where they were going, but soon she felt the blast of the cold night air on her face and knew that they must have emerged from the passages. In the distance she could hear the familiar rumble of plane engines. Kitson had not been lying about the bombing.

'Don't move,' said Mr Kitson laying Emily down on the wet grass. 'You can try and run but you won't get far.'

A car started up nearby and Emily was bundled into the back of it. She was still dazed from the blow she had taken to the back of her head but, as the car raced along the narrow country lanes, she began to regain her balance and gather her thoughts. She forced herself to push aside images of Jack, his bleeding body lying prostrate in the dark of the passages. She felt sick to think of it, but she couldn't allow her concern for him to overwhelm her; it would do neither of them any good. In just a few hours she would be brought aboard a boat bound for Germany. She had to do something soon, she couldn't let herself be taken.

The car began to slow. They had arrived at a checkpoint. It was manned by an elderly gentleman in a uniform that looked like it was last worn during the Boer War. He wasn't exactly the help she had been hoping for. Perhaps if she called out when he took a look at Mr Kitson's papers he could do something. Kitson seemed to have read her intentions however.

'I warn you Miss Cartwright, if you scream I will shoot this man. How long before anyone notices he's gone do you think? A few hours at least, maybe more if the raids on Plymouth do their job. Certainly long enough for us to get off this miserable little island.'

Emily considered what he had said. He was probably right, and she couldn't stand the idea that someone else might die because of her. Her thoughts returned to Jack. Was he dead? Had another person she cared for given their life for hers? She steadied herself. His bravery would be worthless if she gave up now. She needed to stay focused.

'Where are you off to at this time of night?' asked the guard.

'I have to get my niece home.'

The guard glanced briefly at the papers that Kitson had handed over before tossing them back, eager to return to the warmth of his hut.

'On your way then,' said the old boy waving them through.

They drove on, slowly at first but soon picking up speed. Emily knew if she was going to do something she had to act soon. The ropes that bound her wrists had been burned away until in certain places they were barely thicker than a thread. It was time for her to take a chance. As they slowed to approach a particularly sharp bend Emily broke free of her restraints and pulled on the handbrake. The car lurched violently to one side and was sent careering into a thick hedgerow. Mr Kitson, who was not anticipating the impact, was thrown forwards, smashing his head on the steering wheel. Emily was thrown forwards too but just about managed to grip on to the seat in front to stop herself being hurled through the windscreen.

The car came to an almost instantaneous halt. After the crash there was a strange silence, as if the world had a chosen that moment to draw breath, but it was soon broken by a fierce hissing emanating from beneath the bonnet. Emily seized her opportunity, throwing open the car door and running as fast as she could back towards the checkpoint. Perhaps if she got there quick enough they could call the police, or maybe Peterhouse had managed to follow them.

She hurtled along so swiftly she felt as though her feet were barely touching the ground. There was nothing more important than this. Her arms pumped furiously, propelling her on. Her chest began to burn and her legs ached, but still she barrelled forwards, still she pushed harder, desperate to put as much distance as possible between herself and Kitson. She dared not look back less it slow her even the slightest fraction.

Then, just as she thought she might make it, she heard something. It was the sound of a second pair of feet pounding the ground behind her, and they were getting closer. She willed every last reserve of energy to her legs but it was no use. The sound was growing louder and louder, until it was all she could hear in her ears, until it drowned out the furious beating of her heart and smothered her frantic gasps for air. Any moment now she would feel his hot breath on her neck and his hands round her waist as he pulled her to the ground. Finally she chanced a look, hoping somehow that she might yet throw him off or dodge out of his way.

And then it was over. The dark figure behind her reached towards her, and with a mighty swipe, knocked her legs out from under her. For one glorious moment Emily thought she might just manage to stay on her feet but then she stumbled, twisting her ankle, and she fell to the floor, followed instantly by a crushing weight that landed hard on her right leg. She heard a loud snap but felt nothing. Perhaps she was in shock, or perhaps it was simply that she ached so much all over that she had no way of distinguishing one pain from another anymore.

'Du kleine Schlampe. Denkst du, du kannst entkommen? You think you can beat us? It's too late for all that don't you see? It's over, we've won.'

For a moment Emily believed him. After all what else

was left? She had lost her mother, her sister and her uncle, whilst her father existed only as a scribbled name at the bottom of an occasional letter. England was dying, the cities were in ruins, and the country was slowly running out of food. They had stood up to Germany too late for it to do any good. They were on their own. She was on her own. It was over. They would take her, use her, and then destroy her.

Kitson pulled her to her feet like she was a child's rag doll. She could barely stand. The pain that had been missing before was suddenly very much present. She leaned as heavily as she could on her left leg whilst Kitson propped her up.

'What are you going to do?' she gasped. 'I can't exactly walk to the boat can I?'

'The car isn't so badly damaged. It's just a knock. It will get us there.'

Emily's heart sank. She hobbled slowly on, still supported by Kitson. Every step was agony. Surely if Peterhouse was going to catch up with them he'd be there by now. Kitson was right. There was no back up. Peterhouse had been bluffing, he had come alone. They inched slowly closer to the car. If asked she would have sworn she had run across half of Devon, but it seemed she had made it barely four hundred yards.

Then Emily realised something. In supporting her, Kitson no longer had hold of his weapon. She couldn't believe it. It was right there in the side pocket of his jacket. Emily deliberately stumbled, crying out in pain, and grabbed lower down his waist for support, reaching into his pocket as she did so. She allowed herself to be steadied by Kitson, then lifted the gun gently from his pocket praying he wouldn't notice.

The question now was what to do. Emily had never so much as held a gun before, let alone fired one. And where would she fire it? A shot at this range would most likely kill him. Was that really what she wanted? Was that who she was? On the few occasions she had pictured herself firing a gun it was at a distance, and certainly not at a real person. Putting a gun to someone's back felt different. But if she didn't do it, she would be as good as dead.

Emily moved her hand holding the gun to the base of Kitson's spine. She urged herself to pull the trigger, not to give him a chance, to act like the bombers who had killed her family and show him no mercy. In a few more yards the opportunity would be gone. If it came down to a battle of strength she would be done for, and yet she still wasn't sure she could kill someone, even someone like Kitson. She tried to master her thoughts but the pain in her leg was now so bad she thought she might vomit, and she felt as though at any moment she could pass out.

Despite the rain that had begun to fall she was sweating profusely. Simply standing up was becoming increasingly difficult. What would happen if she let him go, if she kept the gun and told him to walk away? Didn't she have a duty to make sure he wouldn't escape? And what about Jack? She could barely bring herself to think of how she had seen him last, a bloody figure slumped on the floor of the passages. She owed it to him to get his brother released, whether he had survived or not, and the only way she could be sure of doing that was if Kitson came with her.

They were almost at the car when Emily finally made her move. She pushed the gun as hard as she could into Kitson's back and at the same time pulled away from his steadying grip, briefly leaning on her broken leg which caused another rush of pain so great she was certain she would collapse. Somehow though, she stayed standing.

'Stop,' she said, pressing the barrel of the gun deep into his flesh.

Kitson made to turn but Emily jabbed at him.

'No. Don't turn around. Don't move. If you move, I will shoot you.'

'You won't shoot me Miss Cartwright, you don't have what it takes. I've seen killers little Emily and you're not one.'

'A bullet doesn't have to be fatal to do an awful lot of

damage,' she reminded him.

Emily was standing at arm's length with the gun to his back. She feared standing any closer in case he made some sudden move. With her leg as it was she could barely keep her balance. If she had to make any quick movements then she would be in trouble.

'What do you really think you're going to achieve here? I've told you, it's over. This is all just... Dunkirk, a defeat dressed up to look like a victory. Even if you kill me we'll come again. We'll come, and we'll keep coming till we get what we want.'

'You know what? I don't think anyone values their life as little as you claim to value yours. I think you're terrified, deep down, and all of this is posturing. If you try and move, if you try to escape, if you try and attack me: I will shoot you. You're right, I'm not a killer, but if you come at me, if you put me in more danger, I don't know what I'll do and neither do you.'

Kitson fell silent.

'So let's be clear about this. I'm not going anywhere with you,' she continued. 'Come again if you like, send all your little men after me, but I'm going nowhere, not with you, not with anyone, not now, not ever.'

Emily had no plan for what she would do next; she had only thought as far ahead as getting the gun. Should she tell him to get in the car and drive her back to Exeter to hand himself in? And what if he refused, what would she do then? She forced herself to move another few agonising steps backwards.

'You haven't really thought this through have you?' said Kitson, and she could hear the snide delight in his voice.

'Be quiet.'

'Come on Miss Cartwright, you can admit it. You're scared. I understand. Let's forget this nonsense and we can be on our way. I can get someone to look at that leg of yours, stop the pain. You'd like that wouldn't you?'

He turned around.

'Stay where you are,' said Emily holding the weapon out in front of herself and trying to ignore how much her hand was quivering.

Kitson's eyes ran greedily up her leg in a way that made Emily feel like prey. She knew she was being sized up. He was working out how quickly he could get to her, and if he could do it without getting injured. She edged backwards but the distance between them didn't seem to alter. She had the gun but she didn't have the power. She knew if she was to survive then that would have to change. She made up her mind in an instant. She wasn't sure she could kill Kitson, but she would make him think twice about coming any closer.

She raised the gun to just above his shoulder and fired. The force of the shot caught her by surprise, in the films it all looked so much easier and she almost dropped the gun. Even so it had the desired effect. Kitson moved back a few feet holding his hands out in a conciliatory gesture. She had bought herself some time, put doubt into his mind. He was no longer certain she wouldn't shoot him, but Emily knew his confidence would grow again the longer the situation went on.

'We're going back to the checkpoint,' she said.

The rain was falling harder now. She had to do something; the longer she waited the more likely she was to lose.

'You say the car works. You're going to drive us.'

Kitson glanced quickly his watch. Good, thought Emily, time is running out.

'Get in the car.'

Kitson scowled but did as he was told. With the gun still trained on him, Emily instructed him to bring the car up to where she was standing. She was trying not to let on, but in truth she didn't think she could walk the final twenty feet to the vehicle. She hauled herself into the rear of the car as she didn't want to be too close to him. That way she could keep the gun to his back. The car was more badly damaged than he had suggested; the bonnet was crumpled, there were scratches all down the side, and one of the tyres was punctured. This made for a distinctly uncomfortable ride, with Emily feeling a sharp bolt of pain in her leg with every pot hole and bump in the road that they encountered.

Kitson drove them back towards the checkpoint in silence. At first Emily was glad about this, she thought it meant he was scared, but as time passed she wondered if he was really plotting his escape, and if keeping him talking might be a better idea. The silence also forced her to dwell on all the things that could still go wrong. It was clear, despite what both of them had said, that they each needed the other alive, but how much damage would be done to them and others in the meantime? Jack was hurt, maybe even dead, she had a broken leg and God knows what else.

Finally they reached the checkpoint. The car rattled and spluttered up to the small hut on the grassy verge. A large figure emerged from the hut but in the darkness Emily could not see them clearly. It was definitely not the man from before as this man was taller, a bigger build entirely. There must have been a shift change, another volunteer had taken over. She hoped whoever it was still had a gun. Her heart leapt for a moment at the thought that it could be Peterhouse, but why would he be waiting there? He wouldn't expect them to be coming back.

'Turn off the engine,' said Emily and Kitson complied. 'Now get out of the car. Slowly.'

Kitson opened the door and climbed cautiously from the car whilst Emily watched him intently. Then, leaning heavily on the door, she started to pull herself out of the car too. As she did so the guard coughed and then cleared his throat and Emily was shocked to hear a familiar voice.

'Had a bit of an accident, have we? Mind if I see your papers?'

Emily looked up in surprise. It was Mr Worthington.

'Mr Worthington!'

'Emily! What are you doing here?'

'I...'

But before she could say anything, Kitson started speaking in his most charming and earnest manner. It was, she supposed, the voice he used in the courtroom.

'My goodness! I'm so glad you're here. This young girl is hurt, she's quite badly injured in fact, and I think she might have suffered some form of upset.'

'Emily?'

'Mr Worthington, you've got to help me.'

'What on earth happened to you? What are you doing with that gun?'

'It's this man, he's a spy. He's a German spy.'

Mr Worthington took the rifle from off his shoulder and pointed it towards Mr Kitson.

'I can assure you, I am no such thing. My name is John Kitson and I'm a solicitor from Exeter. I have offices just off Fore Street. Anyway, I was coming back from some urgent business in Plymouth when I found this girl at the side of the road. She appeared to be hurt and somewhat confused. She has a broken leg I think. Who knows how that could have happened? I put her in my car and was returning to Exeter, but then she produced this gun from somewhere... rather caused me to lose control of my vehicle. I know this must look awfully odd, but I honestly think she's lost her mind, the poor thing. It's this damn war, affects people in the strangest of ways. You know her, do you?'

'She's... she's staying with me. She's an evacuee from London.'

'Ah, well that's very good of you to take her in when you clearly have other duties too. If we're going to win this war, it'll be because of people like you. Still – and don't think I'm criticising – but is it right that she should be left wandering round the streets at night? It's a dangerous world at the best of times and these are clearly not the best of times.'

'No... no... I quite agree,' said Mr Worthington looking befuddled.

'Mr Worthington,' Emily interjected, 'I know how strange this all sounds, but this man is a spy. He kidnapped Jack and he was trying to take me away to Germany with him.'

Mr Kitson merely offered up a shrug as if to say, 'I told you she wasn't well.'

'Jack? Who's Jack?'

'A... a friend of mine....' she stuttered.

Emily realised that Mr Worthington did not know who Jack was, and he was unlikely to be best pleased if he found out. A brief look at Kitson told her that he was already putting the pieces together.

'Where did you get that gun?' asked Mr Worthington.

'It's Kitson's. I took it from him.'

Mr Worthington looked more confused than ever, but he didn't lower his weapon.

'Look, old chap,' Kitson bluffed, 'I am happy to take this girl to the hospital, but I am a bit worried about what she might do with that gun. For all I know it's not loaded, but I wouldn't want to find out.'

'What she says about you–'

'That I'm a spy?'

'Yes.'

'It's not true...' he laughed incredulously. 'I work in Exeter, I've lived in Exeter half my adult life.'

'Emily's not a liar. She's an odd girl it's true, rather too curious for her own good, but she's not a liar.'

'I don't doubt it. I don't know what has happened, or how she got those terrible injuries, but she needs help. For goodness sake surely you can see that?'

Mr Worthington nodded slowly.

'Emily, I think you should put the gun down.'

Her grip on the pistol tightened.

'I can't. This man is a spy. He's a killer. I think he killed Jack. He knows... he knows about me... he knows what I can do... he knows about the others, about the girls... he knows who killed Clara.'

'I don't have the faintest idea what you're talking

about. Who is this Clara? And who is Jack? Jack who Emily?' asked Kitson, mustering a sincerity that surprised her.

'Jack Copleston' she said in the slightest of voices.

Mr Worthington looked like he had been shot, the air had left him entirely.

'Jack Copleston? The brother of Tommy Copleston? What are you doing making friends with that boy? After all I told you... I warned you... Why Emily?'

He lowered his gun.

'Mr Worthington, I can explain everything, but you have to believe me.'

'No, I don't. You listen to me. Tommy Copleston tore my family apart. My wife and child are gone. You of all people, I thought you would understand,' the hurt in his voice frightened her more than the rage. He looked lost. 'I don't know what's happened to you but clearly you've been hurt. We'll talk about this... this other thing when you're better,' he turned away from her and addressed Kitson who was watching them both carefully.

'Did you say you could take her to the hospital?'

'Of course.'

'Mr Worthington please!'

'Would you be quiet?' he snapped. 'I'm afraid I can't come with you, it wouldn't do to leave my post, not tonight of all nights. Looks like Plymouth is taking a battering.'

'Yes, though I suppose if it had been a clearer night it might have been even worse,' he replied, sounding a little disappointed. 'Now your girl is still pointing a gun at me and I'd rather she wasn't. Would you mind?'

Mr Worthington turned his disapproving glare on Emily.

'Emily give me the gun.'

Emily shook her head.

'Give me the gun.'

'He shot Jack. He was responsible for Clara's death, he framed Jack's brother. He is a Nazi spy. I will not give you

326

the gun.'

Emily tried to keep it fixed on Kitson but was having difficulty, the pain was almost unbearable now, dizziness was sweeping over her in waves. The sweat mixed with the rain poured down her face and made it hard for her to see. Mr Worthington had also moved himself in to the line of fire so there was no chance she could get a clean shot away even if she could see straight.

'Emily, please put down the gun. There's a good girl. We can talk about all of this when you're better.'

'You don't understand, he's going to take me out of the country. By morning I'll be in Germany.'

'Please Emily, you'll hurt yourself. Put it down.'

'No.'

Mr Worthington edged nearer.

'Please don't do this Mr Worthington. I know you're upset, but...' an idea seized her, 'you knew my father. You fought together. Captain David Cartwright of the 8th Devonshire's. I... I didn't know until recently. I'm begging you–'

'Captain Cartwright is your father?' he said.

'Yes.'

'But why didn't he tell me about you?'

'It doesn't matter right now, what's important is that you don't let this man take me anywhere.'

'Why would a German spy even be interested in you? It doesn't make sense.'

'You fought with my father at Mametz, is that right?'

She was speaking quickly now. The pain was so great she worried she would pass out before she could finish.

'Yes, I did. He was a good man. He saved my life.'

'And did you ever think there was anything odd about him? Anything different? The dreams, you couldn't explain the dreams...'

A look of comprehension slowly dawned on his face as he remembered the fateful day that the Captain had saved his life. He had been shot and his leg was bleeding heavily. He was sure he was going to die, but then the Captain had rescued him, and carried him to the hospital. Lying in his bed the Captain had disappeared and suddenly his wife was by his side instead, talking to him, whispering little reassurances that everything would be okay. Then he had been transported worlds away, back to the cottage, back to his wife and little girl; the pain had faded into nothing, and for a while he had peace. Of course afterwards he had dismissed it. It was a fever dream bought on by the pain and the drugs, but then he spoke to the other men. Each one confessed that they always had the strangest dreams whenever Captain Cartwright was around, dreams so real they all would have sworn they had truly happened.

'I didn't know until recently,' said Emily, seeing a change in his expression, 'but we share similar gifts, gifts that the Nazis would like to possess.'

Emily hoped she had got through to Mr Worthington. She looked across at Kitson but his face was inscrutable, only his eyes offered any clue as they beadily studied the scene.

'I think I understand,' he whispered, 'now let me have that gun, I'll take care of this.'

Emily finally gave up the weapon. In truth she no longer thought she could shoot it. The pain in her leg was close to unbearable and she thought she might collapse at any moment. Mr Worthington took the gun from her and slipped it into the belt of his trousers. He turned to face Kitson with a smile on his face.

'There we are, no harm done.'

Kitson visibly relaxed.

'My goodness, thank you so much. Now I should really get this young lady to a hospital don't you think?'

'Absolutely,' Mr Worthington agreed.

Emily didn't move. She thought Mr Worthington had understood her, but she was wrong, and now she had given up the gun. She felt the panic begin to rise once more.

'Mr Worthington...' she pleaded, but he ignored her.

'One thing before you go,' he said, addressing Kitson. 'Where did you say you had business this evening?

Plymouth wasn't it?'

'Yes. I got a call earlier today from a valued client of mine and had to rush right over there. I ran into young Emily here on the way back.'

'Funny you should be on this road then, it doesn't go anywhere near Plymouth.'

Hitching his rifle up again, he pointed it at Kitson.

'Open the car.'

Kitson did as he was asked without protest and then stood back to await further instruction, his eyes still scanning the scene looking for an opportunity.

'Emily do you think you can make it to the car with my support?' asked Mr Worthington.

Emily nodded and very slowly, she limped towards the car. It was agony, and every step she took cost her an extraordinary amount of energy and will power. Finally she was able to rest as she waited for Mr Worthington to call for help. Mr Worthington, still pointing the gun at Kitson, indicated that he should step into the guard's hut where he would make a call and have him arrested. Kitson complied without saying a word.

Emily sat in the back of the car trying to suppress the feeling of nausea she felt inside which was partly bought on by her broken leg and partly by the desperation she felt at not knowing what had happened to Jack. Then it occurred to her that she could find out. If he was alive, if he had a future then perhaps she could See it. Her heart lifted almost at once. She closed her eyes, doing her best to block out the pain. She tried to picture Jack, but it was too hard. When the outcome was certain it was so much easier. She tried again. Please let him live, she thought to herself.

She tried once more but each time she found herself picturing him, not as he was, but as she wanted him to be. If she couldn't focus she would never be able to do it. Then she remembered the scrap of his shirt she had taken from his room. It was still up her sleeve. She drew it out and took a long deep breath, waiting for the familiar pull that would indicate a vision, but nothing came. She had to be at fault, she had to be. She just wasn't doing it right. The only other option was that he was dead, that he had died trying to protect her, and that wasn't fair, that wasn't right. She took a deep breath and –

BANG. A hollow shot cracked the night air and Mr Worthington hit the muddy ground in an instant, a look of surprise frozen on his face. Time seemed to have slowed almost to a stop. She didn't understand what had happened, but Kitson was now standing over Mr Worthington with the pistol. Emily opened the car door, then gathering what little strength she had, threw herself at Kitson. She caught him by surprise and he fell backwards but she was no match for him. Within seconds he was back on top of her, pressing on her broken leg, making her scream in agony.

'Das endet jetzt. You've given me enough trouble. You even so much as breathe until we get on the boat and you're dead.'

He pressed the gun into her face. She could feel the cool metal on her skin and she wished that he would end it. Silently she begged him to pull the trigger. Jack was dead. Mr Worthington was dead. Most of her family were dead. The pain that had weighed upon her since the day of bombing grew heavier still. She could feel the fury pulsing within her and it made her sick. She was ready to go. She had lost everything. Kitson was prepared to kill her; she could see it in his eyes, she had pushed him beyond breaking point, beyond obeying orders. She knew if she could just give him the faintest push he would snap and everything would be over. Summoning the last ounce of strength she possessed, she twisted her body, throwing him off balance. His grip loosened and she managed to wriggle a hand free long enough to catch him just on the underside of his jaw.

'Du dumme Schlampe,' he spat. 'I'll...'

He stopped and straightened up as if he had heard some sort of sound. Then without warning he slumped on top of her: dead. Emily pushed his body off her in disgust. A few feet away, propped up against the hut, sat Mr Worthington, swaying gently, rifle on his lap. As the rain lashed down they looked into each another's eyes, exchanging a silent goodbye. Emily could see a bright light in the distance and felt a wave of tiredness overcome her. She tried to speak, to say something to Mr Worthington, but it was all over. She closed her eyes and quietly slipped away.

Chapter Twenty

'Emily!'

A familiar voice called to her.

'Come on, hurry up.'

It was Celia. She was running through a field in the pretty floral dress that she'd been given for her last birthday. The sun grazed her golden skin and for moment it looked as though she was glowing.

'Wait for me,' cried Emily, running after her sister as she had so often done when she was little. When she finally reached her, they were at the edge of the field.

'Let's go to the spring,' said Celia taking Emily's arm.

Within two steps the field had vanished and they were standing beneath a canopy of trees. A small pool of water lay in front of them, and a string of rocks jutted out just above the surface.

'The stepping stones!' exclaimed Emily. 'I'd forgotten about this place.'

'We used to come here years ago. Dad had to help you jump from stone to stone because you were too small to reach them otherwise, and you used to throw a little tantrum if you weren't able to do something I could.'

Emily laughed in recognition, and the spell was broken. Celia sat down on the largest stone and dangled her feet in the water.

'You're dead,' said Emily.

'Yes, I am,' agreed Celia.

'But you're here...'

'And so are you.'

'Am I dead?' asked Emily uncertainly.

Celia suddenly swung one leg out of the spring, sending water crashing over her little sister.

'Do you feel that?'

'Ahhh, that's freezing,' Emily cried as the cold water trickled down her back.

'Then you're probably not dead.'

'You couldn't have just said no?' she grumbled, pulling at her now sodden dress, trying to keep it from sticking to her skin.

Celia grinned and despite herself Emily did too.

'How long will you stay?'

'I don't know, I'm not in charge. Until you wake up I suppose.'

'Then I don't want to wake up.'

The two girls sat looking at one another, neither speaking. Emily felt the hot sting of tears in her eyes, her breathing became heavy and she found she could no longer meet her sister's gaze.

'It's just so much harder without you and mum. Everything's harder,' she said quietly as she stared into the cool, crisp water.

'I know, but you'll be okay in the end. You're pretty tough.'

'I don't want to be tough.'

'But you have to be, otherwise it was all for nothing.'

'You saved my life.'

'So live it. Make it a life worth saving.'

Emily looked up at her sister.

'I don't know how.'

'You'll work it out, you're not as dumb as you look.'

Emily let out a dry, choking laugh, and more tears fell.

'Tell me about Jack,' said Celia with a smirk, taking her feet from the water and crossing her legs.

'How do you know about Jack?'

'I'm translucent.'

'Omniscient,' Emily corrected, drying her eyes on her sleeves.

'Yes. That one.'

'Jack looks out for me and I look out for him. You'd like him. He's brave, braver than me anyway, and he's funny too.'

'He sounds great.'

'He likes cricket and football.'

'He sounds less great.'

'I wish you could meet him.'

'So do I.'

There was nothing left to say, and a silence fell between them. Instead, Emily listened to the noises around her, letting the sounds of her childhood fill her heart. Birds chirruped in the trees, bees hummed, the water gently lapped against the bank, and somewhere in the distance she could just make out the peeling of church bells. It was a sound she hadn't heard since the war started, but she didn't want to think about that. She didn't want to think of anything much at all. Suddenly she was seized by an idea.

'Race you,' she said, and it wasn't a question.

'Aren't we a little old for that?' replied Celia haughtily, though Emily could tell she was readying herself to run.

'Well… if you're scared…' taunted Emily, shooting her sister a sly grin, then she leapt from the bank onto the first stepping stone where Celia was already scrambling to her feet. 'Catch me if you can!'

Emily was determined to win this time, bounding from stone to stone, slipping and sliding on the mossy rocks but never losing her footing completely. Celia followed in her wake and together they played as children once again, their laughter skipping across the water like skimming stones. At times she thought she saw her mother on the bank taking photographs, whilst her father lay on the ground with his hat over his eyes, trying to get some sleep. But they were just glimpses, reflections on the water, and she knew better than to reach out and touch them. They were not hers to hold.

They made it to the other side and collapsed onto the grassy bank, gasping for breath. Emily was not sure exactly how much time had passed, minutes maybe, hours even, but the air was definitely cooler now. The dappled light that shone through the trees had faded leaving only shadow, and when the two girls looked at each other, they knew their time was up.

'Do you really have to leave?' asked Emily, though she was already certain of the answer.

'Everything ends sometime.'

'Celia, I...' she began.

'You too,' Celia replied with a tiny smile, and then she was gone.

For a few moments Emily felt like she had lost her all over again, and her weary heart ached with such sweet a pain she could hardly stand it. Then a gentle breeze picked up as if from nowhere. It danced in the leaves, bringing with it a scent Emily knew and loved, a mixture of soap and tobacco, of wood shavings and freshly cut grass. She breathed it in, soaking it up. And the scent was followed by a song. She didn't know if it was carried by the trees, or whether it had come from within her, but it seemed to appear from everywhere all at once, as if the spring itself was singing. It was a lullaby her parents had sung to her when was she very young and slowly that awful, gnawing hollow she had carried around inside her since that terrible day began to ease.

'Hush, little baby, don't say a word,
Papa's gonna buy you a mockingbird.
And if that mockingbird don't sing,
Papa's gonna buy you a diamond ring.
And if that diamond ring turns to brass,
Papa's gonna buy you a looking glass.
And if that looking glass gets broke,
Papa's gonna buy you a billy goat.
And if that billy goat doesn't pull,
Papa's gonna buy you a cart and bull.

And if that cart and bull turns over,
Papa's gonna buy you a dog named Rover.
And if that dog named Rover won't bark,
Papa's gonna buy you a horse and cart.
And if that horse and cart falls down,
Well you'll still be the sweetest baby in town.'

The song still echoed round her mind as she woke, though the wonderful smell quickly disappeared, replaced by the sharp tang of disinfectant. Slowly she opened her eyes, and as they adjusted to the light she could see that she was all alone in a large room. But where was she? England or Germany? Across the room was a window through which she could see the answer. The sun was slowly rising, turning to pink the river which slithered between the hills and down towards the city of Exeter. She smiled to herself. The rain that had lashed down so fiercely the night before was gone; it was the beginning of a fine spring day. Carefully she pulled herself upright and began to examine her various injuries. Her leg was in plaster and she was covered in cuts and bruises. She wanted to get up, she needed to know what had happened, but there was little chance of that. Somewhere close by she could hear movement.

'Hello?' she called. 'Is anyone out there?'

When there was no response. She called again, louder this time.

'Can someone help me? Please? Anyone?'

There was still no reply. What had happened to Jack and Mr Worthington? She hoped from the bottom of her heart that they had both survived. But what if they hadn't? Or what if Jack was still down in the passages? Perhaps she was the only one who knew where he was. And poor Mr Worthington, how could he have made it through the carnage of the Great War only to die at the hands of a mad man in Exeter? She needed to know, she needed to be certain.

'Hello?' she cried once more. Nothing.

Out the corner of her eye she spotted a small leather-bound book resting on a chair a few feet from her bed. Perhaps if she threw that at the door it might attract someone's attention, she thought. With some considerable difficulty she pulled the chair towards her, wincing as the movement put pressure on her broken leg. She picked up the book and, taking careful aim, hurled it towards the door just as it swung open to reveal Peterhouse.

'Bloody hell,' he said ducking to avoid the hardback missile Emily had launched in his direction. 'You're on the mend I see.'

'Sorry,' said Emily sheepishly.

'What is this anyway?' he said picking the discarded book up from the floor. 'Hard Times? Well thank goodness it wasn't Bleak House or you'd have probably knocked me out.'

Emily wasn't to be distracted.

'How's Mr Worthington? How's Jack?'

Peterhouse leant against the doorframe with a smile on his face, the familiar blond hair startlingly unruffled, not a strand out of place.

'They're okay, just about. They've had a rough time of it, but they'll live, so that's something.'

The weight that had sat like a rock in the pit of her stomach dissolved, turning to laughter that spilled from her like bubbles from champagne.

'Can I see them?'

'All in good time.'

'What happened to Kitson?'

'Dead,' replied Peterhouse with a hint of satisfaction.

Emily's mind raced. If he was dead, did that mean that Tommy would have to stay in prison?

'What about Jack's brother?'

'I should think Thomas Copleston will be released very soon.'

'How? I mean if Kitson is dead then–'

'Once I started looking into Tommy's case then it became clear that Kitson was either incompetent or actively working against him. So I started doing some digging into that man's past, and nothing I found added up. The first record we have of him was when he turned up in a British hospital on the 23rd November 1918, claiming to be Corporal John Kitson. He said he'd been injured in the fighting but disappeared before anyone could question him further. The next time he appears in our records is in the late twenties when he visits Germany and meets senior members of the Nazi party. Shortly after these meetings he somehow finds the money to set up as a solicitor in Exeter. Of course, the intelligence agencies lose interest because it seems like he's just a second-rate solicitor plying his trade in a provincial town in the south west of England. If the Ministry had known about his links to Germany we would have kept a close eye on him, unfortunately we have not been in favour for quite some time now, and relationships with our colleagues in other departments have suffered. But he was here for a reason. He had been sent to Exeter specifically. Then once you discovered the link between Ralph Ferguson and Kitson things began to fall into place. The jewellery matched the missing girls, so Tommy could not possibly be guilty.'

Emily smiled. They'd done what they set out to do. Jack was sure to be delighted but her mind kept wandering back to Kitson.

'How did he hope to get me out of the country?'

'There was a small boat waiting in Exmouth ready to take you out to sea. We must assume he'd made arrangements to have you picked up a few miles out, the boat was hardly suitable for a channel crossing. Perhaps there was a U-Boat patrolling the waters, we'll never know, we couldn't spare the planes to look for it. Plymouth was badly hit last night.'

'Were many people killed?'

'We don't know yet, but a few, and there was a lot of damage to buildings, fires, that sort of thing.'

Emily nodded. The glow of hearing that Mr Worthington and Jack were safe was slowly wearing off as other thoughts took over.

'Why am I in a room all to myself?' she asked.

'You're in this room for your own protection. We think you're out of danger for now but there's no point in taking chances. I've got a couple of guards on the way. They'll stay on the door at all times, day and night. No one will get in –'

'Or out?' said Emily accusingly.

'You're free to leave whenever you please. Of course, you have broken your leg so you might just want to rest up for a few days at least. Your father will be pleased to see you,' said Peterhouse.

'My dad is here?'

'Whose book did you think that was? I like Dickens but I prefer Trollope. He was here a few minutes ago, I expect he'll be back shortly. Your father that is, not Anthony Trollope.'

'So… when do we leave?' asked Emily.

'Leave?'

'For London. I said I'd come and work for you if you got Jack's brother out of prison.'

'I've spoken to your father and I think it's best if you stay here for the foreseeable future, under the care of Mr Worthington.'

'But why? I thought you wanted me to come with you?'

Peterhouse massaged his temples in frustration.

'It doesn't matter what I want. I'm glad you refused to follow me to London as it happens, I think if you had done so you would now be in serious trouble. The Ministry is in a state of flux, and there are those who would seek to take advantage of the current situation for their own ends. Sadly I can foresee a day when those on our own side represent as great a danger to you as the Nazis. That being the case I will do everything in my power to protect you. Anyway, enough of this. For now everything is in place and you may remain here in Exeter if that is what you wish.'

'It is.'

'Very well. Until we meet again Miss Cartwright, please look after yourself. I've left you my card. If there is trouble, or if you See anything you think I should know about, then please call me.'

He offered up a respectful nod, settled his hat gently back on his head, being careful not to disturb a single hair, and left. Emily was alone once more. She began to think about what Peterhouse had said regarding the Ministry. It worried her that he had changed his mind so quickly. Only two weeks ago he had begged her to come to London with him, now he wanted her to stay where she was. She wondered what could have had happened in the meantime, then she remembered something he'd said when he'd called to warn her about Mr Kitson.

'I've been a fool. I thought the danger was from without, but really it was from within.'

What did it mean? Was someone after her? Was it the Ministry? Or someone else? She knew she should feel scared but after all that had happened it was difficult to care. She was just glad everyone was okay. She was going to live in Exeter, she was going to stay with Mr Worthington. It meant she could still see Jack and her grandmother. Her heart fluttered in pleasure at this thought. It was not home, but it was as close as she was likely to get for a while.

Suddenly the door to her room swung open again and her father walked in.

'Emily, I'm so glad you're alright.'

He leant on the side of her bed and embraced her. Emily could smell his familiar scent, a mixture of sweet tobacco and peppery soap, and just for a moment she was transported back to the spring where she had played so happily with her sister. She pulled him in tight, smiling to herself. He was back.

'You were wonderful my darling, I'm so proud of you.'

Emily smiled.

'And I'm sorry. I'm sorry for everything. I shouldn't

have kept all of these secrets from you, and I won't, not anymore. Understand if you can, that I did it for the best possible reasons. I was trying to keep you safe.'

'It didn't work though did it?' she said quietly.

She wasn't looking for a fight, it was simply a statement of fact.

'No. No I suppose not.'

She looked up at him. He looked older than when she had last seen him. In six months he had aged six years.

'I've come to a decision,' she said firmly.

'Oh yes?'

'It's time I started taking control over my own life. I've let others make my choices for me for too long. You didn't tell me the truth, and it ended up making things worse.'

'I know and I've said–'

'I'm not finished,' said Emily cutting him off. 'You weren't always wrong. Grandma Josephine for instance. I like her, I really do, but at times... at times I've seen what it must have been like for you. Occasionally I've felt like a new toy for her to play with, rather than a granddaughter she should love and protect. She's irresponsible, but I need her. She's family and I don't have much of that left. She's also the only person who knows how to help me with my abilities. If they're going to put me in danger, whether it's from the Nazis or from the Ministry, then the least I can do is to learn to use them properly. I want to study with Grandma Josephine, but on my own terms. I will practise, I will get better, and I will be ready for whatever comes my way.'

Her father stroked her hair and nodded. He had tears in his eyes.

'So grown up. I wish I could have kept you a child just a little longer.'

'But you can't.'

'You're right, you're right. If there's anything you want to ask me, then now is the time.'

Emily thought for a moment.

'What is a Projector? What can you do?'

'I can make people see things.'

'What things?'

'It depends. Sometimes I take things I know about them, and I help them to see those things. I used to do it in the trenches. You wouldn't understand what it was like there, no one could hope to unless they were unfortunate enough to live through it. Whilst the men slept I used to give them dreams they could enjoy. I thought it was the least I could do, to make them see there was still some beauty in the world.'

'So that's all you do? You give people nice dreams?' said Emily incredulously.

Her father gave a sad chuckle.

'No. That was how your grandmother saw my ability too, but I can do much more than that.'

'You should have fooled the Germans into thinking there were thousands of you running across the fields at them. They might have surrendered, or else used up all their ammunition fighting daydreams.'

Her father shook his head.

'A Projector's powers are very limited. I can't make more than one person see anything at a time. That's why your Grandma Josephine was never really interested. She couldn't see the point. She thought it was no more than a party trick. I suppose that rubbed off on me, because I never considered doing anything with my abilities either, not until after the war. In fact, it was a conversation with one Private Worthington that got me thinking. He wasn't certain what it was I could do, but he suspected well enough, and he told me that I had a responsibility to make things better if I could. When I left the army I joined the civil service. There I made contacts and rose quickly. I began to look for those with powers like mine and managed to persuade the people that mattered that it might be an idea if we had someone dealing with this sort of thing. That's when I founded the Ministry. It was a real mixture of army, civil service and intelligence people. We tried to take the best elements of all three. To begin with it all went well and we had some significant successes. Anyway, as time passed we grew bigger but as a result we lost our independence: we became just another government department. Too many people with limited abilities were recruited. It led to vast amount of time and money being wasted. Our moment was gone. New weapons were the order of the day and we were shunted to the side. The Ministry as I knew it died in the Munich operation.'

'What was that?'

'A story for another day.'

'You said I could ask whatever I wanted.'

'Ah yes,' said her father with a tired smile, 'but I didn't say I'd answer, did I? I'm not hiding anything from you Emily, I promise, but you need to know more about what we did before I tell you about Munich.'

Emily chewed at the side of her mouth. She knew her father wasn't going to say anything more on the subject however, so she reluctantly moved on.

'Can you show me?' she asked him.

'Show you what?'

'Your power.'

He thought for a moment, then took her hands in his.

'Do you have to be in contact with someone for the vision to work?' she asked.

'No, but it's strongest that way. You do have to be in close proximity though. Sadly I can't beam my thoughts across the sea and convince Hitler to shoot himself.'

'How close do you have to be?'

'Within thirty feet or so.'

He stroked the side of her face and smiled, then took her hands once more. Moments later they were standing on the street outside their old house. Emily could have sworn they were truly there. She could feel the heat of the sun and the gentle touch of the breeze on her skin. She could smell the flowers that were in full bloom in Mrs Sadler's garden. At that very moment her mother walked by them carrying a bag full of shopping. Emily wanted to reach out,

343

to help her, but her father laid a tender hand on her shoulder. Her mother stopped at the door to fish her key from her coat pocket. Someone called from across the road; she turned around so that she was looking almost directly at Emily and her father, then smiled and waved. Emily's heart skipped several beats. She glanced at her father. He looked so sad. Her mother turned back to the door, let herself inside and closed the door behind her.

'Come on,' he said wearily, 'we can't stay here.'

The image disappeared and they found themselves back in the room at the hospital. She pulled her father's hands towards her lips and kissed them gently on the knuckles.

'Do you still miss them?' she whispered.

'Every day,' he replied.

'I still don't understand why you never told mum about what you could do.'

Her father sighed another long, deep sigh.

'It's difficult to explain. There wasn't one reason alone. Early on it was because I feared she might reject me. It's not normal what we can do Emily; I was worried she would think me some sort of freak. It sounds so silly now because she was the kindest, most open-minded person I have ever known. She found the good in everyone. Still, I didn't know that then, and so I kept quiet. I thought I would tell her once we got to know each other better, then the longer things went on the harder it got to explain why I hadn't told her before.'

Emily could see him playing all the missed opportunities over in his head.

'But that wasn't the only reason. Partly it was due to the nature of what I can do, making people see things. I suppose I didn't want her to think that any moment she spent with me might not be real, that somehow I was tricking her into loving me. I never used my abilities on her, you must believe me. I made that promise to myself at the very start. You have no idea how tempting it was sometimes, to make a special evening that much more perfect, to improve the sunset or take a gloomy day and make it golden. But I couldn't bear the thought she would fall in love with the illusion of life with me, instead of life as it really was. I was so good at it; how could she ever be certain what she was seeing when she was alone with me was real? And if, having failed to tell her what I could do for so long, I had suddenly come clean, then it would have been only too understandable if she'd thought I had manipulated her in some way.'

Emily nodded. She felt, at last, that she was beginning to understand.

'But finally, and most shamefully,' he continued, 'I am a man of secrets. I live in a secretive world Emily, and I was raised at the knee of a woman who lies about everything. Nothing of my mother is real. Her name, her titles, her accent; all borrowed from other people. It's a fantastic act of self-creation. She has built herself into the person she wants to be, rather than the person she was born, and she's done it several times over. I think some of that has rubbed off on me. I reach for the easy lie over the hard truth every time. For all his faults Frank was the only one in my family who was truly himself. From now on I shall try and be more like Frank.'

'Okay,' said Emily as she drew him into a hug, 'but not too much like Uncle Frank. I don't think I could take it.'

Her father chuckled and pulled Emily closer, until she could feel their aching hearts beating as one.

'What's it like living with Mr Worthington?' he asked.

'It's okay. It doesn't feel like home though.'

'I'm sorry, I'd love to tell you it will one day, but I don't know if that's true. I hope things will be different now he knows what really happened to his daughter. It won't bring her back but the guilt and betrayal he must have felt thinking that Tommy Copleston had killed her... maybe he'll find a little peace. And, of course, you can see your friend Jack more often can't you?'

'Can I see him now? He is here isn't he?'

'Maybe you should wait; he's been through an awful lot. You both have.'

'Please, I'll be quick. Two minutes, no more.'

Her father reluctantly agreed and helped Emily from her bed. Emily tried not to let on how much effort it was taking. Carefully, and with the aid of her father, she lowered herself into a rickety wheelchair and was rolled out of the room. The guards that had been placed outside for her protection looked as though they were going to protest, but her father intervened.

'She's just going to visit a friend. We won't be long.'

Unsure if this was allowed they decided the best thing to do was to follow her, so now Emily had three grown men trailing in her wake and she drew a lot of strange looks from the other patients.

She found Jack at the end of a busy ward. He was sitting in the final bed closest to the window. Spotting her approach, he grinned, then continued tucking into a large plate of hospital food. Emily couldn't tell quite what it was meant to be; it was brown, that was all she knew, and it smelled like her old PE kit. Still, Jack seemed to be enjoying it.

'Alright?' he said amiably as her entourage backed away to a discreet distance. 'Nice transport.'

'Thanks. How are you?'

'I'm fine. Well obviously not *fine* fine, or I wouldn't be here, but I'm not dying. They're sending me home in a few days.'

'That's great news. What... what happened?' she asked nervously.

'I got shot in the shoulder didn't I?' he replied. 'Bloody hurt I can tell you.'

'Will it heal?'

'They think so. Gonna have a cool scar though.'

Emily shook her head and smiled.

'Sorry. It's all my fault.'

'You didn't shoot me. You tried to stop him. It's not your fault Em.'

'But I feel responsible.'

'Stop being such a girl. We're alive. Can you credit it?

And my brother's getting out of prison. I should be thanking you. You believed in me when no one else did.'

'Yeah well you believed in me too,' said Emily lowering her voice.

Neither one spoke for a moment, then Jack remembered something.

'I erm... I made you this, been working on it the last few weeks,' he said pulling something out of the tiny cabinet beside his bed. 'I thought... well I was going to give it to you on your birthday, but then I realised that I don't know when that is, and now seems a good a moment as any. When were you born by the way?'

'21st June.'

'Right. Do I still have to get you a present?'

Emily laughed.

'I'll tell you when you show me what it is.'

'Got my ma to bring it in. It's not much but...' his voice trailed off and he pressed what looked like a small wooden egg cup into her hands.

Emily frowned. On closer inspection it began to reveal itself. It sat on a wooden base and on the front was a square piece of paper with a short note written out in an untidy hand.

'When Ivo goes back with the urn, the urn;
Studds, Steel, Read and Tylecote return, return;
The welkin will ring loud,
The great crowd will feel proud,
Seeing Barlow and Bates with the urn, the urn;
And the rest coming home with the urn.'

It was a replica of the Ashes cricket trophy that England and Australia had competed for before the war. A grin slid across her face.

'It contains the ashes of the stump – well, stick – you took clean out the ground the day we first met,' explained Jack.

Emily laughed and looked down at the trophy. It was a

rough approximation with none of the polish and gleam of the real thing, but to her it was perfect.

'Thank you Jack,' she said quietly, 'if I could stand I'd give you a hug.'

'Best not then eh? I've been through a lot and I'm not sure if I could take it.'

Emily laughed again.

'What is that you're eating by the way?'

'I dunno, is brown a food?'

Her father approached.

'Right then Emily, I think it's time we got you back to your room.'

'Dad, this is Jack. Jack this is my father.'

'Pleased to meet you Jack.'

'You too Mr Cartwright.'

'I don't suppose I can persuade you to keep my daughter out of trouble in future can I?'

'I'll do my best. She usually does what I tell her.'

'You can't listen to him,' Emily stage-whispered to her father, 'they think he's addled. The bullet did more damage than the doctors are letting on. Next he'll be telling you he can beat me at cricket.'

Jack smiled.

'Come on Emily Cartwright, let's go,' and her father wheeled her away back to her bed.

Emily glanced back to see Jack looking after her. When he was caught watching he glanced away and resumed devouring whatever dubious substance was on his plate.

A few days later Emily was released into the care of Mr Worthington. Her father had already returned to London so it was just the two of them at the Station Master's cottage. Peterhouse arranged for someone to be watching the house at all hours in case anybody unexpected turned up, but no one did.

As Emily was unable to walk or look after herself properly, her grandmother would stop by whenever Mr Worthington was at work. Jack paid several visits too, and they would happily sit in the garden and chat. They even devised a form of cricket she could play from her wheelchair. Spring had arrived, the weather was finally beginning to turn, and for the first time in a long time she felt the smallest sense of anticipation welling up within her.

There would never be a day when she did not miss her family, and some days that hurt would burn in her more fiercely than ever, but she also knew that she could go on without them. She had her father, Grandma Josephine, Mr Worthington and Jack, and they would look out for her, as she would look out for them. It wasn't the family she would have chosen, but it was a family nonetheless, and after all she had been through in the past few months it was enough. It was hope.

Epilogue

It was early one Sunday morning in June when his promotion came through. After much negotiation and cajoling, the Ministry was finally under Trinity's full control. That it had taken as much time as it had was ridiculous. The Munich fiasco in '38 should have been enough to see him take charge, but the Faculty – as they insisted on calling themselves – had somehow managed to retain their independence. He had been brought in merely as an overseer. Well no longer.

He knew some people found his fascination with the place strange, amusing even, but he could see something they could not. As it stood the Ministry was a luxury that could not be afforded in the fight against Nazism. Good men and women running around chasing after people with, for the want of a better term, magical powers, merely to keep them safe? It was a travesty that it had been allowed to continue unchecked for so long. But with the right man at the helm, he was certain it could become one of the Great Offices of State, perhaps even *the* Great Office.

The step-child of a brief and ill-begotten liaison between the army, and the civil and secret services, the Ministry was supposed to give Britain the upper hand on the world stage by finding those with "special" abilities and putting them to use in service of the Empire. Sadly, it had not worked out that way. Those with genuine abilities were few and far between. A couple of early successes saw money and influence pour into the department, but too much time was wasted on those whose powers were at best, weak, and at worst, a simple combination of showmanship and charlatanism.

The Ministry had become a by-word for wastefulness and incompetence. It was the punchline of many a joke at all the right kind of parties. Numerous friends and colleagues had suggested that it would be best to put it out of its misery. But not Trinity. For several years he had been quietly working away in the background, pulling together the information he needed, slowly removing those he couldn't trust, and putting into place others of whose loyalty he was more certain. Now only a stubborn few of the old guard remained.

He had called the meeting at Ministry headquarters the moment he had received the news. Despite the early hour he was sure most would already have heard about his elevation to Chancellor. He had been provisionally in charge ever since his predecessor had passed away, but he had lacked the authority to make the real changes he craved. Now his moment had arrived.

Trinity had gathered together the Faculty for a meeting in the Ministry library. He sat at the head of the table and shuffled his papers whilst they eyed him with a mixture of fear and distrust. He didn't care what they thought of him. It was his responsibility to clear up the mess they had made. They'd had their chance to make it work, but they had squandered it. Now it was up to him. If they hadn't seen the opportunity that was right in front of them, that wasn't his fault.

'Is this all of us?' he asked.

At that moment Peterhouse entered. Trinity had been hoping that he wouldn't show up. Peterhouse was one of the true believers. He'd had the Old Bulldog's ear for a time, but that was before Munich. Some of the other Faculty looked up to him, but Trinity saw him for what he was, a fool whose time had passed, a symptom of the sickness that had withered the heart of the British establishment.

'Sorry I'm late. Dashed cold in here old boy, nothing we can do about that is there?' asked Peterhouse smiling kindly round the table.

'I'm afraid not,' he replied stiffly.

'Ah well, KBO as they say', and he smiled again. 'So, what's this all about anyhow? Strange time for a meeting, first thing on a Sunday.'

There was murmur of agreement from the table.

'I won't keep you long, don't worry. I have some news for you all, although I don't think it should come as any great surprise, especially given the field we work in.'

He laughed at his own little joke but no one else joined in.

'As of 12.01 this morning, I have officially been made Chancellor of the Ministry. As such I have a number of changes I wish to make to the Second Sight programme. You know of course that our role here is protect those in the civilian population with special abilities, and if possible, to bring them into the fold. It is my view, and the view of the army, the secret service and his majesties government, that we have been far too laissez-faire in the manner we carry out our brief. There is a small, but potentially highly dangerous, group of people running around the country unchecked. If just a few of them chose to work for the Nazis, or disagreed with the way that this war is being run, then we could have a catastrophe on our hands. It has been decided therefore that all participants in the Second Sight programme, including those who are known to us but who are not active participants, must be brought fully under His Majesty's protection within the next forty-eight hours. Those who refuse to cooperate will make themselves enemies of the state and will be treated as such.'

'What does that mean?' asked Peterhouse pushing his foppish blonde hair from out of his eyes. 'Brought *fully* under protection? You said it yourself, they're already under our protection.'

'How many of you could say with absolute certainty where each of your charges are right at this very moment?'

He eyed the table challenging them to respond.

'These people are too dangerous to be left out there on their own, and we do not have the resources to protect them adequately, as your most recent escapade proved Peterhouse.'

'If you'd listened when I told you about–'

'Let's not go through all that again,' he said quickly cutting him off. He had perhaps been unwise to bring up that particular case. 'The girl and others like her are a threat to this country. If they do not work for us, then they work against us.'

He addressed them all, taking care to look at each and every one of them in turn.

'It is your job to bring them in. Any of you who refuse will be disciplined in the most severe manner. If you do not feel you can carry out what is being asked of you within the specified timeframe then please let me know, I will be only too happy to help.'

'To be clear,' said Peterhouse, 'you're talking about internment. Locking up people whose only crime is to be different.'

'I am talking about protection, for them and for the Great British public.'

Two of the men, he forgot exactly which ridiculous names they had given themselves, shifted in their seats before one of them spoke up.

'But I promised... I mean to say that we promised –'

'I don't care one jot what it is you promised. Those are your instructions gentlemen.'

He was careful not to use the word 'orders'; even the most placid members of the Faculty seemed to take offence at the term.

'Now look here old boy,' Downing, one of Peterhouse's favourites was speaking now. He had heard rumours about the two of them but he didn't know if it was anything more than idle chatter.

'Look here, if we do this we're no better than the Nazis, rounding people up, putting them in camps. These people mean no harm. Some of them have been quite helpful to the war effort.'

'And they will be rewarded. I do not seek to punish those who cooperate, only those who would aid and abet the enemy, either directly, or by failing to come to their country's assistance when she is at her most vulnerable. It's time to choose a side.'

There were a few mutterings and murmurings but no one spoke up. Peterhouse looked ready to lynch him. Just let him try, thought Trinity.

'I really don't think that forty-eight hours is enough time,' said Downing with a shake of his head.

'It is plenty of time. This is a matter of urgency. After that they will be rounded up and brought in on a non-voluntary basis.'

'And if they resist?'

'I think you know the answer to that,' he replied coolly.

There was another murmur of dissent but no one else dared, it seemed, to put their head above the parapet.

'It falls to me to remind you that if any of these assets disappear in the next two days, you will be held accountable. I would hate for you or your families to be inconvenienced so please do not be tempted to...' he paused to search for the right word, '...assist your people in vanishing. You bring them in. Your loyalty to them is commendable but misguided, your ultimate loyalty is, of course, to the Ministry. Forty-eight hours gentlemen. The clock is ticking.'

Trinity gathered his notes together and left. The library was silent now. The message was clear and understood. One by one the Faculty returned to their desks. Only Peterhouse and Downing remained. They were alone for several minutes before either one spoke. Downing was first to break the silence.

'So... it's like you said.'

'I had hoped it would be different.'

'And you can't have a word with the Bulldog, get him to step in? Put a stop to all this?'

'They won't let me in. Besides he's got enough to be getting on with. You can only fight so many battles.'

'What do we do?'

'Exactly what we said we'd do.'

'You're ready for this?'

'I think I have one big innings left in me. You?'

'Where you lead...'

'Good luck old man. Stay safe. They'll hang you out to dry if they catch you, remember that.'

'You too Rupert.'

Peterhouse smiled at the use of his name. At some point in the past, and for reasons no one could quite remember, each of the Faculty had ceased to be referred to by their Christian names and were instead named after various Oxbridge colleges. Each college represented a different division within the department. It was a sort of shorthand they employed amongst themselves and somehow it had stuck.

'Thank you Charles,' said Peterhouse fondly.

The two men left the library, stopping by their desks only to pick up their briefcases, before exiting the building.

In a small corner office Trinity sat, listening carefully to every word they said. When they had finished he picked up the phone and placed a call.

'Keble? This is Trinity,' he said brusquely, 'it's as we thought. They're going to try and help them go to ground. Peterhouse and Downing must be stopped. Use any means necessary, just bring Emily Cartwright to me. It's time to see what the Seven can do.'

THE END

*Emily Cartwright will
return in
Second Sight:
The House of the Hidden*

Acknowledgements

A huge thank you to everyone who has helped make this book what it is. To Philippa and Lizzie for saying the words every writer longs to hear: 'I can't wait to know what happens next.' To John, for cooking more times than he should have done. To Rich, for giving me the challenge to write a film about witches that he could direct. Sorry to you (and to everyone else) that this is not a film about witches, but without you there would have been no book. Finally, to my mum for her endless encouragement and support, and for the hours she has spent editing and proofing. All errors that remain are mine.

29554335R00209

Printed in Great Britain
by Amazon